Advance pra[ise]

"Lovers of uplifting roman[ce ...] voice Heidi McCahan. Rea[ders will fall in l]ove with the town of Evergreen and its charming residents. Five delicious stars!"
—Kristy Woodson Harvey, *New York Times* bestselling author of *A Happier Life*

"Two shattered hearts find themselves in a confection of trouble when their paths align in Evergreen, Alaska. With family secrets to contend with, and a rivalry that goes back generations, this candy-filled romance is delicious and satisfying."
—Jean Meltzer, internationally bestselling author of *The Matzah Ball*

"With its rootable romance, intriguing family mystery, and irresistible Alaska town full of charming personalities, *A Winter of Sweet Secrets* has all the ingredients we want in a delightful comfort read. Heidi McCahan has perfected the recipe for uplifting and inspirational cozy love stories!"
—Bethany Turner, author of *Cole and Laila Are Just Friends: A Love Story*

"Heidi McCahan shines in her newest offering that will satisfy any readers' sweet tooth. This small-town romance will delight fans of Liz Johnson and Denise Hunter."
—Sarah Monzon, author of *All's Fair in Love and Christmas*

"A glorious Alaskan setting, characters who tug at your heartstrings, and a candy shop of goodies you can almost taste...plus poignant family drama that will keep you turning pages. Heidi McCahan has written the perfect sweet escape."
—Lee Tobin McClain, *New York Times* bestselling author

"*A Winter of Sweet Secrets* is a heartfelt story of family, love, forgiveness, and second chances. This book proves a winner!"
—Amy Clipston, bestselling author of *With This Ring*

Books by Heidi McCahan

Love Inspired Trade
One Southern Summer

Love Inspired

Opportunity, Alaska
Her Alaskan Family

Home to Hearts Bay
An Alaskan Secret
The Twins' Alaskan Adventure
His Alaskan Redemption
Her Alaskan Companion
A Baby in Alaska

For additional books by Heidi McCahan,
visit her website, www.heidimccahan.com.

A Winter of Sweet Secrets

HEIDI McCAHAN

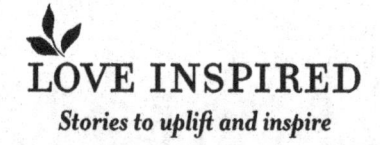

LOVE INSPIRED
Stories to uplift and inspire

If you purchased this book without a cover you should be aware that this book is stolen property. It was reported as "unsold and destroyed" to the publisher, and neither the author nor the publisher has received any payment for this "stripped book."

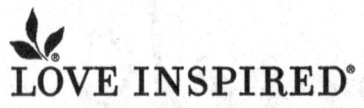

LOVE INSPIRED®
Stories to uplift and inspire

ISBN-13: 978-1-335-99411-0

A Winter of Sweet Secrets

Copyright © 2025 by Heidi Blankenship

All rights reserved. No part of this book may be used or reproduced in any manner whatsoever without written permission.

Without limiting the author's and publisher's exclusive rights, any unauthorized use of this publication to train generative artificial intelligence (AI) technologies is expressly prohibited.

This is a work of fiction. Names, characters, places and incidents are either the product of the author's imagination or are used fictitiously. Any resemblance to actual persons, living or dead, businesses, companies, events or locales is entirely coincidental.

For questions and comments about the quality of this book, please contact us at CustomerService@Harlequin.com.

® is a trademark of Harlequin Enterprises ULC.

Love Inspired
22 Adelaide St. West, 41st Floor
Toronto, Ontario M5H 4E3, Canada
www.LoveInspired.com

Printed in U.S.A.

For my dear grammies, who may have lacked cooking and baking skills but more than made up for it in abundant love and steadfast faith. Your lessons guide me every day, and this story is for you.

Chapter One

There wasn't a chocolate caramel truffle for sale in all of Kansas City that tasted as delicious as her Grammie's. But that hadn't stopped Jovi Wright from sampling the options. The best remedy for heartache had always been her grandmother's sweet treats. Since she was thousands of miles from Evergreen, Alaska, a local candy shop would have to do. She'd stopped at three so far, and none crafted anything close to the amazing concoctions her grandparents offered at Evergreen Candy Company. How hard was it to make a chunk of milk chocolate that contained the perfect amount of smooth, buttery caramel? Grammie and Grandpa had always made it look easy.

Jovi tucked her chin into her collar to shield herself against the frigid air swirling around her and waited for the light at the intersection to change so she could cross. Thick snowflakes fell from a gray sky, and impatient drivers jockeyed for position in the rush hour traffic. She should have been on her honeymoon in Fiji right now, not trudging through a blustery January storm. Alone. She might as well continue her quest.

After one more sample and a sugar rush, Jovi tugged her key chain from the pocket of her puffy black winter coat and climbed the stairs to the over-the-garage apartment she'd rented in August.

August. Back when she'd been hopelessly in love with her then-fiancé, Michael, and thrilled to be living less than an hour from the military base where he was stationed. The paper bag of bakery treats from the cute place on East Third bumped against her leg. Shivering as snowflakes landed on the bare skin at the base of her neck, Jovi quickly unlocked her door and stepped inside. Thankfully, the short-term rental had come fully furnished. This place had been the ideal nest for her. Until she'd been dumped.

Now getting out of Kansas City couldn't come soon enough. She'd only planned to stay six months anyway, long enough to fulfill her contract as a traveling nurse at St. Luke's Hospital and walk down the aisle to marry the man of her dreams.

More like a nightmare. Michael had called the whole thing off in October, only twelve days before they were supposed to say *I do*. Her throat tightened, but she quickly closed the door, hoping the extra forceful slam might banish the painful emotions before they spilled over. Because she couldn't bear feeling this way anymore. She'd wallowed long enough. She'd cried for three days straight when he'd ended their relationship. Then came the coping with plenty of carbs and sweets, and she even let her coworkers from the hospital take her to the domestic thriller movie everyone raved about. Now that the holidays were over and the new year had begun, she just wanted to be over it. Over *him*.

The hollow ache in her chest proved forgetting was easier said than done.

Sighing, she set the bag down on the distressed cream-colored console table in the entryway, then pulled off her wet boots. Her contract had expired. The message in her inbox required a decision. Sign a contract for thirteen weeks in a new location? Or find something permanent here? She made more money as a traveling nurse, but moving now seemed exhausting and stressful. She caught a glimpse of the dark circles under her eyes in the oval mirror, cringed, then turned away to hang up her keys and her jacket on the hooks by the door.

Pulling off the knit beanie, damp with melting snowflakes, she felt her chest pinch at yet another reminder of her ex. She'd bought the hat because he'd insisted everybody rooted for Kansas City's football team. Tomato-red had never been her color, and to be honest, she couldn't care less about football. She preferred downhill skiing or snowboarding or snowshoeing—the activities she'd learned as a child that got her outside enjoying nature. Sitting around watching football hadn't been her thing. It had been Michael's thing, so she'd adapted to fit his preferences.

"A lot of good that did me," she grumbled, then grabbed her bag and strode into the kitchen. The white quartz countertop, stainless steel appliances and modern oil-rubbed bronze fixtures made up for the size of the place. There wasn't room for a table, but that didn't matter because she ate her meals at the bar dividing the kitchen from the living area. The brown leather padded stools were comfy enough. She hadn't bothered to cook much anyway. Takeout was easy to purchase on her way home from the hospital, and when Michael came to visit, he'd preferred a local restaurant that had oversize televisions hanging on every square inch of available wall space.

She'd been looking forward to finding a new place together. Yeah, it was probably going to be military housing, and following him to yet another new location had provoked more than one concerned comment from her family. But it wasn't like she was tied to any particular city as a traveling nurse. So she'd chased their doubts away with daydreams of how they'd be together finally, husband and wife. She could make any house a home with her new husband by her side.

Now here she sat, trying to soothe her heartache with more sugar. As a nurse working in health care, she knew this was the worst possible coping strategy. Her scrubs still fit, though, and the guilt hadn't motivated her to change her ways. Maybe she'd balance out the sweets with leftover beef and broccoli takeout.

While she waited for her food to reheat in the microwave, she filled a glass with water and carried it into the living area. Her landlord had upgraded the furniture before Jovi moved in. The beige microfiber love seat and matching chair with a beige and yellow geometric pattern weren't her favorite, but both were quite comfortable. The wooden coffee table, TV stand, and side table all sported the same creamy purposely distressed finish. Jovi had purchased new spring-themed decor yesterday, including cute throw pillows with fringed edges, and a scented candle that smelled nothing like the sea air or a beach cottage as the label implied, but she sort of liked the images on the box. Maybe her next assignment needed to be in a place where she could dip her toes in the ocean on the regular.

Sighing, she reached for the remote and scrolled until she found a streaming service featuring a one-hour special with an entertaining stand-up comedian. Hopefully, she'd be able to avoid all the commercials featuring couples in love during the weeks leading up to Valentine's Day. Because now that Christmas and New Year's Day had passed, reminders of love and happy couples were everywhere. Her heart wasn't ready. Being unexpectedly single was a very long slog. Growing up in a town called Evergreen, where her grandparents ran a candy company that sold out of their signature chocolate boxes every year, had fueled Jovi's affection for holidays. Until this year. Until Michael's cruel decision snatched the future she'd longed for from her grasp.

The muted sound of her phone ringing stopped her from retrieving her dinner. She pushed to her feet and crossed to the door, patting her jacket pockets until she found her phone. Her sister Isabel's name filled the caller ID. Oh, no. She'd promised to call her back this afternoon.

"Hey, Isabel. I'm sooo sorry. I completely forgot."

"What happened?"

"I was on my way to pick up my wedding dress from the lady who did the alterations but got distracted by a sale for home decor, then I wanted to get some chocolate from a new bakery and..." She trailed off. Embarrassed yet again that she'd been such an airhead. Isabel was in charge of operations at the family's candy company, served as the youngest mayor ever elected in Evergreen, and had a thriving, healthy marriage. She probably never forgot the next task on her perfectly planned to-do list.

"Did you get the dress back?"

Isabel's hopeful tone made Jovi squeeze her eyes shut. She didn't want to admit the truth.

"No, I couldn't bring myself to go inside. I'll call her later and ask her to donate it to charity."

Isabel gasped. "But that's your dress. Don't you want to—"

"Keep it in case he changes his mind? Doubt that will happen."

Not that she hadn't entertained the idea of Michael showing up outside her door, declaring he'd been a fool.

"I just thought you might want to resell the dress," the always practical Isabel suggested. "Maybe recoup some of your money."

In the kitchen, Jovi opened the microwave, but her leftovers had lost their appeal. This conversation always had the same result. Isabel restated her disgust over Michael's choices, and Jovi felt ashamed for somehow defending him.

Jovi pushed the steaming food around on her plate with a fork. "Is my canceled wedding the reason why you called?"

"No." Isabel blew out a long breath. "I need your help."

"Uh-oh." Jovi left the fork on her plate and leaned against the counter. "What's going on?"

"Long story short, the company's been struggling financially for months," Isabel said. "And we'd hoped the demand for our products would increase during the holidays, but sadly, sales aren't where we need them to be."

"I don't understand." Jovi's stomach tightened. "The candy and chocolate have been bestsellers for years. What happened?"

"The recipes for everything we make were all Grammie's. We haven't altered those, other than finding more cost-effective ingredients from different suppliers and changing up our seasonal offerings. But our customers are demanding unique, locally sourced ingredients, as well as gluten-free and sugar-free alternatives. Unfortunately, they seem to expect a lower price than what we can offer."

"Have you considered investing in more social media advertising? Or emailing promo codes for discounts to current customers?"

"We've tried. I had a virtual assistant helping with that last fall, but the outcome wasn't significant. More ads aren't the solution."

"Then what is?"

Isabel paused. "I need you, Jovi."

"Me? I'm afraid I don't have any quick fixes either. Honestly, I wish I did."

"You're a hard worker, and with Valentine's Day coming up, we need all hands on deck. It's been challenging to retain employees lately, and I need someone reliable to take customer service calls and pack and ship orders. And I really need you to help me figure out how to save this company."

Jovi nibbled on her thumbnail. Those were all tasks she could handle. Mostly. Except for that last part.

"We've done everything we can to fine-tune our marketing, including highlighting how we incorporate locally sourced ingredients whenever possible," Isabel said, her voice laced with frustration. "It seems like we're constantly troubleshooting any issues with the production line that might impact our quality control. Sadly, nothing seems to boost our sales. We need a stellar product. Something fresh and interesting that will appeal to a new generation of savvy customers."

Jovi couldn't argue. It wasn't like she'd been around to help run the day-to-day operations. But it sort of sounded like Isabel's expectations were way too high. "What are Mom and Dad saying about all of this?"

Isabel's hesitation sent a jolt of trepidation zipping through Jovi's veins.

"That's the kicker. They've given an ultimatum. If we can't course-correct and increase our sales this quarter, they want to sell. And believe me, there's a global conglomerate waiting in the wings with an appealing offer."

No.

"I'll come home." Jovi sprang into motion, hurrying to the hall closet where she kept her suitcases stashed. "How soon do you need me?"

"How soon can you get here?"

"I'll shop for a plane ticket as soon as we hang up."

What if the hospital in Evergreen needed a traveling nurse? She'd scrolled through the available options for her next contract last week but hadn't seen any openings close to home. She'd check again. Because there was no way she'd let her parents sell the company, and spending the rest of the winter in Evergreen would be better than moping alone here.

Isabel loved her younger sister. Really, she did. But sometimes Jovi's choices made Isabel want to scream. Who gave away a brand-new beautiful wedding dress? Sure, visiting the seamstress was probably a painful reminder of Michael's cold feet and his abrupt rejection, and Isabel didn't blame her for not wanting to keep the dress in her closet. But why not resell it?

Her desk chair creaked as she drew in a deep breath, held it for a count of seven, then released it while she counted to eight. A stress-management technique she'd added to her repertoire when she sensed her blood pressure had spiked. Thirty seemed a little young to be worrying about medical issues, but she couldn't ignore the tension that dogged her lately.

She wasn't going to prod Jovi about her decision. If the girl wanted to give up thousands of dollars, that was on her.

Besides, she couldn't be too critical. Jovi had agreed to come home. Without a fight. Even if she only stayed through Easter, at least there'd be an extra set of hands. Because they were running out of time to save the company. Isabel flipped open her planner, pausing to admire the color-coordinated stickers she'd selected to accessorize her weekly spread.

A reminder she'd written in her planner to check in with the manager at Grammie's new place caught her attention. She rubbed at the tightness in her chest. As soon as Jovi came home and got settled, they'd have to squeeze in a quick trip to Anchorage to visit Grammie. She opened an app on her phone and tapped out a quick email, requesting an update.

The case manager at the care facility had said that the first two weeks of adjusting to life in memory care were challenging. She'd gently but firmly recommended the family stay away and let Grammie get used to her new routine. Isabel never backed away from a challenge, but moving Grammie in there had been the most heart-wrenching thing she'd ever had to do. Even worse than Grandpa's funeral last January. She couldn't fathom staying away for two solid weeks. Tomorrow was only day eight. Thankfully, she wasn't alone in her sorrow. Mom and Dad were upset too. She'd even caught Mason swiping at tears on his cheeks when they'd walked back to their cars after moving Grammie in. And she could count on one hand the number of times she'd seen her husband cry.

Her front door opened and closed. The familiar sound of work boots thumped in the entryway. Mason. Oh, no. Was it six o'clock already? A little late to defrost anything for dinner. Maybe he wouldn't complain if she served frozen pizza and a bagged salad for the second time this week.

"Hey." He stopped in the doorway of her home office, his ruddy cheeks flushed from the cold. His green eyes met hers, and her pulse sped. Funny how she still got the same feeling when he walked into the room. He was more handsome than he was fifteen years ago, but she'd still never forget the day she'd spotted him walking into Evergreen High School. A brand-new ninth-grader who'd just moved to town because his folks had taken jobs at Winterhaven, the local ski resort.

"Hey." She offered a smile. "How was your day?"

He shrugged one muscular shoulder. "I've had better."

"Oh?" She tried not to look worried. He'd been saying that more often when she asked about his job with the Department of Transportation. Sure, things got hectic this time of year, especially when they were already on track to break their record of more than one hundred and sixty inches of snowfall. But he rarely complained about the demanding workload.

"Jake and Wendy invited us out for dinner. I need to shower real quick, and then we can go."

She winced. "I'm sorry, babe. I can't. The board of directors for the library meets at seven thirty."

He scowled. "It's Thursday. I thought you said you were free tonight. And last time I checked, you aren't on that board."

Oh, no. She'd forgotten that he'd asked her this morning if she'd had anything planned. He was right. She had said no. Because twelve hours ago, her calendar was wide-open.

"They're meeting with a team of architects who are in town for a few days." Isabel tried to keep her voice neutral, but she was super excited about the project. "They've drafted a proposal to build an expansion next spring."

"So why do you need to be there?" Mason shoved his hands in the front pockets of his black hoodie. "Are you in charge of the library now too?"

Ouch. She realigned the five colored pens she kept next to her planner to color-code any additional notes. "No, but I am the mayor, and this is a big change for our community."

"You didn't answer my question." Mason's tone had turned icy. "Why do you need to meet the architects?"

"Because they asked me to come to the meeting. It was a last-minute thing."

"Your best friends, who you barely ever see anymore, invited you to dinner. Along with your husband. Aren't we more important than an out-of-town architect?"

"Mason, I—"

He held up his hand, irritation flashing in his eyes. "Don't bother making another excuse."

She jumped to her feet, his words piercing her. "But you don't understand."

"You're right. I don't." He turned to leave. "I don't understand why you've put your friends and me at the bottom of your massive to-do list."

Emotion tightened her throat. "I haven't put you last."

He turned back to face her. His silence and the muscle twitching in his cheek indicated that he did not agree.

How had their marriage come to this? A standoff over a Thursday-night meeting.

"You know what? I'll go without you. But you have to tell Wendy why you said no."

"Mason, wait."

"I need to get in the shower." He left and strode down the hall.

She sank in her chair, propped her elbows on her desk, and

buried her face in her hands. Why couldn't he appreciate that she was working so hard to keep everyone happy? This was their seventh year of marriage, and they'd fought more in the last few months than they ever had in the six years prior.

Her phone chirped. A text message from Jerry, one of the long-time employees at the candy company, filled the screen.

Call me, please. The pulling machine just broke. We need to get a mechanic here ASAP.

"Seriously?" She blinked, then read the message again. Failure of a crucial machine three weeks before Valentine's Day could tank their first-quarter sales completely. Her folks did not need another reason to entertain an offer to sell the company. Thankfully, her strategy with Jovi had worked. Sure, her sister hadn't been involved in day-to-day operations since, well, ever. But that didn't mean Jovi wouldn't be upset if they sold. She'd responded exactly how Isabel hoped she would—by offering to get on a plane.

Isabel jumped up, shrugged into her jacket, then dropped her phone into her handbag and hurried toward the door. On the way to the car, she texted both Jerry and Mason to let them know she was on her way to the factory to sort out scheduling repairs.

Part of her regretted not sticking around and speaking with Mason when he got out of the shower because he'd probably be asleep when she came home from her meeting. But she was tired of fighting with him about how she managed her time. For the sake of the family's business, she couldn't ignore a broken pulling machine.

"But, Daddy, I don't want to move."

Darby Jane looked up at him, chin wobbling. Her blue eyes

filled with fresh tears. Poor thing. She'd cried buckets in the last year. He hated that he'd provoked more sorrow.

"Baby girl, listen." Burke Solomon dropped to his knees beside her on the hardwood floor in their historic home's entryway. He smoothed her pale blond hair from her forehead. How to explain to a five-year-old that he couldn't live here? That Charleston couldn't be home. Not anymore. They had to go where people weren't constantly staring at him. Judging him. And he couldn't possibly live in a house where every single room reminded him of Mary Catherine and Henry.

"We're going to go where huge snowflakes are falling from a sky full of stars." He forced a smile and gently clasped her slender shoulders in his hands. "We'll learn to ice-skate together and build snowmen and get hot cocoa topped with whipped cream and sprinkles."

"I like cocoa." She sniffed. "Candy canes are yummy too."

"I'll take you to Evergreen Candy Company, where they make the best chocolates and the softest sugar cookies ever."

She hung her head. "Not better than Mommy's."

Again, with the punch in the gut. How did she remember Mary Catherine's sugar cookies? "Your mommy's cookies were pretty spectacular, but the ones in Evergreen, Alaska, are equally amazing."

"I don't want to go," she whispered, turning away from him. Bobo, her pink-and-gray hippopotamus, worn and smudged with dirt, dangled from one hand as she wandered toward her empty playroom. The place was packed up. A young couple moving down from New York had already signed a one-year rental agreement. Burke had four suitcases to take with them on the plane, and in a few minutes, the car carrier was scheduled to arrive. He'd sold his vehicle to an acquaintance who planned to resell the car at an auction. If his aunt's truck wasn't still in good shape, he'd have to buy something used and practical when they got to Alaska.

Selling here in Charleston had seemed less daunting than having his car transported to Alaska for an exorbitant fee. And to be honest, he didn't want his luxury sedan. Just one more excruciating reminder of the life he'd once known. Besides, the hefty payments were eating into his savings.

"Darby Jane, let's put on your coat, and you can walk across the street with me."

She turned and stared at him, her face blotchy from crying. "Why?"

"You're going to play with your friend Leah and see her new puppy. You like dogs, right?"

Their neighbors across the street, the Watkinses, had helped him out countless times in the last year. He'd stumbled through his tumultuous grief journey and endured the public scrutiny of being a single dad whose selfish decision had wiped out half his family. Today he had to call in one last favor because he did not want Darby Jane to see his car go away.

"I don't want to play with Leah." She hugged Bobo to her chest. "Why can't I stay here until we have to go?"

He held out her coat like going outside in the chilly air and hanging with a friend she'd likely never see again was a big thrill. Instead of just one more miserable thing he'd have to ask of her. "This will be probably your last visit for a while. It's polite to say goodbye. They've been so kind to us."

Katie Watkins, her husband, Todd, and their daughters, Leah and Grace, were among only a handful of people who'd tempered their harsh words. Who'd chosen kindness and empathy instead of disgust. He stopped short of mentioning that. Darby Jane was too little to understand. Mary Catherine's parents hadn't forgiven him. And at this point, it seemed like they never would. How could they just cut Darby Jane out of their lives, though? He couldn't wrap his mind around that. Still, he'd written them a letter and told them he and Darby Jane were moving to Alaska, and they were welcome anytime. That was the best he could do. Of course, he understood that his in-laws were heartbroken, and he didn't expect them to forgive him, because he couldn't forgive himself. But he wanted them to have a relationship with Darby Jane.

His brother, Shane, had stopped by before the movers came and tried to persuade him to reconsider. Insisted that leaving town wasn't a wise decision. Burke had resisted the temptation to remind Shane that he didn't know the first thing about coping with the loss of a spouse or an infant, given Shane didn't have a wife or children. But it would've been a wasted effort. Instead, they'd exchanged brief backslaps and polite, empty words.

Burke hadn't been convinced Shane's efforts were genuine, anyway. His brother's uneasiness hinted that their father had sent him to convince Burke to change his mind. Dad thought he was bananas for leaving the South and had told him in no uncertain terms that he should get back to the advertising agency where they had worked in tandem for years. Dad didn't seem to understand Burke hated advertising. He'd much rather write books. Well, at least that was how he felt when he'd left the firm. These days, he couldn't seem to string enough words together to make a complete sentence, much less a whole book. Worse, he'd blown past his deadline for submitting his second manuscript months ago. But that was next week's problem. Today, he had to figure out how to get Darby Jane out of the only home she'd ever known.

"Come on, sweet pea. Let's walk across the street. I need you to stay at Leah's house until I handle one last thing."

"What thing? I'll help you," Darby Jane said, moving closer.

He shrugged into his jacket. "This part is going to be kind of loud and scary."

Her chin wobbled again, and her mouth turned into a frown. "What's more scary than losing Mommy and baby Henry?"

Emotion welled, and he wasn't sure if he could tamp it down

this time. He tried his best not to lose his composure in front of his daughter, but sometimes the grief slipped out. He swallowed past the boulder lodged in his throat, then turned toward the door. "Come on. It'll be less than thirty minutes. You can pet the puppy, and you don't have to play with Leah if you don't want to. Miss Katie's going to keep you safe, okay? She probably has a great snack waiting for you."

Darby Jane set her stuffed animal down, put on her jacket, then snatched Bobo up again. They stepped out the front door and walked across the street, a crisp breeze sending dry leaves skittering down the lane.

After he dropped Darby Jane off, he walked down the neighbor's driveway in time to hear the rumble of a diesel engine. The double-decker car carrier eased down the street and stopped in front of his house. Brakes hissed and classic rock played from the speakers through the open window.

A burly guy wearing greasy gray coveralls and a faded ball cap stepped down from the cab. He spit tobacco in an empty plastic soda bottle before handing over an electronic tablet.

"How's it going? Are you Burke Solomon?"

Burke nodded and took the tablet. Why had he expected the standard unassuming tow truck? By now half the neighborhood probably had their noses pressed to their front windows. So much for hoping Katie would be able to distract Darby Jane with snacks and a cute puppy.

He signed all the places on the electronic forms the driver told him to, then stood back watching helplessly as the guy loaded his car into the last vacant spot on the lower deck of the carrier. A few minutes later, the truck pulled away, belching exhaust into the air. Bracing for the worst, Burke turned around to see Darby Jane in the window of the Watkinses' house, sobbing.

The look of disdain on Katie's face as she met his gaze through the window made him turn away. Yep, it was time to go. Moving to Evergreen wasn't going to be easy. He didn't have any idea if his wild notion would work out. He had to go where they could start over, where his little girl could have a delightful childhood. Because he was determined to make that happen for her.

Chapter Two

"Hello, ladies and gentlemen. For those in the gate area waiting for flight 723 from Anchorage to Evergreen, we regret to inform you that this flight has been canceled due to a high wind advisory in Evergreen."

"No. Way." Groaning, Jovi sagged against the column in the middle of the crowded gate.

"We'll rebook you on the next available flight," the gate agent continued, "but tomorrow morning's flight is full. We do, however, have limited seats available on the three-fifteen…"

"Seriously?" Jovi stopped listening. The additional details were difficult to hear over the rising chatter of her fellow disgruntled passengers, anyway.

"The wind? Really?" A middle-aged man sitting nearby yanked his phone from the pocket of his gray hoodie advertising a local brewery. "I didn't see no storm on the radar."

"Did she say tomorrow morning's flight is already booked?" A woman who looked like someone Jovi knew in middle school leaned toward the man sitting beside her. "That can't be. Who are all these people going to Evergreen on a Monday?"

He scowled, lifted his baseball cap and scratched his head. "Probably all the ones who don't want to drive on that new road. I told you that thing was a waste of money. The people that live here don't even want to use it."

Jovi turned away and drained the last sip of her coffee. She'd tried skipping the sugar and going heavier on the almond milk creamer, but it still tasted too bitter. Gross. After tossing the empty cup in the trash can, she pulled out her phone to text her parents and Isabel the latest news.

Maybe they'd recommend a friend she could call to stay with, because she did not relish the idea of spending a night in a lonely hotel room. Sure, she'd been to Anchorage countless times over the years, but rarely by herself. Besides, her now-canceled flight was supposed to be the third leg of a very long journey from Kansas City. The last four days since Isabel had called and asked her to come home had been a whirlwind. She'd packed her few belongings, carted them to the house of a coworker who'd graciously offered space in her basement, then cleaned her apartment from top to bottom so she'd get her deposit back. Her muscles ached from the intense effort. She wanted to fall into her mom's embrace, see her dad's eyes twinkle when he smiled, hug Isabel and Mason, then sleep for days in her bed.

If she could figure out how to get home.

Her phone hummed in her hand. A text message from Isabel popped onto the screen.

Have you left Anchorage yet? I need to find a way to get a replacement part for the pulling machine onto your flight.

Uh-oh. This storm was impacting more than just her travel plans. Poor Isabel. She didn't need another problem to solve. Jovi quickly typed a response.

Flight was just canceled. I can't decide what to do. If I can get a rental car, maybe I can bring the part with me? I'll keep you posted.

The dots bounced on her screen, then Isabel's answer arrived.

That would be amazing if you could pick up the part. I'll text you the address. And yes, please keep me posted.

Jovi didn't want to waste any more time standing around. Heaving the straps of her overstuffed backpack onto her shoulders, Jovi attempted to make her way toward the counter to rebook her flight.

The petite woman working the gate climbed up on a stool and grabbed the handheld microphone. "Once again, ladies and gentlemen, we apologize for canceling the flight. Due to a storm in Evergreen, wind gusts are preventing aircraft from landing safely. When Evergreen reopens its airport, you'll be among the first to know. In case you missed my previous announcement, tomorrow morning's flight is full, and we have limited seating available on the afternoon connection. Please form a line at the desk, and we'll address your concerns as quickly as possible. Thank you for understanding."

If most people were determined to fly, maybe she could get a rental car. When she'd come for Grandpa's funeral last January, Dad had picked her up and driven on the new highway. It was a hundred miles from Anchorage to Evergreen. Doable. Although running into a storm on the way gave her pause. It had been years since she'd navigated a rural Alaskan highway by herself at night in subzero temperatures. Which was exactly why her parents had encouraged her to fly to Evergreen. Neither Dad nor Mom had been willing to come and get her on short notice. Given the current weather situation, maybe driving wasn't the best strategy. Still, she did not want to stick around Anchorage to wait for the next available flight. And if she did rent a car, then she could pick up that part Isabel needed. Turning away from the long line that had already formed, she walked quickly toward the rental car counter in the main terminal.

"But Daddy, I have to find her. She's my Bobo." The distraught little girl standing outside the restroom caught Jovi's attention. Even though tears streamed down her cheeks, she looked adorable in her lavender jacket with faux fur lining on the hood, and jeans tucked into brand-new lace-up snow boots. She carried a stylish purple backpack with a small stuffed turtle dangling from the zipper.

Jovi let her gaze slide to the man standing beside the little girl. He was startlingly handsome. And not from Alaska. His high-end forest green parka, stone-colored pants and trail-running sneakers were dead giveaways.

He pinched the back of his neck with his hand. The poor guy looked exhausted.

The little girl tugged on the hem of his jacket. "Daddy, did you hear me? I have to find Bobo."

Jovi drifted closer. She didn't have time to waste if she planned to rent a car, but the heartrending tone in the precious child's voice kept her from moving on. "Excuse me. I know it's none of my business, but is there anything I can do to help?"

The man's head snapped up.

Oh, hello, five-o'clock shadow. And those eyes. She'd never seen a more perfect shade of amber. His hair was the color of milk chocolate, and he wore it a little shaggier than she'd expected for someone who gave off such a CEO-on-a-ski-trip vibe.

Confusion marred his handsome features. "Pardon?"

Right. She'd overstepped. She scrunched up her nose, then clutched at the straps of her backpack self-consciously. "Yeah, so, I'm sure you've got this. Sorry to bother you."

Heat bloomed on her cheeks as she turned to go.

"Wait. Daddy. Ask her to look for Bobo."

Jovi ducked her chin to hide her smile. This kid. Her exaggerated whisper paired with her cute Southern accent was just too much.

"Sweetheart, she's probably in a hurry to catch a flight," he said.

Jovi whirled back around. "My flight was just canceled."

"I'm Darby Jane." The little girl stuck out her hand. "What's your name?"

The man heaved an exasperated sigh.

Despite the curmudgeon's obvious need to keep his business private, she couldn't resist shaking his daughter's hand. "I'm Jovi. It's a pleasure to meet you, Darby Jane. That accent is the cutest thing I've ever heard. Where are you from?"

"Charleston, South Carolina."

"Whoa. You've traveled a long way."

The oversize white bow with pink polka dots clipped to her ponytail bobbed along with her solemn nod. "I lost my Bobo."

"That's what I hear," Jovi said. "I'm so sorry. May I help you look?" Jovi met the attractive-but-grumpy man's weary gaze again. "Some key details about Bobo might be good to know."

"Her favorite stuffed animal is a pink-and-gray hippopotamus." He surveyed the corridor around the entrance to the restrooms. "We dropped it between our last plane and here."

"I didn't drop it," Darby Jane insisted, swiping at her tears with her hand. "I went to the bathroom by myself because Daddy says that's what big girls do. When it was time to wash my hands, I put Bobo on the counter, 'cept I forgot her. N-now she's gone."

Darby Jane's obvious distress as she stumbled over the last part of her explanation sent a profound sense of loss jolting straight through Jovi. They had to find Bobo.

"And you're super sure you didn't leave her on the plane?"

Jovi eyed the excessively long line of women snaking out of the ladies' room behind Darby Jane.

"This. Bathroom." Darby Jane stomped her foot and pointed.

Okay, then.

"Darby Jane." Her father gently placed his hand on her tiny shoulder. "Don't stomp."

"How about if I go in and take another look?" Jovi formed her mouth into a we're-all-in-this-together smile. "Sometimes when I'm upset, I can't see the missing thing, even when it's right in front of me."

Hope flickered in Darby Jane's blue eyes.

Her father, on the other hand, chose that exact moment to check the time on his smart-looking watch. "I'd like to get on the road, Darbs. Maybe we can order you a new hippopotamus online."

Jovi sucked in a breath. *Oy. You are heartless, dude.*

The child's expression crumpled. Her whole body shook as she started sobbing all over again.

Yikes. He'd dug himself into a deep hole. "I'll check the bathroom."

Without waiting for a response, she left him standing with Darby Jane and squeezed by the women spilling out into the busy corridor. "Excuse me. Pardon me. Sorry. Looking for a lost stuffed animal. I promise I won't cut."

"Hey, hold on," a lady grumbled. "I've been standing here ten minutes."

"I'm not cutting. Need to find a stuffed animal, that's all."

A cacophony of toilets flushing, women talking, and hand dryers blowing greeted her. Jovi stood, deflated, staring at the closed stall doors. Then she scanned the counter beside the sinks. No stuffed animals in sight.

"Is this the one?" An older lady wearing a blue-and-gray sweatshirt with the words *Thankful and Blessed* printed on the front gestured to a changing station for babies mounted on the wall. A well-loved hippopotamus sat on top.

"Oh, my." Jovi clapped her hands together. "I think that might be Bobo. Thank you. I'll take it to the little girl who's waiting outside."

"No problem, dear." Her papery skin crinkled when she smiled. "Happy New Year."

Jovi's frigid heart softened. For the first time this month, she returned the greeting with genuine enthusiasm. "Happy New Year to you as well."

She plucked the stuffed animal from its perch, then squeezed back through the line at the door. When she got out into the hallway, she thrust the hippopotamus triumphantly in the air. "Darby Jane, look."

The little girl dropped her backpack on the floor and ran toward Jovi at full speed.

She grabbed Bobo and hugged it tight. "Thank you. Thank you, thank you. I love you, Bobo, and I missed you so much."

Jovi bit her lip as she witnessed the girl's tender reunion with her stuffed animal. Darby Jane's unfiltered gratitude summoned an unexpected wave of tears. Jovi gulped them back down and forced herself to meet the grumpy dad's gaze. At least he wasn't frowning.

"Wow, I did not think we'd find it," he said. "What did you say your name was?"

"Jovi."

"I'm Burke. Thanks for your help."

Was that a smile? She must've imagined it, because the curve of his lips quickly flattened back into a thin line.

"Not a problem, Burke. Safe travels." She hurried on her way. A canceled flight might keep her in Anchorage tonight, but at least she'd made a small difference in a cute little girl's life. And maybe her kindness would inspire Darby Jane's father to cheer up.

★ ★ ★

He probably should've handled that differently.

"But I didn't even get to say goodbye to her." Darby Jane pooched out her lower lip.

Burke opened his mouth to encourage Darby Jane to pick up the pace, then changed his mind. He'd been short-tempered enough already with her lately. Did it matter if they took an extra fifteen minutes to walk to baggage claim?

He tucked an errant strand of her hair behind her ear. "Maybe we'll see her again."

She eyed him doubtfully. "Where?"

"Well, most people go to the same general area to pick up their suitcases. She might be waiting there. Come on. We get to ride this escalator over here."

"Oh-kayyy." Darby Jane stretched the word out into three syllables, then stifled a yawn. "Look. Yummy treats."

He eyed the snack stand as they passed by. Chocolate chip cookies beckoned from behind a glass case. Premade sandwiches, bottled drinks and bags of chips filled the shelves. Nothing fancy. Burke hesitated. Breakfast had been eons ago, a hurried affair at the hotel where they'd spent their last night in Charleston.

"Sweet pea, as soon as we get our bags and the car, then I promise I'll figure something out for supper."

"Those cookies look so good." Darby Jane slowed again, looking back over her shoulder.

Lord, give me strength.

He hadn't been great about praying lately. All right, to be honest, since he'd lost Mary Catherine and Henry, he'd pretty much stopped speaking to God altogether. But the long trek across the continent had brought prayer to his lips more often in a single day than he'd uttered in the last year.

"They do look good," he agreed. "I'm worried that if we eat cookies for supper, we'll have unhappy tummies later."

And tending to a sick child on the road alone was not how he envisioned his night going.

"Do you have any apples or carrot sticks left in your bag?"

She nodded. "But I'm not hungry for those."

He bit back a smile. "Yeah, me either. Careful, please. Watch your step." Holding her hand in his, he guided her onto the moving escalator. Had he asked too much of Darby Jane? This move was a huge change. One that his therapist and her pediatrician had advised against. He'd turned his daughter's world upside down and expected her to handle it like a grown-up.

As they descended into the airport's lower level, she held Bobo tucked under her chin, her bright eyes taking in her surroundings. Then her breath hitched. "Is that *snow*?"

He stared through the wide windows, trying to get his bearings. The digital clock on the arrivals and departures screens overhead indicated it was just past five in the evening. But outside, light from the streetlamps and vehicles punctuated an unsettling inky darkness. The silvery-blue high beams from a large truck illuminated thick, wet snowflakes.

Oh, my. "You got it, baby girl. Your first snow. How exciting."

But his stomach clenched. Maybe this wasn't a great idea. He'd never lived in a winter climate. Twice he and Mary Catherine had flown to New York City as a splurge to see a Broadway show or enjoy a weekend away. Someone else had handled the driving, though.

All the talk of canceled flights propelled him toward baggage claim. He didn't want to think about having to hole up in a hotel somewhere tonight.

If they could just keep going, hopefully, they'd get safely to Evergreen.

A large sign propped against a stack of three suitcases on top of the baggage carousel reminded passengers to check the names on tags before grabbing their luggage. People milled about, scanning the sea of duffel bags, suitcases, and ski equipment. A steady hum of conversation, punctuated by a baby crying and a dog barking, filled the air.

Burke and Darby Jane's four suitcases had been pulled from the circulating belt and sat waiting for him outside the airline's baggage claim office. Darby Jane patiently trailed after him to the luggage-cart rack. He let her insert his credit card, then showed her how to collect the rented cart and load their bags.

"I'm getting so tired, Daddy. Are we almost done?"

"Yes, I promise." He swiped at the perspiration on his forehead, then turned and gestured toward the orange-and-blue sign glowing at the opposite end of the airport's lower level. "We only have to walk right over there, speak to those nice folks, get our keys to the car we're renting, then we'll be on our way."

Darby Jane yawned again. "But what about Aunt Lois's truck?"

"That truck is waiting for us in Evergreen. We're going to borrow this other car for a little while until we're sure that Aunt Lois's truck will be what we need."

Assuming he could even get it started. His mom, Aunt Lois's only sibling, had remarried and currently spent the winters with her husband in St. John. She didn't care about the house in Evergreen and was thrilled that Burke wanted to assume care. But that meant its condition was a mystery. He'd tried not to stress about what he might realistically find when he got there.

"Can I ride on the cart too?"

"No, that's not safe. Hold my hand, please. We're almost finished with all this walking."

They moved slowly, working their way among the frazzled passengers pushing their overloaded carts and strollers with irritable children.

A dog barked again, deep and loud, startling Darby Jane.

The animal with a white-and-black masked face peered through the opening in a large transport crate, its ice-blue eyes trained on them.

"That's a big doggie," Darby Jane said, clinging tightly to his hand as she hovered close to him.

"That's a husky. Such beautiful dogs."

"No, thank you." Darby Jane sped up, and he kept pace, rolling the heavy cart along the grungy linoleum floor. She'd been a real trouper today. Hopefully, he could keep her awake long enough to stop someplace for supper.

Lines had formed at all five of the rental car counters. Tension crackled in the air. Burke's stomach knotted as he picked up snippets of the conversations. People were clearly not pleased with the news being delivered by harried customer service representatives. He maneuvered his luggage cart toward the company that had a car waiting for him. The woman speaking to the attendant looked like the same person who'd found Bobo.

"That's Miss Jovi!" Darby pointed, a wide smile spreading across her exhausted face.

"See?" He tapped the end of her upturned nose with his finger. "It didn't take long to find her, did it?"

Jovi didn't turn around to speak with them, though. The tone in her voice and the way she clutched at the straps of her backpack indicated there might be a problem. Burke eased the luggage cart to a stop and tried not to eavesdrop.

"How can there not be any more rental cars?"

The older man with thinning salt-and-pepper hair and a robust mustache stared at his computer screen. "I'm sure it's not the news you were hoping to hear, ma'am, but this storm's a doozy. Several flights have been canceled, and the airport's entire fleet has all been rented out." He slid a business card across the counter and tapped it with his pen. "Here's my card.

Call first thing tomorrow, and I can give you a better idea of when I might have a car available. If you don't reschedule your flight, that is."

He craned his neck to see around Jovi and made eye contact with Burke. "May I help you, sir?"

Burke cleared his throat. He didn't want to infringe on Jovi's personal space. But she didn't appear to be in a hurry to move.

"Come on, Darby Jane." He squeezed past the cart then stopped beside Jovi at the counter.

She turned and faced him. "Oh, hello. Bad news. No more cars."

"Oh. Um…" Burke feigned a grimace, then shifted his gaze toward the man and held up his smartphone. "I believe I have a reservation for Burke Solomon."

"Good evening, Mr. Solomon. Let me see what I can do for you."

Jovi frowned. Her vivid blue eyes toggled between Burke and the man at the counter. "But I thought you said you didn't have any cars."

"I don't have anything available to rent for walk-in customers. But Mr. Solomon's had this reservation for months."

Jovi looked as though she'd just tasted sour milk. Darby Jane tugged on her father's hand for what had to be the millionth time today. "Daddy, we should share," she whispered.

Burke pretended not to hear, but Darby Jane was not quiet. Her exaggerated stage whisper was tough to ignore.

Jovi stood rooted firmly in place.

The customer service representative scrolled and typed on his computer for what seemed like an eternity. Finally, he stopped and glanced at Burke again. "We have a four-door crossover SUV waiting for you, Mr. Solomon. I'll need to see your driver's license and verify that the credit card on file is your preferred account. Then you'll be on your way."

"Excellent. Thank you." He fumbled for his wallet, the

weight of Jovi's gaze heating his skin. She had helped him out when he'd been in an exasperating spot, unable to find Bobo or access the women's restroom on his own. But he didn't know anything about her. Sure, she'd been kind and gone out of her way to help him. Should he allow her in his car with his kid? Besides, what if they were going in two completely different directions?

"Daddy." Darby Jane yanked on his sleeve.

He dragged his hand across his face, then glanced down at her.

"We have to share. It's the right thing to do."

"Smart kid you have there, Burke." The amusement lacing Jovi's voice made his face heat with shame. He sighed, then slowly turned to Jovi.

Her brows sailed upward toward her blond bangs.

"Do you need a ride?"

She splayed her palm across her chest. "Why, Burke, I thought you'd never ask. Yes, I most certainly do."

He pinned her with a long look. This was not the least bit funny. "Where are you headed?"

"Home." Smiling, she bounced up on her toes. "I'm from Evergreen."

Well, how about that? Burked tried—and likely failed—to mask his annoyance.

"Yay!" Darby Jane tucked Bobo in the crook of her elbow, then clapped her hands. "That's where we're going too. Come with us, Miss Jovi. It'll be so fun."

Uncertainty flickered across Jovi's face as her smile faded. "Yeah, so fun."

Burke half listened to the instructions about how to collect his rental car, then tucked his wallet back in his pocket and pushed the luggage cart toward the exit. Jovi and Darby Jane followed behind, chatting about their favorite road trip snacks and songs.

The muscles coiled in a tight knot between his shoulder blades. What a way to cap off a grueling day of travel. Driving in winter weather with a nearly delirious five-year-old and the most irritatingly optimistic woman he'd ever met.

Chapter Three

The man drove like he'd never seen snow. At this rate, they wouldn't get to Evergreen until tomorrow. Jovi rattled the ice in her cup, left over from their dinner stop at a fast-food place, then took a long sip through her straw. She tried to discreetly lean across the center console to sneak a peek at the speedometer. They crept along at a lousy thirty-two miles per hour.

Stifling a sigh, she reached for the dial on the stereo and upped the volume on the radio. Some might say this song was overplayed, but she couldn't resist humming along to the iconic country hit.

Burke let go of the wheel just long enough to jab at the button and silence the music. "Do you mind? I'm trying to concentrate."

He resumed his white-knuckle grip and hunched farther over the steering wheel.

"You need total silence when you drive?"

"In treacherous conditions, yes."

"Got it." Jovi squirmed in the passenger seat. Sweat dampened the back of the white T-shirt she'd layered under her cardigan. Burke had the defroster cranked to its highest setting, and the heater pumping warm air into the vehicle. Rather than adjust any of the settings and risk aggravating him more than she already had, she'd have to peel off her outer layer.

She unclipped her seat belt and then shrugged off her jacket.

He glanced her way. The silvery light from the dash illuminated his pinched features. "What are you doing?"

She hesitated, her arm stuck in one sleeve. "Taking off my jacket. It's too hot in here."

"It's not wise to unbuckle while the vehicle's moving." Disapproval clung to every word. "Especially in these conditions."

Oh, dear. He really needed to simmer down a notch. Sure it had been snowing since they'd left Anchorage, but at least the wind wasn't blowing hard. They were totally safe. Ditching her jacket on the floorboard, she pulled her seat belt back on and quickly snapped it into place. "See? I'm safe as can be. Now I won't pass out. Which means I can keep you awake. So really, that was all for your benefit."

His one-syllable grunt made her smile. "Quick question. Have you ever driven in snow before?"

"Not recently. What was your first clue?"

"You're going under the speed limit, clutching that steering wheel like it's our lifeline, and, well, you look terrified. How'd I do? Are my observations accurate?"

"If I may, I'd like to point out that if we hadn't detoured to pick up your precious part, then we'd likely be much closer to our destination by now."

Her scalp prickled. Could he be any more obnoxious?

"Look, I get that you're annoyed I asked you to drive a measly four blocks out of your way to meet a lady who stayed after hours to make sure she handed that package to me in person. By the way, thanks to her willingness to go above and beyond the call of duty, I now have that *precious part* in my possession.

And if we ever get to Evergreen, I'll be able to give it to my sister. Then hopefully, the mechanic will be able to install it, and a small family-owned company that provides several jobs for residents will be up and running smoothly again. So I apologize for the inconvenience, but on behalf of the many customers worldwide who enjoy their sweet treats from Evergreen Candy Company, thank you for understanding."

Whoa. She slumped back against the headrest, slightly out of breath.

Silence hung heavy between them.

Then the corners of his mouth twitched. "Feel good to get that all out?"

Ignoring his snide comment, she took another sip of her diet soda. The carbonated liquid slid down her throat. Maybe she should apologize. That was kind of a lot. Yet she felt lighter somehow. Besides, somebody needed to tell him what was up, because he was kind of grinchy.

Good deeds and generosity didn't really seem like they were his thing.

Bright lights from a truck driving behind them illuminated the interior of their car. Burke held up his hand to shield his eyes from the reflection in the mirror. The other driver passed quickly. A spray of snow kicked up from the truck's tires and coated their windshield.

Grumbling under his breath, Burke twisted the knob and forced the windshield wipers to work at top speed. The truck's taillights glowed red, then disappeared into the darkness up ahead.

Jovi deposited her drink back in the cup holder. "Has anyone ever told you that you're grumpy?"

"Has anyone ever told you that you're sarcastic?"

"Just you." She studied his strong profile, noting the tension settling in his angular jaw. "Let me guess. You're not a fan?"

"It's a challenging communication style and one I find difficult to engage with."

"Oh, that's good to know. Thank you. Perhaps I'll try a kinder, gentler approach. Burke, you must be exhausted after traveling all day with a young child. What can I do to make this final leg of your journey more enjoyable?"

"See? That right there." Burke shot her another exasperated look. "You didn't mean a word of that, did you?"

"Don't be ridiculous. I meant all of it. That was empathy."

"With a generous dose of sarcasm. Again, it's all in the tone."

She blew out a gusty breath. "You sure know how to make a hundred miles feel like a thousand."

"Happy to be of service."

They rode for a few more minutes in a terse silence until Burke cleared his throat. "Does it always snow like this here?"

Laughter bubbled from her lips. He shot her another look. This one fierce. She clamped her hand over her mouth. Darby Jane had fallen asleep about an hour ago. She didn't blame him for being upset if her outburst woke the sleeping child.

"Sorry," she whispered. "But you did just move to Alaska, right? Did no one tell you about the weather?"

"This seems a bit excessive."

She peered into the darkness. Their headlights tunneled into the road ahead, where the snow was now pelting them at a dizzying rate. An ominous feeling danced down her spine. Maybe he had a valid point. Now that she'd taken a closer look, this did seem like a lot of snow all at once.

"We've been on the road for almost three hours," Burke said. "Does it typically take this long to drive from Anchorage to Evergreen?"

"No, it shouldn't. This is only my second trip on this road, though. They finished building it about a year and a half ago."

"Before that people came and went from Evergreen by airplane?"

"Or dog sleds and snow machines. But yes, we relied mostly on planes."

"Wow." He shook his head in disbelief. "I can't imagine traveling anywhere by a team of dogs pulling a sled."

"It's not for everyone," Jovi said. "How did you decide you wanted to move to Evergreen if you're unaccustomed to snow?"

"My aunt has a place there. We visited several times when I was a kid, and those are some of my happiest memories. I wanted Darby Jane to experience an Alaskan winter."

"Who's your aunt?"

"Lois Phillips."

Jovi's breath hitched. "No way. Really?"

"Do you know her?"

Oh, wow. Where to begin? "Well, from what little I've been told, your aunt and my grandmother used to be the best of friends. Until they weren't. The Wrights and the Phillipses have been feuding for longer than you and I have been alive."

Burke drummed his thumb against the steering wheel. "So you're one of Carol and Dennis's granddaughters?"

"Yep. My sister, Isabel, is two years older." Jovi angled her body more toward his. "Forgive me for asking, but did you and I meet when we were kids?"

He shook his head. "Aunt Lois didn't want me to play with Carol's grandkids. Ever. She made that quite clear. To be honest, she had so many activities planned when I visited, there wasn't time to wonder about the kids who lived nearby."

"I still can't believe they live down the road from one another and manage to never speak. Or they used to, anyway." Jovi softened her tone. "I was sorry to hear that Lois had passed."

"Thank you," Burke said. "I hate that Darby Jane didn't get to meet her or my uncle Mac. My mother, Lois's sister, well, they weren't exactly close. Polar opposites, really, and there's a substantial age difference. But I loved to visit Aunt Lois and Uncle Mac."

"They were good people," Jovi said. "Mac and Lois both loved Evergreen and always supported the community. I wish I knew why she and Grammie had a falling-out."

"Yeah, she and my uncle lived in several places throughout the years. He was in the military, and they moved quite a bit. But they seemed happiest in Evergreen."

"Agreed."

He looked over at her again.

"What?" She squirmed in her seat, surprised by the way one side of his mouth lifted in a hint of a smile.

"We agreed on something."

"That your aunt and uncle were good people? That wasn't hard." She twisted the beaded bracelet on her wrist around in a slow circle. "Here's something we probably won't agree on."

"Oh?"

"Why don't you let me drive the rest of the way?"

"Absolutely not."

"Why not?"

"Because I've got this," he insisted. "And your name's not on the rental contract."

"You're a rule-follower, aren't you?"

"One hundred percent."

"Are you coming to bed, or do you want me to throw more wood on the fire?"

Isabel turned from the window where she'd been pacing for the last twenty minutes.

Mason stood in the archway between the kitchen and the living room. He wore his faded Evergreen High School basketball T-shirt and red-and-white plaid flannel pajama bottoms.

"I can't go to sleep. Not until I know Jovi's home."

He ran his hand over his close-cropped blond hair. She yearned for him to move closer. To offer to stay up and wait with her. Maybe watch the next episode of *The Crown*. But he looked worn-out. Hadn't said much at dinner either. Only that he'd had a rough day dealing with the storm and its impact on keeping the roads plowed.

"Have you heard from her?" Barefoot, Mason crossed the room and stopped beside her. The scent of his shampoo, familiar with its hint of spice and citrus, made her pulse thrum.

"After she told me her flight was canceled, she said she'd caught a ride with someone she'd met at the airport." Isabel pulled her phone from the pocket of her robe and scrolled through her messages. "Then I got one more saying she had the part for the pulling machine, and they were on their way. But that was almost three hours ago."

At six feet tall, Mason stood a head above her. She'd always relished the strength of his steady presence. What would he do if she sagged against him? Leaned her head on his chest. Was their relationship so strained that he wouldn't allow her to find comfort in his strong embrace? Things had still felt tense ever since she'd missed dinner with Wendy and Jake. But that had been almost a week ago. To his credit, Mason had been a little more understanding once he'd found out about the broken pulling machine. He'd even stopped by the factory, looked over the unit, and tried to figure out if he could fix it. But neither Mason nor Phil, their longtime local mechanic, had been able to solve the problem. They desperately needed the part riding somewhere between here and Anchorage with Jovi and her stranger companion.

"I'm worried, Mason. This wind is vicious."

"Jovi takes care of herself. She always has." Mason linked his arms across his broad chest, the sleeves of his T-shirt pulling taut around his muscular biceps.

Isabel scoffed. "She caught a ride with someone she doesn't know."

"Didn't you say her flight was canceled? Sounds like her options were limited."

He had a valid point. And maybe she was worrying too much. Isabel pinched her lips shut, pocketed her phone, and turned back toward the window. The wind howled around their house. Snow blew sideways. At least eight inches had accumulated in the yard, and the forecast called for another ten before morning. She rubbed at the ache in her sternum.

She really didn't want to ask Mason for anything. Especially since he'd probably tell her sending out a search party at this point was ridiculous. Dangerous, even.

The wireless speaker nearby played one of her favorite pop songs, but she didn't feel like singing along or swaying to the upbeat rhythm.

Slowly, Mason reached out and pulled her to him. "Babe, it's going to be fine."

He brushed his lips against her forehead. She sighed, relieved to reconnect. Behind them, the fire crackled in the hearth. Maybe she'd misread him.

"What if they run out of gas? Or they get in an accident?"

His strong hand gently rubbed her arm. "Your imagination is on overdrive. They're probably taking things slow. Or they stopped to grab something to eat."

The worn fabric of his shirt felt smooth against her cheek. Mason's heart beat against her ear. Strong and steady. "I just want my sister home," she said quietly.

"I know you do. And she will be here soon."

"It's probably selfish of me, but I want her here because I'm hoping she'll be able to help me come up with a new product. Something that will dazzle our customers and perform so well that we can convince Mom and Dad not to sell the business."

Mason tensed. Isabel lifted her head and stared up at him, trying not to get distracted by the appealing stubble on his jaw. "What?"

"You don't want to sell?"

"No. Of course not."

He gritted his teeth and peered out into the darkness. "But you said the business has been struggling and holiday sales were disappointing. If you sell, imagine the time you'll have to focus on other things."

A lump formed in her throat. "What other things? Mason, my grandparents literally grew that business from nothing. It's not fair to sell out to a global conglomerate just because we've hit a downturn."

"Oh, here we go." Mason dropped his arm to his side.

"Have you not heard anything I've said in the past two weeks?"

"Isabel, take a breath." Mason held up his palm to interrupt. "For the record, I've heard plenty. And by the way, I've been trying to find time to talk to you about what's going on with me. But there's very little space in that packed calendar of yours."

Her jaw drifted open. Seriously?

"Don't look at me like that. I've dropped several hints that I need more from you, but evidently my needs are insignificant."

She sucked in a breath. "When did I say your needs were insignificant?"

He braced his hands on his slim hips. Irritation rippled across his ruddy features. "You didn't have to say it at all. The message came through loud and clear."

"That is *not fair*."

Shaking his head, he turned away. "I'm not doing this with you."

"Not doing what?" She cut quick strides toward him, anger simmering in her belly. "Having a conversation? Clarifying your accusations?"

"I'm going to bed because I have a phone interview first thing in the morning for a job in Juneau," Mason called back over his shoulder. "Good night, Isabel."

At the end of the hall, he slammed their bedroom door closed.

An interview for a job in Juneau? Since when? Her heart heavy at the realization that her marriage might genuinely be in trouble, Isabel blinked back tears, then sent Jovi another text. If Mason chose sleep over talking this out, she wasn't going to stand in his way. It was almost midnight, and the storm seemed to be getting worse. There was no way she could just crawl into bed and fall asleep. Not until she knew for sure Jovi was home.

So maybe his need for control was a bit over the top. All for good reason, though. Reasons he didn't want or need to explain to the chipper woman riding shotgun. Burke stole a sidelong glance. Her blond hair swung forward as she dipped her head and used the flashlight from her phone to rummage through her bag.

"Everything all right?" He didn't want to stop again, not that there appeared to be that option. They hadn't passed a gas station or a café in the last hour.

She held up a small bag of chocolate and peanut butter candy. "Sugar craving. Would you like some?"

"Please." He'd drained the last of his soda a while back. A jolt of sugar and chocolate would help him stay alert.

"I tried texting my sister to let her know we're coming, but I'm not getting any service." Jovi set her phone back in the center console next to their empty cups. "She's going to be worried."

He held out his hand, and she poured half a dozen pieces of candy into his palm.

"Thanks." Burke popped the treats into his mouth, savored the chocolate peanut butter concoction, and tried to ignore the plummeting temperatures indicated on the dash. Thirty-five degrees below zero. How was that even possible?

"Is there typically service out here?" He peered out the side window. Frost on the glass obscured his view. Snow and the dark shadows of trees covered in snow were all he could identify.

Jovi sighed. "I—I don't know."

At least the storm had eased up. His wipers weren't working quite as hard as they had been a few minutes ago. Eyes gritty, he straightened his spine and tilted his head side to side to alleviate the stiffness in his neck. Should he give up and let Jovi take over? Undoubtedly, she had far more experience navigating winter weather than he did. Still, the stubborn part of him couldn't handle relinquishing control. Couldn't handle the notion of anything going wrong. Not with his precious little girl asleep in the back seat.

"Maybe we're in a brief dead spot," he said. "Didn't you say this road was all about progress? Seems odd that you can't text."

"Yeah, I don't get it either." Jovi crumpled the candy bag into a ball and tucked it out of sight. "Mining companies from Australia or someplace like that wanted access to the underground natural resources near here. People who own fly-in fishing lodges and other high-end accommodations felt their exclusivity was being threatened. They cater to a certain kind of client. Anyway, it was a protracted battle."

"Did they think a road would give them more of an everyman clientele?"

Jovi yawned. "Excuse me. Sorry. It's been a long day. I didn't really keep up with all the debates. Evergreen has changed for the better since they built the road, according to my sister."

"Has she lived there her whole life?"

"Yes, she has, and she's currently the mayor."

"Good for her," Burke said. "That's probably an intriguing role."

"She seems to love it. Between that, managing operations at the candy company and keeping up with our grandmother's care, Isabel's a busy lady."

"So about the candy company." He drummed his thumb against the steering wheel. "Is that the place that put homemade marshmallows in hot chocolate and made that incredible chocolate with peanut butter in the middle?"

"Wait. Your aunt wouldn't let you play with us, but you can still remember the marshmallows and the chocolate peanut butter balls?"

He shrugged. "I suspect Uncle Mac sneaked in the goods. That candy and those marshmallows were the highlights of our holiday visits. And the jelly she put on our toast. Man, that was delicious. What was the flavor?"

"Grammie made a mean rose-hip jelly."

Burke snapped his fingers. "That's it. Rose hip. The name used to make me laugh. I still dream about that stuff sometimes."

"I hate to break it to you, but due to recent staff changes and lackluster sales, I'm not sure they'll keep manufacturing all of the signature products."

Whoa. Staff changes, declining sales and a broken machine. Regret knifed at him. Okay, so maybe he should've been more understanding about stopping to get that part they needed. "Is that why you're coming home? To help keep the business afloat?"

Jovi hesitated. "I don't know about that. My sister asked me to come home, help with day-to-day operations, and somehow convince our parents not to sell the company."

"Big-city girl comes home to rescue her family's small-town candy business. Sounds like one of those wretched made-for-TV movies."

She didn't bother to stifle her laughter this time.

"What's so funny?"

"Nothing." Jovi waved off his question, her shoulders trembling as she kept laughing.

"Please. Enlighten me. What's so funny?"

"Oh, it's just..." she tried to catch her breath "...not a surprise that you don't like sweet, wholesome entertainment."

"I need something with suspense," he said. "International espionage. A propulsive plot. Is that so wrong?"

"Nope. Not wrong."

He gave her the side-eye. "You're mocking me."

"Not mocking." She held up her open hand. "It's consistent with what I've observed about you so far, that's all."

"Daddy, where are we?" Darby Jane's sleepy voice from the back seat interrupted their banter.

"Hey, sweet pea. Hang in there. We're almost to Evergreen."

"How much longer?" Darby Jane whined. "I'm thirsty."

Jovi swiveled in her seat. "About thirty more miles. It won't be long."

"I can't wait for thirty miles," Darby Jane mumbled. "Do you have any water?"

Burke fumbled behind his seat for his backpack. "I have some water left over from our flight. It's in the side pouch."

Jovi tapped the overhead light on. "You focus on driving. I'll get it."

"Thanks." He returned his hand to the wheel and blinked against the fatigue.

The plastic bottle crackled in Jovi's hand. "Here you go, Darby Jane."

"Thank you."

"You're welcome." Jovi reached up to turn off the overhead light. She'd been so kind to Darby Jane. A pleasant warmth stirred in his chest. He forced himself to keep his eyes on the road.

Jovi was an attractive woman with delicate features, including a heart-shaped face and a pert, upturned nose. Not that he was interested in romance. At all. And especially not with someone from a family his aunt had been feuding with for decades. Once they were settled, he'd have to do some covert investigating. Because Aunt Lois didn't have a vindictive bone in her body. There had to be a valid reason for the rift between his family and the Wrights. And if there was one thing writing books had taught him, it was how to research. He'd make it his mission to get to the bottom of this feud.

Chapter Four

Finally.

Jovi settled with her family around their favorite table beside the front window at Trailside, Evergreen's iconic diner. The brutal trip from Kansas City, including navigating last night's storm with the persnickety rule-following Burke Solomon, had been worth it. Because she'd been reunited with her favorite people. There wasn't an empty booth in the dining area or a vacant stool at the L-shaped counter. Conversation ebbed and flowed as the servers hurried from the kitchen to tables, serving up hearty breakfasts, coffee and fresh pastries.

Yawning, Jovi reached for the steaming mug of coffee Mom had filled from the carafe, then cast an appreciative glance around the restaurant. "What do you know about Lois and Mac Phillips's nephew?"

Mom's spoon clattered to the speckled beige Formica table, spattering droplets of coffee on Dad's plaid flannel shirt. Isabel, Mom and Dad exchanged pensive looks.

Huh. Interesting.

"Sore subject?" Jovi paused with her coffee halfway to her lips.

"Grammie and Lois were the best of friends," Mom said quietly, dabbing a paper napkin against Dad's sleeve.

Jovi swallowed the first sip of the rich house blend, letting it warm her insides. "So I've heard. But I never understood why they stopped speaking, although that might be the reason why I didn't know Lois and Mac had nephews."

Isabel's phone hummed on the table. She glanced at the screen, huffed out a long breath, then scooped up the device and deposited it in her handbag.

"Everything okay?" Mom asked.

"That was Mason. He's... Never mind." Isabel's tight smile and dismissive shake of her head earned a curious arched eyebrow from their mother. Ignoring her, Isabel shifted her attention back to Jovi. "What brought this on? Your interest in the Phillips family, I mean."

"I rode into town with Burke Solomon last night," Jovi said. "He mentioned fond memories of his childhood visits to Evergreen with his aunt Lois and uncle Mac."

Dad leaned back as their server brought their order to the table. Once she'd departed, they joined hands, and he offered a quick blessing.

After he finished, Jovi unwrapped the paper napkin and cutlery. "Do you remember anything about Mac and Lois's nephews?"

Dad added a dollop of butter to his toast. "Vaguely. I think they came with their mother, often around Christmas or to celebrate the New Year."

Isabel topped off her coffee. "The older brother is named Shane."

"How do you know?"

"Because Charlie Schumacher is their family's point of contact." Isabel sprinkled pepper on her scrambled eggs. "I was in line behind him at the grocery store before Christmas and overheard him talking on the phone. Then he hung up and told his girlfriend that Mac and Lois's nephew planned to move into their cabin after the holidays."

Jovi sliced her utensils through her ham and cheese omelet. "So what you're saying is, if I want more details, just hang out at the grocery store?"

"The electric company might be a better option," Isabel said. "Those ladies know everything."

"Burke and his family must not have visited often, because he didn't know how to drive in the snow, and we can't recall seeing them around town," Jovi said. "Which is odd, because his whole reason for moving here seems to center around his nostalgic memories."

"For as long as I've been alive my folks made it clear we weren't supposed to speak to Lois, Mac, or anyone at their house," Dad said. "My mother was adamant Lois could not be trusted."

"But Lois and Mac volunteered at church and kept score at basketball games. People around town really seemed to love them," Jovi said. "And they lived down the road from your parents for years, so how did Grammie and Lois go from being best friends to not speaking to one another, when they were neighbors?"

Dad shrugged and plucked a slice of bacon from his plate.

"I realize Grammie isn't her usual self," Jovi said gently. "I would never want to do anything to upset her or make her memory loss more traumatic, but this guy moving here as a single dad because he remembers good candy and homemade marshmallows... It's super intriguing."

Thoughts of Burke's piercing gaze and Darby Jane's grateful expression when she'd been reunited with Bobo at the airport spooled through her head. Two highlights from an otherwise miserable travel day. She quickly diverted her attention to her scrumptious breakfast.

"Where did they move from?" Dad picked up his glass of orange juice. "And what does he do for a living if he can afford to move here?"

"Good questions." Jovi swallowed a bite of her omelet, then set her fork down and pulled her phone from her purse. "They came from Charleston, South Carolina. I meant to do some investigating last night, but I was way too tired."

"South Carolina?" Isabel's brow furrowed. "That's a long way to go, especially with a kid. Is the wife coming later?"

The first image that popped up from her internet search featured a beautiful woman leaving a historic-looking home. Jovi scanned the caption and article. "Whoa. Apparently, he's a best-selling author. I had no idea. Have you ever heard of him, Dad? He writes thrillers."

"Nope. Never have." Dad's eyebrows slanted. "Last name is Solomon?"

Nodding, Jovi scrolled on. "Hmm. That's odd. Seems like he's caught up in some sort of scandal. Evidently, there's some speculation about him having an affair or something."

"Well, I'm not surprised." Dad shook his head. "Like I said, my folks did not trust Lois and Mac or their extended family."

Wow, he'd jumped to conclusions quickly. Disappointment tightened Jovi's stomach. "Just because the guy's had some tough times doesn't mean that he's bad news. We don't know what happened with him or with Lois and Mac and your parents."

"Since when do you defend somebody that you shared a ride with for a few hours?" Isabel scoffed. "He's moved as far as possible from his hometown without actually leaving the country, in the middle of winter, with a little kid. That definitely raises some caution flags."

Jovi hesitated. "You're not wrong. I just—"

"Let's get back on track here. Thanks for picking up that part." Dad patted her hand. "Hopefully, we'll get it installed, and the pulling machine will be up and running by lunchtime."

Mom's phone hummed with an incoming call. She glanced at it. "Oh, this is the administrative assistant for the owner of Schmidt's Chocolates."

Jovi's breath caught. They made phenomenal chocolate. "She calls you, like, directly? How often?"

Mom hesitated, then let the phone remain on the table until it stopped ringing.

"Why didn't you answer it?" Isabel asked.

"Because I want us to have a conversation as a family before I take another call or schedule another meeting. Your father and I want to sell. Ideally before the first of June."

Isabel gasped. "This June?"

A knot lodged in Jovi's throat. Surely they didn't mean that. June was less than five months away.

"We understand that this will be hard for both of you," Mom said. "But that's where we stand."

"It's time for us to do other things," Dad added.

"Like what?" Jovi winced. Boy, that came out harsher than she'd intended.

Dad shot her a pointed look. "Travel without being responsible for processing thousands of pounds of cocoa powder every year, maintaining equipment, or creating a sustainable product line. Life is short, and when health issues arise they can be costly. Selling the company will give us a cushion to pay for your grandmother's care and set aside extra for our own needs. We don't want you girls to have to worry about us. My father's death and Mom having to move into the memory care facility have caused us to reevaluate what truly matters." He leaned down and pressed a tender kiss to Mom's forehead. "Candy isn't what makes our world go round. At least not anymore."

"Aww, that's sweet," Jovi said. "But I'm not willing to sell."

Her sister tipped her chin up, determination flashing in her eyes. "Me either."

Dad's expression turned sober. "Here's the bottom line—

declining sales can't be ignored. Not for two consecutive quarters, anyway."

Jovi folded her hands in her lap so they didn't see her trembling. "What if we can come up with a new product? Something that will turn things around?"

Mom frowned. "I admire your optimism, but frankly, I don't think that's possible."

Ouch. "Will you at least give me—" she shot Isabel a quick glance "—give us the opportunity to try?"

Dad and Mom exchanged glances. "All right," Dad said. "You have until Memorial Day to come up with something and demonstrate through focus group feedback that its popularity justifies declining reasonable offers to sell the company."

Jovi thrust out her hand. "Deal."

Something undecipherable flashed in her father's eyes. Then he smiled and shook her hand.

An icy ball of fear settled in her stomach. What had she done?

"Daddy, I'm freezing." Darby Jane tugged the hood of her lavender jacket with the fur trim up over her tangled hair. Her whole body trembled as she stood inside the doorway of Uncle Mac and Aunt Lois's dilapidated cabin. He'd struggled to convince her to leave the warmth and comfort of their motel room where they'd spent the night.

"I know, sweetheart." He tugged his knit hat down over his ears. "We're going to make it warmer soon."

Although he didn't even know where to begin. He eyed the black woodstove in the corner of the living room. How had this place become so neglected? The tipped-over dining room chair with the broken leg, dust on the sheets draped over the sofa, and the uncomfortably cold air chilling his bare face made the beautiful cabin from his childhood memories feel the opposite of cozy.

Sure, the stunning view of the frozen lake still gleamed

through the oversize living room windows. Aunt Lois's beloved romance novels still lined the built-in bookshelves beside the windows. Last night's storm had become a bad memory, and the midday sun shining on the fresh snow outside was so brilliant that he had to squint.

But Darby Jane had made a valid point. They wouldn't last more than an hour or two in a house this cold. And he had no idea how to heat a cabin with only a woodstove.

Charlie, the man who'd met him with the key a few minutes ago, shoved his hands deep in the pockets of his brown Carhartt jacket. He wore a thick red knit beanie, brown heavy-duty pants and winter boots that made him look invincible.

"Yeah, after Mr. Wright passed away last winter, there wasn't anyone to keep an eye on the place. That's why your brother hired me, I suppose."

Surely, he hadn't heard him correctly. "Who?"

"Mr. Wright. Dennis is his first name." Charlie gestured with his thumb over his shoulder. "He and his wife still own the place down the road, and their family runs the local candy company. We were all pretty bummed when he passed."

Burke only managed a nod. He didn't know anything about Dennis Wright, but something told him he was going to learn a whole lot more. Including why Aunt Lois didn't think enough of the guy to ever let him and his brother play with the Wright girls when they were young.

"Super nice of him to look out for Lois and this place after Mac died, since everybody knows those families have been fighting for years." Charlie ducked his head. "Sorry, guess you don't need me telling you stuff you probably already know. But Mr. Wright was a good man."

But he didn't know. That was part of the problem. He needed to learn more about his aunt and uncle if he had any hope of getting to the bottom of the feud. Burke gave him a brisk nod.

First things first. "What do I need to do to get this place livable?"

Charlie hesitated, then glanced around. "Your family paid me and my sister extra to move a lot of your aunt and uncle's stuff to the shed out back. Whatever didn't fit, we just left here."

Burke swallowed hard. The cabin he remembered had stacks of well-loved books on the end table, cozy blankets draped over the sofa and framed photos on the walls of Mac and Lois's adventures. Now the place felt vacant. Unloved.

"I'll show you where we put the key to the shed. FYI, it's stuffed to the gills." Charlie's gaze slid toward the woodstove. "The electricity's been turned on, and I'll double-check that the water heater is working. I've scheduled a delivery of firewood. That should be here shortly, and I've got some old newspaper and kindling in the truck that I'll carry in. Heating with a woodburning fire can be tricky, but once you get the hang of it, this place will be nice and toasty."

"What if the pipes are frozen?"

Not that he'd ever experienced that in real life. Charleston rarely encountered the kind of weather that led to such plumbing-related disasters.

Charlie winced. "I hope that's not the case, but in a few minutes, we'll know for sure."

Seriously? He'd sent word he was coming. Couldn't Charlie have made a little more effort to prepare the place? Burke swallowed his terse words and followed him down the short hallway off the kitchen to a utility closet. Charlie opened the door. "Here's the valve that controls the water supply to the cabin. Let me turn that on, then we'll give the faucet in the bathroom a nudge and see what happens."

See what happens? Oh, he did not like the sound of that at all.

Charlie cranked the valve mounted in the wall, then turned and clapped Burke on the shoulder. "No worries, man. I know what I'm doing."

Did he, though? Burke dragged his fingers along his unshaven chin. Probably best if he didn't overtly question Charlie's abilities. Not if he wanted access to heat and running water anytime soon. His brother, Shane, had supposedly handled all communications with Charlie. Which evidently meant sending an occasional text. Why hadn't Shane or their mother followed up to make sure Mac and Lois's property was being properly maintained? Shane had given him Charlie's number, but only after Burke had pestered him for a week. As usual, he was kept on a need-to-know basis when it came to important details regarding the rental property. His brother seemed to doubt Burke capable of handling anything substantial these days. An attitude he'd probably adopted from their father. And their mother was too preoccupied with her whirlwind love affair to care about her older sister's vacant cabin in rural Alaska. Whatever. He stepped back to let Charlie do his thing.

"Daddy, do you have a blankie?" Darby Jane sank to the worn shag carpet on the living room floor, cuddling Bobo under her chin.

"We can probably find you a towel or something clean. Want to watch a movie on my computer?"

Her eyes lit up. "Yes, please."

"All right. One second." At least he'd thought far enough ahead to plan for her entertainment. A few minutes later, he had her all set up watching one of her favorite animated movies, nibbling on a cinnamon roll left over from breakfast at the motel, and drinking a bottle of water.

"I'll be right back with a blanket." He patted her shoulder then hurried down the hall, pausing when he passed the kitchen. From the looks of things, they'd remodeled maybe one time in the past thirty years. The cabinets, countertops and fixtures weren't anything like the modern spacious kitchen they'd left behind in Charleston. But wasn't that sort of the point? A fresh start in a place that resembled a different planet, scrubbed free of any detail that might remind him and Darby Jane of all they'd lost. Although, despite his promises of ice-skating and drinking the best hot cocoa in the world, he was still acutely aware that he'd plucked her out of an exceptionally comfortable lifestyle.

The oversize farmhouse sink with its chipped enamel and a faucet that resembled something out of the 1890s brought back memories of Aunt Lois washing dishes and Uncle Mac standing beside her, smiling as she handed him another pan to dry. It had been more than twenty years since he'd stood in this kitchen, but that particular memory made it seem like yesterday.

The oven had been a sophisticated model ahead of its time when they had installed it. If he concentrated, Burke could still taste the sweet concoctions Aunt Lois had baked for him when he visited. As soon as Charlie confirmed that all the utilities were in working order, he'd find a way to feed himself and his little girl.

"Daddy, I need a blankie," Darby Jane called out.

"I know, pumpkin. I'm looking." He continued down the hallway and checked out the three cozy bedrooms. At least there were beds, dressers and nightstands in each room. The linen closet beside the master bedroom was completely empty, though. He peeked in the closet in the bedroom that he and Shane had shared. On the top shelf, a crocheted afghan in shades of blue, purple and green yarn sat neatly folded and wrapped in a clear plastic bag.

Perfect. Burke unzipped the bag, pulled out the afghan, and grimaced at the mothball fragrance that greeted him. Darby Jane would have something to say about that. Hopefully, when their household goods arrived in a few weeks, they'd have their familiar blankets and bedding. Until then, he'd have to encourage her to make do with what was available.

"I've found a very special blanket to share with you," Burke said, as he returned to the nook beside the dining table where Darby Jane had decided to sit on the floor and watch the movie.

She clicked on Pause and eyed him with suspicion. "What is that?"

He held out the crocheted blanket. "It's called an afghan. It's handmade. Crocheted by your great aunt Lois. Your uncle Shane and I watched lots of movies with this spread over our legs."

"But it's ugly."

He forced his lips into a smile and draped it over her shoulders. "It will keep you warm until we get the fire started."

"And it smells," she wailed, then burst into tears and squirmed away from the blanket. "I hate this place. Please, Daddy, take me home."

He'd been waiting for that request. It had taken a whole sixteen hours since their plane had landed for her to ask. That was about twelve hours later than he'd expected. Deflated, he turned toward the front door as Charlie stepped back inside, stomping the snow off his boots on one of Aunt Lois's faded entryway rugs. He carried two small logs, newspapers and some kindling in his arms.

He eyed the sobbing little girl clutching Burke's legs and plowed on with his update. "I'll get a fire going, then I'd say this place is move-in ready."

"Move-in ready. Right." Burke raised his voice to be heard above the sound of Darby Jane crying. "Thanks for your help."

"Not a problem."

Charlie crossed the room and carefully set his supplies down, then got to work crumpling newspaper for the fire. Burke dropped to his knees and pulled his little girl into his arms. He didn't bother to offer any uplifting comments about his nostalgic memories in the cabin or empty promises that this would be the best winter of her young life. Because to be honest, he was really starting to wonder if maybe Shane and Dad were right. Had he been so blinded by his grief that he'd made another foolish choice, dragging his little girl all the way to Alaska?

★ ★ ★

"Please, please let that part be the one we need." Isabel stepped out of her sedan, blinking against the bright morning sun as she whispered her plea toward the cloudless blue sky. She'd rattled off more than a handful of desperate prayers lately. Cringing, she shouldered her handbag and pocketed her keys. What God must think of her and her clever little games. This wasn't the first time she'd put her faith on the back burner, pretending to have it all together, only to panic when another crisis landed in her path, sending her back to begging for intervention.

Her boots crunched over the packed snow in the Evergreen Candy Company's parking lot. Another car door slammed as Jovi climbed out of the passenger side and quickly caught up. As usual, her sister looked amazing, even after her marathon trip from Kansas City. She wore her blond hair partially pulled back at the crown, with stylish bangs and a few wispy strands framing her face, but somehow it looked sophisticated. Her ice-blue puffy winter jacket emphasized her gorgeous eyes.

Tamping down her petty jealousy, Isabel flipped her long ponytail over her shoulder then turned and led the way toward the entrance. Two towering evergreens stood like proud doormen on either side of the recently shoveled path. A faux twig wreath with plastic pieces of pink, red and purple candy adorned the glass front door. Isabel pulled it open, immediately basking in the familiar scent of sugar and chocolate that enveloped the rush of warm air.

Jovi followed her inside, then paused. She squealed with delight. "There."

Isabel turned and faced her. "What?"

Jovi's eyes lit up and a broad smile stretched across her face. She drew in a deep breath and released it slowly. "That's the aroma. This is what home smells like to me."

Isabel whirled away, blinking back unexpected tears. Oh,

no, not now. She wasn't about to tell her sister everything. She couldn't unload on Jovi, not on her first day back. Besides, as the older sister, she'd always been the sensible one. Practical. The one who didn't need her sister's advice. Instead, she'd taken great pride in handing out the tips, hacks and guidance Jovi often needed.

She stomped her boots on the mat and then stepped into the lobby. Light streamed through the broad expanse of windows overlooking an outdoor patio with picnic tables. Liquid chocolate poured from the iconic fountain in the middle of the room.

Sandra, their faithful administrative assistant who'd sat at this desk for over a decade, stood near the self-serve beverage bar, restocking the baskets with sugar packets and stir sticks. She turned and smiled over her shoulder. "Good morning."

When her gaze landed on Jovi, her kind brown eyes widened. She dropped the empty cardboard box in the recycle bin nearby. The heels of her black knee-high boots clicked on the ash-colored luxury vinyl tile floor as she hurried to greet them. "Jovi, welcome home, honey. What a thrill to see you today, and Happy New Year."

"Hi, Sandra." Jovi stepped into the older woman's embrace. "It's so nice to see you again."

Isabel stood back, clutching her handbag. Her phone buzzed, but she chose to ignore it, because if it was Mason telling her more about how he'd nailed that interview, well, that wasn't a message she wanted to receive in front of Sandra and Jovi. She still hadn't come up with a kind way to respond to the message he'd sent when she'd been at breakfast. Guilt twisted her insides. She wanted to be happy for him. Oh, how she wanted a husband who loved his job and could advance in his career. But what if it came at the expense of her happiness? She couldn't possibly leave Evergreen. Not now. Not when her parents wanted to sell the family business. Sure, her sister was back, but that didn't mean she was here for good or capable of stepping into the role Isabel so desperately needed her to fill. Not only a confidante but a business partner as well. One who wouldn't leave or agree to sell out when their first-quarter earnings tanked.

"Isabel, did you hear the news?" Sandra pulled her back to the conversation.

"Excuse me. Sandra, I'm sorry." Isabel offered her most contrite smile. "I was daydreaming there for a minute. What did I miss?"

"The part for the pulling machine has been installed, and the team is about to run a test batch of the mints," Sandra said.

"Oh, that's great news. Thank you for letting me—us—know." The knot between her shoulder blades loosened.

"Of course." Sandra turned her attention back to Jovi. "What brings you back to town?"

Isabel shot her a *please do not tell her everything* look.

"I'm a traveling nurse, and I just finished my assignment in Kansas City, so I picked up a thirteen-week position at the hospital here in Evergreen. This seemed like the ideal time to come home."

"That's great." Sandra smoothed her hands over her plum-colored knit sweater dress. "I look forward to hearing more about your time in Kansas City. If you'll excuse me, I need to get back to work."

"Please let me know when those mints are ready for a taste test," Isabel said. "I'd like to sample one."

"Me too," Jovi chimed in. "Even though quality control is not my responsibility, I'd hate to pass on a chance to taste one of Grammie's mints."

Sandra laughed. "I'll be sure to keep you both updated."

Isabel crossed the lobby and turned down the corridor toward her office.

They passed the framed photo of their grandparents posing for the company's ribbon cutting more than sixty years ago, then stopped and looked through the wall of windows onto the factory floor. Employees moved about the machines, monitoring progress as conveyor belts zipped along, packaging and sorting a fresh batch of filled chocolate candies.

"Can I just tell you that Valentine's season is the tastiest and also the most heartbreaking when you're unexpectedly single?" Sadness tinged Jovi's voice.

"Oh, come here." Isabel pulled her in for a side hug. "It's going to be all right. You didn't want to spend forever with Michael anyway."

"You just keep reminding me of that, will ya? My head hears you, but my heart's not quite on board."

Poor thing. Breakups were *so hard*. Isabel pulled away, then found her keys in her bag, crossed the hall and unlocked her office door. She stepped inside and flipped on the lights.

Jovi shrugged out of her coat, then tipped her head toward the hooks on the wall. "Mind if I hang this up?"

"Please do." Isabel set her bag on her desk chair. "I forgot to ask if you want more coffee. Sandra has about a dozen options."

"No, thanks. I had plenty at breakfast." Jovi added her purse to the hook beside her jacket. "All right, put me to work. What can I do?"

Isabel booted up her computer, then flipped open her planner. She'd blocked out the morning to make sure the pulling machine and the production schedule were both back online. But she had a long afternoon meeting planned with the VP of marketing. Diversifying their holiday product line had been the first item on the agenda. What with Mom and Dad's emphatic insistence that they wanted to sell by June unless sales significantly improved, maybe the leadership team needed to invest more in their spring marketing campaigns. Except the advertising budget had already been stretched thin. She drummed her fingertips on her desk. Since Dad had approved Jovi's plea to come up with a new product, now she'd have to allocate money for that and gathering feedback from focus groups instead.

Her head started throbbing.

"Isabel? Did you hear me?" Jovi rubbed her palms together. Her charcoal-gray sweater slipped off one shoulder as she wiggled her legs. Clad in black leggings and gray Ugg boots, with oversize silver hoops dangling from her ears, Jovi possessed a stylish flair that wasn't common in Evergreen.

"How about we discuss specific tasks you can take on?" Her phone rang, and Mason's name and number filled the screen. Sighing, Isabel silenced the device.

"Is everything okay?" Jovi's concerned gaze tracked Isabel's moves as she took off her coat, hung it on the back of her chair, then sat down at her desk.

Isabel hesitated. Tell Jovi everything, or let her figure it out on her own? "I—I'm preoccupied, especially now that Dad wants to travel the world with Mom and stop thinking about running a successful business."

Sadness flitted across Jovi's features. "I still can't believe they want out. I meant what I said at breakfast. There has to be something we can do to boost sales."

Isabel's phone vibrated on the desk. She glanced at the screen. Mason again.

"What about Grammie's salted caramel chews? Those were always my favorite. Even though Grandpa and Grammie said they weren't meant to be sold, I think customers would love them."

Isabel didn't answer. Instead, she eyed the voice mail icon on her phone. Now she had two messages waiting. Her stomach twisted. She couldn't keep ignoring him.

Jovi perched on the edge of her chair, both hands gripping the armrests. "You seem upset. What's on your mind?"

"My struggling marriage."

A heavy silence filled the room.

She pressed her fingertips to her mouth. Oh, dear. "Did I say that out loud?"

Eyes wide, Jovi nodded. "You and Mason are having a tough time?"

"Yeah, but it's fine. We'll get through it. Everybody hits a rough patch, right?"

Jovi opened her mouth, then closed it, and opened it once more. "I'm probably not the best person to weigh in on that." She slowly pulled out a club chair and perched on the edge of it. "Do you want to talk about it?"

No.

"Mason wants to move. He just interviewed for a job in Juneau, but I don't want to leave Evergreen. I love it here. Not just because of the company, but because this is my home. I thought he felt at home here too. Which is why I can't figure out what this is all about. Clearly, he isn't interested in seeing my perspective. And I don't see his. We're at a stalemate."

There. She'd said it all.

"Oh, Izzy." Jovi stood and hurried around the desk, then looped her arms around Isabel's shoulders.

Tears blurred her vision. A sob erupted. She leaned hard against her little sister. "Jovi, help. I don't know what to do."

"It's going to be all right." Jovi gently rubbed her back. "You and Mason will find a way forward."

Isabel plucked a tissue from the box on her desk and dabbed at the corners of her eyes. If only she had a fraction of Jovi's boundless optimism. Then, maybe she wouldn't feel trapped.

Chapter Five

Burke sighed and unzipped his backpack. Why had he said yes to ice-skating? There had to be a better way to distract Darby Jane from her back-to-school jitters. He could've let her eat popcorn for supper and watch another animated movie together. Much less stressful. They wouldn't have to leave the cabin. But she'd begged, and against his better judgment, he'd agreed.

"Come on, Daddy. I want to go." Darby Jane shoved her feet into her boots. "It's going to be dark soon."

"There are lights at the rink," Burke said, taking as long as humanly possible to stuff wool socks, two extra sweatshirts, and water bottles into his backpack.

"Why are you bringing so much stuff?" She zipped up her jacket. "I thought you said we can't stay long. I have to go to bed early. Right?"

He smothered a sigh. Why did she always use his words against him at the most inopportune time? "Darby Jane, here's the thing. I don't know how to skate."

She lifted one shoulder. "That's okay."

"I'm nervous about trying."

"I know." She reached up and tugged on his hand, melting the frigid exterior of his heart. "I'll show you, 'cuz I've already learned."

He couldn't help but smile. "When did you learn to ice-skate?"

"I went to *lots* of skating birthday parties." She turned and reached for the cabin's front door. "It's fun once you get the hang of it."

Skating birthday parties? And when did she learn to say *get the hang of it*? Must've overheard Charlie. Burke studied her intently, trying to make sense of the fog that had been the last two years of his life. Not a single memory came back to him of taking her to or picking her up from a party at an ice rink. Mary Catherine had handled all those details. Or maybe he couldn't remember accurately because Darby Jane's tone, the way she tossed her hair over her shoulder, everything about her reminded him once again of his late wife and all he'd lost. The grief and the memories nearly stole his breath. Even thousands of miles from Charleston, the death of his wife and their baby boy still permeated his existence.

"Come on, Daddy, you promised." Darby Jane stood on the top step of the cabin's porch. "I don't want to wait anymore."

"I know. And I'm keeping my word. See?" He shouldered his backpack, plucked the keys from the hook by the door and followed her outside. Lois's truck had proven to be reliable.

Charlie had even been kind enough to make sure it started and that the oil had been changed recently. The cabin still didn't feel like home, and it needed a ton of work. But he and Darby Jane had managed to make the place livable over the past three days. Hopefully, once their shipment of household goods arrived and they'd unpacked familiar belongings, he'd find his groove.

Darby Jane climbed into the passenger side of the seventies-era red pickup truck, tugged the door shut with a grunt, then reached for her seat belt. "It smells like peppermint in here."

"Yep." Burke slid behind the wheel, then reached across the cab and opened the glove compartment. A stash of plastic-wrapped candy with the Evergreen Candy Company logo greeted them.

"Candy." Darby Jane flashed him a wide smile. "How did that get there?"

"Charlie gave me a package when he was here the other day."

"May I have one, please?"

"Absolutely." He handed her one, then took a piece for himself. As he backed out of the driveway and drove the short distance to the rink, he savored the sweet taste of the soft peppermint candy.

Darby Jane's cheek was plump as she tucked her candy out of the way, squirrel-like, and turned her inquisitive face toward him. "Why can't we skate over there?"

Burke looked out the window and caught a glimpse between the tree branches of the vast snow-covered lake. Although he'd visited Evergreen during his holiday breaks from school a few times, his aunt and uncle had discouraged him and his brother from venturing out onto the ice.

"Maybe it's not safe." Burke shifted his attention back to the road since he hadn't had much experience driving in the ice and snow. "You never know if the ice on the lake is frozen all the way through. Probably best for all of us if we stick to a well-maintained rink."

She nodded, and his shoulders hunched toward his ears as he dreaded her follow-up questions. Because there would definitely be more questions. What a wise, old soul dwelling in a five-year-old's body. His stomach bottomed out at the thought of her starting school with strangers in the morning. He tried his best to mask his fear. He wanted her to feel confident. Brave.

When he'd registered Darby Jane, the teacher and principal

agreed that easing her in and attending two days this week, then only four next week due to having Monday off for teacher in-service, would be good for her. Selfishly, he wanted to homeschool her, but that wasn't what she needed. Besides, he was only kidding himself. He needed every free minute that he wasn't working on the house to somehow wrangle words onto his laptop.

He'd made hardly any progress on his manuscript since they'd arrived in Evergreen. But he had to keep trying. Time was ticking away, and the extended deadline loomed. March 15. Less than eight weeks to pluck more than seventy thousand words out of thin air. A ripple of unease shimmied along his spine. Sidestepping the ominous thought, they arrived at the rink and parked in the lot. Kids in hockey uniforms were skating back and forth.

"Oh, no." Darby Jane groaned. "I thought you said we could skate now."

"At four o'clock we're allowed to skate. That's only five minutes from now. By the time we're ready, I'm sure those kids will be finished."

She grabbed the new pair of skates he'd spent way too much money on at the local sporting goods store and scurried out of the truck.

Slowly, he followed her, carrying his backpack and the vintage pair of ice skates he'd found in Lois and Mac's hall closet.

Hopefully, the parents mingling rinkside would disperse and there would be very few witnesses to his skating debut.

The standard wooden boards rimmed the rink, but it lacked a fancy plexiglass barrier and bleachers. Maybe hockey wasn't a spectator sport here. Someone had provided a few basic benches and cleared the snow away for people to sit down and put on their skates. Darby Jane claimed the end of one and quickly traded her boots for her skates.

The rumbling of an engine caught Burke's attention, and he turned to see three food trucks pulling into the parking lot.

"Yay!" Darby Jane clapped her mittened hands together. "Can we have supper here?"

"Perhaps. Let's see how long we last ice-skating."

"Oh, I can skate a long time, Daddy." Darby Jane grinned at him triumphantly. "And I'll be nice and hungry for a slice of pizza."

He sat down beside her. "How do you know they serve pizza?"

She pointed. "It's painted on the side of the truck, silly."

"Right."

A whistle blew, and two men on the ice gathered the kids around. There was laughter and chatter, then a communal cheer before the kids skated toward the boards and filtered out through the open gate.

A few minutes later, only two other adults and three kids circled the ice.

Good. Hardly anyone to watch him make a fool of himself.

Darby Jane waited patiently for him to help her lace her skates and tie them.

"Why don't you put on your mittens, and I'll be with you in a second." Burke still had to put his skates on.

Her little body trembled with excitement. "Can I skate? I know how."

"Yes, you've mentioned that." He smiled, then patted her shoulder. "Go ahead. Please be careful."

She stood up and walked gingerly across the packed snow, then squeezed through the open door and glided across the rink.

He paused and watched, amazed at her courage. If he wanted her to do new things, then he had to try as well. But oh, how he hated to fail. He'd done plenty of that already. On the other hand, feeling like an incompetent, grief-stricken dad was far worse than falling on his backside a time or two, right?

Sweat made his T-shirt stick to his back as he leaned down and finished lacing his skates. Then he tugged his hat a little tighter over his ears, slipped his gloves back on and tentatively pushed himself upright.

He made his way toward the boards. At least he'd have something to hold on to. Drawing a fortifying breath, he stepped onto the rink with his right skate followed by his left. Oh, this wasn't so bad. The blades scraped across the surface, and the cold air nipped at his cheeks.

"Great job, Daddy!" Darby Jane's encouraging words enveloped him as she slowly spun around him. "You're doing it."

He forced a strained smile and tried to hide his apprehension, but only managed to get three yards before his skate caught in an uneven patch. His body instantly flew sideways, and he hit the ice hard. Pain surged up through his right arm. *Oh, no.*

He ground his teeth to tamp down a yell. This couldn't be happening.

"Help. Please!"

The pathetic yelp pierced the chilly air. Jovi glanced toward the ice rink. Adrenaline spiked through her. She pushed the bag of prepackaged marshmallows through the open service window of the food truck. "Here you go. Jerry from the candy company asked me to drop these off, and now I need to help somebody on the rink."

The guy working the mobile coffee truck ducked down and met her gaze. "No problem. Thanks for the delivery. These marshmallows are a crowd-pleaser around here."

She gave an appreciative nod. "You're welcome. Thanks for stocking our product."

She draped the strap of her canvas crossbody bag over her shoulder and cut long strides across the parking lot. As she got closer to the edge of the rink, her steps faltered. A sense of dread welled up in her chest as she surveyed the situation. Burke sat hunched over on the ice, holding his forearm as Darby Jane clung to him, tears streaking her flushed face.

Jovi took a deep breath before unlatching the rink door and stepping tentatively onto the slick surface. She sensed concerned gazes following her as she walked cautiously toward Burke and Darby Jane.

"Miss Jovi, please help us," Darby Jane wailed.

"I'm here, sweetie. What happened?" Jovi sank to her knees beside Burke. His eyes locked on hers. A mixture of shame and pain washed across his crimped features.

"I think I broke my arm," Burke said through gritted teeth.

"Oh, dear." Jovi scanned him quickly, from his scalp to the tips of his vintage ice skates, checking for other injuries. "Did you hit your head or injure anything else when you fell?"

Darby Jane's wails grew louder.

"Baby girl, listen." Burke pressed his uninjured hand to his daughter's leg. "I'm going to be all right. Miss Jovi and these nice folks are going to help us."

Darby Jane nodded, drew a ragged breath, then swiped at the tears on her cheeks with her mittens.

Poor thing. And Burke was so tender toward her. He'd pushed his pain aside to comfort his little girl. What a great dad. Jovi gave those thoughts a mental shove, then turned and smiled at the young couple still standing nearby. "Do you think you could take her to get some hot cocoa? The coffee truck is open, and I heard they have fresh marshmallows."

Darby Jane's worried gaze slid to Burke. "Can I, Daddy?"

Burke's lips twitched. "Absolutely."

"We'll take good care of her," the man said, holding out his hand toward Darby Jane. "Come on, let's get some cocoa. What's your name?"

Once Darby Jane skated out of earshot toward the side of the rink with the couple and their child, Jovi focused on Burke. Her training kicked in, and she searched his face, assessing him for any signs of concussion. He still hadn't answered her questions about what had happened. Wow, those flecks of gold surrounding his irises were really something. And how had she not noticed the small scar below his right cheekbone?

"Jovi?" Burke's eyebrows slanted up toward his black knit hat. "Would you mind helping me up?"

She hesitated. "Before we move you, why don't you tell me more about how you fell. Is it just your arm that's injured, or is there anything else that hurts? I need to make sure there are no other injuries."

His frown turned into a tight-lipped smile. "Darby Jane wanted to ice-skate. She's nervous about starting school tomorrow, so I thought this might be a nice distraction. Until I actually started skating. Evidently using my arm to break my fall was also a poor choice."

He winced again, cradling his arm to his chest.

"Can you wiggle your fingers?"

He slowly moved all five digits in his gloved hand. "Yes."

"Any numbness or tingling?"

He shook his head. "No, but I'm getting chilly sitting here."

"Makes sense." She pushed to her feet. "I have a first-aid kit in my car. Sit tight, and I'll run and get it."

"So you're certain it's broken."

She eyed his arm again. "I can't say for sure without an X-ray. My plan is to splint your arm, then take you to the emergency room."

"I can't afford to have a broken arm," Burke groaned.

Oh. Her chest pinched. A single dad with tight finances. Was that why he'd moved into Lois and Mac's place? "I'm sure the folks at the hospital here will work with you to set up a payment plan."

"No, it's not that." He blew out a long breath. "I—I'm supposed to write daily, lots of words on my book, but typing will be impossible now."

So maybe the articles she'd seen on the internet about him being a famous author were correct. "Let's not dive into the worst-case scenario yet. I'll put a splint on your arm and drive you to the hospital to get an X-ray so we know what's going on."

He glanced over his shoulder toward the parking lot. "I can't leave Darby Jane with a family we just met five minutes ago."

"Of course not. But you might have to wait to see the doctor. What about leaving her with someone whose family has been feuding with yours for decades?"

A muscle in his jaw clenched as he attempted to stand. "Say more."

"Wait. What are you doing?"

"I have to get off the ice. I'm freezing." His broad shoulders trembled as he shivered.

She clamped her hand on his uninjured elbow to keep him upright. "My sister, Isabel, and her husband, Mason, live nearby. Their place is on the way to the hospital. I can text and ask if they'd watch Darby Jane for you."

Burke hesitated. "She'll need to eat supper soon, and she's terribly allergic to cats."

"I don't know if they have kid-friendly food, but they're definitely pet-free." She walked slowly beside him as they made their way toward the edge of the rink. He smelled good. Like fresh air and laundry soap. She was tempted to loop her arm around his waist to give him extra support.

Stop. It. Now was not the time to admire his handsome features. Or the way his shoulders filled out his winter jacket. And she certainly wasn't supposed to be staring at the muscle clenching in his angular jawline.

Jovi. Enough!

Once he was seated on the bench nearby, she reached into her bag for her phone. "Would you like me to check and see if my sister is available?"

"If it's not too much trouble."

Less than thirty minutes later, Jovi had splinted Burke's arm and collected Darby Jane, and they were on their way to Isabel and Mason's house.

"Thank you for your help." Burke grimaced as he shifted in the passenger seat of her vehicle.

Jovi adjusted the buttons on the dash to amp up the defroster. "No problem."

"That truck had yummy hot chocolate," Darby Jane said from the back seat. "I hope the kids in my class are as nice as that girl."

"I am sure they will be," Jovi said, recalling Burke's comment about Darby Jane's worries over starting at a new school. "Folks in Evergreen usually have big hearts."

"Even the ones who've been feuding for decades?" Burke quipped.

His comment punctured her statement, and the jovial atmosphere inside the car evaporated. Darby Jane took over the conversation, talking up her new school, reporting how many marshmallows she'd had in her hot chocolate, and asking lots of questions about Isabel and Mason.

When Jovi eased to a stop in front of her sister and brother-in-law's house, she sensed Burke's gaze on her. Probably wondering about her family's rift with his aunt and uncle. Not that she had the time or the energy to try to figure out what the man was thinking. She needed to concentrate on helping Burke see a doctor or a physician assistant and possibly get a splint or a cast. Then she'd go back to Grammie's to search for the iconic salted caramel chew recipe. If she could find it, surely she'd be able to come up with a plan to save the candy company. And convince Mom and Dad not to sell the business that had become their family's legacy.

Who knew they'd be such fantastic babysitters? This had gone much better than Isabel had expected.

"She is the most adorable thing ever." Mason's arm brushed against Isabel's as he reached for the can of whipped cream. She couldn't help but feel a rush of warmth inside her chest at the sound of his low and rumbly voice. When Jovi had asked them to babysit Darby Jane while she took Burke to the emergency room, she'd been unsure if Mason would even be willing as they were both so busy. Would he be irritated that she'd put someone else's needs first? Again?

All her worries melted away when she saw Mason's face light up as he interacted with the little girl. He hadn't looked that content in a very long time.

Over a shared meal of grilled cheese sandwiches and tomato soup, Isabel, Mason and Darby Jane had traded silly jokes and riddles. Darby Jane had charmed them both from the moment she stepped into their house with her soft Southern lilt and her *Yes, ma'am*s and *No, sir*s.

Isabel added a second scoop of ice cream to his bowl, then offered him a playful smile as she gently bumped her hip against his. "She wrapped you around her little finger in about three seconds."

Mason set the can back on the counter, then pressed his palm against the small of her back, pulling her in close. She leaned into his touch. His lips brushed her temple. The warmth of his breath against her skin sent shivers down her spine.

"Maybe we need to think about having a little girl of our own."

The spoon in her hand slipped and clattered on the counter. Her pulse sped. She turned and faced him, wide-eyed. "Are you serious?"

Sure, they'd agreed when they were still dating that they both wanted kids. Someday. But then their first pregnancy had led to heartbreak, and now he'd gone and turned her world upside down by interviewing for a job in another town.

He pulled away. Uncertainty flickered in his eyes, replacing the passion she'd glimpsed only seconds ago. "Don't freak out."

"I'm not." Although the squeak in her voice said otherwise.

Was she freaking out? She tried to dispel her uneasiness by clearing her throat, but it didn't seem to be enough. And yet, her skin tingled where he'd touched her, already protesting the void left by his absence.

"Can I have some sprinkles, please?" Darby Jane asked from her seat in the kitchen, watching as Mason added a large dollop of whipped cream on top of her ice cream. After finishing her grilled cheese sandwich and tomato soup without complaint, she had devoured a bowl of red grapes. Now she leaned back against the chair and ran her fingers along the edges of the red-and-pink checkered placemat.

Mason gave her an amused grin. "Of course you can."

He sent Isabel a sideways glance. His amusement vanished, and a muscle in his jaw twitched. "We have some, don't we?"

Now who was freaking out?

Isabel gestured with her thumb over her shoulder. "They're in the cabinet beside the stove."

Part of her felt blindsided by this whole situation. After all, they had barely spoken for almost a week, until Darby Jane's arrival shoved aside any animosity between them. Not only that, but Mason thought he was ready to become a father, thanks to one mealtime with a well-mannered child. As if that was all he'd have to do. Show up for dinner and ham it up with the kid, while she did the rest.

Stop.

She couldn't let resentment fester. They'd agreed to sit down and discuss his job interview tonight, but that hadn't happened yet, not with Darby Jane's arrival coinciding with his return from work. Honestly, she'd rather put off the discussion.

He had probably done well, knowing Mason.

He'd always been confident, articulate and so knowledgeable

about the construction industry. Still, the thought of uprooting and starting over somewhere new made her want to burst into tears. It wasn't just her work as Evergreen's mayor. She'd devoted her life to the place she called home. Even if her family sold their candy business, she'd never planned on leaving Evergreen. Yet she didn't want to give up on her marriage either.

"Ready for dessert, babe?" Mason set a bowl of ice cream with rainbow sprinkles in front of Darby Jane.

"I'll be right there. Just need to wrap up these leftovers," Isabel said without meeting his gaze.

"Got it." He grabbed two spoons and brought the bowls of ice cream to the table. "Here you go, Darby Jane."

The little girl's eyes widened with excitement over the treat. "Thank you so much. This looks yummy!"

"You're welcome." Mason reclaimed his spot across from Darby Jane and scooted his own bowl closer. "So tell me about Charleston, South Carolina. I've never been. What's your favorite thing?"

While Isabel put away the remaining tomato soup, she half listened to Darby Jane describe a giant bridge near Charleston, her favorite beach and a lunch spot they went to after church services. The only detail omitted was any mention of her mother or other family members. Mason didn't pry. He just listened while the sound of spoons clinking in their bowls punctuated Darby Jane's vivid recollection of watching baby sea turtles hatch from their nest.

When Isabel looked up again, Mason raised his eyebrows, silently reminding her that what they were witnessing was *the most adorable thing ever*. She smiled at him before looking away again. He wasn't wrong. She was adorable.

Maybe Darby Jane would become the bond between their families after all. But that didn't mean Isabel was ready to move away or consider trying to get pregnant again.

Chapter Six

He'd checked everything off his detailed to-do list for Darby Jane's first day of school. Except have a plan for how he'd get out of his driveway when it was filled with two feet of fresh snow. Shoveling wasn't an option since he'd indeed broken his arm and had to wear a cast. Burke stood on the cabin's porch and stared at the white snowdrift piled on top of the truck's hood. It wasn't even daylight yet, and he could tell that too much snow had fallen for him to back out. What if he got stuck? His chest tightened. Who could he call? Did Charlie offer snow removal services?

"Oh, no!" Darby Jane's voice trembled as she stepped out of the cabin. "How will we get out? I'm going to be late on my first day."

No tears. Please, no tears.

Burke tugged his knit hat down over his ears, wincing as his broken wrist screamed at him. He scanned the driveway, analyzing his limited options. Why hadn't he arranged for Darby Jane to ride the bus?

"Why doesn't this place have a garage, anyway?" Darby Jane thumped down the steps and stuck her tongue out, trying to catch a snowflake.

"Good question. I guess Uncle Mac didn't want one." He made a mental note to use the key Charlie had left him to check out the contents of the shed out back. It would be nice to know what was stored in there. Once he figured out how to clear a path through the snow. He reached for the shovel leaning against the cabin. Maybe he could knock some snow off the truck's windshield if he only used his uninjured arm.

"Daddy, can we build a snowman?"

"I don't think we have time for that, pumpkin. How about—"

"Good morning." Jovi traipsed through the snow toward them, an insulated coffee mug in one hand and a shovel in the other. "I heard somebody has their first day of school today. Are you excited?"

"Miss Jovi!" Darby Jane squealed. "Can you help us, please? We're stuck."

"We're not stuck," Burke said. "We haven't even tried to get out."

"That's why I'm here." Jovi stopped beside Darby Jane at the bottom of the steps and glanced up at him. "Welcome to winter in Evergreen. Isn't it amazing?"

She had to be well caffeinated. That was the only reasonable explanation. Because how could anybody be this happy at seven in the morning when it was still dark and ten degrees below zero?

He slanted her a look. "*Amazing* isn't the first word that comes to mind."

Not that he wasn't grateful for some help because he desperately needed a way out of his driveway. Quickly. But he wasn't thrilled that he needed to rely on Jovi to solve all his problems.

Jovi cleared a spot off the bottom step and set her coffee down. "I brought an ice scraper, just in case." She pulled a plastic tool from her jacket pocket. "Since you have a cast, I'm guessing shoveling isn't part of your morning routine. Good news: Looks like the snowplow has already been through, so give me about forty-five minutes, and I'll have you all squared away."

"Thank you for rescuing us." Darby Jane clapped her mittened hands together. "I really don't want to be late on my first day."

Burke winced. Did she have to keep mentioning that? School didn't start for almost an hour, right? "What about your driveway, Jovi?"

"I don't have anywhere to be right now." The lone streetlamp at the edge of his yard granted enough light for him to admire her full pink lips. He couldn't look away from the appealing flush clinging to her cheeks either.

Calm down. Bitter rivals, remember? Long-standing family feud? Falling for someone now is the last thing you need, Solomon.

True to her word, less than forty-five minutes later, Jovi had cleared off the truck and carved a drivable path to the road.

Burke stared in awe as she staked her shovel in the snowbank like some kind of warrior princess, then faced him with a triumphant smile.

"There." Chest heaving, she planted her gloved hands on her hips. "Mission accomplished."

He managed to find his voice. "I don't know what to say."

Her smile faded. "How about *thank you*?"

He cringed. "Yes, of course. Thank you very much. I—I couldn't have done this on my own."

"C'mon, Daddy." Darby Jane hurried toward the truck. "We've got to go."

"What do you say to Miss Jovi?" Burke called out.

"Thank you, Miss Jovi!"

Jovi chuckled. "You're welcome. I'll just grab my coffee and be on my way. Hope you have a wonderful day, Darby Jane. Can't wait to hear all about it."

Somehow, her kind words pained him. Like fingers pressing on a fresh bruise. She hadn't meant to, but Jovi's friendly encouragement carried a sharp reminder that his late wife wasn't here to celebrate Darby Jane's milestone event.

"Thanks again." He offered a tight smile, then turned and climbed into the truck.

A few minutes later, he drove down the street toward her new school.

"Daddy, this is so not a good idea." Darby Jane rode beside him, clutching her backpack on her lap.

Wow, her enthusiasm over Jovi's surprise visit had faded quickly. He eased into the line of vehicles snaking back from the elementary school's front door. "What's not a good idea?"

"School. Today." She looked at him, her eyes shiny with unshed tears. "I—I can't."

Oh, Darby Jane. He swallowed hard. "Sweetheart, it's time. I'd keep you at the cabin with me forever if I could, but that's not what's best. For you or for me."

"This is all so new and scary. What if no one likes me?"

Her solemn words, barely louder than a whisper, gutted him. He'd asked too much of her. Saying goodbye to everything she'd known. Moving to the opposite corner of the continent. There was no going back now, though. "Remember our plan? Only two days this week, then a nice long weekend off, and a few more days next week."

"But there will be lots more days after that." She tightened her grip on her backpack straps. "What if I hate it?"

He reached across the bench seat and patted her shoulder. "It's going to be okay. You loved your last school, remember? I'm sure that once you get settled, you'll love this one as well." The words were more to comfort himself, really.

"I'm super scared." She stared out the windshield, her lower lip trembling.

His stomach bottomed out. If only he could scoop her up and protect her from any more hurt. She'd known too much devastation already.

He had to be strong for both of them. Taking her small hand in his, he put on his best brave face as they reached the front of the line much too soon. A young woman with a friendly face opened the passenger door and smiled at Darby Jane, then at him.

"Hi there! Welcome to Evergreen Elementary School. I'm Mrs. Douglas, the music teacher. Are you ready to have a great first day?"

Burke tried to speak, but his throat closed up. He squeezed Darby Jane's hand instead, hoping she'd understand what he couldn't say aloud.

Her blue eyes pleaded with him not to make her go, but she nodded all the same and slid out of the truck with her backpack in tow.

Mrs. Douglas shut the door and then guided Darby Jane toward the school's entrance. With every step, Burke wanted to jump out of the cab and walk with her all the way to her desk. But he couldn't. It was time she did this on her own. Besides, back in the fall in Charleston, she'd marched into school on her first day with her chin up and insisted she didn't need his help. He silently prayed that she'd find that same confidence again.

She glanced over her shoulder one last time before disappearing through the double doors.

He exhaled deeply, then slowly eased away from the curb and followed the car in front of him out of the parking lot. She was bound to find new friends here. The excitement of learning had to outweigh her worries. Right? He had just enough faith left in him to believe that this move might not be so bad after all. Maybe the relocation to Evergreen would turn out to be a good decision.

Back at the cabin, he parked in the driveway and trudged inside. He shrugged out of his coat, then approached the woodstove, holding out his hand to evaluate the warmth emanating from it. Outside the window, thick wet flakes fell from a gray sky, nearly obstructing his view of the lake. His casted wrist made every task more awkward, but he managed to add another log to the fire. He passed through the living room and into the kitchen, where he stopped in the doorway. The tiny space was quiet without Darby Jane.

He ran a hand over his face, then headed for the old coffee maker sitting on a corner of the counter. He refilled it with fresh grounds and cold water.

With coffee dripping, Burke moved to the kitchen table and opened his laptop on its warped surface. He had to write something. Anything. He stared down at the device for several seconds before finally letting out a sigh. Now what?

He had no new ideas. No words. Nothing but doubt and fear that he'd never find inspiration. And yet here he was, ready to try again. If he'd written one best-selling novel, a story he'd knocked out of the park on his first try, why couldn't he create a second?

It had all seemed so easy with his debut, back when life was relatively simple. He'd fit his writing into early morning sessions before he left for work at the ad agency. Mary Catherine had kept life at home running smoothly, allowing him plenty of space to create. She'd been his biggest fan.

No. He couldn't let his grief derail him. Not today.

Burke shifted in his chair and stared at the open document on his laptop. He'd slogged through reading the first four chapters during their flight to Alaska, but his efforts didn't seem like anything worthy of publication. If only he'd known when he was writing his debut how hard he'd have to work the second go-around. The pressure of a looming deadline hovered over him. Squeezed the air from his lungs.

The next word, the next sentence, hung irritatingly out of reach. Nothing he put down felt right. He typed, deleted, typed and deleted again. Then he pushed back his chair and circled around the counter to the coffee maker. His imagination churned, examining a new plot twist. Somewhere the sound of an incoming FaceTime call snagged his attention. He hesitated, not wanting to surrender any of his precious writing time to anyone. But he couldn't keep avoiding calls, texts and emails. He found his phone and checked the caller ID.

Stephanie Miller's name filled the screen. His stomach clenched. Ignoring his literary agent wasn't a wise choice. Drawing a deep breath, he swiped his finger across the smudged glass and accepted the call, then offered a pleasant smile.

"Hey, Stephanie. How are you?"

"I'm well, Burke. Hope you are." Her smile didn't quite reach her eyes. "How are things progressing with your manuscript?"

Oh, dear. He palmed the back of his neck with his good hand, then held up his casted arm. "Experienced a bit of a setback. Minor mishap at the ice rink."

Her brown eyes grew wide. "Burke. No. You're not serious."

"I wouldn't fake a broken arm, Stephanie. You know me better than that."

"I'm not accusing you of faking anything. I just can't believe this. The timing is awful. Why were you ice-skating?"

"Because I'm a single dad, and my daughter wanted to go."

"I see." Stephanie massaged her forehead with mahogany-red manicured fingertips. "So give me a timeline. When can I expect the first three chapters and a polished synopsis? Your editorial team would like to see evidence of your progress."

He cleared his throat. "I understand. I'll have that to you just as soon as possible."

"And how are you defining *as soon as possible* these days, Burke?"

Her frosty tone grated. Wow. She had certainly departed from her Southern sensibilities today. "Steph, I'm doing the best I can."

"Despite your unfortunate circumstances, it's time to perform at a high level. You don't need me to remind you that this deadline is coming up quickly. I so want to believe that you're going to meet it. Because paying back an advance is a challenging endeavor."

His belly knotted again. That fear had seemed so irrational. But with each passing day, he realized that he couldn't afford to return the money. Not if he was going to provide for himself and Darby Jane here in this rugged Alaskan community.

Before he could formulate an answer, footsteps on his porch and a gentle knock distracted him. "Message received, Stephanie. Now if you'll excuse me, there's someone at the door."

"Burke, there's no—"

He ended the call before she could say anything more. Ever since a handful of Southern newspapers and a few social media accounts had featured a photo of Stephanie leaving his house early in the morning a few months ago, their interactions had been strained. She'd only come by to deliver a strongly worded pep talk, but that was not how the images had been perceived. Gossip had circulated, accusing them both of inappropriate behavior. Yet another reason why his mother-in-law refused to speak with him. A fresh wave of shame curdled his gut. Man, he hated that she'd had to call and admonish him for his lack of productivity. Not that he needed a reminder, thank you very much. He was well aware of his personal and professional failures. Somehow he'd prove to his agent and his publisher that he was worthy of a second chance. He had to. Because he'd run out of options.

★ ★ ★

Did Burke not hear the knock? Or was he ignoring her? Jovi rapped harder a second time. What would Grammie say if she knew Jovi had befriended Lois and Mac's nephew?

Jovi shivered against the chilly air swirling around her. She'd brought a frozen chicken potpie and some peanut butter cookies. It wasn't like she'd agreed to cook for the guy for weeks or anything, but he did have a broken arm after all. Besides, how could she not drop off a meal after she'd witnessed him struggling to get out of his driveway? The guy had to eat, and he had a child to feed.

Plus, the few details that she'd pieced together about their families' long-standing feud hounded her. Why had they fought? And how would she ever uncover the truth now that Grammie had dementia, and the other people involved had passed away?

The wind picked up, blowing snowflakes across the modest porch. Jovi sucked in a breath as a few found their way into the exposed skin around her coat's collar. Shifting her weight from one foot to the other, she surveyed the cabin's exterior. The molding around the door frame was chipped and aged, and the paint was faded and cracked from years of wear. A small ceramic planter shaped like a rabbit sat beside a faded welcome mat.

Muted footsteps approached, then the lock turned, and the door opened. Burke filled the narrow gap. Something warm and pleasant unfurled around her fragile heart as his inquisitive gaze met hers.

"Jovi. Hey."

"Good morning. Again." She held out the cardboard box she'd used to transport the food. "I brought cookies. Hope you're not allergic to peanut butter. There's also my mother's chicken potpie. With your broken arm and all, I thought you might appreciate dinner."

"Thank you. That's very thoughtful." He opened the door wider, and his eyes flitted to the bundle in her hands.

"Oh, dear. You can't carry a box. What am I thinking?"

She hesitated, hovering on the threshold. Oh, wow, okay. Now she'd just invited herself in. *Down, girl.*

An amused smile tugged at the corners of his mouth. "Would you mind carrying it into the kitchen?"

"Not at all."

He stepped back, and she entered the cabin.

She quickly scanned her surroundings. The rustic interior wasn't much to brag about. Bookshelves on the opposite wall sat mostly empty, except for a few paperbacks. Yet the worn sofa looked sturdy and comfortable, and a fire crackled in the woodstove.

She tipped her head toward the wide windows filling the opposite wall. "The view of the lake must really be something on a sunny day."

"It's not bad." Burke closed the door behind her. "The kitchen's this way."

Right. She wasn't here for a tour of the cabin. She took the hint to move on and followed him through the living area into a small, functional kitchen. The scent of bacon and coffee mingled in the air.

He wore a blue-and-white checked button-up layered over a white crew neck T-shirt, with one sleeve rolled back to accommodate his cast. Faded jeans hugged his slim hips, and he had donned wool socks.

Stop gawking. She quickly averted her gaze and slid the box onto the worn Formica countertop.

His open laptop and smartphone on the round table nearby caught her eye. "How's the writing going? Must be challenging with a broken wrist."

His features pinched. "It's not going well."

Oh-kay. Heat warmed her cheeks. Point taken. He wasn't interested in chatting today.

"I'll be on my way, then. Hope Darby Jane has a great first

day at school. Just cook the pie at four hundred degrees for about fifty-five minutes." She turned and strode quickly toward the door.

"Jovi, hold up."

Burke's deep voice halted her steps. She turned, with one hand still braced on the doorknob.

His expression softened into something that sort of resembled gratitude. "Thank you for everything. You've been so kind. I don't know why our families couldn't get along, but Darby Jane and I are extremely grateful for all you've done."

Well, how about that? She offered a tentative smile. "You're welcome. To be honest, I really can't stand to see another human struggle. If you need anything else, just holler. I'll be down the road scouring my grandparents' place for a salted caramel chew recipe."

Instantly, she wanted to snatch the words back. Her family probably wouldn't want her to tell Burke her plans. But he was an author, and a successful one at that. Wasn't like he had plans to launch his own candy business or anything.

"Oh, that's intriguing." He smiled. "Keep me posted."

"Will do." She opened the door, then hesitated and turned back. "If you're interested, tonight is Evergreen's annual Frosty Frolic."

His brows sailed upward. "Frosty what?"

Jovi held up her palm. "I know what you're going to say. It sounds ridiculous. The motto is Silly Name, Serious Fun. Seasonal depression is a thing, so a stress-free gathering gets people out of their houses to socialize, since the weather and the umpteen hours of darkness are challenging."

Burke's eyes sparkled with amusement. "The chamber of commerce should hire you for their ad campaigns."

"Thank you." She feigned a curtsy. "My sister trained me well. In case you missed it, she's the mayor."

"Yeah, I think I heard that somewhere."

She hesitated. Was he flirting? "So...is that a yes? I would've mentioned it earlier, but I didn't want to say anything in front of Darby Jane in case you didn't feel up to going out."

Okay, too much talking. And did he think she'd invited him on a date? Ugh. No. Warmth heated her cheeks as she stood awkwardly, wishing for the second time in five minutes that she could take back her words.

"I'll think about it. Maybe we can exchange numbers, then I can let you know after I see how Darby Jane's first day went?"

"Sure." She pulled out her phone. "What's your number? Then I'll text you so you'll have mine."

He rattled off the number, and Jovi added his contact information to her phone then sent him a brief text. "Talk to you soon."

"Thanks again." Burke gently closed the door behind her.

Jovi stashed her phone in her pocket and returned to her vehicle. Snow fell harder now from a granite-gray sky, obscuring the view of his neighbors' property through the trees. She slid behind the wheel of the crossover SUV her mom had loaned her, started the engine, then backed down his driveway and made her way toward her grandparents' log cabin.

Poor Burke. He'd battled one setback after another. She'd rest easier knowing she'd helped by delivering food. Or maybe she'd used him as an excuse to procrastinate. Because as much as she loved her grandparents, she did not want to return to their house for the first time without them.

But she had to find that recipe. Her memory of those salted caramel chews couldn't be wrong. Quite possibly the most delicious candy Grammie had ever made. And yet the company had never produced them.

After she parked in the freshly plowed driveway, she pulled out her phone and texted Mason a quick thank-you for making sure that she'd be able to get to the property. Then she pocketed her phone and turned off the ignition, but stayed in the car, blinking back a fresh wave of tears.

Memories of her last visit home before Grandpa passed away spooled through her head. It had been early fall. She'd tried persuading Grammie to sell the caramels at the candy company, but she had stubbornly refused. Still determined to get her way, Jovi had asked Grandpa to intervene. The irritation that had flashed in his eyes had been surprising. He'd tersely insisted Jovi stop asking. Not that his decision was unusual. He'd always sided with Grammie. They'd been an incredible team. But his impatience had stung. Left her feeling unsettled. Maybe that was why she couldn't shake the notion of adding the salted caramel chews to the current product rotation. In her heart of hearts, she was convinced they'd be a huge hit.

After lunch, she had plans to meet with the person who managed the online candy orders, and she'd get her first training session on how to pack and prep orders for shipping. That left her with a couple of hours to search for the recipe. She didn't start work at the hospital for two more days.

Jovi climbed out of the car. Hunching her shoulders against the blowing snow, she jogged across the driveway and up the steps. Then she pushed her key into a lock, turned it and slowly eased the door of her grandparents' house open. Her chest tightened, bracing for the onslaught of memories. She stepped inside, drawing in a tentative breath. A familiar scent of mothballs greeted her. Thankfully, her family had kept the house in good condition and the utilities connected. Grammie had only been in the memory care facility for a few weeks now, but already a fine layer of dust coated flat surfaces. She swallowed against the tightness in her throat, then shrugged out of her jacket and hung it on the old-fashioned coatrack that Grandpa had made.

A forgotten scarf still hung there, one Jovi was sure Grammie had knitted. The turquoise yarn was a shade that Grammie had adored. Jovi reached out and touched the twists of thread. *I miss you, Grammie.*

She'd have to get Isabel to take her to visit soon.

Even though Mom and Dad had explained to her that Grammie was supposed to get situated in a new routine and adjust to her new living arrangements before anyone came to visit, the guidelines just about broke Jovi's heart. If their sweet Grammie's condition had deteriorated and her memory was failing, what difference did it make if her family visited her? But she hadn't argued. After all, she wasn't the one doing the heavy lifting here day in and day out, making the tough decisions. She hadn't come home for the holidays or helped move Grammie. Still, she was eager to visit, and not just because she wanted to know more about the recipe.

She crossed the living room to the thermostat on the wall. Mason had told her just to give it a nudge and the heat would kick on. Thankfully, her grandparents weren't like other folks who lived near the lake who only heated with the woodstove. Sure, she could still start a fire with the best of them, but there wasn't any wood in the wood crib, and she hadn't brought matches or a lighter.

Her family had given her the blessing to move in and get situated, and she was more than ready. Her parents had grown accustomed to being empty nesters, and although they'd graciously let her stay with them in her old bedroom for the past four days, she felt like she'd stayed a little too long.

As soon as she bought groceries, she could settle in here nicely.

She rubbed her hands together to warm them up, then turned and faced the kitchen. This time, she couldn't stop the tears from falling as she surveyed the worn oak cabinets, the faded floral curtains framing the window above the sink, and the ceramic ring holder sitting on the counter. A gift Jovi had made in a high school art class out of pottery. It was crooked and ugly, but Grammie had still used it.

In the corner, a vintage milkshake mixer sat tucked under the cabinets. Grammie had always kept plenty of supplies on hand to crank up a milkshake whenever Grandpa had wanted one. Jovi sniffled as the sweet memory provoked more tears.

The heat kicked on, pumping warm, dry air through the vents.

Mental images of two people who'd loved one another deeply and adored their family swirled around her, nearly bringing her to her knees. Coming here was even harder than she'd anticipated.

She swiped at her tears with the cuff of her sweater, then dragged the step stool out of the pantry and over to the cabinets above the refrigerator, where Grammie had always kept her recipes. The ones she shared, anyway. Jovi had long suspected that Grammie had a few recipes that she'd never let anyone know about. What if the salted caramel chews had been kept top secret? She opened the cabinet.

Her breath hitched. The metal tin. The one she'd spent countless hours sorting through as a kid. A snowy, downtown bustling Christmas scene was painted on the outside. Black paint had been rubbed off the handle, probably from overuse.

She pulled it from its place, stepped down from the stool and carried the treasured container to the counter. She popped off the lid.

Several recipes were still inside, written on index cards and pieces of yellowed notepad paper with frayed edges. Her grandmother's familiar scrawl documented portions of ingredients for various cookies, cakes and a few main dishes. A couple of pages of magazines had been torn out and folded to fit in the box. When Jovi was little, she and Isabel used to sit on this counter and help make cookies and candy.

She flipped the stack over and started thumbing through

the recipes and magazine clippings again. She set aside one for a white chocolate and pretzel bark that might be fun to try.

No evidence of any recipes with caramel could be found. She sighed and tucked everything back in the box. Maybe she could broach the subject with Grammie on her first visit to the memory care facility, although that was probably something she should clear with her family first. The last thing she wanted to do was upset her grandmother. She'd always said they were special candy for family and friends.

Jovi closed the box, then turned in a slow circle, examining the kitchen for more places to search.

Grammie, where did you hide your secrets?

He might have mocked the name silently when Jovi had extended the invitation, but if he could, he'd thank every single person responsible for making Frosty Frolic happen. Because Darby Jane had been whiny and irritable since he'd picked her up from school. But now that they were making their way along Main Street in Evergreen, bundled up in every piece of winter clothing they'd packed, she'd morphed into the most delightful five-year-old on the planet. He cast a sideways glance at Jovi walking beside him. Was this the Jovi effect? Did having an adult female around make that much of a difference to his daughter?

Burke gritted his teeth, bracing against the onslaught of guilt that often accosted him like a cunning villain, lurking in the shadows. Always ready and leering, eager to remind him of his failures. He'd moved across the country. It had been two years since the accident. Would he ever forgive himself for not being the one who picked up Darby Jane from preschool that day? No, he wasn't responsible for the other driver's erratic behavior, but he had been the selfish dad who'd insisted he couldn't be bothered to stop writing his novel to look after his children.

"Happy Frosty..." Darby Jane looked up at her father. Her curious gaze met his. "What's that word?"

Burke cleared the unexpected tightness from his throat. *"Frolic."*

"It's a fancy word for *fun*." Jovi did a silly little skip move in the middle of the sidewalk that drew a laugh from Darby Jane. "Here, watch me. This is how we frolic."

"Maybe we could frolic inside?" He tipped his head toward the gift shop. "It's freezing out here."

The digital sign outside the bank across the street said minus twenty-five degrees. Was that accurate? Jovi hesitated, pressing her lips together. He didn't miss the irritation that flashed in her blue eyes. He looked away and pretended to admire the painted-on display temporarily decorating the gift shop's front windows. A talented artist had designed a wintery scene featuring a snowman on a white fluffy snowdrift with a perfect carrot nose and a scarf draped around his rotund figure. The traditional black hat and Y-shaped sticks for arms completed the oh-so-frosty vibe.

"Darby Jane, tonight's scavenger hunt is all about finding paw prints," Jovi said. "This store might be a good place to look."

Burke held open the door for Jovi and Darby Jane. "What's the significance of the scavenger hunt again?"

"We have some local mushers who live here year-round. It's dogsled racing season, so this is just something fun we can do to celebrate and support them. If Darby Jane gets a stamp on her card every time she visits a store with a paw print hidden somewhere," Jovi said and gestured to the card the little girl clutched between her mittens, "she can drop by the community center and pick out a prize."

"Got it." Burke followed them inside the store. The pungent smell of scented candles filled his nose. He leaned closer to Jovi and dropped his voice low because, honestly, he wasn't sure how much longer they'd last. "How many paw prints does she need for a prize?"

Jovi carefully scraped her boots on the doormat, then peeled off her gloves. "She only needs seven to get a prize. I think there are twelve or fifteen hidden, but it's your call how long you want to hunt. I know it's a school night."

She offered an empathetic smile before stepping aside to allow a young couple to squeeze past them and exit.

His pulse blipped and then sort of stumbled. Probably alarmed that he'd suddenly decided to pay attention to someone who made him feel…happy? Because Jovi had the most appealing smile. It wasn't just the lovely curve of her pink lips or her white teeth. No, it was more than that. When she was happy, she didn't hide it. Her whole face lit up.

It sort of made him nervous. And a little jealous.

"Daddy, come on, we have to look around. I don't have any clues yet." Darby Jane tugged on his jacket, yanking him back to reality.

"All right, I'm here." He trailed behind her through the store's crowded center aisle. The gift shop carried Alaskan arts and crafts, books and a selection of Evergreen Candy Company products. He paused beside an endcap stocked with plastic bags filled with candy and red-and-pink boxes of chocolate wrapped in white satin ribbon for Valentine's Day.

"How about that?" He turned to Jovi. "They're selling products from your family's company."

Jovi surveyed the display with a satisfied smile. "Some of our most loyal customers are local small businesses."

"Found one," Darby Jane squealed, drawing amused glances from other customers.

A kids' storytime area was tucked in the back corner of the shop. A silver-haired woman wearing jeans and a pale blue sweater smiled at the four children squirming around her, asking for a special stamp from the store. The paw print was prominently displayed on an easel next to her.

She caught Burke's eye. "If you'd like to stay, I'll be reading *Balto* in just a few minutes."

Burke swallowed back a groan. He must've forgotten to tell his face not to frown, because Jovi chuckled.

"Don't look so excited." She gently nudged him. "Aren't you an author? And a parent? I thought you'd be thrilled about a quiet indoor activity like this. It's a great story, by the way. Balto is one of the famous sled dogs who led his team through harsh winter conditions to Nome years ago. The dog musher, Balto, and his team saved the whole town from diphtheria."

"Can I buy my own copy and read it to Darby Jane at home?"

"Sure."

This time her tight smile didn't quite reach her eyes. Burke winced. Was he being too much of a party pooper? Probably. Did he have to get an exhausted kid in bed tonight and then up again early for school tomorrow? Also yes. And he didn't want to be grumpy. Not when Jovi had been nothing but kind and generous.

"Alpenglow Espresso is right next door." Jovi gestured over her shoulder. "I could—"

"I am not drinking espresso at this hour."

"They sell decaf. What I was trying to say, before you interrupted, was I'll pop over and grab us some hot decaffeinated drinks while you stay here and buy a copy of the book. Sound good?"

"All right, one pit stop, but then we have to keep going. I don't want to keep her out too late. Tomorrow's going to be rough, especially if she's all hyped up on hot cocoa and giddy from collecting clues."

Jovi's eyes narrowed. "Your festive attitude is delightful. I'll meet you outside in a few minutes."

Before he could respond, she turned and left. He stared after her. Torn. Okay, so maybe his less-than-stellar attitude grated. But she didn't know what he'd endured. Maybe if she'd lost half her family, she wouldn't be so ridiculously happy all the time.

Chapter Seven

"A hidden recipe?" Isabel stared at her sister. Jovi always had some wild ideas, but this topped the charts.

Jovi set her disposable coffee cup on the counter. "Hidden or missing. What other explanation is there? Grammie's salted caramel chews were so good. She made them in small batches and we always ate them way too fast." Her lips twisted into a smile that fell away just as quickly. "But I can't for the life of me remember how she made them, and I scoured her kitchen. No salted caramel chew recipe."

Isabel hesitated. "Why would Grammie hide a recipe?"

They didn't need more complications at this point. They were barely hanging on.

Isabel took a flattened cardboard box from the giant stack against the wall. Irene, their longtime packing and shipping manager, came into the room carrying a six-pack of clear packing tape.

"Irene, do you remember our grandmother ever bringing

you a salted caramel chew?" Isabel handed the unassembled box to Jovi. "You've probably worked here the longest."

Smiling, Irene slid the carton onto the counter. "Jerry on the production line has worked here a year longer than me. But thank you for the vote of confidence. I do remember the salted caramel chew. And Jovi's right. They weren't for sale. Your grandmother brought them to share at staff meetings sometimes."

Irene's oversize earrings bobbed against her slender neck as she used scissors to punch a hole in the plastic shrink wrap, then extracted a roll of tape for her empty dispenser.

"I think we should sell them." Jovi pushed out the flaps for the bottom of the box. "But I don't have Isabel convinced."

The dispenser squealed as Isabel tugged the tape across the cardboard, sealing the bottom closed. She really hated to dismiss Jovi's suggestions. Her sister had been willing to leave Kansas City and come home to help. And saving the company from being sold to a global conglomerate was still a priority. But without a recipe, how could they roll out a new product on a tight deadline?

"I know you did a quick run-through yesterday, but let's go over how we receive an online order, pack it and prepare it for shipping again. I want to make sure you're feeling confident with the entire process." Isabel gestured toward the empty cardboard box. They needed to stick to the task at hand before chasing down a missing recipe.

Jovi pulled a few sheets of tissue paper from the supply Irene had carried over to the counter. "I'm ready when you are."

"Not much has changed over the years." Irene slid the laptop closer. "Except we use laptops and more automation."

"Remember when Grammie used to take orders by phone on that cute little notepad?" Sadness tinged Jovi's smile.

Isabel wiggled the mouse on the computer, then clicked to open the program that tracked their inventory. She didn't have time for a jaunt down memory lane today. As soon as she finished here, she had to get on a call with a customer in Cincinnati. Then on to a quick meeting with the chamber of commerce to approve Evergreen's digital summer ad campaign.

"Well, like Irene said, we've gotten a little more advanced." Isabel nodded toward the computer screen. "This is a fairly simple order. The customer wants one box of twelve of our peanut butter chocolate eggs, which we almost always have in stock."

Irene pointed to the box of candy already sitting on the counter.

"Next, we make sure every box has the signature ribbon with our logo on it."

Isabel pointed to the forest green ribbon imprinted with Evergreen Candy Company's logo wrapped snugly around the white box.

"Got it." Jovi nestled the candy inside the tissue-paper-filled box they'd assembled.

"The next step involves directing the software to print a mailing label and an invoice." Isabel completed those steps with two clicks of her mouse. "Any questions?"

Jovi shook her head. "How many people are responsible for packing and shipping?"

"Ideally, there are six of us working in here." Irene crossed to the printer stationed on a stand in the corner to retrieve the label and invoice. "Lately we've had trouble retaining employees."

Isabel winced. The truth stung. They offered competitive wages, good benefits and a clean facility. But staffing shortages had become the norm in recent months. And with their decline in sales, they hadn't needed six staff members to fill orders.

Jovi layered more tissue paper into the box, added the invoice Irene brought her, then taped the box shut. "Is there a quality control process?"

Isabel nodded. "Double-check the mailing address on the box matches the one on the spreadsheet."

"We put all outgoing packages in that giant plastic bin." Irene gestured to the container beside the door. "When we're finished filling today's orders, we wheel that out to the lobby, and the receptionist orders a package pickup."

"Cool. Thank you for the refresher," Jovi said, shifting her attention to Isabel. "What do you think of my salted caramel chew suggestion?"

Not going there. Isabel blew out a slow breath. "Why don't we go visit Grammie. She's allowed to have visitors starting tomorrow. Maybe we'll catch her in a moment of lucidity, and we can ask her about that recipe."

Jovi's face lit up. "Seriously?"

"It's worth a try." Although, those moments of clarity had become more and more rare in the past six months. Isabel refreshed the computer's screen to check for any new orders. Jovi had been gone so long, she had no idea the version of Grammie they might encounter. "We won't know until we ask, right? We can stop at our specialty supplier and pick up a case of food coloring we'll need for the Easter seasonal orders too. I'll have to hurry back, though. I promised Mason a date night."

"Deal." Jovi reached for her coffee again. "Are there any more orders to fulfill?"

As they worked with Irene to pack and ship additional orders, Isabel's thoughts wandered to Mason, and her pulse ramped up. He wanted to start a family. Now? His words still had her reeling. She didn't feel equipped to be a mom yet. She wasn't sure if she'd ever feel ready.

Her uncertainties, combined with Mason's interest in a new job that possibly meant relocating, had robbed her of more than a little sleep the previous night. How could he ask her to not only leave her family, her community, and her work but toss in becoming a parent too?

She'd barely kept from having a meltdown.

He'd brought her breakfast in bed this morning, though, and

sent her a sweet text inviting her to dinner at their favorite restaurant tomorrow. She had to give him credit. He was at least trying to bridge the chasm between them. So she'd meet him halfway. It was the least she could do for the man she loved.

This visit had seemed like such a great idea when her sister had offered it yesterday. But now, she couldn't bring herself to go inside.

"Wait." Jovi's voice broke, and she clawed at Isabel's coat sleeve. "I'm not ready."

Isabel offered an empathetic smile. "Me either."

They stood outside the memory care facility in Anchorage, their breaths leaving puffy white clouds of vapor in the wintry morning air.

"We have to see her, though." Isabel tilted her chin up. "Grammie needs to know we haven't forgotten her. And I need to know that she's all right."

Jovi swallowed against the tightness in her throat, then took tentative steps forward. "You're right. At least we're doing this together."

Isabel blinked several times, then sniffed. "Right. Together."

They trudged toward the entrance. The double doors parted, and they entered the building. A familiar antiseptic smell, one she'd grown used to over the years working in health care, greeted her. Soft instrumental music streamed from a speaker. A woman wearing a fuzzy charcoal-gray sweater smiled from her place behind the wide faux wood reception desk.

"Good morning, ladies. Welcome to Oasis Care. How can I help you?"

Her berry lipstick, neat silver bob and kind hazel eyes propelled Jovi forward. "We'd like to see our grandmother, Carol Wright."

"This will be our first visit," Isabel added. "She just moved in two weeks ago."

"Give me one minute, please." The woman slid her reading glasses into place. Her manicured nails clacked over the keyboard on her computer. "Mrs. Wright finished breakfast recently, and she's sitting over there by the windows."

Jovi turned and scanned the lobby. A grand piano and comfy beige furniture filled the seating area, with a broad expanse of windows overlooking a beautiful snow-covered courtyard.

"I'm Gretchen, by the way. I'll need to see your photo identification, please."

Jovi and Isabel handed over their driver's licenses. After Gretchen entered the data into her computer, she passed the cards back. "We recommend you keep visits short. Twenty to thirty minutes is ideal, and we have a client liaison on hand should you need additional support."

Additional support? Jovi's scalp prickled. Was Grammie going to be combative? Prone to make a scene? Guilt swept in. Wow. She'd missed out on a lot, being so far away. Relying on Isabel, Mom and Dad to keep her up-to-date on Grammie's health had seemed like the right thing to do, but clearly she had no idea how far Grammie had declined. Because she couldn't imagine her sweet, independent grandmother getting out of hand.

"Thank you for the pointers," Isabel said. "It's helpful to know what to expect."

"Of course." Gretchen clasped her hands on the desk. "Enjoy your visit."

Isabel turned away, and Jovi trailed her across the lobby. Lush, green plants filled every nook and corner. A beautiful arrangement of fresh flowers adorned a coffee table situated between two sofas. Their wet boots squeaked on the linoleum as they approached a woman sitting in a rocking chair.

Jovi's breath caught. Her grandmother's hands, frail now, clutched the arms of the rocker. A pink striped blouse layered under a purple cardigan reminded Jovi of a similar outfit Grammie often wore. Maybe it was the same one? She'd draped a beautiful multicolored quilt over her lower body. The trademark voluminous curls were absent. Instead, Grammie's hair had been trimmed short in a pixie cut that would be super fun to style. Jovi made a note to bring gel next time. Maybe Grammie would let her do a mini spa day.

"Grammie." Isabel stopped beside the chair and sank to the floor in front of her. "It's me, Isabel. How are you?"

Grammie's lips curved downward into a frown, and her eyes, once so vibrant and full of life, skittered between Isabel and Jovi.

Jovi spotted an empty folding chair nearby and pulled it closer. "Hi, Grammie. So nice to see you again. I've missed you."

Grammie tightened her grip on the arms of the chair. "I don't believe we've met," she said, her voice a tentative warble.

Ouch. How could Grammie not know them? Jovi settled her purse next to her boots and forced her mouth into a smile. "It's me, Jovi."

Grammie's expression hardened. "Are you here to talk to me about my taxes? Because I'm afraid I can't help you. My husband and son handled all of that."

Oh, dear. Jovi and Isabel exchanged worried glances.

"Grammie, we're your granddaughters. Your son's children." Isabel reached out and ran her fingers across one corner of the quilt. "We stopped by to say hello."

Glaring, Grammie pulled her feet out of reach like she'd been pinched. "Please don't touch my quilt."

"I'm so sorry." Isabel's hands trembled as she fisted them in her lap. "It's beautiful."

"Thank you. My friend Lois made it for me."

The mention of Lois snared Jovi's curiosity. "Were you and Lois pretty good friends?"

Grammie looked at her like she'd sprouted a third eye. "The best. I've known her for years."

Jovi hesitated. Lois's passing didn't seem to be a detail her grandmother was aware of right now. It would be cruel to mention it, right? She'd always been instructed to converse with dementia patients, rather than argue with them over the accuracy of details. "What kind of things do you and Lois like to do together?"

"Oh, we love to bake. She makes the best candy. During the holidays, you know, our treats are the talk of the town." Grammie chuckled, a familiar sound that wound around Jovi's heart.

"Indeed." Jovi nodded. "Your candies and cookies are legendary."

Grammie's smile faded, and she shot Jovi a suspicious glance.

Undeterred, Jovi pressed on. "Do you know any recipes by heart? Like maybe your salted caramel chews?"

Grammie harrumphed as she plucked a tissue from her cardigan pocket. "I don't give away my recipes to anyone, least of all strangers."

"Right. I understand."

"Like I said, if you're here to talk about the taxes, you've got the wrong gal. My husband or my son will be home from work this evening, so you'll have to come back later."

Jovi stood and gently tugged her sister to her feet. "Of course. We'll visit again soon. Come on, Isabel. We need to go."

"But it hasn't even been twenty minutes," Isabel whispered.

"We don't want to upset her. She doesn't know who we are." Jovi gave Grammie one last smile, but Grammie turned her head away, rocking gently, twisting the tissue between her gnarled fingers.

They crossed the lobby, waving at Gretchen as they passed her desk. Together, they made their way outside.

"That was awful." Isabel fished a pack of tissues out of her purse. "How can she not know her own grandchildren?"

Jovi's phone hummed inside her jacket pocket. "We tried. That's what matters."

"I just can't believe she's losing her mind." Isabel dabbed at her tears. "She's barely been sick a day in her life. Why dementia? And why her?"

"If only I knew." Jovi pulled her phone out. A text from Mason filled a bubble on the screen.

Please don't leave Grammie's place yet. I have a surprise. See you in a few.

Did he expect her to stall? Jovi bit her lip and snuck a glance at her sister.

Isabel's eyes narrowed. "What's going on?"

Thankfully, the rumble of a car approaching saved her from answering.

"Is that Mason's car?" Isabel shoved the tissues back in her purse, then strode to the edge of the sidewalk. Exhaust floated into the air as the dark blue sedan slowed to a stop in front of them. The driver's-side door opened, and Mason stepped out.

"Mason," Isabel said, "what are you doing here?"

He flashed a sheepish grin. "My boss sent me to exchange a part we need for one of the loaders. When you said you were going to be in town today, I thought I'd surprise you. I've already made reservations for our date. How was your visit?"

Scowling, Isabel shouldered her purse. "It was terrible. She thought we were accountants or something, and she fussed at me when I touched her."

Mason's smile evaporated. "That's tough. I'm so sorry."

"But now we know what to expect, right?" Jovi gently nudged Isabel's shoulder with her own, infusing her voice with optimism she didn't quite feel.

His gaze swung to meet Jovi's. "Would you mind if I whisked Isabel away for the weekend? We could use some time alone."

Isabel stiffened. "I thought you had to pick up a part?"

The doubt in her tone made Jovi cringe. Uncertainty flickered across Mason's features. Before Isabel crushed him with her excuses, Jovi looped her arm through her sister's and steered her toward the vehicle's passenger side. "What a thoughtful guy you have. He's taking date night to the next level, right? Go on. Enjoy yourselves. I'll drive your car back to Evergreen."

Isabel wrenched her arm free. "But what about—"

"Babe, I've thought of everything. Packed your bags, cleared your calendar and made all the arrangements." Mason opened her door with a gallant flourish. "You don't have to plan a thing. And I'll deliver the part when we get back to Evergreen."

"Oh, that is so sweet." Jovi pressed firmly on her sister's back and guided her into the car. "Can't wait to hear all about it."

Mason closed the door as Isabel voiced another concern. Blowing out a long breath, he closed his eyes for a second.

Her heart pinched. Poor thing. "She's not going to make this easy for you."

Mason opened his eyes. Something that looked like sadness flickered there. Then it was gone. He reached out and gently squeezed her arm. "Thank you for your help."

"Anytime."

After they drove out of sight, Jovi turned and trudged across the parking lot to Isabel's car. She had to get back to Evergreen and get ready to start work at the hospital. Envy seeped in. It sure would be nice to have someone to plan an extravagant date. Instead, she'd been dumped by her fiancé. Isabel didn't appreciate how good she had it with Mason.

Thoughts of Burke spooled through her head.

"Ha! Not happening." She kicked a small chunk of ice in her path. Darby Jane was a cutie, but her father? A total grump with a ton of baggage. Not to mention, their families had a turbulent history. ~~Besides, she hadn't come back to Evergreen~~ to fall in love. The last thing she needed was a man in her life.

"Daddy, I'm full." Darby Jane pushed away her plate loaded with an unfinished Belgian waffle and then slumped against the booth's buttery vinyl cushion.

Burke hesitated, awkwardly lifting a fork full of omelet to his lips. Eating while wearing a cast was more of a challenge than he'd expected. And they'd waited forty-five minutes for this table. A mistake he'd not make again. Evidently, half the town showed up at Trailside on Saturday mornings. "You've hardly eaten anything, love. How about a few more bites?"

She usually gobbled up any kind of sweet breakfast. Besides, her meal easily cost him eighteen bucks, including her orange juice and the side of bacon. It would be nice if it didn't go to waste.

Darby Jane shook her head. "Can't."

Their server stopped at their table, a carafe of coffee in hand. "Would you like a refill?"

"Please." He nudged the mug toward the edge of the table.

Steam curled from the mug as she slowly topped it up. Hovering, she eyed the little girl. "What's wrong, sugar? I thought you'd love that waffle."

"My tummy is real sad." Darby Jane's chin wobbled.

Oh, no. Burke pinched his mouth shut to stifle a groan. *Please, not the stomach flu.*

"Do you have a fever?" The woman pressed her palm to Darby Jane's forehead, then gave Burke a look. "Don't mean to be in your business, sir, but she feels a little warm."

He surveyed his daughter's flushed cheeks and glassy eyes. Now that he studied her, she didn't look well. How had he missed the usual signs? Setting his fork down, he dabbed his mouth with his napkin and looked up at the server. "Thank you for letting me know. We'll be on our way home in a few minutes."

"I'll bring your check right over." She offered a kind smile. "I'm Connie, by the way."

"Nice to meet you, Connie. I'm Burke, and this is Darby Jane." He fumbled for his wallet. "We'll take two boxes, please."

"Sure thing." She moved on to the next table.

"Thanks." Did Darby Jane need to go to the doctor? The last time she had a fever, she'd come down with strep throat. Maybe they could wait and go tomorrow if she still felt bad. Except tomorrow was Sunday, which meant another emergency room visit, since he hadn't taken her to a local pediatrician yet. Ugh. He had that delivery coming today too.

"Excuse me, Connie?" Burke called after her. "May I ask a favor, please?"

"Daddy, no," Darby Jane groaned. "I want to go."

"Darby Jane." He kept his voice low, but pinned her with a serious look. "This is important. Please don't fuss."

Her lips formed a pout.

Connie returned, wearing a concerned expression. "How can I help?"

"Do you have any advice on who I might speak with about moving furniture and boxes? I just found out this morning our household goods will be delivered this afternoon." He held up his casted arm. "I'm not in a position to be particularly useful."

She bit the corner of her lip. "Let me text a few friends."

He twisted his mouth into what he hoped was a grateful smile. "Appreciate it."

Connie moved away, stopping at an adjoining booth to refill coffee mugs and speak to several customers.

He hated asking for help, he really did, but the barge traveling from Seattle with their belongings had been delayed indefinitely. But then the moving company had called and informed him that they'd made a mistake. Instead, delivery of his pod containing everything he'd shipped from Charleston was happening today. Once he took delivery, he didn't want their precious cargo just sitting there in the cabin's driveway. What if three more feet of snow fell overnight? Then he'd have to find people to shovel, unload and unpack. Highly unlikely. Charlie had gone out of town for the long weekend, and he hadn't met his neighbors yet. Except for Jovi. And he'd rather not rely on her again.

She'd done plenty to help already.

Besides, he still felt guilty for having such a lousy attitude at Frosty Frolic. Blowing out a long breath, he reached for his coffee. Maybe more caffeine would soothe the headache forming behind his eyes. Because this all felt impossible to manage. If only he hadn't lost Mary Catherine. She'd always stayed on top of the details and knew exactly what to do when Darby Jane didn't feel well. He swallowed against the tightness in his throat.

"Daddy, I need to go." Darby Jane yawned. "I'm so tired."

"Hang on, sweet pea. I haven't paid yet. As soon as Miss Connie comes back with the boxes and our check, then I promise we'll get going, okay?"

"Oooh-kaaay." She rubbed her eyes with her fists.

Poor thing. It had been ages since she had gotten sick. They'd had plenty of other obstacles to overcome, but remarkably, they'd been healthy for months. Maybe starting at a new school had exposed her to different germs. At least she'd have three days to recover.

A few minutes later, Connie returned with his bill and a small card. "I jotted down a couple of names and numbers, and I texted them already. Both are good guys. If they're in town, I'm sure they'd be glad to come by and help."

"Perfect. Thank you so much." He tucked the card inside his coat pocket, then awkwardly boxed up their leftover food. After he paid the cashier near the front door, he guided Darby Jane outside.

"I'm cold," she whined, her teeth chattering as they moved slowly toward the truck.

"We'll be back at the cabin in just a few minutes." Burke held the truck's door open while she climbed inside. Then he buckled her seat belt for her. She wrapped her arms around her trembling body.

Burke paused before closing the door. Uncertainty swept through him. How sick was she? He touched his palm to her forehead. Connie wasn't wrong. Darby Jane's forehead did feel quite warm. Maybe he needed Jovi's help after all.

Nope. He'd handle this. It wasn't the first time Darby Jane had had a fever. Surely wouldn't be the last. Besides, their brief discussion about their families not getting along had stayed with him. Sure, she'd been exceptionally kind. But could he trust her?

As he drove away from the diner, he mentally analyzed his meager resources. Hopefully he still had children's fever-reducing medication tucked away in his shaving kit. And he'd bought crackers and ginger ale on his last grocery store run.

When he rounded the corner on the road leading to the cabin, he tapped the brakes because a semitruck blocked his access.

"Oh, my." He slowed to a stop behind the massive trailer carrying a forklift and a large rectangular box. Two men in dirty brown coveralls and orange beanies stood on the snow-packed ground, chatting and gesturing with their hands.

"What's happening?" Darby Jane sat up straighter, craning her neck. "Are they stuck?"

"I don't think so." Burke gingerly shifted into Park and then unbuckled his seat belt. "This might be our delivery. Please stay here while I speak to them."

Darby Jane gasped. "I hope my favorite striped jammies are in that big box."

Burke chuckled. "I'm sure everything we packed is in there."

If only he could get some help hauling everything inside the cabin. His broken arm was becoming a problem. He climbed out of the truck.

Another vehicle pulled up behind his. Super. Burke gritted his teeth. Now he'd blocked traffic for everyone who lived on this road. Not a great way to make friends.

The woman behind the wheel waved, then got out of the car. Jovi. Her cheery smile made his heart kick against his ribs.

"Hey, Burke." Snow crunched under her gray boots as she strode toward him. "What's going on?"

"Hey." He tried not to stare at the way her silver-blue jacket made her eyes sparkle. Or get distracted by the silky blond hair framing her face.

"Are you all right?" Concern flashed across her features. "Where's Darby Jane?"

He cleared his throat, then palmed the back of his neck. "She's in the truck. And yes, we're fine. Mostly. She doesn't feel well, and evidently we're about to get a delivery."

Her gaze slid past him. "Is that all your stuff from South Carolina?"

"Yes, except I'm not quite sure how I'm going to get it all unloaded and inside the cabin." Warmth heated his skin. "I didn't want to pay extra for movers to come and unload. In hindsight, I wish I'd made a different choice."

She pulled her phone from the pocket of her jacket. "If I ask around, I can probably find some people to help."

"I asked Connie, our server at the diner, if she had any contacts. She gave me a few names and numbers, but I haven't had time to call." He fumbled in his coat until he found the note.

"Here. Let me take a look." Jovi took it, her fingers brushing against his. A pleasant warmth zipped up his arm.

Pull yourself together, Solomon.

"I can't ask you to do anything else," he said. "You've gone above and beyond already."

Jovi glanced up from her phone. "I haven't done anything except be a decent human."

Right. Of course. Clearly, her generosity wasn't because they'd bonded on their unexpected road trip or because she had any interest in a relationship. And *why* was he even thinking like this? Admiring her appearance, responding to their fingers touching like he was eleven years old, second-guessing her kindness—ridiculous. All of it.

Because he certainly didn't plan on dating. Guilt over his obsession with his writing career and its result in Mary Catherine's and Henry's deaths still dogged him. He and Darby Jane had plenty to deal with already, and he'd been scandalized for having a meeting with his literary agent.

If he ever did decide to get involved with a woman, he sure wouldn't start with someone who belonged to a family that Lois and Mac had fought with for years. There had to be a reason why the Wright and the Phillips families had parted ways. As soon as he had his stuff unpacked and Darby Jane felt well again, he'd start investigating. Someone in this close-knit community knew the juicy details. And that might spur the fresh idea he needed to finish his novel.

How long did it take to unload a pod from a semitruck? Jovi tried not to express her impatience, but the forklift operator had been blocking the road for over thirty minutes. And fatigue was getting the best of her. She really wanted to get back to her house and take a long nap. But Darby Jane's pathetic expression and the news that she didn't feel well niggled at her. A nasty virus had inflicted several patients at the hospital. What if Darby Jane had come down with it?

"I'm sorry about this. I hate that we're blocking access to your grandparents' place. Seems as though there's an issue with the forklift." Burke gestured for her to follow him. "Come on inside the cabin. Darby Jane fell asleep. I need to wake her up and get her settled inside. Besides, I have an article I want to give you."

Jovi stifled a yawn. "If they don't move soon, I'm going to leave my car here and walk down the road to the house. I'm worn-out."

"Tough week?"

"I just finished working a night shift at the hospital."

He paused beside the truck's passenger door and gave her a confused look. "I thought you were working part-time at your family's candy company."

"I'm trying to juggle both." Jovi followed him. "I signed another contract as a traveler. Keeps me here for thirteen weeks, gets me a nice paycheck, benefits, you know, the whole nine yards."

"What's a traveler?"

"A temporary health care worker. We're paid a premium for being willing to relocate every thirteen weeks to fill a position that would otherwise go unfilled. We have a critical nursing shortage in this country and..." Why was she telling him this now? He needed to get Darby Jane inside. "Never mind. You don't need to hear me get up on my soapbox."

He smiled gently. "Some other time, perhaps. Again, I'm sorry about the inconvenience. If you'll just pop into the cabin for a minute, I'll give you that article. It's an old newspaper clipping that I found tucked in a book featuring my aunt Lois and the woman I believe is your grandmother."

Oh. Jovi shivered, jamming her hands deeper into the pockets of her coat. "I would like to see that. I guess I can come in for a minute."

The beeping of the forklift interrupted them.

Another truck drove down the road, then slowed to a stop and pulled over behind her car. A man got out. He was in his midtwenties and wore a gray hoodie, faded jeans and black work boots.

"Hey. I'm Jensen. Connie from Trailside sent me a text, said you might need some help moving?"

"Here's the man you need to speak to." Jovi tipped her head toward Burke, who'd opened his truck's door. Darby Jane stirred. She opened her eyes, blinked, then rubbed her eyes with her fists. She did not look well at all.

"Thanks for coming by, Jensen." Burke gave a quick nod. "I'm Burke Solomon. This is my cabin. We're taking delivery of our household goods today, and with my arm in this cast, I'd appreciate the help. If you've got a couple of hours."

Darby Jane groaned.

"Here, why don't you let me take her?" Jovi held out her arms. "Are you all right, Darby Jane?"

"Uh-uh." Darby Jane's lip quivered. "I don't feel good. But I wanna watch the guy move our box."

Poor baby. She looked so pitiful.

Burke smoothed his hand gently over her forehead. "She started looking ill when we were at breakfast. Pretty sure she has a fever."

Yikes. "Come here, pumpkin." Jovi scooped the little girl into her arms. Boy, she felt really warm. "I'll take her inside. Is your front door unlocked?"

"Here." He handed over the keys. His expression softened. "Thank you for doing this."

"No problem." Jovi turned toward the cabin with Darby Jane wedged on her hip. "How long have you felt bad?" Jovi's breath came out in little puffs of white as she worked her way around the truck and forklift.

"Since I waked up." Darby Jane leaned her head against Jovi's shoulder. "I'm hot and cold at the same time."

"Yeah, I know. It happens. Your body's fighting those germs."

"Germs are icky."

"Indeed." Jovi sidestepped the truck driver as he directed the forklift operator to maneuver the pod off the truck.

When she got to the porch, she fumbled with the key, managed to jam it into the lock, and then carried Darby Jane inside. She settled the girl on the couch and plucked her boots from her feet.

"Let me get you a blanket." She pulled an afghan from the back of the couch and draped it over Darby Jane's trembling body.

"That one's ugly."

"I know, but it will have to do. I'm sure your favorite blankets are going to be unpacked shortly."

"Will you stay with me until we're all unpacked?"

The words pierced Jovi's heart. As much as she wanted to say yes, exhaustion weighed her down. And Burke wouldn't want her to make promises she couldn't keep. "I don't know about that. I've been up all night working, helping take care of other sick people at the hospital."

"Can you help take care of me too?"

How could she say no to that? "Of course. Do you like crackers and ginger ale when you feel yucky?"

Darby Jane nodded and tugged the afghan up over her lap. "And a movie on my daddy's laptop."

"We'll have to wait for him to come inside to handle that part. I'm sure he'll just be a minute. I'll look for the ginger ale and the crackers while we wait. Okay?"

"Okay."

Jovi set the kid-sized boots and jacket by the door, then toed off her own. Shivering, she padded into the kitchen. When Burke came inside, she'd ask about starting a fire in the woodstove. It was chilly in here.

On the counter, she spotted a yellowed newspaper article, obviously clipped from a larger section ages ago. Her breath caught. The photo in the center of the page was blurry, but she could still make out the familiar outline of Grammie. Just a much younger version. She looked beautiful with a sweet smile on her face. Lois stood beside her. They both grinned at the camera as they held out boxes of cookies or candy.

Jovi leaned closer and scanned the caption.

Lois's and Grammie's names were there in print. They'd won a local contest in Evergreen with their confections. She checked for a date at the top of the article, but for some reason, whoever had clipped the story out hadn't included it. The women couldn't have been more than twenty-one or so in the picture.

So when had they stopped being friends? And why?

"Jovi?" Darby Jane called out. "May I have something to drink, please?"

"Be right there." She opened the pantry. A box of saltine crackers stood on its end. She pulled out a sleeve, then added a few to a bowl she found drying beside the sink. Thankfully, a can of ginger ale was already chilling in the fridge. Did Darby Jane have a favorite cup? Or did she need to use a straw inside the can? Jovi peeked inside a few of the almost bare cabinets until she found a plastic mug with a sturdy handle. That would probably work. After pouring half the liquid into the mug, she carried the soda and crackers into the living area just as the front door opened and Burke came inside with three guys behind him, all loaded down with large boxes. Chaos ensued with the men trampling in, trying to figure out where to place the stacks. Boy, Burke had a job ahead of him. Especially with his arm in a cast. Darby Jane watched wide-eyed from the couch. Jovi made her way around the obstacles and sat beside her.

"Which one has my special blanket in it?" Darby Jane shivered, and her voice held a whine.

Jovi eyed the first stack of boxes. Even though they were all labeled, this wasn't the time to start digging for things. They'd only be in the way. Besides, something told her the girl wouldn't want to stop once they got started.

"Want to try the ginger ale and crackers I brought for you?" Jovi held them both out. "You might feel better after a little snack."

Darby Jane nodded and selected one cracker. Her little body trembled. Chills from the virus or just too cold? Jovi set the bowl and the mug on the coffee table, then crossed to the woodstove. She'd start the fire herself. After locating the box of matches tucked away on a high shelf, she put a log from the neat stack nearby, some kindling and crumpled newspaper inside the stove, then lit the paper and stoked the fire until flames licked the wood.

Jovi couldn't stop a huge yawn as she sat back down on the couch. Darby Jane mimicked her action.

"After you finish your crackers and soda, why don't you curl up and take a little rest?"

"Can't." Though her eyes drooped, Darby Jane shook her head. "Too loud."

Jovi stroked her flushed cheek. "You'll feel better after you rest."

Her own body ached with fatigue. She just wanted to go home and sleep. Except she felt bad leaving Darby Jane here, and Burke was distracted, giving the moving crew instructions on where to place things. As soon as he came back in from the other room, she'd ask for a thermometer to take Darby Jane's temperature.

She settled into the corner of the couch. It wouldn't hurt to close her eyes. Just for a few minutes.

Burke stood in the living room of the cabin, debating his options. Jovi had fallen asleep on his couch. Darby Jane, at some point, must've snuggled close, because now she slept with her head on Jovi's lap. His heart swelled at the sight. Jovi's peaceful expression, the pink bow of her full lips, and the warmth from the fire sent his thoughts all sorts of places they shouldn't go. Then logic immediately stormed in, like a drill sergeant on a mission, determined to restore order.

He couldn't be with Jovi. Not like this, not now, and maybe not ever. Did he want to be a single dad for the rest of his life? Of course not, but it seemed like the only way. Besides, he'd barely waded into investigating their families' mysterious feud. Even though he hadn't come up with any concrete details on the cause, the existence of the rift served as enough of a warning. They couldn't get involved with one another.

Yet here he stood, wondering if maybe he should just turn around and go fix himself something to eat. What was the harm in letting her sleep a little longer? His head spun as he stood there in limbo, not sure what to do.

Except, what was he supposed to do with his oh-so-conflicted emotions? He couldn't pretend he hadn't caught himself stealing peeks out the window to see if she was around. Or that his heart hadn't expanded at the sight of her doing all the maternal things for Darby Jane that his late wife had once done. And don't even get him started on what happened to his insides when she smiled. Or laughed.

He bit back a strangled groan. Yeah, he had to put a stop to this.

Pulling in a deep breath, he stepped closer. Instantly, Jovi's eyes opened. She blinked, then looked down at Darby Jane. Her mouth parted, but when her gaze flicked to his, she found her voice.

"What's going on?" Jovi asked, her voice thick with sleep.

"You fell asleep." Burke kept his voice low. Waking Darby Jane was the last thing he wanted to do.

Jovi's brow furrowed as she sat up. When Darby Jane stirred, whimpering, Jovi winced. The little girl sighed, then curled into a ball on the couch and hugged the afghan tighter.

"I guess I should go," Jovi whispered.

No. Shoving the petulant thought right back where it came

from, Burke offered her his hand to help her stand up without disturbing his daughter.

Jovi hesitated for a moment before accepting his offer and allowing him to help her up to her feet. She stood close enough that he breathed in a pleasing vanilla-scented aroma. Her eyes roamed his face. The sensation of her fingers still clasped in his kicked his pulse up a notch, and his stupid traitorous eyes dipped toward her lips.

Jovi angled her head slightly. She peeked up at him through dark eyelashes. It wouldn't take much for him to lean in and—

"I'll walk you out."

Somehow, he forced himself to let go of her and turn away.

Without another word, the two of them moved toward the door. She stopped long enough to shove her feet into her boots. But when he held the door open for her, Jovi paused and looked at him with an expression that seemed almost…hopeful? Burke's heart skipped a beat as their gazes locked, but he quickly looked away, not wanting to succumb to temptation. He had already made his decision: he wasn't going to take a chance on a relationship with her.

Instead, Burke cleared his throat and stepped aside so she could leave without him blocking the way.

Outside on the porch, a bitter cold swept over him. He shivered, but he'd be a gentleman and walk her to her car. Overhead, millions of stars spilled across a black velvet sky. A bright round moon had crested the mountains silhouetted in the distance. They walked in silence until they reached Jovi's car where Burke opened the door for her.

Except she didn't get in. "Burke."

As his name left her lips, the air around them shifted. Burke froze as their gazes locked again, scared at what might unfold. He wanted so desperately to reach out and take her in his arms, but a paralyzing fear kept him still.

No. He couldn't. Not after the horrific losses he'd endured. Stepping away, he shook his head. If he allowed himself to get too close to her, there would be no turning back.

"I'm sorry." Her expression was difficult to read in the silvery moonlight as she scrutinized him. "For whatever I did to make you uncomfortable."

"It's all right," he said quickly. In a tone far too abrupt for his liking. He could almost feel the heat radiating from her as she stood there in silence. One hand gripping the car door's frame. The seconds ticked on in agonizing silence.

Suddenly, there was nothing else to say. Jovi slid behind the wheel, barely mumbling *good night* before she slammed the door.

As she started the engine and then drove away, Burke couldn't help but feel both relieved and saddened at the same time. Relieved that she was leaving so he could remember why they couldn't be together—they were all wrong for each other—and sad because he wanted nothing more than to keep talking with her for hours.

He watched her taillights until she pulled into her driveway before finally letting out a deep breath and walking back inside the house.

He'd pushed her away. But what might've happened if he'd kissed her instead?

His stomach tightened. Yeah, okay, so tonight had proved that he wanted to open up to her, but fear held him back every time. Fear of getting hurt, fear of feeling vulnerable, fear of how falling in love might impact his daughter's life.

His thoughts raced on endlessly as he retrieved the thermometer and fever-reducing medicine from the bathroom. Darby Jane, his manuscript, unpacking all these boxes—those were the things that mattered. Not pursuing a relationship with his beautiful, available neighbor. Especially since she'd only signed a contract for thirteen weeks. What if her family sold the company and she left town? He and Darby Jane couldn't afford to get attached. Besides, his selfish choices had resulted in catastrophic consequences. Time had softened the edges of his grief, but not his guilt. He didn't deserve to find love again.

Chapter Eight

This view. Mason's attentiveness. Their three glorious days together in the resort's luxurious suite reminded her why she'd married him. Her husband sure knew the way to her heart. How to spoil her. Isabel nestled against him as he draped his arm around her shoulders and pulled her closer. The glass-enclosed gondola glided up the Alaskan mountainside. This sightseeing trip was the last item on Mason's well-planned itinerary before they headed back to Evergreen. Everything had been perfect.

In the distance, whitecaps dotted the gray Pacific Ocean. From her side of the gondola, she spotted a glacier spilling down a craggy, snowcapped mountain. Countless peaks and valleys bordered the ski resort, and a brilliant blue sky brushed with wispy white clouds stole her breath.

"This has all been incredible, Mason. Thank you."

Mason's grin creased his clean-shaven, ruddy cheeks. With a gleam in his eye, he leaned over and brushed his lips against hers. He tasted like coffee and sugar. The appealing spicy fragrance of his aftershave made her body tingle and brought back memories of their previous night together.

He leaned back.

"Wait," she whispered, her eyes trained on the curve of his full lips. "Don't stop."

His hooded gaze and the pad of his thumb drawing lazy circles on the back of her hand clouded her thoughts.

She slid one hand along the sleeve of his puffy jacket, across his broad shoulder, then cupped his jaw in her palm and claimed his mouth again.

"Be careful." His gruff voice carried a teasing note when they broke apart. "We're going to fog up these windows. The operator will have something to say when our ride's over."

Laughing, she snuggled closer and rested her head against his chest. "We are married, you know."

"I'm well aware." Mason affectionately squeezed her knee. "We're also riding to the top of a mountain overlooking a very busy ski resort in a mostly transparent box, and I don't know how much longer I can keep my hands to myself."

"Noted. I'll behave."

They rode in comfortable silence. Until her conscience got her attention. She swallowed against the dryness in her mouth. "I'm sorry I was so critical when you surprised me with this trip."

"No problem. I understand you don't like surprises, but to be honest, it was the only way to get you out of Evergreen for the weekend."

"You're right. It wouldn't have happened any other way."

They climbed higher, the view only getting more stunning.

"I haven't been here in years. Look." Isabel pointed toward a snowboarder below them, surrounded by yards and yards of untouched white snow, carving a path down a steep valley. "That's quite a ride." She sighed. "I wish I still skied. We used to go all the time when I was in high school."

"Winterhaven is open," Mason reminded her. "It's practically in our backyard, and we have all our gear in the garage."

"I know. It's just..." She stopped herself before blaming her schedule. Such a pitiful excuse. "I want to make time to do more fun stuff with you, Mason."

His body stiffened. Silence filled the small enclosure. "Do you mean that?"

She pulled back, studying him. "I wouldn't have said it otherwise."

Mason looked away. "We've avoided all the hard topics so far this weekend, but since we're headed home in a couple of hours, maybe now would be a good time to talk about our future."

Despite the heat in the gondola and the lingering warmth from their kiss, not to mention the exquisite couples' massage they'd enjoyed after brunch, an ominous chill racked her frame. "What do you mean?"

A muscle in his cheek twitched. "I've been invited to a second interview. For that project manager position I told you about. It's with a well-respected construction business in Juneau."

"What?" She gasped. "You're still thinking that you want that job. Even though you'd have to move?"

He removed his hand from her leg and twisted on the bench seat to face her. Irritation flashed in his eyes. "*We* would move. Together."

She shook her head. "No."

"Isabel, we've talked about this. I don't want to stay in Evergreen forever. The place is suffocating."

"*Suffocating?*" Anger spiked. "Wow, that's quite the thing to say when you're married to the mayor."

"It's because I'm married to the mayor that I feel this way. Between the business, your responsibilities with the town council, and your family commitments—"

She held up her hand. "What do you mean by my family

commitments? I thought you liked spending time with my parents."

Mason palmed the top of his head. "Your parents are great. And I'm really sorry about everything you've been through with your grandmother. I hate that she's losing her memory and had to move. I wish I could change it, but at the same time, we have our own lives. If your parents want to sell the company, now's the perfect time to make a fresh start. It's important that our kids experience more of Alaska than just our tiny town."

"You mean the kids we don't have yet?"

He winced. "I want to start a family with you, Isabel. Sooner rather than later. I thought you wanted kids. When we dated—"

A terrible grinding noise interrupted their conversation, and the gondola jerked back and forth.

She gripped the sleeve of his jacket. "What's going on?"

Mason's chin lifted as he scanned their surroundings. "We're making an unexpected stop."

"But we're suspended in midair." Her chest tightened, and her pulse sped as she craned her neck to assess their location. Up ahead, the mountaintop restaurant's roof glinted in the sun. Below them, skiers in bright colored ski jackets and snow pants zipped down the runs, oblivious to their plight.

Mason threaded his fingers through hers. "It's going to be okay. We might be stuck here for a few minutes, though."

"Can't you call someone?" They needed to get back. She had to prepare for Tuesday's town council meeting.

"I wish I could, but I didn't bring my phone." Mason's eyes roamed her face. "Did you bring yours?"

She shook her head. "We agreed to leave them in our room."

"Why don't we make the most of our time together and keep talking?"

This time, his thumb caressing the back of her hand aggravated her. She tugged free, fisting her hands in her lap. "Because honestly, Mason, I don't know what else to say. You're asking me to give up everything I love."

"Everything? What about me? Don't you love me? I'm your husband."

"That's not fair. You know I love you."

"Do I, though?"

Hot tears pricked the backs of her eyes. "How can you ask that?"

Mason's expression hardened. "It doesn't feel very loving when I'm the last on your list."

She flinched. "I just spent an entire weekend with you."

"After Jovi prodded you to agree, and she had to shove you into the car to get you to comply." His voice grew louder. "Don't you dare pretend like you were excited about this."

"I'd just come from a heartbreaking visit with my grandmother, Mason. Less than ten minutes ago, I apologized for my attitude, and you said, 'No problem.' When in reality, it seems as though we have a much bigger problem on our hands."

They sat there, side by side on the bench seat, staring each other down. Tears blurred her vision.

At last, he spoke. "You're right. We do have a big problem. I want to go. You want to stay."

"So what are we supposed to do?" she whispered. "Wh-what are you suggesting?"

Mason blew out a long breath and looked away. "I don't know where we go from here. But I'm going to the second interview."

She stared at her hands. His declaration squeezed the air from her lungs.

Unbelievable.

Isabel wriggled uncomfortably in her seat, the heat in the enclosed cable car and the strong coffee she had drunk that morning finally taking its toll.

Sighing, she unzipped her jacket, feeling the sweat already

starting to collect on her forehead. Oh, she should not have had all that coffee at breakfast. She tugged off her jacket and flung it on the bench beside her.

Mason studied her. "Everything okay?"

"I really need to use the restroom. How much longer do you think it's going to take for them to fix this?"

Mason softened at the desperation in her voice. "Sweetheart, I don't know. I'm sure they're working as quickly as they can. We're not the only ones who are stranded."

Isabel nodded, trying to take comfort in the fact that they were not alone in their predicament. She glanced over at the other gondolas, seeing the couple behind them smiling and enjoying themselves. She felt a pang of envy for their contentment. Why couldn't she be happy for this prolonged date with her husband instead of wishing for it to be over?

"We'll have to just wait it out," Mason said finally. "Maybe the maintenance crew will come soon and get us going." He reached out and took her hand. "We could try talking some more. Do you feel comfortable with that?"

Panic shot right through her. *No.* "Um, okay. What do you want to talk about?"

"Can you say more about your fear of having children?"

Tears pricked at the backs of her eyes. He always managed to find just the right words to cut right through the armor she used to shield herself. Her breath hitched, and she bit down on her lip. She didn't want to talk about this. It was too painful. "You know why."

"Babe." His compassionate gaze held hers. "Lots of people lose babies. You're not defective or broken. I've done some research, and many people go on to have healthy, uneventful pregnancies."

His eyebrows scrunched together over his beautiful eyes that always saw more than he let on. "The doctor said there's no way for us to know why you miscarried. We're both perfectly healthy."

"I'm not ready," she whispered, barely squeezing the words out.

"It's been five years." Mason's voice was tight. "Don't you think it's time to at least try again? To give us a chance to have a family?"

"That's easy for you to say. You're not the one who has to worry every single second, wondering if you're eating the right things or if you stood on your feet too long or lifted something too heavy."

His hand tensed. A muscle in his jaw clenched. He was disappointed, but she just couldn't bring herself to take that leap of faith yet.

Mason pulled away and stood up, then settled on the bench opposite hers. Blood roared behind her ears. They were going to argue again. She sensed the tension building.

And she was so tired of conflict.

After a few minutes, Mason's troubled gaze found hers. "Listen, Isabel, I know this isn't easy for you, but I want us to have a family. You don't have to do this alone. I'll be here right beside you every step of the way."

His words hung in the air.

Couldn't he see how vulnerable they made her feel? Sure, he'd be right there every step of the way, but he couldn't control the outcome. Couldn't control the fear that plagued her daily. Couldn't soothe the deep sadness she'd have to wade through if she lost a baby. Again.

She tried to avoid his gaze, but he returned to the seat beside her, gently cupped her chin and forced her to look at him. "Talk to me," he said softly. "What is it that you're afraid of?"

She took a deep breath and let it out slowly. If she was super honest, maybe he'd finally understand. "I'm scared of not being able to control the outcome." She bit her lip before continuing. "I know it's irrational, but I worry that if we try again and things don't work out, then I'll be back in that same miserable, hopeless place. It's too risky for me right now."

Mason nodded and released her chin before pulling her into an embrace. She sank into his chest, feeling a wave of love and comfort wash over her.

He spoke quietly into her hair. "We're supposed to trust the Lord's timing, right? Even when we think our plans and our timelines are ideal, He knows what's best for us."

Isabel closed her eyes as the truth of Mason's words hit home. Yes, trusting God was what she needed to do. But it was so hard! She pulled back, then looked up at him.

His strong, calloused hands cupped her face. She leaned into his touch. He thumbed away a tear. "This is exactly why I want to move somewhere new. Somewhere without all these connections and obligations. The hard memories. We could find a new doctor this time around. Then, we'd start fresh without worrying about being under such scrutiny or pressure here in our hometown. We'd be free, to find our own path forward together without fear or expectations hanging over us. Doesn't that sound exciting?"

Shocked, she pulled away. Anger pulsed through her veins. She shook her head. "It sounds terrifying. Why would we consider giving up our community and all the safety it brings? Who would help us if something happened? Why are you asking me to do something that sounds so awful?"

Mason sighed and hung his head. "Because I want something more than just driving snowplows and being someone else's employee."

"Then why don't you stay in Evergreen and start your own business or try to get promoted?"

He rolled his lips together and fixed her with his strongest gaze. "Are you kidding? You know Jonathan will be working until he can't anymore. Retirement isn't really in his vocabulary. And if I'm honest, I don't want to wait that long either before making plans, Isabel. I have dreams and ambitions too, and I won't put them off forever."

"What do you mean?"

"I don't know what to do." Mason flung his hands in the air. The anger simmering between them came out in his words. "We both want different outcomes, and neither of us is willing to yield. I'm going ahead with the interview, regardless of what you say."

She tried to keep her voice from shaking. "And I won't give up my role as mayor just because you want me to."

The air between them felt thick and heavy. How had they gotten here? Fog coated the windows of the gondola from their heated exchange.

As the cables above them began to groan and creak, Isabel let out a sigh of relief. They weren't anywhere close to resolving their conflict. If anything, the situation had become dismal. But she had to get out of this cable car.

Was this how it was going to end—in separation? Divorce?

Even now, those terms made her insides churn. But with Mason being so unreasonable, what could she do?

"It has to be here somewhere." Jovi sighed and sank back on her heels. "That's the fourth box I've sorted through and haven't found any recipes."

"Here, I brought you a latte from the coffee shop." Isabel stood in the doorway of the company's storage room, holding a to-go cup with a cardboard sleeve. "Why don't you take a break? There's something I want to talk to you about."

Jovi eyed the white bankers' boxes stacked in the corner that she still hadn't looked through yet. "I'll take a short break, but then I'm going to keep searching. So far I've found receipts, user's manuals and old Christmas cards from loyal customers. I feel like they saved everything around here except for the one recipe we need to keep the place going."

She stood and took the cup from Isabel. "Thanks for the coffee, by the way."

"You're welcome." Isabel stifled a yawn. "Grammie did like to save stuff, especially recipes. But I'm starting to wonder whether the salted caramel chews were something she just experimented with and we happened to be around to taste them."

Isabel led the way out of the storage room and continued. "Or she kept a lot of the recipes in her head. Come on into the workroom. Irene's bringing fresh samples of candy and cookies we want you to try."

"When do you want to go see Grammie again?" Jovi paused in the doorway, lifted a lid on a box and peeked inside. Ugh. More files overstuffed with papers. "Maybe she'll know us this time."

"I forgot to tell you," Isabel said over her shoulder. "Gretchen from Oasis left me a voice mail message. There's been a flu outbreak. No visitors allowed until further notice."

Jovi groaned. Poor Grammie. "That sounds awful."

As they walked down the hall, Jovi scanned the production floor below through the windows. Jerry stood on the concrete floor, gesturing to a young man beside him as the conveyor belt cruised by, transporting sweet concoctions. "You just mentioned Irene bringing in samples to try. I've been thinking about our conversation with Mom and Dad, and that looming deadline. If I can't find the recipe, is there anyone who works here who can help me come up with the key ingredients?"

"We have a small team that develops new products. Usually it's Jerry, Irene, me and one other person. But I'm afraid we're spread too thin already, prepping for Valentine's Day and Easter. If you want to try developing the salted caramel chews, you're going to have to do that on your own." Isabel's phone hummed. She glanced at the screen, frowned, then kept walking.

"I'm not super confident that I'll be able to recreate Grammie's version, but I'm willing to try. The salted caramel chew I remember was so tasty. I just can't imagine why she kept something that good to herself." Jovi slowed down long enough to take a sip of her latte. Whoa. So delicious. The perfect combination of bold yet sweet.

"What if it wasn't hers to begin with?" Isabel walked faster. "What if she used a recipe that she'd found in a book or a magazine? Then she wouldn't have been able to claim the candy as her own and sell it here."

Jovi took another sip of her coffee to keep from blowing out an exasperated sigh. Every time she thought they might be onto something, Isabel introduced another possibility Jovi hadn't considered yet. "Wait. What did you want to talk about?"

Isabel slowed, then turned and faced her. "I hate to bring this up, because I know how gossip flows in this town, but a few people have mentioned to me that they've seen you and Burke Solomon together. A lot."

Really? Jovi stared at her sister. "You're joking."

Isabel frowned. "I don't make jokes about people gossiping. Especially when my family's involved. Are you spending a lot of time with him?"

She picked at the cardboard sleeve on her coffee cup. "Not... like that. I've helped him out a few times because he's had to deal with one catastrophe after another, and he gave me a ride to Evergreen so I didn't have to spend the night in Anchorage. We're just being neighborly."

Doubt swam in Isabel's eyes. "I know you don't need me to remind you that our family and his had a falling-out. It must've been a big deal to sever a friendship, so please, proceed with caution. Especially after what you found on the internet about him."

Oh, brother. Why was Isabel getting worked up about this? Wasn't a weekend away supposed to rejuvenate? Isabel looked more exhausted—and irritable—than when she'd left. "I appreciate your concern, but there's nothing to worry about. I wouldn't give a clickbait story on the internet much credit. Besides, Burke isn't interested in a relationship with me."

Was he? A reminder of the way his eyes had held hers a beat too long filled her head. Then when she'd fallen asleep on his couch with Darby Jane and he'd walked her to her car, she'd been almost positive he'd wanted to kiss her. Warmth heated her skin.

Ridiculous. She brushed off the notion, then offered a bright smile. "He's not my type. Honest."

Isabel studied her. Awkward silence hung between them. "Happy to hear I don't need to worry. Let's go. Irene's waiting for us."

When they entered the brightly lit tasting room Irene greeted them with a warm smile. "You're just in time for our latest samples."

The smell of sugar and chocolate made Jovi's mouth water, and she took a deep breath, inhaling the sweet aroma.

Irene stood at the counter. She nudged two white square plastic trays closer to Isabel and Jovi. Jovi clutched her sister's sleeve. "Is that what I think it is?"

Isabel smiled. "Look familiar?"

"I used to beg Mom and Dad to buy a whole batch when we went to the fair in Washington." Jovi plated the layered chocolate bar. "Nanaimo bars are scrumptious."

"It's a prototype," Irene explained. "Not a salted caramel chew, of course, but it has the potential to be a crowd-pleasing favorite."

"And don't get too attached to the idea," Isabel cautioned. "We're in the early stages of development."

Jovi took a small bite of the dense bar. The crunchy base layer carried hints of almond and coconut, but it was the chocolate and vanilla combo as well as the salty garnish on top that made her want more.

"Would you like some?" Irene offered water as a palate cleanser from a portable pitcher and a plastic cup.

Jovi swallowed, then nodded. She set her coffee aside and took the cup from Irene.

"What do you think?" Isabel propped one hip against the counter.

Jovi hesitated. She really hated to be critical, but they weren't as tasty as she'd hoped.

"It's fine, I guess."

Irene frowned. "Just *fine*?"

Jovi cleared her throat. "I mean, it's good, but it's not exactly what I was expecting. I remember it being sweeter and creamier."

Isabel nodded. "We're still tweaking the recipe, so we'll keep that in mind. Vanilla pudding mix is the most economical for the middle layer. However, the traditional recipe calls for a specific custard powder that we're struggling to source."

Irene jotted down notes on a yellow notepad, then looked at Jovi. "We're always looking for honest feedback, so thank you for that. Do you want to sample anything else?"

Jovi scanned the counter. On an oval plate, there were sugar cookies shaped like flowers, decorated with elaborate glazed frosting. "Now, what are these?"

"We're rolling out our first batch of sugar cookies for Easter." Irene set her pen and notepad aside. "This is a trial run. Would you like one?"

"We've worked very hard to come up with locally sourced ingredients. As you can imagine, that's tough to do in the winter in Alaska. But, as I've already mentioned, our customers have become a bit more discriminating, and it's important to them that we incorporate things like berries and all-natural sweeteners in our products whenever possible." Isabel plated a sugar cookie for herself.

Jovi picked up the cookie and took a bite. It was soft, yet held its shape and tasted like a mix of honey and vanilla. The frosting was smooth yet delicate and had the perfect amount of sweetness.

"This is amazing."

Isabel smiled. "Glad you like it. We use honey from a beekeeper who lives here in Evergreen. Last year they were a hit with customers."

Jovi took a few more bites of the cookie before putting it down. "I'm impressed."

Isabel's smile faltered. "But…"

"I love that you're honoring Grammie's legacy. She'd be so proud. But I'm not giving up on finding that salted caramel chew recipe. To me, they'd sell better than the bars and the sugar cookies."

"Thanks for sharing your thoughts," Isabel said. She pressed her lips into a thin line and looked away.

That didn't sound like a consensus. Jovi finished her coffee and stood up from the stool. "Well, I'd better get back to it. Thank you for the treats."

As she headed back to the storage room, Jovi couldn't shake her disappointment. The Nanaimo bars and sugar cookies were delicious, but they weren't going to turn things around enough to keep her parents from selling. She was determined to find that missing recipe.

Chapter Nine

"I need a costume for tomorrow." Darby Jane put the empty salad bowl and the container of dressing on the counter beside the fridge.

The serving spatula slid from Burke's hand and fell into soapy water in the kitchen sink.

He turned and stared at her. "Beg your pardon?"

She trailed the tip of her finger through the frosting on the edge of a cupcake.

"Whoa, whoa, whoa. Hold on." He held up a dripping hand. "Before you dive into your dessert, what do you need a costume for?"

She licked the frosting from her finger and challenged his gaze. "My teacher sent a note about it." Something that looked an awful lot like irritation flashed in her eyes. "It's the hundredth day of school. Everybody wears a costume, and then we get to parade through the hallways. It sounds super fun."

Darby Jane grinned, but no amount of charm could outweigh the fear sneaking through him. A costume by tomorrow?

He still couldn't quite wrap his mind around what she'd said. He dried his hand on a towel and then wiped at the beads of sweat forming on his forehead. "Tell me again what we're celebrating?"

"We've been in school for one hundred days," she said, punctuating each word with intentionality as if he was supposed to just know. "Well, I haven't been there for one hundred days, but everybody else has, so we're supposed to make a big deal. It also helps us learn to count. But I already know how to count to one hundred."

"Educational and festive. How delightful."

Her little brow crinkled. "Why are you mad?"

"Because you're just now telling me at—" he glanced at the clock "—seven o'clock that you need a costume for an event I'm not familiar with. Forgive me, but I'm panicking, Darby Jane."

She blinked twice. "The note was in my communication folder."

He tunneled his hand through his hair. "What's a communication folder?"

She blew out an exasperated breath and stomped out of the room.

"Don't stomp away from me like that," he called after her. "I'm trying to help you solve this problem."

She returned a moment later, her cheeks flushed, eyes glassy with unshed tears. "My communication folder." She thrust a red plastic folder at him with her name printed on the front and a sticker. "It comes home every Monday. You're supposed to look inside because it tells you everything you need to know."

"Thank you." He set it on the counter and opened it.

"There." She pointed. "See?"

Sure enough, a flyer along with the letter from the teacher. His stomach sank.

She popped her little fists on her hips. "I also got a star for doing my math worksheet properly."

He tried to smile and pat her on the shoulder, but he was still too freaked out to properly congratulate her. "That's great. Way to go."

Burke pulled the flyer out and studied it. The info he needed was all there. Costume recommendations, guidelines about what to avoid, and the deadline in bold print and emphasized with a yellow highlighter.

Splendid.

How had he messed up so badly? Again? He set it down, then dragged his palm across his face. "Well? Any suggestions?"

"No." She hung her head and scraped her toe over the faded linoleum. "You have a good imagination. Don't you have an idea?"

He barked out a laugh. "Darby Jane, I write novels. I appreciate the compliment, but I'm not a set designer or a costume coordinator. What are your friends wearing?"

She lifted one shoulder. "I don't know. Maybe Jovi can help us."

Outside, a snowplow barreled down the road, its blinking lights casting a glow through the window. The chains on the tires jangling and the motor rumbling reminded him that at least another foot of snow had fallen.

"Jovi works nights at the hospital now, remember?"

"But not every night." Darby Jane turned and hurried toward the living room windows. "I saw her car when we came home from school. Maybe she's home now."

"Maybe. Or maybe we can try to figure this out on our own?"

Since Jovi had mentioned the feud between his family and hers and the candy company, he'd wondered if maybe somebody had done something untenable to create the rift. And he wasn't sure who he could trust. Had Mac or Lois been the offending party, or had it been someone in the Wright family? He hadn't had time to do a thorough investigation, but when

Jovi had shared she wanted to find an iconic recipe, well, it had inspired him to write. He'd cranked out more words this week than he had in the past five months, and it felt good to be productive again. If only he could keep up this pace, he might make his deadline.

"Why don't we just ask her?" Darby Jane turned from the window, a hopeful look in her eyes. "You could send her a text. She used to live here, right? Maybe she has her old costume."

His girl had never been one to give up easily. Burke couldn't help but smile. "It's possible."

"Jovi always has an idea about how to fix things, even when me and you don't."

He couldn't argue with that. But still. Thoughts of the pretty blonde with the infectious smile and oh-so-sunny outlook on life whipping up a last-minute costume for his daughter? He wasn't sure how much longer his heart could resist. Worse, the more time they spent together, the more Darby Jane gravitated toward Jovi. He'd hate for his little girl to get too attached to someone who might not stay in Evergreen.

The whole situation literally seemed like a recipe for disaster.

She was going to make a delicious batch of salted caramel chews if it was the last thing she did.

Jovi unpacked the sugar, brown sugar, maple syrup and honey from the bag. Groceries had set her back a few bucks. Man, she'd forgotten how expensive it was to live here. But she wanted to support the local store, and she had to admit that being back here in Evergreen had been fun so far.

Sure, her hands ached, and she wore three Band-Aids on her fingers from all the paper cuts she had from helping pack and ship the last-minute orders for Valentine's Day next week. Not to mention she'd spent about six hours in the car this week delivering cookies and special orders all over town.

She'd been scheduled to work tonight at the hospital, but

thankfully, they'd called her off because they said they didn't need her. She probably shouldn't have committed to working at the hospital and packing orders at the business, but to be honest, she wanted to stay as busy as possible this month.

Anything to keep distracted, because she didn't want to dwell on how this would have been her first Valentine's Day as Michael's wife. How this would've been their first Valentine's Day as newlyweds. How she wouldn't have had to cope with living in different cities, as they'd done for most of their engagement.

They could have been together and happy. Hopefully. Probably. Maybe.

Instead, he'd rejected her with a ridiculous excuse about how he wasn't ready to commit. Why had he waited until twelve days before the wedding to reveal his fears?

Now she was alone.

The hurt and anger threatened to swallow her.

No. Not going there tonight.

She opened the kitchen drawer and retrieved Grammie's candy thermometer. She held it in her palm and turned it over. Oh, how she wished she could call her up and ask about making those chews. She and Isabel planned to visit again soon, but for now, she'd settle for trying a couple of recipes that she'd found online.

So far her quest to recover Grammie's recipe had gone nowhere. She'd looked in every cabinet and every closet in the house and only succeeded in making a mess. There were still a few more boxes to sort through in the storage room at the company, but Isabel had encouraged her to take a break. The problem was, they didn't really have time to take a break. It was the first week of February already, and their parents had moved forward with their plans to sell. Mom and Dad had had dinner with a representative from a European candy company owner just the other night. Jovi had declined an invitation to attend. She didn't want them to think she was interested.

She lined up the ingredients and reached for her phone to pull up the recipe she'd bookmarked. Whatever she came up with had to be tastier than those strange Nanaimo bars she'd taste-tested.

A text message from Michael filled her screen.

Her heart kicked against her ribs. A text from her ex-fiancé—how ironic. She flipped the phone over, not wanting to deal with it. Except she needed to look at her phone for the recipe. And besides, she didn't have to respond, right? She could just read it and then carry on.

Sighing, she reached for her phone again.

Hey, Jovi. How are things?

I'd love to talk sometime. I know you probably don't want to hear from me, and I understand that. But the thing is, I really miss you. And anyway, just thinking about you. Hope you're safe and well.

Anger pulsed through her veins.

Now he was thinking of her? She pushed the phone away and crossed the kitchen to where Grammie kept her saucepans and baking dishes. She pulled out the most robust pan she could find, quickly wiped it out with a damp paper towel to remove any dust, and then set it on top of the stove.

Then she found a glass baking dish and a couple of glass measuring cups. Perfect.

Her phone hummed. Jovi's mouth ran dry. Not again.

She added water to the kettle to boil. This called for some tea. She'd already put aside some frosted sugar cookies from the business and added some chocolate truffles, bypassing the heart-shaped ones, thank you very much. She huffed out a breath. Who told their ex-fiancée they missed them? In a text message? Especially a few months after calling off a wedding at the last minute?

She lit the burner under the kettle as her phone hummed again.

"Seriously," she growled, then crossed the kitchen in three quick steps and grabbed the phone again. "What do you want from me, Michael?"

Two more messages greeted her.

There's a small chance I could be sent with special ops to one of the bases in Alaska.

I ran into a friend of ours, who mentioned that you were going back to Alaska for a while. If our schedules sync, it would be great to see you in person. Let me know if you're interested. Here are the dates...

"No, I am not interested." She set the phone down and then glared at the device. *Was* she interested, though?

If she was honest, it felt good to have some attention from him. And a tiny part of her was feeling quite smug that he was having second thoughts. Okay, a huge part of her wanted to shout *I told you so*. But the rational side of her brain couldn't fathom why she'd even entertain talking to him, much less meeting up with him.

Honestly, could he be more insensitive?

Surely he knew it was almost Valentine's Day. Did he choose this month intentionally to reach out? Maybe he was lonely too.

Good for him.

So many questions spooled through her head. Instead of responding, she found the recipe she needed and gathered the ingredients.

Cutting the stick of butter into smaller pieces was so satisfying. Once she added them to a glass bowl, she slowly poured in the heavy cream. Then she put the bowl in the microwave, set the time, and turned it on. Turning away, she eyed the corn syrup and sugar on the counter. Working with sweet sticky substances wasn't her gift. So much could go wrong. But playing it safe and not attempting to make the salted caramel chews didn't get her anywhere either.

"Just try," she whispered. "How bad could it be?"

The kettle came to a boil, so she paused to fix her tea, then went back to heating the sugar, corn syrup and water in a pan on the stove. The appealing aroma of sugar mingled with the scent of the melted butter, making her mouth water. As soon as the concoction started to boil, she double-checked the recipe.

Oh, no. She didn't have any parchment paper. She peeked inside the empty grocery bags, then searched all the cabinets. Nothing.

Really? Couldn't one thing work out? She'd have to substitute wax paper or aluminum foil, because that was all she had, and these ingredients were too expensive to waste.

Her phone pinged yet again. Nope. Not looking.

Lost in the memories of helping her grandmother make candy, Jovi measured the temperature, stirring almost constantly until she had the concoction to the appropriate consistency. Well, the consistency she thought looked right.

After lining the glass baking dish with foil, she poured in the hot, smooth mixture.

As the caramels cooled on the counter, she added a bit of honey to her mug. Soft knocking on the door got her attention. What now? She'd planned to hunker down, enjoy her desserts alone and try to pretend that Michael hadn't reached out.

The knock sounded again. Maybe it was an emergency. She'd better answer. Cradling her tea in both hands, Jovi crossed to the door and opened it. Her heart skipped to find Burke and Darby Jane standing on the porch. Their breath left puffy white clouds in the night air.

Not a bad surprise. Maybe they could help pull her out of her Michael funk.

"Hey there. It's two of my favorite neighbors. Come on in." She stepped back and waved them into the house.

Burke smiled, although there was something in his eyes that she couldn't quite name. He seemed slightly guarded. He sure looked handsome, though, in his red-and-gray plaid lined button-up over a gray thermal Henley. His jeans had the perfect amount of fade in the denim, and he'd invested in some practical winter boots. Darby Jane looked cute as ever, all dolled up in her head-to-toe pink and purple winter garb.

"It smells good in here," Darby Jane said, quickly making herself at home by shedding all of her stuff.

"Darby Jane, please pick up your coat and hat." Burke gestured to her coat that she'd tossed on a chair.

"It's fine." Jovi smiled. "I'm glad you feel comfortable here, sweetie."

"We're sorry to interrupt." Burke unlaced his snowy boots, then nudged them against the wall. "I tried texting, but when you didn't answer, we decided to invite ourselves over. Because frankly, I'm desperate."

A muscle in his jaw twitched as his eyes met hers, then darted away.

Desperate. Interesting. She glanced between Burke and Darby Jane, silently assessing them both. They looked well. "Oh, you're not interrupting. I'm trying to make this candy that I remember from my childhood, but—"

"Ooh, I like candy." Darby Jane craned her neck to see past Jovi into the kitchen.

"Yes, she does. But that doesn't mean she needs to eat any." Burke firmly clamped his hand on Darby Jane's shoulder. "You just had a cupcake, remember?"

Jovi chuckled. "Why don't you both join me in the kitchen? Burke, can I offer you some decaf coffee or hot tea?"

"Either works," Burke said. "Please don't go to any trouble."

"It's no trouble. I have plenty of decaf coffee." She quickly prepped the coffee maker for a fresh pot. "Darby Jane, would you like milk, water, or, if it's okay with your dad, hot cocoa?"

"Hot cocoa, please." Darby Jane climbed up onto a stool next to Burke and eyed the box of goodies Jovi had brought home from the candy company.

While Jovi waited for the coffee to brew, she found some hot cocoa mix in the cabinet for Darby Jane, then retrieved her phone from the counter. "I'm sorry I didn't respond to your texts. I got caught up in the candy-making."

That was true. She had. No need to mention Michael, though. She quickly scanned Burke's message lamenting a last-minute need for a costume for Darby Jane, a plea for help, and a confession that he had absolutely nothing to offer other than his gratitude.

She chuckled, then tucked her phone out of sight. "Wow, you are in a pickle. So tell me about this project."

"I need a costume to celebrate the hundredth day of school, which is tomorrow." Darby Jane rested her chin on her hands.

"Oh, wow. I didn't know that was a thing." Jovi combined the cocoa mix and hot water from the kettle in a green mug with the Evergreen Candy Company logo printed on the outside.

Amusement gleamed in Burke's honey-brown eyes. "Darby Jane was hoping you could help her."

How could she say no to these two? There had to be something in this old house Darby Jane could wear. Jovi retrieved the cream and sugar and then brought them to the counter. "My first-grade teacher, who was also my kindergarten teacher, really wanted us to read, so I think she gave us stickers for every book we finished. But I don't remember celebrating the hundredth day. Have you come up with any ideas?"

"Nope." Burke leaned his elbows on the counter. "We've mostly just panicked."

"You panicked." Darby Jane slanted a look in Burke's direction. "I'm not worried at all."

Jovi pressed her lips together to hold back another laugh. The child said the funniest things.

"Some of us were supposed to stay on top of the communications coming home from school." Two splotches of color appeared on his cheeks.

"Well, that someone is also a single parent who recently moved across the country, broke his arm and probably has a few other responsibilities to juggle. Right?"

"All true." Burke's genuine smile made her pulse speed up. "Thank you for understanding."

"You're welcome." Jovi gave the hot chocolate a quick stir, then eased the mug across the counter toward Darby Jane. "Has anybody tried an Internet search? Scrolled through Pinterest, perhaps?"

Burke's brows drew together. "What's Pinterest?"

Jovi gasped in mock horror. "Haven't you marketed your novel on Pinterest?"

"Evidently not." Burke sighed. "But maybe I should?"

"We'll talk marketing strategies later. Let me get your coffee, then we'll see what we can come up with."

Isabel's warning about spending time with Burke echoed in her head. Was she getting too involved? Probably. Was this a nice distraction from Michael's texts? Also probably. But who could resist a handsome single dad in need? Besides, she couldn't bring herself to disappoint Darby Jane. So she'd help out. Just this one last time. Because she wouldn't let her heart get broken again.

Chapter Ten

Family feud. Families fighting. Longtime family feud. Alaska feuds in Evergreen. Burke scrolled through the search results filling his screen. Nope. Nothing useful. How about *Hatfield and McCoy*? Or *Montagues and Capulets*?

Ugh. Too depressing.

His phone slipped from his grasp and landed with a soft thud in his lap.

"Are you kidding me?" He glared at the device as if it had somehow leaped from his hand of its own free will.

The two women sitting diagonally across from him in the cramped medical clinic waiting room gave him curious looks. Burke formed his mouth into a tight-lipped smile. They tipped their heads closer and whispered to one another.

Hopefully, after this afternoon's appointment, he could say goodbye to the restrictive cast on his wrist and transition to a hard splint. Typing with a cast for almost three weeks had been nearly impossible, crippling his productivity and dampening the small amount of motivation he'd cultivated.

He retrieved his phone and then resumed his internet search. Not that his quest had been fruitful at all, and pecking away at the tiny keyboard with his nondominant hand really made him cranky. This whole unfortunate situation made him cranky. If Jovi didn't know why his aunt and her grandmother had stopped being friends and his messages to his brother and his mother had so far gone ignored, how in the world would he ever find any helpful clues?

Burke's aggravation grew with every futile search result. The rift between his aunt and Jovi's grandmother had consumed too much of his mental energy lately. Last night, when he'd been falling asleep, he'd almost convinced himself that the conflict had likely been petty and insignificant. But, today, it still gnawed at him. Like Darby Jane and her stubborn allegiance to Bobo, he had latched on to the notion that a propulsive story might somehow materialize.

A thread he could spin into a completed manuscript.

Okay, so maybe his agent and his publisher expected something a little darker. A story that meshed with the genre expectations of domestic thriller readers. But he'd fallen so far from his debut bestseller pedestal. Did it matter if he changed gears and tried something new? He'd already aggravated nearly everyone in his professional life. They probably wouldn't be at all surprised if he proposed a completely different novel.

Stop. This is madness. What are you thinking?

Sighing, he raked his hand through his hair and leaned back in the uncomfortable plastic chair. The murmurs of other patients waiting alongside him blended into a dull background noise. Jovi's pretty face flashed in his mind. A pleasant warmth bloomed in his chest.

She was part of the reason he wanted to resolve this feud. Okay, most of the reason.

Burke glanced at the two women. They both quickly looked

away. Ignoring their prying eyes, he pecked out a new query in the search bar.

Alaska family feud Evergreen history

He checked the time. His appointment started in five minutes, but the assistant at the front desk had already let him know they were running behind. Might as well use the time he had to keep sleuthing. He thumbed past several articles about the history of the area, then paused when an obscure blog post title buried deep in the search results caught his attention.

"'Tragic Tale of Betrayal Soils a Remarkable Life of Service,'" he whispered.

Yes, please.

He tapped the phone, eager for the slow-loading screen to produce more juicy details. As the text appeared, he quickly scanned the words. The blog post recounted the story of two prominent families in Evergreen, Alaska, the Montgomerys and the Harrisons.

Disappointment tightened his chest. Frankly, not the names he'd hoped to read. But he kept going. It described their once-close friendship that had spanned generations, only to be shattered by a devastating betrayal.

Tragic tales? Betrayal? Essential ingredients for a compelling story.

According to the author, there had been rumors of a massive vein of gold running through the heart of the Montgomerys' property that they'd homesteaded in Evergreen. Allegedly an unimaginable fortune, even by 1897 standards. The Harrisons possessed the tools necessary to mine the gold, so they convinced the Montgomery family to form a partnership, and they embarked on an arduous journey together, united by their shared pursuit of this elusive treasure. But somewhere along the way, darkness seeped in, and a misunderstanding swelled until it consumed both families. The animosity trickled down to the next generation like a poisonous inheritance and—

"Burke Solomon?"

A young blonde woman wearing purple scrubs stood in an open doorway nearby. She held a laptop and offered a polite smile.

He stood and pocketed his phone. "That's me."

"This way, please." She led him down a wide hallway lined with closed doors. The muffled sound of a baby crying, followed by a woman's soothing voice, filtered from the last room on the left.

"Come on in here." She turned into the last exam room on the right side of the hallway.

Burke complied. The room was small and clean, furnished with medical equipment and the standard padded exam table. A framed photo of a famous athlete dunking a basketball paired with an inspirational quote hung on one wall. The air carried that distinct antiseptic smell that always made him feel a bit uneasy. He sat down on the vinyl chair by the counter as the medical assistant took a seat on the rolling stool, then glanced at her laptop.

He waited for her to ask the usual introductory questions, his mind quickly wandering to the information he'd just gleaned. Did the history of that particular family feud have any connection to the mystery behind his aunt and Jovi's grandmother's severed friendship?

"All right, Burke," the medical assistant said with a warm smile, "how's your wrist been feeling since we last saw you?"

"It's been okay." He tried to sound positive. "The pain has subsided, but wearing this cast is a hassle. Any chance I can transition to something more flexible?"

She nodded sympathetically and clicked away on her computer. "I get that. Casts can be quite restricting. I imagine the doctor will request an X-ray, and if everything looks good, she might transition you to a hard splint."

That sounded like progress. Sort of. "Will I be able to do more with a splint on? Like typing?"

She stood and turned to the blood pressure machine on a rolling cart nearby. "Yes, the hard splint allows for slightly more range of motion. Hopefully, that will allow you to increase your daily activities and encourage the fracture to heal. We always tell patients it takes between six and twelve weeks for complete healing."

Burke nodded. "Got it."

While she checked his vitals, his thoughts wandered back to the captivating post he'd read. The more he thought about it, the more the tragic tale of betrayal that had torn apart the Montgomerys and the Harrisons sounded familiar. And it felt like the perfect fork-in-the-road inspiration he'd been seeking for his novel.

There had to be somebody in town who had the inside scoop about her family's feud with Mac and Lois Phillips. Marriages, divorces, spring break vacations, engagements, juicy secrets and the latest special at Trailside—nothing stayed concealed for long. At least that had been the way things went when she'd grown up here.

Jovi set her latte and her berry granola parfait on a small round table near the front door—the last empty spot in Alpenglow Espresso—then took off her coat and sat down. The whir of the beans grinding and the hiss of the espresso machine mingled with the cries of a fussy infant in a car seat nearby. Shiplap walls painted an inviting shade of crisp white showcased an impressive collection of framed photos and art created by Alaskans. The large windows granted customers a gorgeous view of a bustling street corner in Evergreen with a glimpse of Winterhaven Ski Resort in the distance. A fireplace filled the opposite wall, inviting guests to enjoy one of the overstuffed chairs flanking its river rock hearth. One of the coffee shop employees added another log to the crackling flames.

She stirred the granola and berries into the vanilla Greek yogurt and then took a bite. Stifling a grimace, she forced it down. She'd talked herself into making a healthy choice to offset the calories from her latte, but the fresh blueberry scone with the coarse sugar sprinkled on top still tempted her through the glass bakery case nearby.

Maybe she'd order one to go and save it for later. But thoughts of her patients back in Kansas City who'd struggled with diabetes and cardiovascular disease raised a warning flag. A scone probably was too decadent. Besides, she needed protein to fuel her brain for her quest. Jovi put her spoon down and opened the browser on her phone to start an internet search. Except, where to begin? She paused, took another bite of her parfait and reflected on the stories she recalled her family talking about when she was younger. Fights about land, gold mines and unrequited love. Those were the scandalous tales that had been passed down from previous generations. She'd heard a few stories about people making piles of money during the oil pipeline construction, and locals falling in love with workers who'd moved to Alaska, only to find out the men had families waiting for them back home. More than one book had been written about that part of Evergreen's history, but she'd never heard anything about her family being involved. Besides, the pipeline didn't run through town. She'd learned early on to believe only half of what she'd heard about messy situations anyway.

Jovi typed her grandmother's name into the search bar, then scrolled through the results. A few articles from the Anchorage newspaper popped up, all featuring the candy company's outstanding reputation. An unexpected wave of emotion crested inside.

"Oh, Grammie," she whispered, touching a grainy image of her grandmother holding up an award-winning jar of rose-hip jelly at the 1998 state fair. "How can Isabel and I save your company?"

The door opened, and Burke Solomon stepped inside, his computer bag in one hand. He paused in the doorway and surveyed the coffee shop. Her pulse skittered at the sight of his handsome, clean-shaven face. The corner of his mouth tipped up in a smile when their eyes met.

"Good morning." His gaze slid to the chair opposite hers. "Is that seat taken?"

Yes. "No." She reached for her latte. "Unless you're in a bad mood."

"I beg your pardon?" He lowered his bag to the floor, then pulled off his knit hat. Her eyes followed the path of his hand as he pushed his fingers through his tousled dark hair. Her mouth went dry. She quickly reached for her latte.

Seriously, Jovi. Don't let him catch you staring.

From the corner of her eye, she spotted three women sitting together casting curious glances their way. They had all been in Isabel's class in high school. One gestured with her hands as she spoke. Then laughter erupted.

Super. Jovi averted her eyes. *And that's how rumors get started.*

Her cheeks flushed. She took a small sip of the sweet, hot beverage then sat back in her chair and did her best to look displeased. "Sometimes you're grumpy. And high maintenance."

His mouth drifted open. Surprise flashed in his eyes. "High maintenance? How?"

"Oh, please. Frosty Frolic? First, you were mad that the lady who owned the gift shop wanted to read *Balto.* Then you—"

"I wasn't mad. I just wanted to keep things moving." He fumbled in his back pocket and awkwardly produced his wallet.

"Then you didn't want caffeine because it was too close to bedtime."

"Hardly a crime to be mindful of that," Burke grumbled.

"As I recall, there was a fair amount of whining about the frigid temperatures."

Amusement glinted in his eyes. "Darby Jane whines a fair bit, I'll give you that."

"Ha." She narrowed her eyes. "Don't be cheeky."

Okay, so maybe he deserved a little empathy given all he'd been through. But she had found a missing stuffed animal, shoveled his driveway, sat with him in the ER, brought him dinner, invited him to Frosty Frolic, and whipped up a last-minute costume for Darby Jane. And still. He managed to get under her skin.

"If you want me to sit somewhere else, I can. I'd hate to ruin your morning."

She picked up her spoon and dipped it in her yogurt. "You haven't ruined anything, and you don't have to change seats. Besides, there aren't any open tables."

"All right, then. I'll go place my order." He turned away, then turned back. "Jovi."

She hesitated, her spoon halfway to her mouth. His gaze held hers. "Yeah?"

"I'm sorry about my lousy attitude at Frosty Frolic." He blew out his breath and then sat back down. "Moving here and up-ending our whole lives has been harder than I anticipated."

"You've mentioned that. If you don't mind my asking, why move here? Did something tragic happen in South Carolina?"

His features pinched.

Oh, no. She held up her palm. "Wait. You don't have to tell me anything. It's really none of my business. I just saw something online and…"

She trailed off, but the headlines from that article she'd read when she'd first come back to Evergreen flashed through her head. Even though she'd told Isabel not to worry about it, a small part of her still wondered what was actually true.

"My wife passed away in a car accident, along with our infant, Henry."

Her heart plummeted. "Oh, Burke. I'm so sorry."

"Thank you." He looked away. His Adam's apple bobbed as he swallowed hard. "To be honest, it should have been me."

"What? What do you mean?"

"I was working on a novel and facing a tight deadline, but I'd promised I would go get Darby Jane from preschool so Mary Catherine, my wife, could stay home with Henry. Except I lost track of time, and at the last minute, she plucked Henry out of his crib, put him in his car seat, and hurried off to get Darby Jane from preschool."

Burke pressed his lips together.

Oh. She reached across the table and blanketed his hand with hers. "I'm... I don't know what to say. That's awful. But you can't blame yourself."

"Oh, yes, I can. I mean, it was a dump truck driver who crossed the center line and caused the accident. But if I had been the husband and the father that I was supposed to be, life would look very different now."

"Jovi?"

She glanced up to see her father standing just steps away. How had she not noticed him come in? He gave her hand on top of Burke's a shocked look. Adrenaline pulsed through her. She quickly pulled away.

"Dad, this is Burke Solomon. He's Mac and Lois Phillips's nephew, and my new neighbor." She forced a bright smile, but it did almost nothing to erase the thick tension hanging in the air. "Burke, this is my father, Greg Wright."

Dad kept his hands in his pockets and offered Burke a curt nod. "Burke, it's nice to finally put a face to the name."

"Likewise, sir." Burke's gaze darted between her and her father. Uncertainty lingered in his expression.

Not that she blamed him. Dad wasn't exactly rolling out

the welcome mat. She glanced up at her father. "What brings you by?"

"I'm grabbing coffee and scones for your mother and me. You?"

"I just ran into Burke. He was telling me more about his life in Charleston." She shifted in her chair. "Since you're here, maybe you can answer a pressing question. Burke and I have both been wondering what our families have been fighting about all these years."

Burke stiffened.

Dad tucked his tongue in his cheek and dragged his fingers along his jaw. He hesitated. "I'm not aware of any specific details, only that my parents and Burke's aunt and uncle had a bitter falling-out. It seemed to impact every area of their lives." His phone hummed. He pulled it from his pocket. "I've got to take this. Jovi, we'll talk later."

He turned and walked away.

Her scalp prickled, and an uneasy feeling danced along her spine. What was that supposed to mean?

Burke cleared his throat. "That went well. If you don't mind, I'll wait until he places his order before I get in line."

"Good call."

Why did her dad care if she sat with Burke and chatted about his life? He'd just shared a vulnerable part of his past, leaving her with more questions about the picture online of a woman leaving a house, and his alleged scandal back in Charleston.

They'd had enough drama for now, though. She'd save her questions for later. "By the way, I see you've transitioned to a splint. That's great. And how did the hundredth day of school thing turn out?"

"Yes, I'm thrilled about ditching that cast. Thanks for asking. And Darby Jane's costume was a huge hit, all thanks to you." Grinning, he fumbled for his phone. "Let me show you the pictures."

Warmth bloomed in her chest. When he smiled at her like that, she almost forgot his curmudgeonly ways. Almost.

A looming deadline and the imminent threat of financial ruin should be enough to keep him on task. But no. Burke couldn't seem to stay focused on his manuscript. Images of a certain blond neighbor smiling, helping Darby Jane and laughing at his daughter's comments infiltrated his thoughts.

He sat in the public library in Evergreen, an inviting building tucked away on a side street one block from the downtown area. The place reminded him of a rustic ski chalet, with vaulted ceilings, exposed wood beams and trim on the exterior that made the building look like a fairy tale gingerbread house. He'd chosen a table for four situated near the front door with a view of the parking lot to wait for a high school student that he'd agreed to tutor. The boy, Alex, was allegedly failing his eleventh-grade English class and had lost his eligibility to participate in sports, so his teacher and his parents both wanted him to elevate his grade.

Tutoring wasn't Burke's idea of a good time, but he couldn't afford to say no. Besides, there were worse ways to supplement his income. He checked the time on his laptop. Three forty-five. The kid's mother had assured Burke her son would show up by four. Burke had come early, straight from picking Darby Jane up from the elementary school, and told himself he'd write the next scene in his novel.

So far, he'd written three new sentences and deleted a whole paragraph. The opposite of productivity. At this rate, he'd never meet his March 15 deadline.

Stephanie would ream him out.

He blew out a long breath and then glanced at Darby Jane, nestled on a red beanbag in the nearby children's nook. She had a stack of books at her feet and one on her lap. Her eyes roamed over the pages, but she'd flipped through the first book far too quickly. He probably should have arranged for childcare, but that defeated the purpose of charging for tutoring, and he'd been optimistic that the library could keep her occupied.

Determined to write at least one decent paragraph before his new student showed up, Burke reread the most recent words he hadn't cut from the scene. The library door opened, stealing his attention. An older woman and a preteen girl walked in, both carrying fabric tote bags filled with books. Cold air accompanied them and circled slowly around Burke. He shivered and then adjusted the zipper on his gray fleece pullover jacket.

A pleasant aroma of paper mingled with the not-so-pleasing scent of wet socks. Burke wrinkled his nose and discreetly glanced around, unable to identify the source of the odor.

Stay. On. Task.

The keys were smooth under his fingertips. After enduring three weeks with a cast on his wrist and then graduating to a splint, he'd progressed from pecking out a few words at a time to typing at a respectable rate. Nothing close to how quickly he'd once moved at the keyboard. That felt like another lifetime ago. But at least he'd added a few more words to his manuscript. The time inched closer to four o'clock, so he clicked Save and closed the file. It was pointless trying to concentrate. Instead, he reached for his phone.

He owed Jovi a thank-you. The thought had niggled at him since they'd shared a table at the coffee shop yesterday. So far he'd procrastinated in reaching out. Mostly because telling her about Mary Catherine and Henry had made him feel vulnerable. And he didn't like it. Not one bit. Then her father's reaction at seeing them together somehow made him feel guilty. More guilty than he already felt over losing his wife and child. How was that even possible?

The other problem was that he couldn't overlook the feelings that flowed through him like a warm summer breeze. Feelings that invited him to say and do things he should not. That jeopardized the precarious safety net he'd relied on to protect him and Darby Jane.

He hadn't been on a first date or pursued a woman since he'd met Mary Catherine nearly twenty years ago. The thought of asking a woman out terrified him. And then, after the debacle with those photos of his agent leaving his house, he'd doubled down on his plan to avoid anything that might be misconstrued as dating. Folks had said terrible things on social media about Stephanie. He couldn't put anyone through that again.

Mostly, he just wasn't ready to put himself out there.

Except his reliance on neighbors back in Charleston and here in Evergreen had spotlighted an impossible-to-ignore dilemma: Darby Jane needed a strong female presence in her life, and he'd gone and plucked her out of her community.

Guilt sauntered into his belly like a spaghetti Western villain through the swinging doors of an old saloon. Audacious. Pretending to own the place.

Burke had grown weary of kowtowing to the ugly emotions. So he created a new text message to Jovi. First, he attached a picture he'd taken earlier of the sun bathing the mountains west of town in shades of pink and lavender. It offered the perfect backdrop for her family's cabin nestled in a grove of trees at the end of their road. But sadly, words failed him. He scowled at his phone's screen. It shouldn't be that hard to tell someone he appreciated their kindness.

Besides, she'd rescued him multiple times. Now he needed to repay her generosity. He tapped out an invitation to have dinner at his house on Friday. Made it clear that he wanted to thank her. There. Casual, low-pressure, and frankly the least he could do. He hesitated. Their families had been at odds for decades. Mr. Wright had mentioned a bitter falling-out. Just enough information to aggravate him. Was there some diabolical secret associated with Jovi's family that he had yet to uncover?

Chuckling, he promptly dismissed the notion. Jovi didn't have a mean bone in her body.

Before he pressed the icon to send the text, a teenage boy approached, uncertainty in his expression. He hesitated beside Burke's table. "Mr. Solomon?"

Burke set his phone down, then rose and extended his uninjured hand. "Yes, and you must be Alex."

Alex offered a nervous smile and a firm handshake. "Yes, sir."

Wow, impressive manners. "It's nice to meet you. Have a seat."

"Thanks." Alex shrugged out of his letterman jacket, then sat and unzipped his backpack. "I appreciate you doing this."

"Not a problem." Burke closed his laptop and pushed it aside. "Sorry to hear you're struggling."

Alex hesitated, then reached up and adjusted the folded edge of his black beanie. "I don't know that *struggling* is the right word. Then again, I'm not too great with words." He shrugged. "Guess that's why I'm here."

"Let's see what we're up against. Do you have a syllabus or something that hints at what we're aiming for?"

"Uh, maybe." Alex opened a folder and riffled through some papers.

Darby Jane picked that exact moment to trot over to the table. "Daddy, I'm bored."

Burke swallowed back an irritated groan. "Alex, this is my daughter, Darby Jane. Darby Jane, this is Alex." He leaned closer to her ear. "Sweet pea, we talked about this. You said you'd be fine with a stack of books."

"But I'd be even better if you'd let me play a game on your phone." She hopped from one foot to the other, flashing her most charming smile.

Oy. This kid.

Alex hid a laugh behind his hand.

Burke passed her his phone. "All right, but keep the volume turned off."

"Awww, man." She tipped her head back and glared at the ceiling. "Shoulda brought my headphones."

"I can't help you there. No headphones. Sound *off*. Got it?"

"Yes, sir. Thank you." She clutched the phone in her little hand and skipped back to the beanbag.

"She's funny," Alex said.

"Thank you." Burke stared after her. "A real handful, that one."

"I always want to play games on my phone instead of reading, too," Alex said. "Probably another reason I'm in the mess that I'm in."

"Noted." Burke smiled. "Any clues or objectives for your project in that folder?"

Alex slid the paper across the table. "Here's what my teacher wants me to do."

Burke read the assignment. A three- to five-page paper analyzing the themes of *The Great Gatsby*. Whoa. He'd have to go way back in the dusty files of his memory to even remember what that classic novel was about.

"Not going to lie, this is a tall order." He gave the paper back to Alex. "Let me do a quick internet search for a plot summary."

"So you haven't read it either?" Alex sat back in his chair, looking somewhat victorious.

"Not in about two decades."

"I don't get why she makes us read the old stuff. But my dad says if I want to be eligible for wrestling season, I have to do exactly what my teacher asks." Alex frowned. "No complaining."

"Do you have a copy of the book?"

"Yeah, I think I brought it." Alex dug through his backpack. More papers rustled, and he set aside a three-ring binder.

Before he could start up his computer, Darby Jane hurried back to his side. "Daddy, guess what? I sent Jovi that pretty picture. Plus I added one of me all dressed up in my hundredth-day costume. And I did it all by myself."

Oh, no.

Panic arced through him, white-hot and razor-sharp.

"Darby Jane." He cleared his throat, not wanting to lose his composure in front of Alex. Or hurt his daughter's feelings. "Now's not the best time to discuss this. I'm sure Jovi will love seeing the pictures. Will you give Alex and me a few minutes so I can help him with his project, please?"

"Yep." She went back to her beanbag.

"No more texting without permission, though," he called after her.

Burke refused to meet Alex's curious gaze. So that was that. He'd just offered dinner to Jovi. How would he ever pull that off?

Alex leaned across the table, studying him. "Dude, your face just got, like, super pale."

Burke dragged his hand over his face. "Well, to be honest, my daughter just sent a text from me offering a beautiful woman dinner this Friday night." He lifted his splinted arm. "Not exactly a whiz in the kitchen."

Alex grinned. "I got you. My mom could probably help you out."

"Your mom?"

"Yeah, she makes most of the food for all the big events around town. Want me to text her and ask?"

"Uh, sure."

Alex fished his phone out. His thumbs flew over the tiny keyboard.

Burke stared, trying not to be envious. Typing he could do. But he'd never picked up the texting dexterity like kids these days.

Less than a minute later, the whoosh of an incoming message held Burke's attention.

"She says she'd be glad to help," Alex said. "She'll text you some information about her Valentine's Day special. Mom's an amazing cook. I don't know who your girl is, but she'll be high-key impressed with the food."

Valentine's Day. Oh, no. His stomach twisted in a hard knot. Was that this Friday? Why hadn't he paid more attention to the date? Or deleted the message before he'd handed a five-year-old his phone? He had no idea what *high-key impressed* meant exactly, but he'd take whatever assistance Alex's mother offered. Especially since Darby Jane had put the plans in motion, and he only had four days to come up with something brilliant.

She couldn't keep working this hard.

The sun had long since set when Isabel trudged through the front door of her house, weary to the bone. Her feet and her lower back ached from rushing between her office and the factory floor, and her stomach grumbled, reminding her she'd skipped lunch to troubleshoot a production line issue with Jerry. Under Irene's watchful eye, they'd kept the supply chain humming right along.

But with nearly a hundred orders still left to fulfill in just three days, Isabel couldn't help but feel overwhelmed. As much as she loved making candy for Valentine's Day, the added pressure of having to hit projected sales numbers made it the most stressful time of the year. Would they be able to deliver everything on time and maintain their reputation for high-quality candy?

Her phone chimed, announcing an incoming text. She groaned, then slipped off her shoes and pulled her phone from her purse. She braced for more bad news as she read the message from Jerry.

I wanted to let you know that we just took a fresh batch of chocolate-covered peanut butter hearts off the line. Everything's running smoothly. Have a great night.

"Thank You, Lord," she whispered. At last. An encouraging update. She scrolled down to catch up on the rest of her unread texts. The group text thread with Wendy and two other girls they'd grown up with had three new messages. Somehow, she'd missed this conversation from a couple of days ago.

What's up with your sister and that mysterious hot new guy?

Seriously, we couldn't get over how great they looked together at Alpenglow.

Until your dad walked in and caught them holding hands. Yikes. He did not look happy.

Isabel, where has she been hiding him? He's yummy. We need details!

"Oh, Jovi." Sighing, Isabel jammed her phone back in her purse and set it on the floor. They'd just talked about this. Why didn't Jovi get that her timing—and her choice of men—was lousy? And why had Dad gotten involved?

Not wading into the drama tonight. Too exhausting.

The savory aroma of fast food wafted from the crinkled paper bag in her grasp, making her mouth water. She couldn't wait to devour the crispy fries, juicy cheeseburgers and creamy vanilla milkshake. After today, she'd earned it.

But as she entered the dimly lit kitchen, she gasped when she spotted Mason, leaning against the counter and greedily devouring the cake she had made earlier. He didn't even bother using a plate, just scooped up forkfuls directly from the pan. The frosting container lay open next to him, and he was about to take another bite when he looked up and met her gaze.

Neither of them moved to embrace. A pang of regret throbbed in her chest. "You're back. How was your trip?"

"Interview was great, but then my flight was delayed. It took me all night to get home. I came in early this morning, but you'd already left."

Not the best time to mention she'd cried herself to sleep from sheer exhaustion. And the fact that he went to Juneau to interview for a new job, despite her protests about moving. She walked slowly toward the counter, her tote bag bumping against her leg. "It's almost Valentine's Day. We're short-staffed."

Mason's eyes widened. Had he just remembered?

She slid her takeout onto the counter and set her bag on the floor at her feet.

"Is that your dinner?"

She nodded. "Is that yours?"

His mouth twitched with a smile. "Just my first course. Thanks for baking it, by the way."

"You're welcome. I had planned on chicken parm as well, but...that didn't work out."

She took a long sip of her thick creamy shake. No need to fuss at him for eating the cake. She was worn-out and honestly, he couldn't be blamed for her disaster of a day.

But she still didn't feel like sharing her food.

"You can have one of the cheeseburgers." Isabel took two plates from the cabinet. "I'm feeling oddly possessive about the fries and the milkshake."

"Only if you don't want it." He rubbed his hand slowly across the back of his neck. There was a glimpse of the Mason that she knew and loved. Strong and capable on the outside. But kind, considerate, and a heart as soft as melted caramel inside.

"I probably don't need to eat two cheeseburgers." She removed the food from the bag, divided the order between the plates and handed him one. His eyes pinged between her and the food.

"You said you didn't want to share."

She offered a half smile. "I can't bring myself to eat all of the fries in front of you."

His eyes sparkled with amusement. "Appreciate it."

They carried their plates to the table. Mason got them both glasses of water and brought them over. Then she eased into the chair across from him.

Without waiting to ask the blessing, she quickly unwrapped the cheeseburger and took a generous bite. "Mmm. So good."

The sesame bun, melted cheese, salty patty with the stack of lettuce, tomato and pickles plus the extra ketchup and mayo provided everything she needed to cope with her never-ending day. Wow, what was going on with her appetite? She hadn't been this happy about a meal in ages.

"You know...I could help you," he offered.

Isabel stopped midbite and stared at him. "With what?"

His smooth brow crinkled. "The Valentine's Day orders. Didn't you say you guys are shorthanded?"

Was he serious or just trying to appease her? "Don't you have to work this week?"

Mason shrugged. "I've got plenty of paid time off."

She winced at the unspoken reminder that they hadn't taken a vacation other than their weekend away together in a long time.

His offer tempted her. She was grateful that Jovi had come home to help, but it had been a struggle to keep up with her sister's sporadic schedule and handle all the issues that popped up at the candy company. Mom and Dad hadn't stepped away completely from day-to-day operations, but they weren't exactly offering suggestions to address the waning sales either. Still, uncertainty swirled in her mind.

She set down her burger and studied his hopeful expression. He seemed genuine, and he'd be a tremendous asset. Efficient, hardworking, and more than willing to tackle a task he wasn't proficient in. She couldn't overlook the unresolved issues simmering between them, though. Especially their tense conversation when they'd been stranded in the gondola. Their relationship had been strained for what felt like forever. Was working together a solution? Or would it only stir up more strife?

But then she looked into his eyes, the earnestness shining through, and something inside her softened. This was Mason, after all. The man who had always been there for her, supporting her dreams and goals. Maybe she was being too hard on him.

"Isabel?" His voice broke through her thoughts.

"Are you really sure about this?" She couldn't hide the hope in her voice.

Mason's eyes filled with determination. "Absolutely. I'll do whatever you need. Besides, we make a great team, remember?"

Their gazes held. Despite his reassurance, doubts gnawed at her. Yeah. They had made a great team. But that was before. Back when they were young and naive and used helping out at the candy company as a way to sneak off and find time alone, plus earn a little extra money. Their deliveries had taken twice as long and earned suspicious glances from her mother when they'd finally returned the van.

She tamped down the memories and picked up her burger again. Maybe, just maybe, this was their chance to reconnect and mend what had been broken. "If you're willing to use your vacation time, we could use the help. *I* could use your help."

Ugh. She hated admitting that last part.

Relief washed over Mason's face. He reached over and took her hand in his, caressing her skin with his calloused thumb. "I won't let you down."

Her pulse hummed, and she dropped her gaze to her plate. Did he mean that? She longed to savor the rare moment of peace they'd carved out, so she swallowed the question and then pulled away. After adding more ketchup to her plate, she nudged it toward him for his fries.

"So. Tell me more about Juneau."

Chapter Eleven

News of her coffee shop encounter with Burke had spread. Just as she'd feared. Jovi thumbed through the text messages from her dad and Isabel.

We need to chat about why it's not wise to spend time with Burke Solomon.

What's up with the rumors I'm hearing that you're dating a hot guy? Is that Burke?

"Thanks for your input, guys." Frowning, Jovi shoved her phone in her back pocket without responding. So maybe she'd been a tiny bit selfish, accepting Burke's dinner invitation.

She leaned over the pedestal sink in her bathroom and outlined her lips with a mauve lip pencil. But she couldn't bring herself to say no. Deep down, she couldn't deny the attraction she felt toward the handsome, brooding single dad who also happened to be from the family her own relatives distrusted.

Was it worth the risk of spending time with him? Or would sharing a meal add more complexity to their already complicated relationship? But then again, he had invited her as a way to show his gratitude for all her help with Darby Jane.

Honestly, since their paths had crossed at the airport in Anchorage, she'd done a lot for the man. He owed her.

But she'd also said yes because she didn't want to spend Valentine's Day alone.

The past four days had been intense. She'd worked an overnight shift at the hospital and helped pack and ship over a hundred express orders of cookies, candy and chocolates. Then she and Jerry had spent several exhausting hours yesterday fulfilling last-minute deliveries around town. As they'd finished, she couldn't ignore a pang of longing. As much as she loved bringing joy to others, it only amplified her loneliness.

She'd made a promise to herself that she wouldn't succumb to the comfort of staying at home, wrapped in her soft flannel pajamas, binge-watching her favorite show. Because if she stayed here alone, she'd constantly check for messages from Michael, and it would only make the pain worse.

But being alone also hurt. Which option was worse? Facing her loneliness or facing the memories of her failed relationship?

So she'd painted her fingernails a stunning midnight blue, then carefully smoothed out any imperfections. The blue cashmere sweater she'd borrowed from Isabel was the perfect shade of sapphire. Could she convince her sister to let her keep it? The soft fabric clung to her skin and brought out the vibrant color of her eyes.

She might as well look good, even if this wasn't a date. Jovi spritzed on some floral perfume, its sweet scent lingering in the air around her. She'd put on her favorite jeans because the bootcut style elongated her legs and gave her an elegant silhouette. She took one more long look in the mirror. Not too shabby.

She made her way to the front door, slipping on her favorite puffy winter jacket for added warmth. Then added her best scarf. Nothing wrong with a touch of sophistication to enhance her outfit. Before leaving, she popped a breath mint and grabbed her purse along with a small box of sweet treats.

Stepping outside, the chill of the winter air pierced her lungs. Above her, a full moon illuminated the inky black sky, casting a soft glow over the snow-covered ground. As she made her way down the driveway, each step crunching through the powdery snow, anticipation coursed through her veins like a steady stream. But as she reached the halfway point to Burke's cabin, doubt and nerves slowed her steps.

Was this really a good idea?

After all, she wasn't exactly in the best place for a relationship right now. Even if she were ready to date again, Burke was the last person she should consider. Their families had been tangled in a sticky web of lingering suspicion for decades. But at least Darby Jane would be there, so they wouldn't be alone. The little girl's bubbly personality would surely steal their attention away anyway.

Relax. Have fun. There's no need to worry.

She smoothed down her freshly styled hair before climbing the steps of Burke's porch, her boot heels thumping against the wooden planks. She knocked, expecting Darby Jane's enthusiastic welcome. But instead, Burke opened the door, his mouth dropping open as his eyes roamed over her. A spark of attraction flared in her stomach.

Jovi. No!

She quickly stuffed down the absurd notion.

Burke cleared his throat, drawing her attention to the way his Adam's apple bobbed. A slow smile parted his lips. "Hey. You look stunning this evening."

Oh, boy. Not helping. Might be a long evening. "Thank you."

He motioned for her to come inside. She stepped into his cabin, inhaling the familiar scent of pine and woodsmoke.

He closed the door behind her with a soft click.

She handed over the white cardboard box wrapped with the company's signature ribbon. "A little something for you and Darby Jane."

"You didn't have to do that." Burke accepted the box, eyeing the label.

"I wanted to." She shrugged out of her coat. "Besides, I get a family discount."

"Hard to pass that up, right?" He extended his hand. "Let me hang that up for you."

As he draped her coat and scarf on a nearby hook, she snuck a glance at him. He wore a purple sweater over a gingham-checked button-up, dark-washed jeans with tasteful distressing, and buttery leather driving moccasins. And he smelled incredible: spicy and clean and undeniably masculine.

She quickly looked away when he faced her, feigning interest in the floorboards at her feet. Had he caught her staring? Suppressing a coy smile, she followed him to the kitchen. A girl couldn't help but notice a well-dressed man, could she?

As she stepped into the room, she was met with a warm and inviting glow.

"Oh, my." She stopped in the doorway, scanning the comfortable space. Her eyes slid from the dining table to the kitchen counter, where six different candles flickered, casting dancing shadows on the walls.

"Sorry. It's a bit much." He winced, his prominent cheekbones tinged with pale pink. "Darby Jane helped set the table before she left. The candles were her idea."

Jovi swallowed hard. *"Left?"*

The timer beeped, and Burke placed the treats on the counter before shutting off the noise. "She had a last-minute offer to spend a few hours with some girls in her class tonight. One of the other moms will bring her home later."

"Sounds fun." Her voice came out in a squeak. So awkward. Unease settled in her stomach. The buffer she'd hoped for between them was gone, leaving them alone. Romantic, first-kiss alone. In his cozy cabin surrounded by flickering candles and Adele's soulful music streaming from a speaker somewhere. A delicious smell wafted from the old stove, making her heart race and warning bells sound in her head. The chemistry zinging between them was undeniable. Now would be a great time to leave.

Instead, her feet stayed rooted to the floor. "Is there anything I can do to help?"

"Would you mind slicing the bread?" He angled his head toward a package of French bread, a knife, and the tub of butter beside a cutting board on the counter.

"Sure." Easy enough. She washed her hands at the sink, then dried them with a paper towel, humming along to the familiar pop hit.

"What can I get you to drink? There's sweet tea, lemonade, milk or water." Burke's voice sounded closer than she expected. "Or feel free to combine the lemonade and sweet tea, if you'd prefer."

"Yes, please. That's my kind of combo." Jovi smiled at him over her shoulder. Their gazes locked and held. Her palms started to sweat. She quickly averted her gaze and reached for the bread knife.

"So." She cleared her throat. "Since Darby Jane's not here, maybe now is a good time to ask. Have you figured out why our families stopped speaking to one another?"

Ice cubes rattled inside a glass. Then the fridge door squeaked. Adele kept on crooning. Burke didn't answer.

Oh, no. Had he discovered something scandalous? She set the knife back down and slowly turned to face him. He stood at the counter beside the refrigerator and calmly poured tea over the ice in the glass.

Jovi wiped her damp palms on her jeans. "What is it?"

Burke traded the tea pitcher for a carton of lemonade, his expression unreadable. "A woman I've never met spoke to me at the grocery store. Evidently, she'd heard we'd been to Frosty Frolic together and had coffee at Alpenglow."

Jovi winced. "Seriously? Who was it? And please tell me she wasn't rude."

Burke hesitated.

She accepted the drink he offered her, but carefully set it aside. "My dad and my sister sent me texts as well. I—I had no idea my family had strong feelings about us…hanging out."

"Me either." He rubbed his fingertips across his chin. "The woman at the store made it clear she wasn't pleased that you and I have been spotted in public together."

"Whatever." She shook her head. "I'll speak to my parents and Isabel about their concerns. But strangers in the grocery store? That's absurd. People need to find something else to do besides gossip about who we're having coffee with."

Burke chuckled. "I'm quite flattered that they care."

"I'm glad you can laugh. I find it irritating. You've survived the unimaginable. Moved across the country with your sweet little girl to find a fresh start. It's quite impressive."

Something undecipherable flashed across his face. The music, the refrigerator's hum, a truck driving by outside, all of it faded into the background as they stood in his kitchen, staring at one another. A fluttery sensation started in her stomach and spread to her extremities.

Candlelight danced across the planes of Burke's face, highlighting the sharp angles and shadows of his chiseled jawline. The small divot in the center of his chin was like a miniature valley, drawing her gaze in and holding it captive. As he moved closer, her breath caught in her throat. Did the neckline of her sweater expose the rapid beat of her pulse in the hollow of her throat? She stood pressed against the corner of the L-shaped counter, unable to move.

Burke stopped in front of her, his striking golden-brown eyes darkening as they roamed her face. She clenched her fists, determined to resist this powerful pull sparking between them.

"Jovi." Even the sound of her name on his lips made her nerve endings light up.

Her fingers itched to tunnel through those glorious waves of his hair, feeling the soft strands between her fingertips. She admired the chiseled curves of his jaw, the strong lines of his face that were both rugged and refined.

Burke gently leaned in, his breath warm against her skin as he braced his arms on either side of her. "I hadn't planned on—"

She didn't give him time to say another word. Closing the remaining distance between them, she pressed her palms against his broad chest, closed her eyes, and then savored the perfect collision of their lips meeting.

He'd never claimed to be an easygoing, tranquil man.

Kissing Jovi made Burke downright agitated. Impatient. Eager for more. Especially when her palms slid from his chest to the nape of his neck and delicately tunneled in his hair. The way she leaned into him, the welcoming sound she made when he deepened the kiss, and the heady fragrance of her floral scent enveloping him—yeah, he'd take more of all of it.

He wanted this kiss to never end.

The world around them seemed to fade away as he found solace in Jovi's soft, pliant lips. His heart thundered in his chest. He pulled her closer, his palm splayed against her back, as time slowed. Each delicious second elongated. The weight of his past mistakes and regrets vanished as he surrendered to this newfound connection.

When they parted, both their chests heaving, Burke stared

into Jovi's eyes. He gently brushed back a strand of hair that had fallen across her face. "Thank you for that. As I was saying, I hadn't planned on kissing you tonight."

Her trembling fingers touched her mouth. Uncertainty swam in her gorgeous eyes.

A trapdoor in his stomach gave way. Had he crossed the line? Except, she'd kissed him. He took a step back. "I'm deeply sorry if I misunderstood. I didn't mean to make you uncomfortable."

She blinked, her gaze searching his face. Slowly, she lowered her hand to her side, then shook her head. "I kissed you first, and I shouldn't have. I'm the one who needs to apologize."

"You have nothing to be sorry about. That kiss was incredible." Boldly, he tipped her chin up with one finger. "*You* are incredible."

He couldn't bear the thought of losing this connection before it even had a chance to fully blossom.

"I should go." Her gaze skittered away, and she scooted past him.

"What? Why?" The vulnerability in her expression and her attempt to distance herself sent panic surging through him. They'd had a moment. No, more than a moment. A *connection*. Hadn't she sensed it too?

He forced himself to remain standing near the sink when everything in him wanted and needed to bridge the chasm between them. "Jovi, please. Tell me what's wrong."

She stopped beside the vintage refrigerator, faced him and crossed her arms over her stomach. "We can't do this, Burke."

Her words knifed at him. "Why not? What's stopping us?"

Jovi's eyes flickered with a mixture of emotions—longing, regret and something he couldn't quite identify. Fear?

"This is going to sound pathetic, but, I mean, less than six months ago, I was engaged to someone else, and you've endured horrific loss. And there's Darby Jane to consider. Not to mention I still don't know how long I'll be here, especially if my family sells the company. I just... I don't think this is a good idea."

Her mouth turned down in a frown. A gorgeous, kissable mouth that just a few moments ago he'd ardently claimed with his own.

He couldn't believe what he was hearing. Had her family's comments about them bothered her more than she'd let on? "I get that you're worried about dating again. It's scary to put ourselves out there. But our past relationships shouldn't dictate our futures." He took a step closer, his voice filled with determination. "We deserve to explore what we're feeling for each other, right?"

She looked torn. "What if it doesn't work out? How will Darby Jane handle that? And what if we uncover something that makes us realize we're better off apart?"

A tight knot of frustration formed in his chest. He had never been one to back away from a challenge, but Jovi's resistance addled him. The intensity of their kiss had been undeniable, and he couldn't simply ignore the magnetic pull between them.

"I agree, there are risks involved. But sometimes, taking risks is the only way to truly live. And if we never try, won't we always wonder *what-if*?"

Tears welled in Jovi's eyes. "I just can't. I don't want to get hurt again."

Me either.

He knew all too well the sting of past hurts.

A painful silence settled between them. The passionate connection they had shared only minutes earlier now felt like a distant memory.

"I won't push you into something you're not ready for." Resignation laced his words. "Your apprehension is valid, and I never want to cause you pain."

"Thank you for saying that," she said softly, blinking away her unshed tears. "I don't want to spend the rest of my life wondering *what-if*. But I also can't ignore the fears that are holding me back." She drew a ragged breath. "I appreciate the dinner invitation, but I—I think it would be best if I went home."

Don't go.

He understood her hesitations, but it didn't ease the ache of losing something that felt so right, even if it had only just begun. Didn't ease the longing to grab her hand, to pull her back into his arms and persuade her that they could find a way forward. "I won't try to convince you otherwise."

She offered him a small, sad smile before turning to leave. As she put on her coat and scarf and then reached for the door, he couldn't bear to let her go without being scary honest.

"Jovi."

She hesitated, then turned to face him, her eyes filled with a mix of curiosity and apprehension.

"I don't know what's going to happen next, but I'm grateful for tonight. For that kiss."

Her gaze softened. "Happy Valentine's Day, Burke." She slipped out the door before he could respond.

He closed it behind her and pressed his forehead against the sturdy wood. How had their perfect evening taken such a wrong turn?

As he walked slowly back to his empty kitchen and replayed her words, the weight of her concerns anchored deep within his chest. She was right. There were obstacles between them, tangled threads of past relationships and family animosity that threatened to unravel any chance they had at happiness together.

But he refused to let their connection be severed so easily. Her concern for Darby Jane's well-being was admirable, and he'd never want to do anything to harm her. Because he'd certainly caused his little girl a lifetime of heartache already. But he'd meant what he'd said about not letting their pasts define them. Besides, he couldn't shake the feeling that Jovi was someone special, someone worth fighting for.

He blew out all the candles, then paced back and forth in his dimly lit living room, pondering the next steps. Research for his previous novel had taught him that the most interesting facts often resided in old books and dusty documents. Remnants from generations past. His aunt had always been fully present during his visits. Never once had he asked her to share anything about their family history, but if there was any chance of uncovering the truth, it lay hidden within these walls. Or within this town.

Somehow he had to find a way to unravel the mystery of their families' feud.

She had to forget about that kiss.

The next morning, Jovi found an empty table nestled in the back corner of Alpenglow Espresso, then slowly lowered her blue coffee mug onto the distressed wood surface. An adorable heart shape swam in the foam of her vanilla latte.

She cringed. So not in the mood for love-adjacent details today.

Shrugging out of her jacket, she draped it over the ladder-back chair and sat down. Danielle, a friend she'd made when they'd been lab partners in tenth-grade biology, stood at the counter, patiently waiting for the barista to finish making her drink. They'd kept in touch over the years and had been trying to get together ever since Jovi had come back to Evergreen last month. Thankfully, their schedules synced up for this morning's coffee date because she needed to overanalyze last night's kiss with a trusted friend.

She couldn't possibly tell Isabel or Mom and Dad that she'd kissed Burke Solomon. Not after the text messages she'd received questioning her decision to hang out with him. The kiss wasn't a betrayal. Was it? She'd have to address those texts soon. Between Isabel's issues with Mason, and Mom and Dad's eagerness to follow through with selling the company, she dreaded initiating a tense conversation.

Besides, it had only been one kiss.

One incredible, time-stood-still kiss. A kiss that left her craving more.

Warmth climbed her neck as thoughts of Burke's lips on hers filled her head.

Stop.

She desperately needed a distraction.

Thankfully, Danielle weaved her way through the crowded café, pausing occasionally to say hello to someone she knew seated at a table.

Jovi sighed and then reached for her coffee. She could sit here all day. Except she had to head over to the candy company and help clean up the post–Valentine's Day mess. They'd left the workroom a disaster, too exhausted to put away the extra boxes, packing tape and discarded packing materials.

"Sorry to keep you waiting." Danielle put a plate with an oversize chocolate chip muffin and a blueberry scone in the center of the table. "I bought these for us to share."

"Aw, that's sweet." Jovi smiled. "Thank you."

"It's a big deal for me to get out of the house on a Saturday morning without the kids, so I'm treating both of us." The lines beside her vibrant green eyes crinkled as Danielle grinned, then slid into the seat opposite Jovi's. She unwound her striped scarf, then took off her green puffy jacket. She wore a short-sleeved purple sweater that complemented her beautiful skin and long red curls. Impressive for a busy mom of three young children.

"I'm so glad this worked out." Jovi sipped her coffee. Wow, that was good. She let the warm, sweet beverage slide down her throat, soothing some of her angst about Burke.

Danielle nudged her coffee gently out of the way to get access to the pastries. "Justin agreed to handle basketball practice at the rec center this morning and we hired a sitter to stay at the house with the baby so I could squeeze in some girl time with you."

"Well, please tell Justin I appreciate him." Jovi broke off a corner of the scone and set it on her napkin. "We need to catch up."

Danielle reached over and squeezed Jovi's arm, her head tilting as she offered a genuine smile. "It's great to see you. So bring me up to speed. What's going on?"

Jovi leaned forward. "I kissed my handsome neighbor last night, then fled the scene like a complete coward."

There. She'd said it. But somehow revealing her juicy news didn't ease the tension knotted between her shoulders.

Danielle blinked rapidly. Then her pink lips curved into a knowing smile. "Now, that's the way to get a coffee date started. No small talk, no details about your life in Kansas City. Just *bam!* There it is. Tell. Me. More."

She punctuated the last three words with enthusiastic handclaps.

Despite her conflicted emotions, Jovi couldn't help but laugh. "Where would you like me to start?"

Danielle paused, part of the muffin's top halfway to her mouth. "Is that a trick question? At the beginning, of course."

Jovi drew in a fortifying breath. "I ran into him and his daughter at the airport in Anchorage when I first got back to Alaska. This little girl is adorable, by the way. Her name is Darby Jane, and she has the cutest Southern accent. She's just starting school. Anyway, she'd lost her beloved stuffed animal, so I helped her find it. Then we shared a ride to Evergreen because he had a rental and I did not. Then—"

"Oh, forced proximity." Danielle's eyes sparkled. "Was there a snowstorm? Please tell me there was. And did you get stranded?"

"Slow your roll there, friend," Jovi teased. "*Yes* to the snow, but a *no* on the stranded part. Although, it seemed like a distinct possibility because he drove like a grouchy old grandpa."

Danielle's smile faded. "Grumpy, huh? You can probably work with that."

"No, I can't work with anything. Our families have been feuding for eons. There has to be a valid reason."

"Hmm, that's intriguing." Danielle cupped her coffee between both palms. "Any clues?"

"Nothing definitive." Jovi broke off the end of the scone and set it on an extra napkin. "Burke found an article about how his aunt Lois and my grandmother apparently were recognized locally for their candy-making talents. And we already know they were best friends, but we don't know how or when the falling-out occurred."

"Can you ask somebody?"

"Well, Grammie is the only one still alive, and her memory's not great. My family recently moved her to Oasis, a memory care place in Anchorage. She did mention that Lois made candy and also a lovely quilt, but no reference to an argument or anything like that."

Danielle winced. "That's right, I saw her name listed in the prayer requests at church. I'm sorry. Dementia and Alzheimer's are so tough to deal with."

"You're telling me. She didn't even recognize me and Isabel when we visited."

"Maybe you'll catch her in a lucid moment next time."

"Maybe." But she wouldn't get her hopes up. Jovi took a bite of the scone. The coarse sugar crystals sprinkled on top added a nice texture, and the moist sweet pastry saturated with tart blueberries left her reaching for another bite. She'd make a mental note to ask Isabel, Irene and Jerry if they had any tips on how to find the best sugar for her salted caramel chew experiments. The batch she'd made the night Burke and Darby

Jane came over for help with the costume had been hard as a rock, and not at all edible.

"So back to the handsome neighbor. Have you guys been hanging out?"

Jovi nodded. "That's how we got to the kiss. I've helped him with his daughter several times, so he offered dinner as a thank-you, and he invited me to his place. On Valentine's Day."

"That is so romantic." Danielle pressed her palm to her chest.

Jovi's cheeks heated again. "That's the problem."

Danielle's pencil-thin brows flattened. "Why? I mean, other than this alleged fight between your relatives. Do you like him?"

Jovi hesitated.

Danielle chuckled. "That means *yes*."

"No. I mean, yes, I like him, but... I don't know." She pressed a palm to her forehead, struggling to find the right words. "My ex-fiancé really did a number on me when he called off the wedding. I don't know when I'll be ready to date again. Now I'm embarrassed that I just spontaneously planted one on him."

Empathy etched Danielle's expression. "I hate you had to go through that. Michael's loss. One hundred percent."

"Thank you," Jovi said. "He's a decent guy, and it's probably for the best that he called things off, but—"

"Oh, no." Frowning, Danielle pushed aside the muffin then leaned her elbows on the table. "You're talking to him again, aren't you?"

Jovi tucked a strand of hair behind her ear. "He started texting me again, but I haven't responded."

"Please don't let him worm his way back into your life."

Danielle's earnest gaze made Jovi's stomach clench. "You don't even know him."

Ugh. Could she sound any more desperate?

"I don't need to know him personally. I'm speaking up because I'm your friend and I care about you. He called off your wedding, Jovi. That's not a guy who deserves a second chance."

Jovi scraped her fingernail against a sticky substance glued on the table. "Not even if he's contrite?"

"Not even then." Danielle picked up a chunk of the muffin, then paused, her hand halfway to her mouth. "He should be sorry. He blew it. But that doesn't mean you have to take him back."

Jovi leaned back in her chair and rubbed her fingertips against the tightness in her chest. "I guess I've always had a soft spot for someone who regrets their choices and wants a second chance."

"But you just kissed somebody else. It sounds like you're quite open to the possibility of dating someone new."

Jovi shook her head. "Not *this* someone new."

Danielle finished chewing, then reached for her coffee again. "All I'm saying is if there's an element of attraction between you and Burke, then you probably are ready to move on from Michael. And that's okay. Just tell Michael it's over and he does not need to contact you again."

"Would now be a bad time to mention that he might transfer to a base here in Alaska?"

Danielle rolled her eyes. "Oh, please. Is that what he's telling you?"

"Nothing's for sure, but yes, he mentioned it."

"I wouldn't believe a word he says, but that's just me. And even if he does move here, Alaska's a big place. We're more than a hundred miles from the nearest military base. It's not like he's going to be your hot single-dad neighbor."

"Ha. That's cute." Jovi sipped her coffee, trying unsuccessfully to banish the thought of Burke's eyes searching her face.

"Maybe you need to allow this Burke fella to kiss you again."

Jovi choked on her drink, then feigned a mock glare. She grabbed a napkin and mopped at her chin. "Don't say that. I can't rush into anything."

"Why?"

"I already told you. As much as I don't like my family meddling in my business, there's a reason the Wrights and Burke's relatives don't get along, and I need to know what it is. Besides, I've only committed to staying here for thirteen weeks. It's not fair to him, his daughter, or me to get attached."

"I didn't realize you weren't planning to stick around." Her gaze flitted toward the window. "Um, describe that neighbor for me."

"He's about six feet tall, with broad shoulders, and wavy brown hair."

"Carries a leather briefcase type of bag and has a splint on his arm?"

Jovi froze. "Yeah. Why?"

"Because he's coming this way."

"No, no, no." Jovi panicked, desperate for an exit strategy. "I'm not ready to speak with him yet."

Her adrenaline spiked as Burke walked by outside the window. *Please keep going.*

"Relax." Danielle grinned. "You've got this."

But it was too late. Burke paused at the entrance and waited for a young couple to exit, then he stepped inside. Jovi slid lower in her chair. Seeing him frothed her conflicted feelings into a convoluted mess. Her lips tingled with the memory of his touch. She couldn't deny the connection she felt with Burke, but she was terrified of getting hurt again. Michael had shattered her trust, leaving her hesitant to let anyone else in.

Chapter Twelve

Why hadn't he planned for this?

Burke's gaze locked with Jovi's. He couldn't move. Couldn't look away. He tightened his grip on his bag's shoulder strap, debating what to do. Yeah, okay, turning around and leaving was certainly an option. Except he'd made plans to meet Charlie's sister, Denise, here. She'd been the last person to help care for Aunt Lois before she'd passed. And if he had any hope of discovering the impetus for this mysterious feud with the Wright family, then he needed answers. Denise had graciously agreed to chat, so he wasn't about to text her now and ask her to meet someplace else last minute. Besides, he'd made arrangements for Darby Jane to play at a friend's house this morning, and selfishly he wanted to capitalize on having two whole hours free.

Surely he and Jovi could handle being in the same coffee shop together. Right?

It had been one kiss.

Swallowing hard, Burke tore his gaze away from Jovi and took a place at the end of the line. Three customers stood ahead of him, waiting to place their orders. He forced himself to focus on the menu, but from the corner of his eye, he saw Jovi leaning forward, talking quietly with the woman at her table. The temptation to give in, to walk over there and speak to her, was almost too strong to resist.

But a feeling he couldn't quite name kept his feet rooted in place.

Had he been reckless? Inviting her over? Kissing her? That part of the evening had been even better than he'd anticipated. And his heart beat faster at the memory, so there was that. Okay, and maybe the air had nearly crackled between them. Still, she'd said they shouldn't have kissed. That she wasn't ready. To be honest, maybe he wasn't ready either. Even though he'd felt like a half-dead man who'd come alive when her lips brushed against his.

Enough.

Burke clenched his jaw. He couldn't let his emotions cloud his judgment. He had to stop thinking about Jovi. About that kiss.

He took a deep breath, inhaling the aroma of freshly brewed coffee that filled the air. The sharp whir of the blender whipping up a fruit smoothie punctuated the low hum of conversation flowing around him. Two women at the counter surveyed the bakery case, quizzing the barista about the gluten-free options on display. Pushing aside his thoughts of Jovi, he studied the menu once again, determined to keep his mind occupied. Burke tapped his thumb against the strap of his bag, shifted his weight from one foot to the other, and stifled an impatient sigh.

As he waited, his eyes wandered back to Jovi's table. She was still engrossed in conversation with the woman, her gestures animated. Man, she had a gift for connecting with people. How did she make it look so easy? And the way her presence just sort of warmed up the whole room. She hesitated and looked up from her conversation. He offered a tight smile and the smallest of nods. Her mouth opened, closed, then opened again. She didn't look real pleased to catch him staring.

Regret twisted in his stomach. He forced his gaze back to the menu.

They'd crossed that line from friendship to something more, and now he desperately needed to drag his emotions and his heart right back where they belonged. Except that seemed impossible now, given how much he enjoyed spending time with her. How much Darby Jane had settled into the comfortable routine of calling out for Jovi whenever she needed help. Mary Catherine had been gone for two years, and Darby Jane definitely needed a mother figure in her life. Someone other than people who volunteered at church or taught her at school.

Icy fingers of dread crawled up his spine. What if Jovi was the person Darby Jane needed? Jovi was beautiful and sweet and kind, but she seemed to enjoy being a roaming health care provider. What was he supposed to do with that? As much as he hated to admit it, Jovi had made a valid point. What if she left and took a job somewhere else? He couldn't uproot Darby Jane, not again.

Neither of them would survive that.

He had to press on. Recalibrate. Caring for his daughter, meeting his looming deadline and delivering a compelling manuscript—that was what mattered. And there had to be a way to get to the bottom of whatever it was that had permanently divided his aunt and Jovi's grandmother. A niggling sensation told him that this conversation with Denise might give him plenty of fodder to work with. Jovi's father's frigid reaction toward him at the coffee shop implied a deep distrust of the Phillipses. But how could anyone know for sure that Mac and Lois were solely responsible for whatever had gone wrong? Maybe the Wrights had played a role in the feud as well. These things usually had two sides to the story. After speaking with Denise, he'd start looking for more clues. Since he'd read that blog post about the Montgomerys and Harrisons, he hadn't been able to let go of the notion that this town had secrets and a rich history.

"Sir, may I help you?" The dark-haired young woman standing at the register offered a friendly smile.

"Large black coffee, and a plain toasted bagel with cream cheese, please."

"Absolutely. No need to leave room for cream or sugar?"

"No, thanks." He fumbled with his wallet, removed his debit card, then tapped it on the screen provided.

The woman's fingers flew over the keys of the register. "We'll have that up for you in just a few minutes."

"Great. Thank you." He left a tip, declined the receipt, then put his wallet away. When he turned around to find a table, a petite woman with her dark hair pulled back in a sleek ponytail stood behind him, hands jammed in the pockets of her maroon puffy jacket.

Her brown eyes widened. "Excuse me, are you Burke Solomon?"

He hesitated. "I am."

Smiling, she extended her hand. "I'm Denise Schumacher, Charlie's sister."

"It's nice to meet you." Burke awkwardly shook her hand with his. "Pardon the splint."

"No worries." She gestured over her shoulder. "I've already snagged a table. It's the one there with the hefty tote bag." She gave a nervous laugh. "On my way to the library after this."

"Perfect. I'll grab a seat and wait for you there."

"Sounds good." She scooted around him to place her order.

He weaved through the crowded tables to the spot that Denise had claimed, sensing Jovi's eyes on him. This time he didn't look her way or make eye contact. Let her wonder what he was up to. He didn't owe her an explanation. He had every right to investigate this feud because there was nothing wrong with being curious, especially if the information gleaned helped them resolve the conflict. And helped him write a better novel.

A few minutes later, Denise sat down with her coffee and brought him his. "Hope you don't mind that I grabbed your drink for you. It was ready. She said your food will be up in a minute."

"That's kind of you, thank you." Burke slowly drew the mug closer. "Appreciate you meeting me here."

"Happy to help." She set her to-go cup to the side and then rummaged in her hefty tote bag. "Your aunt and uncle were so sweet. And I have to tell you right up front that my dad loved your book. Is it tacky if I ask you to sign his copy?"

"Not tacky at all. I'd be honored to sign it for him."

Denise's smile widened, her relief evident. "Thank you, Burke. It means a lot to my dad." She slid the paperback across the table, then handed him a pen.

As he carefully signed his name on the title page, an unexpected feeling of accomplishment enveloped him. Despite the chaos in his personal life, his writing had resonated with readers. He needed that reminder.

"So where should we start?" Denise tucked the signed book back into her bag.

Burke took a sip of his coffee, savoring the rich flavor that warmed his insides. "Since I'm guessing you've lived in Evergreen a long time, do you know anything about ongoing family feuds? Either between the Harrisons and the Montgomerys or between my aunt and uncle and the people who run the candy company?"

Denise's expression grew serious. "I've lived here my entire life, so almost thirty years. Somebody's almost always fighting about something—gold, girlfriends, boyfriends, building the highway—you name it, there's probably been a dispute."

She tapped her finger against her cheek. "The Harrison–Montgomery feud is a legend in Evergreen, passed down from generation to generation. But it's hard to know what's true anymore when the details get more salacious with every retelling."

Well, that didn't surprise him, but it also didn't provide any clear direction for his investigation. "Anything specific about the legend that you'd like to share?"

Denise took a thoughtful sip of her coffee before answering. "To be honest, I never paid much attention. Most folks around here don't take it too seriously. Especially since someone tried to write a tell-all blog post about it a few years back."

"Tried?"

"Yeah, I only read a few paragraphs. It wasn't that interesting." She lifted one shoulder. "That's how people around here usually react when someone from outside writes about Evergreen or makes a movie or a TV show supposedly set here."

Burke squirmed in his chair. "Say more about that?"

"Alaska is misrepresented in film and television all the time. And *someone from outside* refers to anyone living in the lower forty-eight."

"Ah. I see." He paused as the woman who'd taken his order delivered a toasted bagel and cream cheese on a cheery yellow plate.

"Here you are, sir." She offered an apologetic smile. "Sorry about the wait."

"Not a problem," Burke said, easing his coffee out of the way to make space for the plate.

Denise's sculpted brows scrunched together. "I thought you wanted to ask me questions about your aunt and uncle?"

Burke offered his most charming grin. "That's absolutely what I want to speak with you about. Forgive me for the rabbit hole. How would you describe my aunt Lois in her final days?"

A wistful expression flitted across Denise's face. "She was sweet. Mostly. Spent a lot of time talking about her life. She and your uncle lived a few places before they settled down here."

"With the military, right?"

Denise nodded. "Have you dug through any of the boxes out in the shed? Charlie and I moved almost all their personal belongings out there."

"Right. The shed. I haven't had a chance to poke around in there yet. Charlie gave me the key. I just need to clear a path through the snow. Anything else you can think of that I should know?" Burke took a bite of his bagel, enjoying the creamy texture paired with the warm, crunchy bread. Maybe if he let her talk, she'd unwittingly share something useful.

Hesitating, she glanced around the coffee shop, as if making sure no one was eavesdropping on their conversation. Then she leaned in closer to Burke. "You know, it's interesting that you asked about feuds. I don't recall there being a connection between the Montgomerys, the Harrisons, and your family. But your aunt was real bitter about whatever went down between her and the Wrights."

Now they were getting somewhere. "Do you know what happened?"

Denise shook her head. "I wish I did. Unfortunately, she wasn't specific. The only reason I know about their...conflict is because I brought her a box of chocolates from the Evergreen Candy Company, and she started to cry. Insisted I throw it away."

Burke's scalp prickled. He leaned in, unable to hide his intrigue. "Did she say why?"

"She was crying too hard to make out anything coherent, but I got the sense that it had something to do with grudges and not being able to let go." Denise wrinkled her nose. "Not much to work with, right? Like I said, I wish I knew, because she really was hurting."

Poor Aunt Lois. And to think she might've carried that heartache with her for the rest of her days. "Thank you for sharing that."

It wasn't much, but it was something. The kind of solid information he needed to help uncover the truth.

What a disaster.

Jovi stood alone in the workroom at the candy company, the remnants of the holiday rush still scattered around her. She turned in a slow circle. Why had they left the place in such a mess? Discarded flat cardboard boxes, stray ribbon imprinted with the trademark logo and empty cardboard tubes from used-up packaging-tape dispensers littered the normally pristine workspace. A few empty soda cans and wrappers that once held trail mix and protein bars sat forgotten on the counter. Two plants drooped in their clay pots on the windowsill.

Even the plants seemed to have given up, their leaves wilting and brown at the edges.

She draped her coat over a folding chair and plopped her bag down. Amped up on sugar and caffeine, she kept moving to maintain her momentum, even though she sensed exhaustion creeping in. Sighing, Jovi retrieved her phone, opened a music app, and scrolled until she found an upbeat pop playlist that might spark some motivation. She jabbed the Play icon with her finger and balanced her phone on a stack of books. Isabel wasn't in and hadn't responded to Jovi's text either, so this method would have to do since she couldn't get into her sister's office to borrow a portable speaker.

She just needed something to distract her, to keep her body in motion. Her coffee date with Danielle had been refreshing. A balm to her soul, really. Until Burke had shown up. Not that she didn't expect to run into him. They were neighbors, after all, and Evergreen was a small town. But when he'd sat down at a table with Denise Schumacher—the beautiful, single, and lovely Denise, who'd only become more attractive since she'd been a popular cheerleader in high school—Jovi had struggled to stay engaged in her conversation.

Why did Burke want to hang out with Denise?

Stop. Just stop. She braced her hands on her hips and surveyed the scene. Where to begin? Movement out in the hallway pulled her attention toward the door. Mom strode in, her pink jacket draped over her arm and a stylish handbag in her other hand.

Mom's smile didn't quite reach her eyes. "Hi there. I didn't expect to see you here, sweetie."

"I felt bad for leaving the place like this." She gestured to the mess. "It's not fair for whoever has to process the next round of orders."

Mom set her purse and coat on the counter. "That's thoughtful of you. Easter is right around the corner."

Jovi's chest tightened at the mention of Easter. It was still weeks away, but it felt too soon. She rubbed her fingers against the ache in her chest. She wasn't ready. Not for another round of seasonal candy orders, the end of her projected stay, or the thought of saying goodbye to Burke and Darby Jane. Besides, they hadn't found the recipe. Or convinced Mom and Dad not to sell. This wasn't how her trip home was supposed to go.

"I'm here for pretty much the same reason." Mom swept some crumbs on the counter into a neat pile with the side of her hand. "Well, that and Isabel sent me a text saying she wasn't coming in today."

"Is she okay?"

Mom hesitated. "She didn't mention anything specific, but you know how she is. The girl goes a million miles an hour. Wouldn't hurt to take a day off."

True. Jovi bit her lip. Something felt off, though. Had she and Mason had another argument? She'd check in on her sister later. "So I thought I'd start with picking up the garbage. Sound good?"

Mom nodded. "The trash bags are under the counter, lower cabinet on the far right. We sort the recycle and trash ourselves, so keep that in mind, please."

"Got it. Thanks." Jovi retrieved a bag and then shook it open. "How was your coffee date with Danielle?"

The bag slipped from Jovi's hands. She bent and scooped it up, grateful her mother couldn't see her face. The heat climbing her neck would give away her complicated feelings about seeing Burke. Then she'd have to explain why the mention of coffee with her old high school friend made her blush. Ugh. Why did one impulsive kiss wreak so much havoc?

"Jovi?" Mom's voice carried a hint of concern. "Is Danielle all right?"

Jovi stood and forced a bright smile. "Yes, she's great. We had a wonderful time catching up. Have you heard anything from the people at Grammie's new place? Is the flu outbreak over?"

"Good question." Mom pulled her phone from her bag. "Gretchen sent me a text, but I didn't have a chance to read it yet."

Jovi paused, an empty aluminum can in her hand, and shot her a look. Grammie was Mom's mother-in-law, so not technically her responsibility, but Mom had always been the one to keep up with family logistics, appointments, doctor's visits, etc. Wasn't she worried?

Mom fumbled with her reading glasses, then slid them into place and tapped her phone screen. "Let's see… Gretchen says this is the fourth day that none of the residents have had any symptoms, fever, etc. If they can go five days with no one symptomatic, then visitors will be allowed back in. She recommends we call ahead and double-check before we make the drive."

"I'm glad things are improving." Jovi added three more cans and two plastic bottles to her collection. "I would really like to see Grammie again."

"I'm sure she would like to see you too."

"I can wait if you and Dad want to go first." Jovi stopped short of mentioning she had several questions to ask her grandmother and didn't necessarily want an audience.

Mom pressed her lips into a thin line, then shook her head.

Oh. Mom and Grammie had always had a very kind and loving relationship. "You don't want to visit her at all?"

Mom avoided eye contact. "I—I can't."

"Because..."

Sighing, Mom leaned against the counter and crossed her arms over her chest. "Because if she's lucid, then we're going to have to confess that we're selling the company, and I don't think she'll ever forgive us."

"It's her legacy," Jovi said quietly. "I wouldn't blame her for feeling betrayed. But don't you think she deserves to know the truth?"

Her mother's eyes filled with tears, and she looked away. "I know this isn't what you want to hear, but your father and I still believe selling is the best decision for our family."

Mom's words nearly gutted her. She tried to hold back the wave of anger and disappointment that surged through her. "How can you do this? How can you disregard the legacy, our own family's history, for the sake of profit?"

Mom's spine straightened. She swiped at her cheeks. "It's not just about money, Jovi. Sometimes we have to make difficult decisions for the sake of our future."

"But what about all the memories? Everything Grammie and Grandpa built?" Jovi's voice wavered. She gestured to the scattered mess around them. "We're just going to throw it all away?"

Anger flitted across her mother's features. "We're not throwing anything away."

"No, you're handing it all over to a global conglomerate that doesn't care about Evergreen or understand what it means to be a small-business owner. Please. Help me understand how that's different."

Mom turned and plucked her coat and her bag from the counter, then pinned Jovi with a long look. "Your fierce loyalty to a company you've barely been around to help run is admirable. Really, it is. But a comfortable retirement and financial security means something too."

Jovi gasped. Before she could come up with a response, her mom left.

Her mind reeled. What had just happened?

She drew a deep breath, then finished cleaning up the mess. Memories of the hours she'd spent helping her grandparents, working alongside Grammie in the kitchen, tasting her delicious recipes and witnessing the joy it brought to customers' faces renewed Jovi's determination. This was more than just a company. It represented family, tradition and love. If her parents wouldn't listen to reason, and they were willing to sacrifice everything for the sake of a comfortable retirement, then she'd have to double down on her quest to preserve her grandparents' legacy.

Chapter Thirteen

Burke burst through the heavy wooden door of the cabin, leaving behind a trail of snow on the weathered hardwood floor. With a sigh of relief, he peeled off his snow-covered beanie, then ran his hand through his damp, disheveled hair.

The winter storm had dumped another four inches of snow since he had cleared the driveway with his new snowblower in the early hours of the morning. An indulgent purchase for sure, but still cheaper than hiring someone to come plow or shovel every time it snowed. Besides, he needed to do whatever he could to carve out more time to write. He had less than a month until his deadline.

He'd spent the last two days since his visit with Denise at Alpenglow Espresso pouring every spare ounce of his time and energy into drafting a new manuscript. One hundred and fifty-five pages in and he'd never felt more inspired, more eager to get back to creating his first draft.

Adrenaline zipped through his veins as he shed all his outerwear, hung it up to dry, and then toed off his boots. He'd just dropped Darby Jane off at school and made it home with three minutes to spare before his crucial video call with Stephanie. He padded into the kitchen and quickly reheated a cup of coffee from the pot he'd brewed before breakfast. Doubts began to nag at him. Would Stephanie see the potential in his idea? Or would she shoot it down as just another unoriginal concept? The pressure was on, and he couldn't afford any missteps. He had to convince her that this could be a massive bestseller.

Because he sensed deep in his bones that his encounters with the Wright family and decades-old family feuds provided the kind of intrigue readers loved. He'd tried, but he couldn't ignore an idea that had woken him from a dead sleep more than once. A concept that stole his thoughts when he was supposed to be paying attention to Darby Jane.

After retrieving his mug from the microwave, he slid into his chair at the kitchen table, then opened his laptop and found the link for the video call. A moment later, Stephanie appeared on screen, seated at her desk and wearing a crisp white collared button-up under a teal blazer. He caught a glimpse of Charleston through the window behind her. Envy slithered in. Before long, it would be spring in South Carolina. Warm breeze blowing off the water, azaleas blooming, and not a flake of snow in sight.

No. There's no going back. Remember?

"Good morning." Burke held up his coffee on camera and flashed his most charming smile. "At least it's still morning here."

"Hello, Burke."

Her inscrutable expression and polite smile made him shift in his chair. Had she reviewed the new plot summary he'd emailed her yesterday? Did she like it? His heart thrummed in his chest.

"So? What did you think?"

She scratched at her cheek with a well-manicured fingernail, a sure sign that she was not impressed.

His palms turned clammy.

"I'm thrilled that your creative juices are flowing and you've produced new content, but I have to say, this is a last-minute change that might not work in your favor."

He stifled a groan. "How can you say that? This is a phenomenal concept."

"But it's not a domestic thriller." She looked down and riffled some papers. "It's more of a mishmash between a family saga and historical fiction."

"Those are popular elements that readers adore. Right?"

Stephanie let out a small sigh and shook her head. "I don't know. Seems to me you're reaching here, and time is of the essence. We can't expect your team at the publishing house to bend to your whims."

Irritation zipped through him like a bobsled careening down a slick run. "This isn't a whim."

She blinked twice, clearly taken aback by his tone.

Frustrated, he took a sip of his coffee to buy time and gather his thoughts. He had always been straightforward and respectful in his professional interactions. Was it the looming deadline that made Stephanie risk-averse? He valued her perspective, but he still felt so passionate about this concept. He couldn't compromise. "I know I'm testing your patience, and I understand the consequences if this doesn't work out, but I have to trust my instincts. This idea is too brilliant to let go."

Stephanie leaned forward with a serious expression. Her intense gaze matched her professional tone. "As we've discussed before, you haven't delivered. There won't be another chance for an extension."

"But I'm making progress now. This could be the book that sells millions of copies. Just look at Nicholas Sparks. He's built a successful career on writing heart-wrenching love stories."

"You're not Nicholas Sparks," she countered. "You are bound by contract to deliver what you promised."

"So you're telling me you've never had a client sweep in at the last minute with a brilliant idea that went on to be a bestselling novel?"

Stephanie opened her mouth, then closed it, then opened it again. Her gaze skittered away from the camera. "I can't say that it's never happened, but it's a long shot."

"Forgive me for being blunt, but I'm a single dad who already survived the unimaginable loss of my wife and our baby. Overcoming obstacles is kind of my thing."

A small smile tugged at Stephanie's lips as she looked up at him. "As your literary agent, it's my job to give you sound advice and guide you toward success. I want what's best for you."

"But let's not forget that you also stand to gain from any potential success."

Stephanie's smile faltered slightly before she regained her composure. "Yes, there is that. And I consider myself partially responsible for preventing you from failing."

"I was already teetering on the brink of failure," Burke said. "That other story idea? I mean, I'm not going to say it's garbage, but it's not the story I want to write. I don't feel passionate about it. Maybe in the future, I will."

"Do you feel passionate about the idea you just sent me?"

"Absolutely. This is the story I want to tell right now, and the one that I can write under pressure and deliver on time. If I send you a full proposal, will you please look it over and then pitch it to my editor?"

Stephanie wrinkled her nose. "Burke, I—"

"I'm aware of what I'm asking, and I understand what's at stake." He lowered his voice and infused it with as much persuasiveness as he could muster. "Stephanie, please. Just give my proposal a read-through, and if you're not at all moved by the story and eager to read more, then by all means, we'll go back to the original idea."

"You just said you hated it and you didn't want to write it."

"*Hate* is a strong word. If that ends up being the manuscript I need to deliver, then I can make that happen. But it will be very much a formulaic effort. Nothing unique or especially—"

Stephanie covered her ears. "Stop, just stop talking."

"So is that a *yes*, then?"

She sighed and leaned back in her chair. "Honestly, this whole thing is insane."

He couldn't help but grin. "I know, but it's also brilliant."

"At least we agree on something," she grumbled before meeting his gaze again. "Fine, I'll read your new proposal."

Burke pumped his fist in triumph. "Yes! Thank you, Stephanie."

"I'll need it by end of day tomorrow."

"Consider it done."

She ended the call, and he opened the file for his latest story idea, still chuckling. She'd agreed.

But then guilt walloped him. Jovi probably hadn't given up on her quest to find her grandmother's missing iconic recipe. Would she be angry if she found out he'd incorporated that into his story? He promptly gave those thoughts a mental shove. Wasn't like he was stealing intellectual property. This was a unique idea, a story he'd crafted all on his own based on details he'd observed since arriving in town. Besides, what if, in writing this book, he uncovered the secrets that had divided both their families for decades? Wouldn't she be grateful?

And did it even matter, considering she'd kissed him and then pushed him away? This was his chance at redemption and repairing their families' broken relationship. And deep down, he believed this story had huge potential. He couldn't walk away from it now, even if it meant he had to write for sixteen hours a day. Time for him to leave behind his desert of writer's block and create something truly remarkable.

"Jovi. Wait." Sabrina Johnson's voice echoed through the church atrium. Jovi hesitated. A few more steps and she'd be out the door and on her way to lunch. She had been looking forward to a relaxing afternoon spent with Danielle and her family, away from the chaos that seemed to follow her everywhere. But she couldn't ignore Sabrina. Her tone had sounded urgent. They'd grown up together and been friends until they lost touch after high school.

Jovi turned around and saw Sabrina standing near the tall faux wood table that served as the church's informal welcome center, gesturing for her to come closer. "Do you have a few minutes? I need your help."

Jovi crossed the room and greeted her petite blonde friend with a quick hug. "Hi, Sabrina. It's good to see you."

"You too." Sabrina's dangly earrings bobbed as she pulled back. Her friendly smile faded. "And I know this is super last-minute, but if I don't find one more female chaperone, we'll have to cancel our ski trip tomorrow."

Jovi stifled a groan. Chaperoning so wasn't her thing. Memories of loud music, eating too much junk food, not sleeping and people coping with motion sickness filled her head. Ugh. Just…no. Sabrina had the biggest heart, though. It was hard to say no to someone who volunteered to run the kids' ministry program.

Jovi shifted from one foot to the other and fidgeted with her purse strap. "I know you're in a pinch. It's just that…selfishly, I'm not sure I want to spend all day chaperoning a ski trip."

"Well, the good news is we're just going to Winterhaven, so you're spared the three-hour ride in a packed van." Sabrina's blue eyes sparkled. "The resort instructors will handle the lessons. I just need people who are willing to hang out with the kids, ski with them and offer encouragement. This is an outreach for the parents, by the way. They'll get a few hours to themselves, and we'll get the kids outdoors. They spend so much time on their devices these days, and we—"

"All right." Jovi laughed and held up her palm. "Your sales

pitch worked. I'm not working tonight or tomorrow, so I'll be able to help."

Sabrina's face lit up. "Perfect! Thank you so much."

"Do you need to see my driver's license?"

Sabrina nodded. "I'll take a picture of the front and back. I'm assuming you've passed a background check since you work in health care?"

"Yes, ma'am." Jovi pulled her license from her wallet and slid it across the counter.

"Good." Sabrina picked up her phone and snapped a photo of Jovi's license. "Put your current phone number in here, please."

Jovi winced as Sabrina handed over her phone. "Sorry, I haven't been great about keeping in touch."

"No worries. I understand. I'm glad you're back for however long you plan to stay."

Jovi updated her phone number in Sabrina's contacts and passed the phone back. "What do you mean?"

"Jovi." Sabrina angled her head to one side and gave her a knowing look. "You never let too much grass grow under your boots. Aren't you just here temporarily to help sell the candy company?"

"That's the problem," she said, lowering her voice. "We don't want to sell. Isabel and I are trying to convince our parents to hold on to the company."

"Oh?" Sabrina's brows sailed upward. "How's that going?"

"Not great." Jovi sighed and leaned against the counter. "I had a rough conversation with my mom recently. She and Dad insist that they want to retire and deserve the financial security that comes with selling out."

Sabrina scrunched her nose. "That's tough. I'm sorry. I'll be praying you guys get that all sorted."

"Thank you." Jovi squeezed Sabrina's arm. "Enough about me. What's new with you?"

"Not much. I'm a long-term sub at the high school this semester because one of the English teachers is out on maternity leave. Hopefully I'll—"

"Miss Jovi. Hey!" A familiar little girl's voice echoed across the atrium.

Several people turned as Darby Jane dodged around people milling in clusters, her boots thumping on the laminate floor. An oversize red bow clipped to her ponytail flopped in time to her steps, and the hem of her skirt billowed around her legs. Burke wasn't far behind, his face a mask of uncertainty.

Jovi's breath hitched.

"Well, well, what do we have here?" Sabrina said under her breath.

"Nothing." Jovi gave her the side-eye. "They're my new neighbors. That's all."

"He's the hottest neighbor I've seen in the history of…well, forever."

"Hush." Jovi elbowed Sabrina. Warmth heated her neck as she sensed Burke's gaze on her. Darby Jane rushed to her and hugged her legs. "Hey, Darby Jane."

She straightened and then smiled at Burke. "Hey. I didn't realize you were coming to church here."

It was true. She hadn't. Until the congregation had stood to sing the first song, and she spotted that dark hair and those broad shoulders from ten pews away. More blood rushed to her face. Yes, he was undeniably attractive, but that was the last thing she wanted to acknowledge right now.

"We needed to get plugged in somewhere," Burke said, his smile guarded. "Darby Jane, give Jovi some space, please."

"But I haven't seen her in forever." Darby Jane untangled her arms from Jovi's legs and grabbed her hand. "Where have you been?"

Jovi's smile faltered. "Working. Mostly."

"Hi, I'm Sabrina Johnson." She shook Burke's hand. "Welcome to Evergreen Community Church."

"Burke Solomon." He tipped his head toward his daughter. "This is Darby Jane."

"Sabrina runs the children's program," Jovi said, desperate to keep the conversation moving so she didn't have to explain to Darby Jane that the real reason they weren't spending time together was because Jovi had kissed Darby Jane's handsome, brooding father.

"I hope Darby Jane can join us tomorrow. Since there's no school, the youth will be skiing all day at Winterhaven. Did you get a flyer?" Sabrina pulled a light blue half-sheet of paper from a stack on the counter and handed it to Burke. "Here are the details."

Frowning, he took the flyer and scanned it.

"Daddy, I really want to go." Darby Jane twirled in a circle. "Can we, please?"

Burke shook his head. "Pumpkin, I can't go skiing with a sore wrist."

"You don't have to come," Sabrina said. "It's a day trip to our local ski resort. Jovi and I learned to ski there. It's great! Not to mention a reasonably priced outing."

"No experience required?"

"None. There will be instructors offering lessons, and plenty of grown-ups to hang with the kids." Sabrina clasped her hands in front of her. "Think it over, but please let me know by tonight so I can make arrangements. My phone number's on the bottom there."

"That's very kind of you. Thanks." Burke offered a tight smile. "We'll talk it over."

"Please, Daddy." Darby Jane stared up at him with the most adorable gaze. "I love the snow."

Jovi bit her lip to keep from smiling. She was a persuasive little thing. "If it helps at all to ease your worries, I'm going along as a chaperone."

His gaze toggled from Darby Jane to her. "Oh?"

"If your work schedule is flexible, you can come and sit in the lodge." Sabrina bounced up on her toes. "The view is stunning, and there's good food and delicious coffee."

Jovi silently willed Sabrina to stop with the encouragement. Chaperoning she could handle, but being near Burke? Not a wise choice.

"Sounds like an offer I can't refuse."

Burke's charming smile made her heart turn cartwheels. Oh, wow. She shouldn't be feeling this way. But her mind and her heart clearly hadn't forgotten that kiss.

Or her family's concern that she'd spent time with Burke.

She wanted to believe there was a good reason for the feud, but she couldn't shake off the doubt gnawing at her. Or keep dismissing her growing feelings for him. How could she uncover the truth without betraying her family?

He so didn't want to be *that* parent—the hovering, anxious dad who pelted the volunteer with a dozen questions. But he couldn't help it. Any shred of calm he'd clung to had evaporated when they drove into the ski resort's parking lot and he'd been forced to claim the only vacant space at the end of the last row.

Burke glanced out the crowded café's window again. Gray clouds billowed overhead, obscuring the mountain peaks. He'd forgotten to check the forecast. What if a storm swept in and Darby Jane got separated from the others?

Skiers of all ages filled the bunny hill. If she fell down, would anyone even notice? A long line snaked across the packed snow as people waited for the chairlift. Why had he assumed a youth group outing on a Monday might have the resort to themselves?

"Will someone show her how to get on and off the chairlift?"

"I promise we'll take good care of her." Sabrina gently patted Darby Jane's shoulder. They lingered beside the table Burke had scored next to the window inside Winterhaven's café. Sabrina had patiently tolerated his questions.

"She's going to have a blast."

A blast. Right.

"I'm sure you will." Burke swiped his damp palm on his jeans and forced a smile. "It's just that she's never skied before and—"

"Daddy, stop." Darby Jane punctuated her groan with a dramatic eye roll. "If I don't hurry up, I'm going to miss my lesson."

Shame swept in. "All right, then. Have fun and be careful."

Sabrina offered an empathetic smile and then whisked Darby Jane toward the exit.

Burke eased into the closest empty chair and sagged against the hard wooden spindles.

One visit to a new church and his girl had already gotten plugged in. He should probably be grateful for the invitation to come skiing with the other kids in the children's program, but honestly, he had a serious case of FOMO right now. Not that it would be safe for him to ski, anyway. His wrist still throbbed, despite his regular use of the splint. Probably because he'd spent several hours on Saturday editing the last fifty pages he'd just written.

Darby Jane sure looked adorable. He spotted her walking beside Sabrina. Somehow he'd had the presence of mind to order her ski gear before they'd left Charleston. Of course she'd picked neon green and hot pink. Certainly wouldn't be hard to locate her in the sea of skiers and snowboarders.

Regret twisted his insides. Man, he hated that he couldn't be a part of teaching Darby Jane to ski. Part of him suspected he could handle an hour or two on the bunny hill, but the thought of reinjury if he fell or someone else ran into him kept him glued to his chair. So here he sat, sentenced to a day of watching from the wings.

He slowly unpacked his laptop and set it on the table, worn and scraped and repolished from years of use. Overhead, rustic unfinished beams ran the length of the dining area's vaulted ceiling, making the place feel much larger than it was. The swish, swish, swish of people's snow pants as they walked by, the clinking of silverware against plates, and the aroma of hot cocoa mixed with fried food coming off the grill reminded him of his last ski trip in Utah almost eight years ago.

Thoughts of his late wife cutting down backcountry hillsides, her skis carving through the powder as she dared him to take a black diamond route, replayed in his head. He closed his eyes, straining to hear echoes of her laughter as she beat him to the bottom of the run, her cheeks pink from exertion. Warmth bloomed in his chest as he recalled the perfect end to their outings, cozied up by the fire after his brother, his mom and her boyfriend had all gone to bed.

"Mind if I join you, young man?"

Burke flinched, then opened his eyes.

A stranger with a full head of white hair, brilliant blue eyes, and ruddy cheeks stood beside the table. He held a plated cinnamon roll as big as Burke's face and a large disposable cup of coffee.

"Uh, I... Well, I'm—"

The man pulled out the chair opposite Burke and sat down without waiting for him to stop stumbling over his words.

His broad smile split his craggy face, revealing yellowed teeth. "You look like you're new around here. Thought maybe you could use a friend."

Burke cleared his throat against the unexpected tightness. "Suppose I could."

The stranger retrieved plastic ware, two sugar packets and three creamers from the chest pocket of his fleece-lined plaid shirt.

"How can you tell I'm new here?" Burke reached for his large mocha that he'd purchased from the coffee bar and took a tentative sip. The barista had convinced him to add some white chocolate flavoring, and Darby Jane highly recommended the whipped cream and sprinkles. He grimaced. More sugar than he was used to in his coffee, but he had to admit the sweetness was nice.

Eyeing him, the man tapped his sugar packets against his large palm. "Something kind of fancy about you."

Burke glanced down at his red plaid shirt that he'd layered over a black turtleneck. His jeans had that heavy, just-shoveled-a-roof consistency, and weren't any brand that he'd ever wear back home. "Moved here from Charleston, South Carolina, last month. Guess I don't quite have the jeans, work boots and plaid shirt look down to a science yet."

He laughed, his whole body humming with amusement. "Well, good gravy, son. You're off to a strong start." His bushy eyebrows knit together. "What'd you say your name was?"

"Burke Solomon. And you are?"

"My friends call me Walker." He tore the ends off the packets and dumped both into his coffee. "Oldest granddaughter runs this place, so she lets me hang around."

Maybe that explained the giant cinnamon roll.

"It's a pleasure to meet you, Walker."

"Likewise, young man." Walker stirred the cream in next. "You've got a nice computer there. Let me guess. Day trader?"

"No," Burke said. "Novelist and single dad."

Walker's eyes widened. "Oh, did I take your child's chair?"

"No, sir, you did not. My daughter, Darby Jane, is out there learning to ski."

"Oh? Not a fan of skiing?"

"Actually, I'm very much a skier, but I broke my wrist trying to learn to ice-skate, so I'm sidelined for the time being."

"More time to write, then." Walker winked, then sipped his coffee.

"Indeed." Burke silently hoped Walker's conclusion would propel him to get up and find another table, but he couldn't bring himself to ask, and to be honest, the guy was intriguing.

Between taking care of Darby Jane and researching what little he could find about Lois and Mac, and the Wright family's history in the area, he wasn't sure where to go next with his story. But a late-night email from Stephanie giving him the green light to pursue his current story idea because his publisher wanted the full manuscript meant he needed to crank out several thousand words. Soon.

"How long have you lived here, Walker?"

"Oh, about seventy-seven years."

"Would that be your whole life?"

Nodding, Walker cut a corner from his cinnamon roll with his knife and fork. "You betcha. Parents moved here from Minnesota as homesteaders, and I've never left."

"Wow. Do you have family in the area?"

"Oh, yeah. Three kids, four grandkids, and hopefully there will be some great-grands soon."

"That's wonderful." Burke smiled. "Say, did you ever know Mac and Lois Phillips?"

Walker hesitated, his loaded fork halfway to his lips. "Sure did. Knew them both. They were good people."

"Lois is my mother's older sister."

"No kidding." Walker grinned. "How about that? So how'd you get here from South Carolina?"

"That's a long story for another day. Basically, I wanted a fresh start, and I heard their cabin was vacant."

Something Burke couldn't quite identify flickered in Walker's eyes, but he just nodded and ate his cinnamon roll.

Burke mentally scrolled through his list of unanswered questions. Walker didn't seem standoffish or guarded about Evergreen's history. Maybe he wouldn't mind answering a few questions. "So if you knew Lois and Mac, then you must also know the Wrights."

Walker's expression grew serious. "I do. I've been meaning

to get by and see Mrs. Wright. You know she lives at the Oasis down in Anchorage."

"Yes, her granddaughter Jovi is my neighbor. She mentioned that her grandmother had some neurological issues."

"She's a real firecracker, that one." Walker shook his head and then took a sip of his coffee.

"Do you remember when they were friends? Mrs. Wright and my aunt?"

Walker swallowed and looked off in the distance.

Burke leaned closer, his fingers tightening around his mug's handle. *Please remember something. Anything.*

"They're a few years older than me, so I don't recall all the details, but there was a time when those ladies were thick as thieves. Sadly, they let a man get between them." Walker met Burke's gaze again. His pale blue eyes sharpened. "Your uncle Mac destroyed that friendship."

Whoa. Didn't see that coming. "Can you say more?"

Walker hesitated. "The way I heard it, Lois and Carol both took a liking to Mac. He invited Carol to a dance at the community center but left with Lois. After a whirlwind courtship, they married and moved away."

"And Carol married Dennis Wright?"

"Eventually." Walker carved the side of his fork through the cinnamon roll. "But before Mac was in the picture, Lois and Carol had a small candy business together for a little while. Then after Mac and Carol fell in love, the ladies couldn't agree on who the recipes belonged to. They had quite a spat, and as far as I know, they were never friends again."

"Not even when Mac and Lois moved back to Evergreen?"

"Nope." Sadness flickered in Walker's eyes. "Those ladies were good at two things: making candy and holding grudges."

Chapter Fourteen

She had to find that recipe.

Jovi flipped through the pages of a borrowed cookbook, desperately searching for any combination of ingredients that might produce a similar sweet treat. It was a long shot, but maybe someone in Evergreen had tasted Grammie's salted caramel chews and tried to replicate them.

Jovi eased onto the sofa, wincing as her sore muscles protested. Skiing with the kids from church had been so much fun. But today her whole body ached. Michael had never been interested in skiing and convinced her not to risk getting injured, so they had stuck to safer winter activities like hiking and snowshoeing.

Yesterday was her first time back on the slopes in over three years.

Just one more way she'd let him influence her choices. A knot formed in her belly. Why had she put aside her preferences and allowed him to dictate how they spent their free time?

Except a small part of her still missed him.

Pushing the notion aside, she shook her head and opened the vintage cookbook, then scanned the table of contents until she found the section featuring cookies, cakes and candy. A movie about a big-city girl who moved back to her small hometown just in time to save the annual spring festival played on the television. The plot sounded vaguely familiar. The heroine had to devise clever ways to raise money for the festival, and the hero, a single dad, grudgingly helped her. Even though Jovi knew how it would end—spoiler alert: they save the festival and fall in love—she couldn't help but get caught up in the story. Eager for the happily ever after that came as a satisfying conclusion.

The actor playing the hero's little girl in the movie wore bows in her hair that reminded Jovi of Darby Jane. She quickly banished all thoughts of the small-town single dad and his adorable daughter living right down the road. Yeah, okay, so kissing Burke had made her weak in the knees, and Darby Jane had been a hoot learning to ski with absolutely zero fear, but that didn't mean they had a future together.

She dog-eared a page with a recipe that had potential, then set the cookbook aside. Sighing, she eyed the other cookbooks stacked on Grammie's coffee table. Two she'd found on a shelf in the storeroom at the candy company, one she'd borrowed from a longtime member of the women's group at church, another she dusted off the shelf here in the house, and another Mom kept in her kitchen.

Since her tense conversation with her mother in the workroom, she hadn't spoken with her parents. They'd texted an invite to a family dinner tonight, which she'd accepted. Not that she relished the thought of getting together. There would likely be some tense conversation, especially since her parents and Isabel didn't sound pleased that she'd been seen in public with Burke. And she wasn't ready to accept their reasons for walking away from the candy company. Financial security and a pleasant retirement were admirable goals, but the thought of selling their family's legacy still turned her stomach.

She flipped through the next cookbook, recognizing names of families that had lived in Evergreen for ages. Wow. The stories that one cookbook could tell just by ingredients and black-and-white photos. They were like time capsules. Too bad none of the recipes featured anything close to the chews she was after. She slapped the book shut and put it on the coffee table.

Massaging the ache forming above her eyes, Jovi reached for another cookbook when her phone pinged with an incoming direct message. She grabbed the remote, muted the television's volume and fumbled in the squishy cushions until she retrieved her phone.

It pinged two more times in quick succession. Weird. She didn't spend much time communicating with people via DMs but as a traveler she'd met all kinds of interesting folks, and occasionally they became social media pals. She opened the message. The woman's name didn't sound familiar, but maybe they'd worked together and she'd forgotten.

Or maybe it was spam. But she was invested now and couldn't not look. She scanned the first message.

Hello. I know this will come as quite a shock, but I heard from a friend that you and Michael are planning to get married, and I felt like you should know that he has a child. My baby is his, and I want to make sure that you are aware of our child's existence and what that might mean for you and your future.

Blood roared behind her ears. "What?!" Her hands shook as she scrolled to read the second message.

I debated about whether to reach out, but during my recent conversation with Michael as we were working out visitation and coparenting plans, I got the sense that you were unaware that he even had a child, and I don't think that's fair to you. If you're going to marry him, I want to know that you are fully informed about what you're stepping into. Here's my number if you'd prefer to text me...

"Oh, Michael," Jovi whispered. "How could you?"

She dropped the phone on the couch without responding. The woman would be able to see that she'd read the messages. So she'd have to come up with a response. Messages like that deserved at the very least a follow-up. Michael had a child. Had he not known? Did he not want to tell her? And what was all his talk about reconnecting with her? Maybe even choosing his next post based on her location? Did he think she'd never find out he was someone's father?

Unbelievable.

Was this the reason why he'd called off the wedding? Had he found out about the baby?

The questions piled up. Should she confront him? But the thought of calling now sparked more anger. She turned up the volume on the movie, desperate to lose herself in the storyline. An unfinished slice of toast and a cup of coffee sat on the table, getting cold. She'd lost her appetite. The shock of this news had floored her. What had Michael been thinking, concealing a life-changing secret? Betrayal and heartache gnawed at her. Jovi buried her face in her hands and sobbed.

He'd left her a note. Two measly sentences.

Isabel's hands shook as she reread Mason's handwritten missive printed in neat block letters.

STAYING AT GARRETT'S FOR A FEW DAYS. NEED TIME TO THINK.

She stood in the middle of the kitchen, staring at the lime green square stuck to an envelope and propped against her favorite coffee mug. A sour taste rose in her throat. Fifteen years together and now he needed time apart?

Panic ballooned in her chest. She couldn't move. Couldn't think. Couldn't breathe. How could this be happening? What would she do without him? Tears threatened to spill over as she stood frozen, unsure of what to do next. Their love had always been unbreakable, but now she feared it was about to shatter into irreparable pieces. They had shared everything—from their hopes and dreams to their darkest fears and insecurities. Together they'd survived a painful miscarriage, and he'd supported her through the heart-wrenching decision to help move Grammie to the memory care place. But now, suddenly, he was gone.

What did he possibly need to think about? With a fierce growl, she yanked the note free, then stormed across the kitchen, opened the cabinet under the sink and tried to stuff the note inside. It stuck to her finger.

"C'mon!"

She shook her hand rapidly. The paper fluttered, but didn't budge. Blinking back tears, she shredded the note into tiny pieces, then released the fragments into the bin. There.

Isabel stumbled to the couch and sank onto the cushions, feeling as if her world was crashing down around her. She had loved Mason since high school and never imagined being without him. Now here she was, alone and confused, unsure of what to do or where to turn.

The note had been infuriatingly cryptic. Had he been vague on purpose? Did he receive a job offer and needed to think about his response? Surely after all they'd been through, he'd at least tell her he'd gotten the offer. Right?

Or was he thinking about a more substantial decision? Like moving out?

She sobbed, her chest heaving, as she remembered their last argument. She'd tried so hard to express genuine interest in the job he'd interviewed for in Juneau. She'd even shared the options she'd found for herself there and taken the time to create a new spreadsheet illustrating how the cost-of-living changes and their projected salaries might impact their family budget.

But when he'd noticed that she hadn't included any line items for baby and childcare needs, he'd gotten angry. And then very, very quiet. What if he had decided that staying together wasn't worth it anymore? Isabel swiped at the tears on her cheeks. How could he leave without talking things out?

She needed to do something, to take some sort of action. She got up from the couch and walked to the kitchen, trying to make sense of Mason's sudden departure. She had never felt so lost and alone. But amid the confusion and pain, she knew one thing for sure: they were going to have to sort out their issues. Soon. Because she couldn't stand living with all this uncertainty.

With a squirt bottle in one hand and a roll of paper towels tucked under her arm, she tackled a cleaning project. Scrubbing, scraping, wiping... Nothing was more satisfying than restoring order to her home when her emotions spun out of control. As she cleaned, her mind raced with thoughts of what could have caused Mason to leave so abruptly. Was it something she'd said? Did she do something wrong? She couldn't shake the feeling that she had driven him away, and the guilt was crushing her.

Lost in thought, she didn't even notice the knocking at the door until it turned incessant. She rushed to answer, her imagination entertaining ideas of a bouquet of flowers or a surprise gift from Mason waiting on the other side. But when she opened the door, she was met with a distraught Jovi.

"Oh, no." Isabel stepped back and invited her sister inside. "What's wrong?"

Jovi's hands shook, and she struggled to catch her breath. Isabel gently guided her toward the couch, thankful that she'd shredded the obvious evidence of Mason's departure.

"It's...it's Michael," Jovi finally managed to say.

Isabel's stomach knotted. Really? Leave it to Jovi's former fiancé to somehow weasel his way back into her life. "What about him?" she asked, too worn-out to even try and hide the disdain.

Jovi pulled a crumpled tissue from her coat pocket. "He sent me a text before Valentine's Day, saying he missed me and might be stationed in Alaska soon."

Isabel shook her head. "Oh, Jovi."

"I know, I know." Jovi held up both hands. "But there's no need to worry about us getting back together because I just found out that he had a child he forgot to mention."

Isabel gasped. "You're kidding."

Jovi gulped in a ragged breath. "I wish I was."

"I'm so sorry." Isabel placed a comforting hand on her sister's back. "You deserve so much better than him."

Jovi looked up at Isabel, her red-rimmed eyes full of pain and confusion. "What did I do wrong? Why wasn't I enough for him?"

Huh. How ironic. She and Jovi wrestled with the same questions. "You didn't do anything wrong. He is just a jerk. You're beautiful, Jovi, and so talented. You didn't deserve to be treated like that."

"I don't know." Jovi shook her head. "This isn't the first time a man has lied to me about something significant. Why does this keep happening?"

"I'm the last girl who should be handing out relationship advice," Isabel murmured.

Jovi pinned her with a long look. "What are you talking about? I mean, you'd mentioned you'd hit a rough patch, but you guys are so good together."

Isabel's chin wobbled. More hot tears pricked her eyes. "We're not anymore."

She could barely squeeze the words past the tightness in her throat.

"What?" Jovi's eyes widened. "What happened? Isabel, if something's wrong, you can tell me."

Isabel sniffed. "He left to stay with his buddy Garrett. Needs some time to think." She quoted the air with her fingers, her voice thick with emotion.

Jovi reached out and grabbed Isabel's hand. "Why? Is this about the moving-to-Juneau thing?"

"There's that, yes. But we had a huge fight when we went away for the weekend. He wants kids. I really...don't."

Jovi's eyes softened, and she squeezed Isabel's hand. "Oh, wow. I'm so sorry."

Isabel leaned close and tipped her head against her sister's. "Thanks. I don't know what to do. I love him so much, but I just can't imagine having kids."

Jovi leaned back on the couch, lines marring her brow. "As in...never? Or not right now?"

"I guess when we were young and so obsessed with each other, I imagined having a family. He says we definitely agreed, but then I had that miscarriage, and I've been too scared to commit to having a baby."

"Your feelings are valid. I get that you're worried you might have trouble conceiving or carrying to full term. On the other hand, I've had plenty of patients who go on to have healthy pregnancies and uneventful deliveries."

Isabel bit her lip and looked away. "Yeah, I get that advice a lot. Mason and I have talked about that before, but it always ends up in an argument. I don't want to lose him. At the same time, I don't want to compromise on something that's a huge part of our future."

"That's a tough spot to be in. How long do you think he'll be gone?"

Isabel let out a sigh. "Sadly, I don't see how a few days apart will change anything. He wants to have kids now, and I just don't feel ready yet. I don't know if I ever will be. I feel like such a terrible partner for not wanting the same things that he does."

"That doesn't make you a terrible partner, Isabel. Everyone has their own timeline for major life choices. Maybe you just need some more time."

"That's the thing. I feel like we're running out of time to resolve this. There isn't an easy answer. It's not just about me, it's about him too. I don't want to hold him back from something he really wants."

"So what are you saying?" Jovi whispered.

Isabel hesitated. Just thinking the words made her stomach churn. Could she possibly say them out loud? "I think we're going to separate."

"Oh, Izzy. No." Jovi's eyes welled with tears, and then she pulled her in for a hug.

For the second time since Jovi had come home, Isabel sobbed in her little sister's arms. She cried for the helpless corner she'd backed herself into. Cried for the countless ways she'd hurt the man she loved most. And cried because she was so disappointed in herself for not being a better, braver wife.

He had to tell Jovi about the information Walker had shared.

Burke paced the small cabin, his mind churning as he strong-armed his conflicting thoughts.

"Hey, so, funny story, while you were skiing with my kid, I made a new friend. Maybe you've met? His name's Walker, and he said—"

No. Too…chipper. And he didn't *do* chipper.

Burke stopped pacing and scrubbed a hand over his face. If Jovi heard his upbeat tone, she'd immediately suspect something was up. Not that he had anything to hide.

"Hi, Jovi, sorry to bother you, but I thought you should know that Walker says this whole feud thing is all my uncle's fault."

He growled, then resumed pacing. He wasn't sure if he could trust Walker's words. After all, there was no solid evidence to back up his claims. And even if there was some truth to what Walker said, Burke couldn't shake off the doubts and suspicions he had about the Wrights. If the whole feud hinged on a love triangle, then didn't that mean Jovi's grandmother or grandfather had played a role somehow? Walker's declaration might be accurate, but Burke still clung to his suspicions. How could they know for sure who had ignited the initial spark?

He sighed and tried again. "Hey, Jovi. I want to have coffee with Walker. He seems to know a thing or two about the history of Evergreen, including whatever went down between our families. Care to join us?"

"Daddy, who are you talking to?" Darby Jane hurried into the kitchen from her bedroom, a hopeful look in her eyes. "Is Miss Jovi here?"

Guilt pinched his insides. "No, sweet pea, she's not."

Her face fell. "Then, why do you keep saying her name?"

"Well, I'm..." Heat flushed his face. "I need to ask her something, and I'm practicing so that I get the words right."

"Why don't you text her?"

Because I want to see her. I miss her smile, and the way her eyes light up when she tells me something funny. I like the way her hair skims across her shoulders.

"Daddy, I know! I can text for you. I'm good at that." Darby Jane skipped toward him, her twin pigtails bouncing. She craned her neck, already scanning the kitchen counter to find his phone.

"No, no." Burke stepped into her path and held out his hand. "I can do this. It's important, so I need to practice what to say."

Oh, brother. He sounded like he was about fourteen, rehearsing how to ask a girl to dance for the first time.

Darby Jane's expression turned sour. "Well, don't take too long."

"What? Why not?"

"Because I miss her." Darby Jane's voice wavered. "I thought we'd ski together the whole time, but sometimes she went with the other kids on the big mountain, and I couldn't go." Her lower lip quivered. "The ski teacher said I didn't have enough lessons for that."

"It's okay, sweetie." Burke sank to his knees on the kitchen floor and held out his arms. Darby Jane walked slowly into his embrace, sniffling. "We can figure something out if you want to see Jovi."

Except even as the words left his lips, uncertainty slithered in. Jovi likely did not want to see him. But he couldn't ignore his gut feelings. And he still felt compelled to share what Walker had told him. As much as he resented the idea of his family bearing the blame for whatever had gone wrong between the Wright and the Phillips clans, Jovi still deserved to hear the whole story. Especially since Walker had mentioned that Lois and Carol had fought over recipes and that their friendship never recovered. Burke had come up with some additional questions for Walker, and he wanted Jovi to be there when he asked.

"Daddy, did you hear me?" Darby Jane pulled away, and used the cuff of her red sweater to swipe at her damp cheeks. "When can we see Miss Jovi?"

Poor thing. She was so upset. Burke sat back on his heels and placed a comforting hand on her shoulder. "What would you like to do with her?"

"Maybe we could have breakfast at the diner. I want to talk to her about being in a play."

"What kind of a play?"

"It's a fractured fairy tale."

He rubbed his hand across the back of his neck. "Tell me again why Jovi needs to know about this?"

Darby Jane propped her fists on her hips. "Because you're busy, remember? I'll need someone to help me learn my lines.

You said you have to write a long book super fast. And sometimes I get out of bed at night and tiptoe out here, and you're making your mad face at your computer."

She scrunched her face up in a hilarious imitation.

Burke chuckled. "We'll talk about the getting-out-of-bed part in a minute. Back to your theatrical aspirations. Please remember that Jovi has a job. Two of them, really."

"But she still helps us when she can. My teacher says a play needs teamwork. And we already know you're not too good at costumes."

Ouch.

"I only messed up that one time."

She raised both eyebrows at him.

"Okay, so I've overlooked a few key details lately. I'm truly sorry."

Darby Jane quirked her lips to one side.

Yeah, she was not impressed. Man, this girl—still a child yet she had the expressions and the tone of a thirty-year-old woman. "Okay, so I'm going to text Miss Jovi and tell her that we both need to speak with her as soon as she's available. Sound good?"

Darby Jane nodded, but she stayed rooted.

"What? What did I miss?" Burke stood up.

"Are you going to do it now?"

"Um, sure." He crossed to the cluttered kitchen counter. Where had he left his phone?

"Or do you need more time to think?"

Wow, she was nothing if not persistent. "I'll text her right now."

He lifted up a newspaper, then a stack of mail, and found his phone under an overturned opened magazine. Darby Jane stood, arms linked across her chest like an impatient hall monitor, making sure he followed through.

He quickly pecked out a text to Jovi, asking if she might

have a few minutes to chat with Darby Jane, and letting her know that Walker had shared some information that she might find helpful. There. Polite, yet intriguing enough to hopefully provoke a response.

He hit Send before he could change his mind. "Done."

"Thank you." Darby Jane rewarded him with a satisfied smile. "Please let me know as soon as you hear back."

She turned and left the room.

Burke watched her go, a hopeless sensation blanketing him. He had been owned by his kindergartner. Again.

Sighing, he stared at his phone, hoping for a quick reply from Jovi. A ridiculously high expectation, really. After all, she had made it clear that she needed space. Surely she'd want to know what Walker had said? Even if the details didn't help her locate the missing recipe, the information pointed them toward the cause of the rift. And selfishly, he hoped that if they got to the bottom of how the whole feud started, maybe she'd reconsider her stance on a relationship with him.

Chapter Fifteen

"Let's go see Grammie," Jovi said, tugging the packaging-tape dispenser across another box of candy. "I have two more orders to pack and ship, then I'm finished." She cast her sister a hopeful look. Isabel stood on the other side of the counter in the workroom at the candy company. Dark circles under her eyes, the cup of peppermint tea she'd been sipping for over an hour, and her lack of enthusiasm about anything work-related all hinted at her dismay. Jovi's heart pinched. She couldn't do anything about Mason leaving, short of driving by Garrett's place and giving her brother-in-law a piece of her mind, but she'd do whatever she could to draw her sister out of her funk.

Isabel lifted one shoulder. "Can't."

"Can't or won't?" Jovi double-checked the address on the box, making sure it matched the data entered in the spreadsheet, then carted the package over to the neat stack she'd assembled near the door.

"What if he comes back and I'm not there?"

"Then he can heat a frozen pizza for dinner and watch TV

alone." Jovi crossed to the row of boxes on the counter Irene had already packed. "He's a grown-up. He'll survive if you're not home."

She stopped short of mentioning it would serve him right if he came back and Isabel wasn't there, but her snarky commentary probably wouldn't help. After their tense dinner meeting with Mom and Dad last night, she didn't need to pile on any more stress. Even though Isabel had presented updated data indicating a solid bump in recent sales, their parents hadn't been swayed to change their minds about selling in June. And although she'd tried to reassure her family that nothing was going on between her and Burke, they hadn't appeared convinced.

"Come on, it'll be good for you to get out of here for a bit. You've been working nonstop. Besides, we need more vanilla extract and sugar. Jerry says both are cheaper and in stock at one of the wholesale warehouses in Anchorage." Jovi glanced at the clock. "If we leave now, there will be plenty of time to visit Grammie before she eats dinner."

Isabel heaved a pathetic sigh. "All right. Fine. But you have to drive."

Yes. Jovi pumped her fist in the air. "Sure, I'll drive. Just let me grab my coat and we can go."

She finished packing the remaining boxes while Isabel collected her purse and keys from her office. A few minutes later, as they walked out of the candy company, Isabel trailed behind.

Jovi stopped and turned back. "Everything okay?"

Isabel frowned and didn't look up from her phone.

Uh-oh. Jovi returned to her sister's side. "Isabel, what's wrong?"

Isabel pressed her lips together then shoved her phone in her pocket. "I texted Mason that I was going to Anchorage for the afternoon. Hoping he might care enough to call or at least check in. Is that pathetic or what?"

Jovi put her arm around her sister, steering her toward the

parking lot. "Hey, you're not pathetic. You and Mason are going through a tough time, and it's okay to be sad."

They walked the rest of the way to Isabel's car in silence.

Once they were on the road, Jovi turned up the radio and sang along to a pop song. The snow-covered wilderness flashed by outside, bathed in pinks and purples of the early sunset. Isabel looked out the window. It hurt to see her sister struggling, but what else could she say? The news about Michael's secret baby still stung, but she wasn't going to dwell on that. At least not right now.

As they drove on the highway toward Anchorage, Jovi's thoughts turned to Burke. She hadn't seen him or Darby Jane in over a week, and part of her kind of missed them both. He'd asked her to meet at the diner for breakfast on Saturday because Darby Jane wanted to tell her something important, and Walker had information about Grammie and Lois to share. That was an invitation she couldn't resist. Walker was sweet, but he had a reputation for meddling in other people's business. He probably didn't have anything to tell her that she hadn't heard before. Still, her curiosity was piqued. And she wouldn't say no to Darby Jane.

She'd suggested that they meet outside first and watch the dogsled teams passing through town on their race to Nome. She hadn't been back home to watch the race in ages, and it was definitely an experience she didn't want Burke and Darby Jane to miss. A smile tugged at her lips as she imagined their reactions. Darby Jane would have a zillion questions, and Burke would probably frown at all the noise and chaos.

So okay, Burke was a little uptight. Maybe a lot uptight. He also had a certain charm that drew her to him. Hence that mind-blowing kiss. Or was it the way he looked at her—part amusement and part wonder? As if what she had to say truly mattered. Michael had never looked at her like that. Or made her feel the way Burke did.

Warmth heated her skin. What was she doing, thinking about him like this?

Jovi shook her head, trying to rid herself of the thoughts. She didn't need any distractions right now. Not with Isabel hurting and the mess with Michael still fresh in her mind. Besides, she'd meant what she said when she told Burke they couldn't possibly be together. But as they drove farther down the highway, her mind kept drifting back to him. She couldn't deny the way he made her feel. Her feelings had often led her astray, though. A one-way trip that dead-ended in heartache.

Isabel glanced over, irritation etched on her face. She turned down the radio. "Why are you smiling like that?"

Bummer. Caught swooning by the disillusioned married one. This was not the time to confess she'd kissed Burke. Jovi cleared her throat and tried to morph her expression into something less happy. "No reason. I guess I just love this song."

Isabel's frown deepened, and she returned to staring out the window.

When they arrived at Oasis Care, Jovi greeted the woman sitting at the reception desk. After showing their IDs and signing in, she directed them to Grammie's apartment halfway down a long corridor.

As they walked toward her door, Jovi couldn't help but notice the sterile smell in the air. She glanced at the artwork on the walls featuring tastefully framed, peaceful-looking watercolors of natural scenery. Classical music filtered in from the pianist performing in the atrium. There were worse places for an elderly person struggling with dementia to live. Her gut still twisted with regret. Why did this have to be so hard?

Isabel knocked on the door.

"Come in." Grammie's voice sounded more frail than last time.

Isabel stepped inside. Jovi followed, then quietly shut the door.

Grammie was lying on her bed, her eyes closed. The same

quilt they'd admired during their last visit had been draped over her slender body. Jovi approached, gently placing her hand on Grammie's.

"Grammie, it's me, Jovi," she said softly.

She opened her eyes. Then her lips curved down into a frown. Panic flared in her eyes. "We have so much to do and so little time."

Grammie's sudden outburst caught Jovi off guard. She looked at Isabel, who'd stepped up to the bed beside her.

"What do you mean, Grammie? What do we have to do?" Isabel adjusted the blanket over Grammie's legs.

Grammie tried to sit up, her eyes frantically scanning the room. "They're trying to steal things from me."

Dread washed over Jovi. "Who is trying to steal?"

"You know who." She lowered her voice to a whisper. "Don't say their names. But we have to stop them. It's so important."

Isabel set her purse down, then slipped off her coat and draped it over the arm of the recliner near the window. "Can you tell us what you're looking for? Maybe it's been misplaced. Jovi and I have plenty of time. We can look around."

Grammie shook her head, her eyes darting around the room. "No, no, no. They took it. They've been taking things from me for years, but I've never been able to catch them. Now they're planning something. I know it."

Jovi exchanged another worried glance with Isabel. Mom and Dad had mentioned that Grammie had been exhibiting paranoid behavior for the past few months.

Jovi clasped Grammie's hand between both of hers. "We believe you, Grammie. Do you remember anything else about the person who took it this time?"

Grammie's eyes filled with tears. She looked away, her gnarled hand trembling as she reached for the intertwined gold hearts dangling from her necklace that Grandpa had given her years ago. "Someone I trusted," she whispered. "Someone I never thought would do such a terrible thing."

Her eyes drifted shut. Jovi stood at the bedside, staring in disbelief as Grammie began to snore.

"Wait. No." She nudged Isabel with her elbow. "Do something. I still have questions."

Isabel gave a helpless shrug. "You're the nurse. I—I don't know what to do. Waking her up usually doesn't help, though. I've learned the hard way that she'll likely be confused and extra irritable."

Jovi blinked back tears. Poor Grammie. Even if what she'd said wasn't entirely true, how frightening to keep reliving the same terrible scenario over and over. She sniffed then leaned down and pressed a gentle kiss to Grammie's soft cheek.

"I love you, Grammie. I'll be back soon," she whispered. Turning away, she trudged after Isabel toward the door. This was heartbreaking. Even if she couldn't do anything about Grammie's dementia, she had to figure out what went wrong between her and Lois all those years ago. Maybe discovering the truth would finally bring their families some peace.

Who would steal from Grammie?

Isabel shivered, then sidestepped an icy patch in the parking lot of the warehouse in Anchorage. When they'd moved her to Oasis, they had intentionally kept most of her valuables in Evergreen at Mom and Dad's house. There wasn't much of value in her tiny apartment, so Grammie's paranoia didn't make any sense.

Beside her, Jovi pushed the shopping cart across the lot, carefully navigating the snowpacked ground in the semidarkness. Bright lights from the overhead poles cast a silver-blue glow over their path. The crisp air swirled around them, carrying a hint of car exhaust. Isabel walked beside her sister, carrying two disposable cups full of soda. They'd just eaten pizza at the food court before they'd shopped, and then she had rushed Jovi out of the store, eager to get back to Evergreen. Fatigue dogged her steps, and a headache pressed against her temples. She wasn't sure she could stay awake for the next two hours. Hopefully the caffeine in Jovi's soda would keep her alert.

"Good call buying vanilla extract and sugar here," Isabel said. "Jerry's right. It's much cheaper than our usual supplier."

"Really?" Jovi squeezed the button on the key fob to open the vehicle's hatch.

Isabel nodded as she handed Jovi one of the soda cups. "Yeah, and we're running low on both, so it's perfect timing. Like I said, we try to stick with locally sourced ingredients whenever possible, but for staples like this, we can't beat the competitive pricing of a wholesale place."

Jovi nodded as they loaded the groceries into the back of their SUV, their breath fogging in the cold air. As they got back into the car, Jovi turned up the heat and rubbed her hands together.

"Are you okay to drive?" Isabel asked, noticing the exhaustion in Jovi's eyes.

"Yeah, I'll be fine." Jovi took a long sip of the soda. "I can't get over what Grammie said about people stealing from her. Especially the part about how it's been happening for years. Who do you think she's referring to?"

Isabel shrugged. "Who knows? She's been saying ridiculous things since Grandpa died. Unless she proves that something specific is missing, I'm going to ignore it."

Jovi sucked in a breath. "How can you say that? She was… distraught."

Oh, here we go. Isabel took a sip of her drink and then shifted in her seat. "Jovi, you've been away for almost ten years. We're the ones who've been here caring for Grammie, running the business, and watching her slip away an inch at a time. Trust me, we can't just drop everything and chase a wild story every time Grammie concocts something new."

Heavy silence filled the car. Lights from the dash illuminated Jovi's crinkled brow. Isabel sensed she'd gone too far. But she wasn't about to apologize either. Sometimes her sister needed a hard dose of reality.

Jovi's grip on the steering wheel tightened, and she pressed her lips into a thin line. Isabel had always admired that Jovi had been the sensitive one, the one who cared deeply about others and their feelings. But Isabel was too exhausted to fall into the trap of letting Grammie's dementia ruin her day. She had enough issues of her own to deal with.

"I know you're trying to protect Grammie," Jovi said finally, her voice tight. "But I can't just ignore her. She was genuinely upset. Doesn't that bother you?"

"We're not ignoring her," Isabel said, trying to soften her tone. "This is what dementia is like. I'm sure you've worked with patients who suffer from this condition. Later tonight, or tomorrow, or next week—whenever you see her again—she won't remember what she said. So for the sake of your own mental health, don't let her paranoia consume you."

Jovi sighed and shook her head. "I guess you're right. It's just hard to see her like this. And I can't help but wonder if this is all linked to that missing recipe and her falling-out with Mac and Lois. I'm going to have breakfast with Walker tomorrow. Allegedly he has a juicy story to share."

"Oh, dear. Well, Walker has always had a knack for exaggerating his stories, and he's probably not real happy with us right now. You know Jerry had to let his grandson go, right?"

"Why?"

"He wouldn't show up for work. Kept coming in two hours late or not at all." Isabel reached over and squeezed Jovi's shoulder. "I know you want to get to the bottom of what happened between our families. We'd all like to hear the truth. But..."

Her phone chimed in her purse. Isabel shoved her soda into the cup holder. "What if that's Mason?"

She dug through her bag until she found her phone, pulled it out and scanned the screen.

Hey. I came home to do some laundry and let you know that I'm switching to night shift effective immediately. 7pm to 4am Tuesdays through Saturdays. See you around.

See you *around*? Around where? They weren't casually dating. He was her husband. Anger and confusion surged through her veins.

"Any news?" Jovi asked.

Isabel's hands shook as she reread the message. "He's switching to nights without asking me."

Jovi eased the car out of the crowded parking lot. "Mason?"

"Yes." Isabel blinked back tears and dropped her phone in her lap. "He sent me a text saying he's going to start working nights, and he only came home to do some laundry. No *I love you* or *I'm sorry about our fight*... It's like we're roommates or something. How could he do this?"

"Maybe there's more to the story. We won't know anything until you talk to him. What if there's a good reason for this? Is the Department of Transportation short-staffed? They might need more people to work nights to keep up with snow removal or something."

Isabel wiped away a stray tear. "I—I don't understand. We fought, but is this his way of punishing me? Or is he just so selfish that he didn't even think to discuss this with me? We're supposed to be a team, and yet here I am, completely in the dark."

Jovi nodded. "I get that it doesn't make sense now. Maybe he's just going through something and doesn't know how to put it into words."

"Night shift." Isabel shook her head, still in shock. "That means he's going to sleep when I'm at work. We'll hardly see each other. Maybe that's why he did it."

"Isabel." Jovi's voice carried a note of warning. "Don't do this."

"Don't do what?"

"Assume the worst when you haven't even talked to him yet."

Isabel sighed. Jovi was right. But it was hard not to. Making a major change in his work schedule without asking her was a caution flag. A giant warning sign that they'd grown further apart. Was Mason trying to tell her that he had given up?

Early Saturday morning, Burke circled the crowded lot at the elementary school, searching for a place to park.

Darby Jane sat up straighter, trying to see over the dashboard. "There isn't school today. Why is it so crowded?"

"Folks want to see the dogsled race, I guess. It's a big deal. The teams are on their way through town, racing as fast as they can to get to Nome." Burke slowed to a crawl, scanning the rows of cars on his left and right. "Evergreen is an important checkpoint for the mushers. It means they're halfway to the finish line."

At least that was what he'd gleaned from a quick internet search. Other than a brief glimpse of the race on the news over the years, he'd never paid attention to dogsledding.

"Oh, look, Daddy, there's a spot." She pointed. "Get it. Quick!"

Had she heard anything he'd said about the dogsled race?

Squelching his irritation, he followed her tip. Sure enough, one open spot remained at the end of a row in the farthest corner of the parking lot. It would be a cold walk to the place designated to watch the race, but if he didn't park soon, he was afraid they'd miss meeting up with Jovi.

And he wasn't about to let that happen.

Besides, he'd planned for this. They'd bundled up and put on three layers of clothing to combat the subzero temperatures.

"I've seen pictures, and I think dogs are scary," Darby Jane said emphatically. "But I still want to see the race."

He paused, eased the truck into the opening between two SUVs, then cut the engine. "Make sure you have your hat and your gloves and those hand-warmer things I bought online for us."

"Yep, got it." She opened the squeaky door and hopped to the ground.

He pocketed his keys, grabbed his insulated mug filled with coffee, then slid his aviator sunglasses into place and climbed out of the cab. Winter sunlight reflected off the snow. A brilliant blue sky stretched overhead. In the distance, the snow-covered peaks of the Alaska range filled the horizon. Cold air nipped at his cheeks. He set his coffee on the hood of his truck and tugged his beanie down over his ears.

Darby Jane hopped up and down, singing a song he couldn't identify. The fringe of her pink and purple scarf flopped against her jacket. If only he could harness half of her energy. Maybe he wouldn't feel like death warmed-over. Staying up writing until the wee hours of the morning, desperate to meet his deadline, had robbed him of too much sleep.

Burke snatched his mug from the hood, then angled his head toward the line of people trekking across the parking lot toward the street. "Come on, sweetie. Let's go."

"What about Miss Jovi? Is she still coming?"

"She said she would." Burke braced his hand on her back and guided her around a slick spot. "I'm sure she'll keep her word."

"How many dogs will we see? Aren't they going to get hungry? Who feeds them?"

Darby Jane kept firing off questions faster than he could answer. He tried to listen patiently, but his mind kept wandering to Jovi and how she'd react when they met Walker for breakfast later at the diner.

"Daddy, there she is." Darby Jane tugged on his jacket sleeve. "I see her."

Jovi stood on the street corner by the bank, hands tucked in the pockets of her jacket. Her navy blue knit hat sported a fluffy faux fur pom-pom. Adorable leopard-print sunglasses shielded her eyes, and she had the same scarf she'd worn that night they kissed draped around her neck.

A pleasant warmth spread through his chest.

"Miss Jovi. Over here!" Darby Jane called out and waved.

"All right, all right." Burke chuckled. "Take it easy."

His words were as much for Darby Jane as himself.

She spotted them and smiled. His pulse tripped, stumbling over itself, as his legs propelled him across the street. It had been far too long since he'd seen her. Heard her laugh.

"Hey," he said, stopping in front of her. Man, she was so beautiful it almost hurt to breathe.

"Hey, guys. Are you ready? I haven't watched the race in ages." She gestured with one mittened hand toward the people walking in groups. "Come on, let's go find a place to stand with a great view."

No need. Already found it. He forced himself to look away.

"I'm glad you dressed warm. Thirty-five below zero is no joke, right?"

Darby Jane slipped her hand into Jovi's. "How do the dogs stay warm?"

Burke hesitated, waiting for Jovi to pull away and put some distance between them. Instead, she squeezed Darby Jane's hand tighter, swinging their arms in unison as they walked. "I'm not an expert, but I've always been told the dogs live for this race. It's what they've trained for, and their humans take excellent care of them."

Snow crunched under their boots, conversations ebbed and flowed around them, and a uniformed police officer rerouted traffic through the intersection to accommodate the pedestrians. Kids squealed and darted around the adults. A spontaneous snowball fight broke out, and Jovi inched closer to Burke, shielding Darby Jane between them. That was thoughtful, how she instinctively knew to protect the little girl. Darby Jane would probably have a meltdown if she got hit by a snowball flung by an impulsive boy.

Once they'd passed the line of buildings that composed the businesses on Main Street, they walked toward an open expanse of undeveloped land.

"The dog teams will race right by us." Jovi swept her arm in front of her. "The official checkpoint is about a quarter-mile west of town, but traditionally the people of Evergreen line up along the course here."

They managed to find open space next to the multicolored strand of plastic flags stretched between stanchions.

"Darby Jane, I want you to be close to the front so you can see, all right?" Jovi gently guided her forward.

"Thanks for meeting us," Burke said. "It's fun to hang out with someone who knows what's going on."

"Of course." She braced both hands on Darby Jane's shoulders. "You can't miss this."

Dogs barked in the distance, then a cowbell rattled. Darby Jane's face puckered. "What does that sound mean? Are the dogs coming?"

"Pretty soon." Jovi pressed up on tiptoes and craned her neck. "You'll hear them, don't worry."

Burke forced himself to turn and scan the snowy flat surroundings, instead of staring at Jovi. Even though they both wore sunglasses, he didn't trust that she wouldn't still be able to catch him.

Darby Jane leaned over the dangling flag barrier, trying her best to see.

Applause and cheering washed over the dozens of people lining the route. Had the whole town turned out to watch?

"Here they come. I see one, Daddy. I see the front guys!" Darby Jane looked up at him, her eyes wide with excitement.

Another dog team broke through the trees in the distance, only a few yards behind the leader. More cowbells rang, and the cheers and whistles grew louder. Burke slanted another glance at Jovi. An appealing shade of pink clung to her cheeks, and her full lips curved into a smile as she clapped for the mushers.

He couldn't deny how much he enjoyed standing beside her, catching a faint smell of her now-familiar sweet yet citrusy scent. The family beside them pressed in, forcing him to move even closer to Jovi, their shoulders touching now. Oh, how he wanted to put his arm around her and draw her close. Shield her from the cold. But it wasn't his place.

So he'd settle for letting the slippery fabric of their puffy jackets' sleeves whisper against each other. And maybe wish for the crowd to force them even closer together.

Someone with a megaphone called out the name of the first musher leading the pack into town.

"How exciting!" Jovi clapped faster. "I love it when a woman is leading the race."

Burke grinned, then released an appreciative whoop.

The musher and her sled zipped by, sending clumps of snow flying in all directions. The dogs panted, their pink tongues lolling, as they responded to the musher's verbal commands.

Darby Jane stepped back, retreating into the comfort of Burke's legs. It was quite the sight. Jovi had been right. A not-to-be-missed, unique experience. They sure didn't have dog-sled races in Charleston.

He fumbled for his phone. The traditional sport, its rich history, and the against-all-odds determination to reach the finish line inspired him. A few quick photos and some notes pecked out were all he needed to fuel his next writing session.

Jovi offered her hand. "Want me to hold your coffee?"

"Yes, please." Burke grinned, then handed over the mug.

Leaving himself a voice memo would be much easier, but he didn't want to share his observations about the event with Jovi. Or let her know he'd funnel this outing into his story. He tugged off his gloves. The cold air stung his bare hands. He quickly snapped half a dozen photos, then typed a short note into an email drafted to himself. Sometimes inspiration struck at the most unusual time. He couldn't afford to ignore these ideas.

As the mushers and their dogs raced past, Burke hurried to capture all the details before his fingers got too cold. The adrenaline-infused atmosphere, the determination of the mushers and the sheer beauty of the dogs working in perfect synchrony—all of it fueled his creative fire. He wanted to remember this day, not only for himself but also for the countless readers who would eventually dive into his story.

But as he snapped another photo, an unexpected wave of guilt washed over him. Should he tell Jovi that he intended to use all of this in his writing? As the race continued, he snuck another glance at her. Her enthusiasm was infectious, and he found himself drawn to her energy and warmth. It was as if they were the only two people in the world, surrounded by the exhilarating chaos of the race.

Darby Jane clung to Burke's leg, her small hand gripping his pants tightly.

"Daddy, can we get a hot chocolate after this?"

Burke tore his gaze away from Jovi and smiled down at his daughter. "Of course, baby girl. We're going to meet my new friend Walker at Trailside right down the street."

Darby Jane beamed, satisfied with his answer. But after the last of the mushers sped by and the crowd dispersed, Burke couldn't silence the voice inside him that longed for more than just sharing another meal with Jovi. Surely she sensed their undeniable spark?

To be honest, he yearned for deeper conversations. A genuine connection. She bent closer to listen to Darby Jane. The sunlight bounced off her golden hair, making it shimmer. When Darby Jane said something clever, Jovi's laughter echoed through the crisp winter air. And every time she smiled, his heart flipped in his chest.

The guilt nagged at him, pulling his attention away from the budding feelings he had for Jovi. He had to tell her about his intentions to use her family and their small business in Evergreen as material for his writing. Especially the parts inspired by their families' grievances. But he couldn't shake the fear of rejection or the possibility of ruining their newfound friendship. Besides, he hadn't even finished writing the book yet. And even though his publisher wanted to read the finished manuscript, that didn't mean they'd accept it. No need to borrow trouble.

Instead, he'd focus on the present.

They neared Trailside, and he waved to Walker, already sitting inside at a table by the window. Burke's mind raced ahead, anticipating the struggle of sitting close to Jovi in the crowded café. Battling his attraction to her as he tried to get Walker to recreate their conversation from the ski resort.

Gritting his teeth, he held the door open for Jovi and Darby Jane. He couldn't will his feelings for Jovi away, no matter how hard he tried. There was something undeniably special about their connection, something that went beyond friendship. But he couldn't let himself fall too deeply either. His heart was still way too fragile to risk another catastrophic loss.

Unbelievable.

Over the years, Walker had told some whoppers, but this story might be his most absurd. With a heavy sigh, Jovi pushed aside her empty plate and moved her coffee mug closer.

"So you're telling me that my sweet grandmother and Burke's feisty aunt Lois had a falling-out over a man?"

Walker nodded, a mischievous twinkle in his blue eyes as

he dragged his fork through the last remaining bits of pancake and syrup on his plate. "Yep, that's the gist of it."

"But that doesn't make sense." Jovi shook her head and then glanced at Burke. "How could they both have been married for so long yet have such a complicated history with Mac?"

A crevasse formed in Burke's brow as his gaze bounced around the table. Walker paused midbite, his eyes narrowing in hesitation. "There was definitely some unrequited love involved. Your grandmother had been head over heels for Mac, but he picked Lois to be his bride."

Jovi's heart pinched. Oh, Grammie. She must've been crushed. And she'd never said a word. Maybe because Walker wasn't telling the whole story?

"Daddy, this is boring." Darby Jane slumped in the booth next to Burke, her small frame nearly swallowed by the oversize banquet seat. "Can we go?"

"In a few minutes." Burke leaned in closer, his voice low and urgent. "Please finish your breakfast, sweetheart."

Jovi couldn't blame the girl for being antsy. She wanted to leave as well. Because she'd heard enough of Walker's mysterious claims. She shifted uncomfortably in the worn booth and scanned the crowded diner for any excuse to escape. Or find a voice of reason to refute this ridiculous notion.

Trailside's heavy door swung open with a creak, flooding the restaurant with a gust of wind and six new customers. Jovi glanced at their faces. They weren't people she recognized and they looked too young to have known her grandmother personally. The clatter of dishes grew louder as the teenage girl bussed the only empty table. How Walker had managed to secure his usual Saturday morning booth on race day was beyond her. She had to give him credit for saving their seats. They'd been able to order and receive their meals relatively quickly.

"Walker, were you at the dance at the community center

the night Mac left with Lois? Or did you ever hear or see Lois and my grandmother arguing?"

Walker sighed, setting his fork down on his empty plate. "Jovi, I know it sounds far-fetched and you might not want to believe this story about your grandmother, but I promise you, everything I've told you is true," he said, leaning back in his seat.

Jovi crossed her arms and raised an eyebrow skeptically. "You're right. It is hard to believe because I know she loved my grandfather deeply."

He wiped his mouth with a napkin, then grinned. His leathery skin crinkled around his eyes. "She did indeed. Dennis loved her as well. If you're wanting some sort of proof, you'll probably find that stashed somewhere. Like I told Burke, your grandmother saved everything."

Then why hadn't they discovered any evidence of the feud? Or located Grammie's salted caramel chew recipe? Jovi's skepticism grew with each passing second. "I don't know, Walker. Grammie never said a word about Mac."

Walker shrugged, unfazed. "Believe what you want, but I've got more to this story. You see, after Lois married Mac, your grandmother couldn't bear the loss. So she started making candy and cookies from Lois's recipes and selling the goods around town but took credit for herself."

Jovi gasped. "That is not true."

The older man's blue eyes filled with empathy. "Well, facts are hard to accept sometimes, I suppose."

He tucked his napkin under his plate, then pushed back from the table. "Thanks for breakfast. Hope you all have a real nice day." He reached over and patted Darby Jane's shoulder. "Be good, squirt."

"I'm not a squirt," Darby Jane grumbled.

Walker chuckled, his belly jiggling as he shrugged into his parka then moved toward the door.

As Walker left the diner, Jovi exchanged a bewildered glance with Burke. Her mind reeled from the outlandish tale. Grammie had always been so kind and loving. How could she have engaged in such deceitful behavior?

"Jovi, are you okay?" Burke's concerned voice broke through her thoughts.

"I don't know what to make of all this," she said. "Walker has always been known for exaggerating. Maybe he just got carried away this time. Or else he's bitter. His grandson just lost his job at the candy company, and it's no secret that he didn't like all the attention Mac received from his woodworking."

But deep down, she couldn't shake off the nagging feeling that there might be some truth buried within the layers of Walker's story.

Burke studied her, his eyes roaming her face. A pleasant warmth unfurled in her chest. There was no denying his rugged handsomeness. Or the unspoken tension lingering in the air. Yeah, okay, so she shouldn't be drawn to him, not when they stood on opposite sides of a messy conflict. But as he stared at her, she found herself torn between logic and her growing attraction toward him.

"Jovi," he said, his voice steady, "I know that was a bit of a wild tale, but what if Walker's telling the truth? And what if this information he's shared leads us to the rest of the story?"

She held his gaze and hesitated. Could she really trust him? Or would it only lead to more disappointment and heartache? They were both equally invested in uncovering the truth about their families. That had to count for something.

"You're right. We owe it to our families to find out the truth."

She'd start by searching through the rest of Grammie's belongings and visiting her again. Because she needed answers.

Chapter Sixteen

This couldn't be real.

Isabel looked at the fourth positive pregnancy test lined up on the bathroom counter. Then she pulled the box out of the trash and reread the directions. Lots of tiny print, but not much information about false positives. Maybe a quick internet search would offer additional guidance. Sighing, she tossed the box back in the trash along with the others. Four tests couldn't be wrong, could they? She didn't talk to that many people about pregnancy tests. Okay, so to be honest, she talked to zero people about pregnancy tests. But she'd never heard of four in a row being incorrect.

How? She sank down on the edge of the tub. How had she become pregnant? They'd been fighting so much when— Oh.

She pressed both palms to her flaming cheeks. Their weekend away at the resort.

Although it had ended with their painful disagreement while they'd been trapped in the gondola, she hadn't stopped to think about how their intimate encounters before their epic standoff might have led to pregnancy. A baby.

The one life change she'd feared had happened.

Tears pressed against her eyes.

She gulped back a sob. This was supposed to be a happy event. But here she sat in her bathroom, alone, alternating between shock and dismay. She couldn't be pregnant now.

They were hardly speaking. Yes, sure, Mason had made it very clear that he wanted to have a family. But she hadn't been ready, and they had finally agreed to take a break from discussing the subject because they were just getting more and more upset with each other. Neither of them were making any effort to appreciate the other person's perspective.

But now. Well, these test results changed everything.

She went and found her phone, came back to the bathroom, took a picture, and then swept all of the sticks into the trash can. She had to tell him. It wasn't something she could keep a secret, not with the way she'd been feeling. Last night during the meeting for the library's expansion, she'd almost fallen asleep. It had been so difficult to get out of bed and get ready for work this morning.

Jerry, Irene and the rest of her crew at the candy company would hold things together. Like they always did. Production had ramped up for the spring and summer demands. But now Jovi spent every spare minute trying to find that recipe. Not that it mattered. She still hadn't come up with a product they could test with focus groups. Time was running out, so any hope of convincing their parents not to sell was fading fast.

Oh, this was not a plot twist she wanted to encounter, but it was happening. There must be some sort of lesson she was supposed to learn from this.

Where was Mason today? She started entering his number, and when his name popped up, her finger hovered over the call icon. This really wasn't something she could tell him over the phone, but she certainly wasn't going to send him a text. She needed support. Encouragement. She needed to tell her family. But first she'd have to tell Mason.

Isabel took a deep breath and pressed the call icon. The phone rang once, twice, before Mason finally answered.

"Hey, babe," he said, his voice filled with weariness.

"Hey," she replied, her voice shaky. "Are you busy right now? Can we talk?"

There was a brief pause on the other end of the line. Was he still at Garrett's? Or had he moved back in with his parents?

"Yeah, I just wrapped up a meeting online, and I don't have to work until tonight. Is everything okay?" Concern laced his words.

She swallowed hard, trying to find the right words to say. "No, everything is not okay," she finally admitted, her voice trembling. "Mason, I'm pregnant."

Silence hung in the air. *C'mon, say something. Anything.*

"Mason, I'm pregnant," she repeated, her voice barely above a whisper this time. The silence on the other end of the line stretched on. Her heart pounded. She couldn't decipher his reaction. She knew how much he wanted to start a family, but she also knew how strained their relationship had become lately. Could he see this as an opportunity to reconcile? Or would it push them further apart?

Finally, after what felt like an eternity, Mason cleared his throat.

"Isabel... I don't know what to say. Are you sure?" he asked gently, as if afraid that even the slightest wrong response could shatter her fragile emotions. His hesitant voice provoked more tears.

She took a deep breath to steady herself before answering. "Yes, Mason. I've taken multiple tests. They're all positive." Her voice wavered, betraying her vulnerability. She braced herself for his reaction. "I understand if you need some time to process this," she whispered, struggling to keep her tears in check. "I just thought you had the right to know."

"No, no." There was a pause before Mason's voice came through the phone, steady and determined this time. "Okay," he said firmly. "We'll figure this out together. We always do."

Oh, he was so loyal. A sob broke free. Tears blurred her vision. "I know."

"I'll be home in a few minutes."

She ended the call. Mason's words brought a surge of conflicting emotions: relief and fear all at once. They had been through so much together, but this news changed everything. Her mind swirled with doubts and uncertainties. This wasn't the way she had imagined their strained relationship mending. How would they navigate this new chapter as parents?

Soon enough, she heard the familiar sound of Mason's keys turning in the lock, followed by the creak of the front door opening then closing. His eyes found hers. Without a word, he crossed the room and enveloped her in a warm embrace.

She melted into his arms. Clung to him, seeking solace in his familiar presence. Oh, how she needed him. Wanted him. Desperate for the sense of comfort and security he'd always provided. Was the love they shared still there, buried beneath layers of miscommunication and unresolved conflicts?

"Are you okay?" Mason murmured, pressing a gentle kiss to the top of her head.

"I'm scared," she admitted, her voice trembling. "Scared of what this means for us."

He pulled back slightly to look into her eyes, his gaze filled with tenderness. "I'm scared too. Your miscarriage was tough for both of us. We'll take things one day at a time. And you're going to be an amazing mother."

His eyes drifted to her lips. Then he leaned in and claimed her mouth with his.

Their kiss was filled with a mixture of passion and reassurance. Her worries and doubts faded, and she relaxed into his touch.

When they broke away, both breathless and flushed, Mason caressed her cheek with his thumb. "We may not have planned for this, babe," he murmured, his voice filled with sincerity, "but that doesn't mean it's not meant to be. We'll face whatever comes our way, together."

"I know." She sniffed, then slid her arms around his waist and rested her head on his chest. "So what was your meeting about?"

He hesitated, and his breath hitched. The small circles he'd been tracing with his palm on her low back slowed. "I was speaking with the hiring manager in Juneau. He offered me the job."

Add shed access to his list of reasons to justify buying that snowblower.

This morning, Burke had used the nifty device to carve a clear path through the towering snowbank to Mac and Lois's shed. He inserted the key Charlie had given him into the padlock and turned it, feeling a satisfying click as it loosened. With a strong push, he swung open the metal door. It creaked loudly in protest. He grabbed the first thing he saw—an old vacuum cleaner—and propped the door open. Darby Jane had gone home after school with a friend, but he expected her back soon and didn't want to miss her arrival. She'd be upset if she went inside the cabin and he wasn't there.

Inhaling deeply, Burke took in the earthy scent of dirt and sawdust that permeated the air inside the shed. Then he fumbled around on the wall until he found a light switch. When he nudged it, two fluorescent lights flickered overhead. Wow. He surveyed the sturdy building's interior. Charlie and Denise had accurately assessed the situation: stuffed to the gills. Stacks of cardboard boxes, plastic crates filled with books and discarded small appliances claimed nearly every inch of space. Burke put down the space heater he'd carted over from the cabin, found an open outlet on the wall and plugged it in.

"Please, please work," he whispered, then tapped the power button. The device clicked and groaned, but soon the coils glowed orange and hot air warmed his skin.

"Excellent."

Through the shed's windows, the sky had turned brilliant shades of pink and lavender, announcing another late February sunset with glorious fanfare. It was a balmy twenty degrees below zero. Even though he wore a T-shirt and a sweater under his coat, he relished the idea of shedding at least one of his layers.

Shouldn't you be writing?

He mentally squashed his nagging conscience. So he had eighteen days to write forty thousand words if he wanted to meet his deadline. Concerning, but doable. Especially now that he'd figured out how to use voice to text to dictate most scenes, and his wrist didn't ache every time he typed. Besides, his conversation with Jovi and Walker at Trailside three days ago still pinged around in his head. She hadn't been nearly as impressed with Walker's revelation as he'd hoped. Her skeptical reaction had really thrown him. Especially the part about how Walker might have an agenda, given his jealousy over Mac's woodworking prowess and his relative's job loss.

The tension between the Wright and Phillips families over Mac's choice to marry Lois instead of Carol seemed ridiculous, yet it wasn't uncommon for old wounds to resurface and ignite into full-blown feuds. He had witnessed firsthand how something as trivial as a family heirloom could tear relatives apart.

But reminiscing about past conflicts back home did nothing to help him in this current predicament. Did Mac and Lois have any secrets hidden away here that could prove Walker wrong?

Woodworking was clearly Mac's passion, judging by the lathe

and collection of hand tools. The beautiful bowls on the shelves caught Burke's eye, but he couldn't shake off the feeling that there was something more hiding in this workshop. He examined a few half-finished projects abandoned on a table near the window. Was there still unfinished business simmering between the two families? Mac had passed away in his sleep nearly five years ago, so it made sense that things were still kind of how he'd left them. Or how Burke imagined he'd left them. Guilt pinched his insides. He should have come back to visit more often. If his mother had maintained a more meaningful relationship with her older sister, would he even be dealing with this right now?

Stop.

He raked his hand through his hair. Lamenting past mistakes did nothing to help make progress.

Warmth from the space heater made the shed quite toasty. He shrugged out of his jacket and draped it over a metal stool. Denise and Charlie had done a passable job of boxing things up and stacking them in a haphazard tower in the middle of the floor. Someone had scrawled generic terms on the outside, hinting at the contents.

Burke sighed. He still had boxes of his own in the cabin to unpack. He wasn't the least bit interested in pawing through his late aunt and uncle's possessions. But what if information he needed to resolve the feud and make space for a relationship with Jovi was somewhere in this shed?

Snow crunched under tires as a vehicle pulled into the driveway.

Uh-oh. Was it five fifteen already? How had he lost track of time?

He walked to the shed's entrance and peered out. A car had pulled into the narrow driveway in front of the cabin. Its headlights sliced through the darkness and illuminated the fat wet snowflakes falling from the evening sky. He let out a resigned sigh. So much for having a clear driveway. This looked like the kind of snow that could pile up.

A car door slammed, then Darby Jane ran toward him, clutching her backpack. He waved in the general direction of the driver.

"Hi, Daddy!"

"Hi, pumpkin." He pulled her in for a hug, smiling at the snowflakes clinging to her hair. "How was your day?"

"Good, except I had to come home early because Olive has to go to her piano lesson now."

"Ah." He straightened. "Makes sense."

"Oh, what is that?" Darby Jane dropped her backpack on the floor and squeezed past him.

Ugh. He'd meant to throw a blanket over that thing before she came home. Too late now.

"I think it's a dollhouse."

She stood in front of Mac's workbench, her eyes fixed on the intricately carved two-story house sitting beside some tools. "But where are the dolls?"

"Maybe the person who was supposed to receive the dollhouse has her own dolls."

Darby Jane stared up at him, her brow furrowed. "Who is this for?"

"I don't know." Burke shrugged. "Uncle Mac passed before he could tell us, I guess."

"That's sad." She tugged at one end of the wooden structure. It didn't budge.

"It's heavy, sweetie."

"Then, how can I see inside?"

"Just peek in the window or open that little door on the end there." He glanced around then nudged a step stool closer to the workbench. "Here, climb up so you can get a better look."

She scrambled up the two steps, then leaned in. "Wow, can we take this to the cabin, please?"

"No, we shouldn't. I'll have to ask around town and see if anybody knows if it was for someone special. It's quite fancy."

"But there's stuff in here. Maybe the papers say who it's for."

His stomach tightened. "Papers?"

She pointed. "They're in there, but I can't reach."

Straining, he leaned around the other end of the dollhouse and peeked inside. Sure enough, a stack of large note cards sat wedged next to a miniature staircase. He pulled them out, gently blew off some dust, then scanned a note paper-clipped to the first card.

His lungs compressed. "The note says this dollhouse is for the Wright girls to enjoy and share with their families someday, and the cards are recipes."

"Cool. Can we make something?"

"Not right now. These are for candy."

Darby Jane clapped her hands. "I love candy. Do we have any?"

He forced a smile, then ruffled her hair. "Come on. Let's go inside. We have some leftover lasagna and chocolate chip cookies. No candy, though."

"That's okay. Cookies are good."

Holding the recipes for safekeeping, he unplugged the heater, turned off the lights, then locked the door and followed Darby Jane back to the cabin. His mind raced, only half listening as she told him all about her playdate and how they'd decorated suncatchers or something and played dress-up. Maybe that explained the excessive amount of makeup she still had on her cheeks.

Inside, they took off their boots and hung up their jackets. "Please wash your face and hands, and get ready for supper."

As Darby Jane skipped into the bathroom, humming a song, he paused and flipped through the stack of ten recipes. Peanut butter, molasses, honey and root beer were the most common ingredients featured on the cards. Nothing with caramel, though. The slanty cursive looked like his aunt Lois's handwriting. At the top of each card the words 'Evergreen Candy Company' had been printed in dark green letters. A small logo featuring three evergreen trees filled the lower left corner of each recipe card. Tucked between the last two cards, he found a photo of Lois and Carol, smiling and standing side by side wearing nice dresses. Burke flipped the photo over. He squinted. *New Year's Eve, 1960* was written in faded ink.

He set the recipes aside and pulled his laptop closer. His head spun. An idea for a new scene in his novel bubbled up. He couldn't think too hard about what this meant. Otherwise he'd talk himself out of it. But his deadline loomed, and he'd learned to trust his gut when a new idea started brewing. Burke hesitated. Had he just discovered the evidence needed to support part of Walker's story? Were these recipes the originals that Carol and Lois used when they'd been in the candy business together? But why were they stashed in a dollhouse Mac had built and labeled for Isabel, Jovi and their families? He started typing again, his imagination crafting a new scene faster than he could enter the words into his computer. Darby Jane needed supper soon, so he didn't have much time before he had to stop and reheat the leftovers. As he added another paragraph and the story unfolded, adrenaline surged through his veins. Finally. He'd captured the story's elusive essence. Readers were going to love this.

Thoughts of Jovi's skeptical expression as she'd listened to Walker over breakfast at the diner flitted through his head. Burke paused, his fingers hovering over the keyboard. He'd tell her about what he'd found. Soon. But first he had to get these words down.

Grammie was *not* the jealous type.

Jovi hadn't been able to move past her conversation with Walker and Burke. The implication that Grammie and Lois might've behaved badly because they both loved Mac was so unsettling. Inside the cabin's primary bedroom closet, she lifted the lid from a cardboard box that used to hold fruit. The faint smell of moth balls and old paper greeted her. She sorted through a stack of patterns for doll clothes, an unopened counted cross-stitch kit, and some neatly folded fabric remnants. A large photo album sat at the bottom of the box.

"Bingo." Jovi pulled it out, and the sunlight filtering through the bedroom window hit the faded gray cover. The corners were frayed, and the edges rubbed smooth from years of handling. As she gently opened the album, the spine crackled. The black ink captions written in Grammie's flowery cursive scrawl had faded some, but the pictures were still visible in muted colors and sepia tones. Her fingers brushed against the clear, slick page protectors as she slowly turned each page, the plastic slightly cold against her skin.

Most of the photos featured her dad. Like typical parents of an only child, Grammie and Grandpa had diligently documented his childhood. Jovi smiled as she flipped through the pages and watched her dad's progress from early elementary school through his high school days. It was like a highlight reel of his life as an athlete in Evergreen. She'd known he played a lot of sports but had never realized the extent of his success. Between hockey and basketball in the winter and baseball in the spring and summer, Dad had racked up trophies and medals several years in a row.

She smiled at their family photo posed in front of the candy company. Her dad looked to be about fifteen then. The rest of the album featured postcards from field trips they had taken to amusement parks in California, another to Yosemite, and four whole pages devoted to their visit to Mount Rushmore.

Another two-page spread had been devoted to the candy company's best-selling products. Judging by Grammie's outfits, this must've been back in the late nineties. Jovi vaguely remembered one of the sweater sets and slacks Grammie wore in the photos as her frequent Sunday morning outfit. Jovi squinted and leaned closer, studying each of the products' containers and labels. A carefully preserved newspaper clipping proudly documented the release of the iconic rose-hip jelly. So Grammie didn't mind devoting a page or two to her accomplishments. Or had she taken credit for something that wasn't even hers?

Jovi's gut cinched tight.

Oh, Grammie. If only you could tell me the truth.

She traced her fingertips around the plastic overlaying a photo of her grandparents exchanging a kiss. They stood beside a table, maybe at the church, Jovi couldn't be sure, featuring an array of products from the candy company. Every photo that she found of her grandparents together with her dad, they all looked happy. Content.

As Jovi examined photos of her grandparents, conflicting emotions flooded her mind. On one hand, they looked so happy and in love, standing beside a table filled with treats from their family business. But she couldn't shake the feeling that something was off. She had always believed that her grandmother's radiant smile was genuine, but what if it was all just a facade? And her grandfather, whom she had always idolized, did he really never feel like he came second to Mac Phillips? The photos that had once brought comfort now left Jovi questioning everything she thought she knew about her family.

What was she supposed to do now?

With a heavy sigh, she closed the album, then flipped it open again hoping to find something that would ease her troubled mind. But all she found were more familiar photos and mementos. No secret recipes or hidden messages.

A muffled knock at the front door interrupted her mission. She left the album on the bed and walked down the short hallway, through the kitchen and over to the door. She peeked out the window. Her sister stood on the porch. Jovi unlocked the dead bolt, then opened the door and welcomed her inside.

"Hey, this is a nice surprise. What's up?"

Isabel offered a tired smile. "I have news I wanted to share in person."

"Great. Good news, I hope."

Isabel shrugged out of her coat and hung it on the hook. "Yes. Mostly."

"Can I get you something to drink? More water?" Jovi gestured to the giant green plastic bottle with a straw her sister carted around like a beloved accessory. "I can make hot tea or coffee."

"Just more water, please." Isabel thrust the container toward her. "Thanks."

Isabel sat down on the couch and kicked off her boots then propped up her feet and stifled a yawn. "Sorry. I'm so tired."

"No problem. I'll be right back."

She refilled Isabel's water, poured a glass for herself, then grabbed a container of cranberry and white chocolate sugar cookies she'd brought home from work and carried them back to the living room. Isabel slumped in the corner of the couch with her head tipped back on the cushion.

"Are you feeling all right?" Jovi left the cookies on the coffee table, then handed Isabel her water and sat down beside her. The girl did not look well.

"I have an excuse for being exhausted," Isabel said.

"Uh-oh. Do you have mono?"

Isabel's eyes sparkled with amusement. "No, this isn't mono. Jovi, I'm pregnant."

Jovi gasped. "Really?"

Unexpected tears sprang to her eyes. She clapped, then leaned over and hugged her sister, rocking them both back and forth. "This is the best news ever!"

"Okay, okay." Isabelle chuckled and patted her shoulder. "Thank you. I'm glad you're excited."

"Oh, my. I get to be an aunt." Jovi pulled back, sniffling. "How far along are you?"

"I'm not sure exactly, but I'm guessing about eight weeks. I've had some weird cravings, so I took four pregnancy tests. They were all positive."

Jovi plucked a tissue from the box on the table, then dabbed at her face. "Okay, then. Never hurts to be sure, I suppose. How's Mason? He must be thrilled."

"He is." Isabel's smile faded. "But I have more news."

Jovi's stomach dropped. "I'm sure you're feeling extra cautious since you've miscarried before. Is the baby okay?"

"I haven't been to the doctor yet. That appointment's scheduled, though." Isabel hesitated, picking at her thumbnail. "Mason got a job offer in Juneau."

"Whoa." Jovi sucked air through her teeth. "That's a plot twist for sure. What are you going to do?"

"We haven't decided yet. He's been looking for a different job, and he said he wants to move, and we were starting to argue about it a lot."

"Yeah, you'd mentioned that."

"But now that I'm pregnant, he's feeling torn. So he asked the hiring manager for an extension to think about the offer. Now he has to let them know in two days."

Jovi swallowed hard. "That's soon."

"I came by because I wanted to talk about your plans. Since you don't have too many more weeks here, and if you and I both make plans to leave town, Mom and Dad will sell the candy company in a hot minute."

"Yeah, I know." Jovi rubbed at the tightness in her chest. "I have five weeks left on my contract. I could re-up for another thirteen weeks. The clinic has plenty of work, and the manager already asked me if I would."

"How do you feel about that?"

Images of Burke and Darby Jane filled her head. She quickly batted them aside. They couldn't be the reason she extended her visit. "I'm happy to stay another three months. But after that, I'll need to take a new assignment elsewhere."

"I understand." Isabel massaged her forehead with her fingertips. "Any idea where you might go next?"

Jovi reached for a cookie. "To be honest, I've kind of got my eye on this opportunity in Southern California."

"That sounds fun." Isabel's smile appeared forced. "If I figure out how to travel with a newborn, I'll come visit."

"That's sweet." Jovi hesitated, the cookie halfway to her lips. "I won't hold you to that. By the way, I've been meaning to tell you about the conversation Burke and I had with Walker the other day. He insists the reason Lois and Grammie stopped being friends was because Grammie was secretly in love with Mac, but he picked Lois instead. That caused a huge rift and they fought over who owned the candy recipes."

All the color drained from Isabel's face. "Seriously? That's what he said? Well, remember I warned you that we had to let his grandson go, and Walker has a reputation for stretching the truth. His recollections are like fishing stories—they just get bigger and more outlandish with time."

Jovi nodded and took a bite of the cookie. Man, that was yummy. She'd have to tell Jerry this was some of their best work. The moist consistency plus the perfect texture of white chocolate and dried cranberry made her want to reach for another. "I told Burke about Walker's tendency to exaggerate, but we all are so intrigued by this feud. I'd like to find proof of whatever destroyed their friendship."

"Here's the thing. We agreed you'd help come up with a product that would impress our focus groups enough to change Mom and Dad's plans to sell. Frankly, we're running out of time. I don't know if more research about the feud should be your priority right now."

"I know. But between the feud, that missing recipe, and Walker's suggestion that Grammie and Lois's friendship fell apart because of Mac... I can't move on with everything that's unresolved. Can you?"

Isabel offered a helpless shrug. "I really don't want to move, and I don't want the company to sell. But to be honest, Jovi, I love Mason, and our marriage comes first. I'm out of justifiable reasons to decline an offer."

Jovi's mouth went dry. She had always been the peacemaker in the family, the one who tried to keep everyone together. But now, as she sat there with Isabel, facing the prospect of losing their family legacy, a renewed sense of determination welled up inside her. "I'm going to find that salted caramel chew recipe, and it's going to be such a success that Mom and Dad won't want to sell even if you do move."

Isabel stared up at her like she'd lost her mind. It wasn't the first time her sister had looked at her like that and probably wouldn't be the last. But she wasn't giving up.

Chapter Seventeen

"Guess what?" Darby Jane's blond pigtails bounced as she hopped from one foot to the other in the middle of Jovi's kitchen.

Jovi and Burke exchanged amused glances.

"Tell me," Jovi prodded. "I need all the juicy details." Jovi slid a measuring cup full of sugar closer to the mixing bowl. "But while you're at it, I need you to climb up here and mix some ingredients. Can you help with that?"

"Yep." Darby Jane stepped up onto the stool.

"Hold on." Jovi quickly intervened and pushed Darby Jane's sleeves up to her elbows. They'd hand-sanitized thoroughly before they started baking sugar cookies. "Your shirt is so cute. I would hate to get flour or sugar on those ruffles."

Darby Jane's pink-and-white top had adorable ruffles on the cuffs, and she had a bow pinned at a jaunty angle on the top of her head. What a cutie.

"Thank you." Darby Jane tucked her tongue in her cheek and reached for the sugar. "Can I pour this in now?"

Jovi nodded. "Okay, where were we? You wanted to tell me about those boys in your class who tricked your teacher?"

Darby Jane added the sugar to the eggs and butter in the bowl. "They hid toothpaste in her Oreos."

Jovi grimaced. "Are you serious? What happened when she ate the cookie?"

"It was yuck." Darby Jane scrunched up her face and shook her head. "I thought she was going to be sick in the trash can."

"Oh, dear." Jovi looked at Burke, who sat at the table holding a cup of coffee.

He'd just taken a bite of a chocolate truffle she'd brought home from the candy company. "What's going to happen to the boys?"

"Big trouble," Darby Jane declared, stirring the ingredients together like a professional.

Burke cleared his throat. "There will be consequences. Maybe some in-school suspension or handwritten apologies."

"That's quite a prank," Jovi said. "Did you prank people like that when you were a kid?"

His cheeks turned red, then he cut his eyes toward Darby Jane.

Ah, a silent plea for a subject change. She bit back a smile. "I don't like pranks."

"Me either," Darby Jane said.

"Let's see. What's the next step?" Jovi slid the recipe card closer. "We need to—"

"Oh, wow," Darby Jane said. "These look like the recipes at my house."

Darby Jane's words made her scalp prickle. "What recipes at your house?"

Burke's sudden stillness only added to the confusion swirling in her body.

"We have recipe cards sort of like this." Darby Jane tapped her finger on the stained card. "The little pictures of the trees match. Daddy found them inside the dollhouse that was in the shed behind the cabin."

This didn't make sense. Why hadn't he said something? "You found a dollhouse filled with recipes?"

"Yeah, it's huge. So heavy Daddy can't carry it." Darby Jane let go of the spatula just long enough to spread her arms as far as they possibly could go. "And we found a stack of cards with fancy handwriting. It's cursive. The kind I can't read yet. There's a note and an old picture of two ladies too."

Her whole body trembled. Jovi turned to face Burke. "Anything you'd care to share?"

Guilt swam in his eyes. "There is a dollhouse in the shed."

"That tracks. Mac was a master woodworker. But that's not the part of the story that interests me the most." Jovi fought to keep her voice from rising. "You found a photo and some recipes that look like this?" She held up her grandmother's recipe for sugar cookies.

Burke's features had turned ashen. He managed a brief nod.

"There's a whole stack," Darby Jane said. "Candy recipes. Right, Daddy? I forget the names, but there's a lot. Miss Jovi, what's the next step?" She craned her neck to see the card.

A wave of betrayal crashed over her. How well did she really know him? Was he hiding something from her? The weight of suspicion pressed down on her shoulders as she fought to maintain her composure.

"Burke, we've talked about this. You do know that I'm looking for a recipe, right?"

"You may have mentioned that, yes. I didn't find any recipes for candy made with caramel, though."

"But you're well aware that our families have had some issues." She stopped before she revealed any more information than Darby Jane needed to know. Her fingers trembled as she tucked her hair behind her ears. His calm demeanor infuriated her. How could he just sit there, sipping his coffee, when she was on the edge of unraveling?

Burke stared down at his coffee. "I'm aware."

"So when were you planning to share that you had recipes that belong to my family?"

"Who says they belong to your family?" Burke's chin lifted. His steely gaze sparked with something that resembled doubt. Or maybe defiance? "They could be my aunt's recipes."

"Whose handwriting are they in?" Her voice sounded sharp. Accusatory. Not that she was even the least bit sorry, because he'd intentionally withheld the facts from her.

"Looks like it's Lois's."

"So are you implying that my grandmother stole your aunt's recipes?"

"I'm not saying anything for sure," Burke said quietly, his gaze locked with hers. "Your grandmother and my aunt are in the photo labeled 1960. Darby Jane's correct. The cards all have an Evergreen Candy Company heading and the same icon that yours have—three trees in a cluster. But I'm holding on to the recipes until we get this all sorted, since I found them on property that belongs to my family."

Jovi's hands clenched into fists at her sides. What was he saying? The candy company had been owned by the Wrights for three generations. "Maybe the recipes belong to my family since we started the candy company."

"Remember what Walker said? What if Lois came up with the original recipes and then your grandmother swiped them then made and sold the candy as her own?"

His words stabbed her. "You cannot be serious. You're withholding information because you think that my family is complicit in some sort of intellectual property scandal?"

"Those are your words, not mine, and I don't know what to think, Jovi. That's why I didn't tell you. The ingredients listed on the recipes are for hard candy. Ingredients you might still use in your products now. Molasses, root beer, honey. By the way, the note clipped to the recipes says the dollhouse is for the Wright girls and their families."

A mixture of anger and hurt simmered inside. "That's totally irrelevant. Besides, I don't want or need a dollhouse."

"Are we going to make these now?" Darby Jane tugged on Jovi's sleeve. "What's the next thing we put in?"

Burke shoved back his chair and stood. "I think we'd better be going, Darby Jane."

"Daddy, no." Darby Jane's eyes welled with tears, and her chin wobbled.

Jovi's heart ached. Poor thing. She'd been caught in the middle. "Why don't you go on home. I'll bring Darby Jane over when we're done."

Burke hesitated. "Are you sure?"

"There's no need to deprive her of the chance to bake. I told her we would do this together, so I want to keep my word. When she's finished, I'll walk her home with the cookies."

Regret filled Darby Jane's eyes. "I'm sorry that I made you mad, Miss Jovi." She looked at Burke. "Did I do something wrong?"

"No, sweetie. It's not your fault at all." She tried to keep her voice light and gave her a reassuring smile. Turning to Burke, she said, "I'll bring her over in about an hour."

He nodded tersely and brushed by her, his shoulders stiff and his jaw clenched.

"This is a grown-up situation, baby girl. We'll figure it out." He kissed the top of Darby Jane's head. "Be good. I'll see you soon."

He left without another word. Jovi stared after him. He'd deceived her. How could he accuse her family of stealing? And why was he so hesitant to share those recipes?

What had he done?
Burke paced the cabin, panic sluicing through his veins.

Why hadn't he coached Darby Jane not to tell anyone about their discovery? And how had she noticed the similar details on the recipe cards, anyway? He'd tried to be cautious when he'd removed them. Then he'd stashed the whole stack away in a cupboard and only gave them a second look when she wasn't around.

Not that it mattered now. She'd spilled all their secrets tonight, and he didn't know how to fix it. Thinking about the look on Jovi's face still made him wince. This wasn't how he'd wanted her to find out, and he couldn't blame her for being angry. He'd never intended to keep the truth from her forever. But after their conversation with Walker and his research about historic feuds in Evergreen, he'd needed more time. Time to investigate. Time to make sure that the Wrights hadn't stolen something from his aunt and uncle. This whole thing was so convoluted. Especially since he didn't really know if he could trust Jovi. She'd given him no reason to be suspicious. But what if the recipes had belonged to Mac and Lois all along?

Did he have a valid reason to claim them as his own? Did a recipe have a copyright? He wasn't about to get a lawyer involved or anything, but it seemed like there was more to the story than what he had discovered so far.

He massaged the ache throbbing in the center of his forehead.

He'd been so flustered by Darby Jane's revelation and Jovi's reaction that he hadn't been able to formulate a reasonable defense. Yeah, okay, so from her perspective he wasn't exactly surprised that she felt betrayed. His stomach cinched into a hard knot. He raked his hand through his hair. How could he uncover the truth and convince Jovi not to hate him?

Because that kiss had been nothing short of remarkable. Spontaneous? Absolutely. He'd invited her over on Valentine's Day, feeling absolutely wretched. But when she'd pressed up on her toes and kissed him, her touch made him feel like he could conquer the world. Then he'd spent the last month trying to devise clever ways to see her again. The anticipation of being alone with Jovi, even for a couple of minutes, had propelled him to action in a way nothing else had for months.

So why had he been foolish enough to throw all that away?

His phone pinged with an incoming DM. He glanced at the screen. The notification offered a snippet of a message from his mother. Burke hesitated. They'd traded voice mails and exchanged a few texts but hadn't spoken since he'd left Charleston. He wasn't sure he wanted to know what was on her mind. But he did love her. What if something unfortunate had happened? Part of him needed to know that all was well in her world. He opened the DM.

Darling,
I hope you and Darby Jane are getting settled. I still can't believe you moved to Alaska. Why haven't you sent any photos yet? I'm dying to see how the two of you look, no doubt all bundled up. It's been ages since I visited Lois, but I'll never forget how cold it was outside. Or how dark.

That reminds me...proceed with caution regarding the family that lives down the road. I believe the woman's name is Carol Wright. She and Lois had a terrible falling out, and if any hard feelings linger, well, I'd hate for Carol or her family to do or say something hurtful to our precious Darby Jane.

Love you to the moon and back. Send pictures, please!

Huh. Interesting timing on his mother's part. He'd answer her later. He put his phone on the coffee table and resumed pacing. A few minutes later, a knock sounded at the door, and he peeked out the window. Darby Jane and Jovi stood on the porch in the light. They both held reusable plastic containers.

With a shaky hand, he turned the knob, then opened the door. "Hi."

Jovi's guarded expression increased his unease.

"We brought cookies." Her voice lacked its usual upbeat tone. "You're welcome to keep both boxes."

"Oh, no thanks." He held up his palm. "You can keep some yourself. We'll never eat that many cookies."

"I will so." Darby Jane pushed past him, shoved the box at his chest, then quickly took off her coat and her boots. "Daddy, it was super fun. You have to try the cookies. They are amazing."

Burke eyed the box. They did look good. Thick sugar cookies with swirls of pink and vanilla frosting and generous sprinkles of coarse red sugar crystals tempted him.

"She did most of the work, so maybe she can share some with friends," Jovi suggested, her expression as ice-encrusted as the lake outside.

"Great. Thanks." He turned to his daughter. "Darby Jane, what do you say to Miss Jovi?"

"Thank you." Darby Jane smiled politely. Flour dotted the front of her shirt and she had a ring of something that looked like frosting around her mouth.

"She may have eaten a few too many cookies." Jovi frowned, then turned to leave. "I wasn't paying attention. Too distracted by your big news."

"Jovi, wait. Please."

She turned back.

"Daddy, did you tell Miss Jovi that you finished your book?" Darby Jane hung up her coat. "And that there's some stuff about her in it?"

Oh, no. Darby Jane's careless comment sent a jolt of shock through his body. *Wow, Darbs, you're two for two tonight.*

All he could do was pray for mercy as Jovi stared at him with a mix of disbelief and fury.

"Seriously? I thought you wrote domestic thrillers."

"I can explain," he said, barely managing to squeeze the words out before she silenced him with another dark look.

"Don't bother. I've heard enough."

"But there's a plausible explanation."

"Not one I want to hear." She turned and stepped outside.

He followed after her, tugging the door shut behind him. It was nearly thirty-five degrees below zero outside, but he'd suffer for a few minutes. They needed privacy. He couldn't afford for Darby Jane to hear another word he said to Jovi.

"I really thought we had a shot at a meaningful relationship." He gritted his teeth to resist shivering.

She paused on the cabin's bottom step and whirled to face him. "Yeah, me too. Which makes your deception twice as painful."

"I didn't mean for any of this to happen."

"That can't possibly be true." Jovi shoved her hands deep into her coat pockets. "If you didn't intend to keep secrets, then why didn't you tell me about the recipes right away? Or that you're writing a book about me?"

"I'm not writing a book about you," he insisted. "And I didn't tell you I'd found the recipes because we don't know who they really belong to. Yes, it appears Carol and Lois had a short-lived partnership selling candy. But we don't know exactly what happened or how their business dissolved. There's nothing wrong with looking out for my family's best interests. Part of me hoped that if I figured out what had really happened, maybe our families would call a truce. Then we'd be able to…"

He trailed off. She glared icicles at him, her breath leaving little puffs of white clouds in the cold night air. His porch light illuminated half her face in a yellow glow, hinting at her barely contained rage.

"Why did you move here, Burke? To root out dysfunction and save us from our petty small-town drama?"

He gritted his teeth. "You know why I moved here."

"I'm wondering if the real reason you're here is because you're still running from a scandal you've tried your best to conceal."

"How dare you." The words rumbled low in his throat, his

anger threatening to boil over. How could she accuse him of such a thing?

"I'm just saying, it seems like a convenient coincidence that you move to Alaska, settle into your aunt's cabin, all under the guise of making a fresh start. Especially given the well-documented scandal you left behind in Charleston."

Burke took a step closer. "What are you trying to say? Not too long ago, you acted empathetic. Told me people should be rooting for me. So what changed?"

Scoffing, Jovi bit her lip and looked away. "You're really something, you know that? You've been lying and manipulating me this whole time. How did I not see it?"

"I haven't been manipulating anything," Burke protested.

"Really? Because it seems like you had no intention of telling me about the contents of your book or the recipes you found until Darby Jane revealed all your secrets."

"That's not true. I was just waiting for the right time."

"When exactly was the right time? After I fell for you?"

He reeled back. Her words stung. "No, that's not it at all." Burke forced himself to calm down. He didn't want to fight with Jovi, but her accusations were unfair.

"Then what is it?" Jovi challenged, stepping closer to him again.

He took a deep breath, trying to control his temper before he said something he would regret.

The silence between them thickened as they stood facing each other in the freezing cold. Finally, he broke the tense stillness.

"I wasn't trying to hurt anyone. I just want answers."

"And you're willing to betray my trust to get them?"

"Betrayal's a bit strong, isn't it? There's no harm in protecting my family. Isn't that what you're doing?"

"Oh, how clever you are, Burke, twisting words to justify your selfish behavior." Her voice dripped with sarcasm. "I applaud your efforts. You almost succeeded in charming me and making me look like a fool. This is the third time a man I cared about chose not to tell me the truth. I'm sick of it, and I'm done falling for men who lie."

He winced. Man, he hated that she'd been betrayed twice before. Or that she'd lumped him in with her exes. "Jovi, I—" He reached out to touch her arm, but she shook him off.

"Leave me alone." She stormed down the driveway and into the darkness.

Despite the freezing temperature, sweat beaded on Burke's forehead. His breath came in short gasps, and his heart pounded against his rib cage. He clenched his jaw, trying to calm himself down.

Jovi's harsh words cut deep. He'd truly believed they had something special. Until she'd called him a liar. Just like the last two men who'd broken her heart. He had to make things right. His actions had been for the good of his family, but she couldn't see that. She probably never would.

"You are never gonna believe this." Jovi slipped off her boots, hung her coat up, then padded across Isabel and Mason's living room and flopped in the overstuffed chair beside the fire.

Her sister reclined on the sofa, her feet propped up, and her giant water bottle tucked in close to her side. "Oh, I don't know." Isabel stifled a yawn. "I've heard some pretty wild things lately."

"Darby Jane asked if she could come over. She wanted to tell me about the school play she'd auditioned for. So I asked her to help me make cookies. Burke came too, and he was eating a piece of chocolate and enjoying his coffee when Darby Jane lets it slip that they found a dollhouse in Mac and Lois's shed. Inside was a whole stack of recipes."

Isabel sat up. "You're kidding."

"I wish I was." She frowned. "Our conversation got a little heated."

Now that she'd had time to think about it, she wasn't exactly proud of the way she'd spoken to him. But she just couldn't look beyond the evidence: Burke had intentionally concealed the truth. What else was he not telling her?

"Are these recipes for products we sell at the candy company?"

"Darby Jane said the recipes are for candy. Burke said the ingredients on the recipe cards are likely some of the traditional ingredients we still use today."

Isabel sat forward, her eyes gleaming. "Do you think Burke has the salted caramel chew recipe?"

"I don't know." Jovi heaved a sigh. "I got upset. He's not real eager to hand over whatever he found."

Isabel's excitement morphed into disappointment. "He should at least give us the opportunity to look at them. Did he say why he hasn't been more straightforward?"

"He said there's a note that the dollhouse is for us, then he mentioned something about protecting his family's legacy and all that. But what about our legacy?" Jovi's pulse sped as anger surged through her all over again. "I'm angry with him for keeping those recipes from us because he said they're labeled with Evergreen Candy Company and the little trees logo. But he argued that based on what Walker told us, maybe the recipes originally belonged to Lois. He also said something about we don't know how their partnership dissolved."

Isabel's eyes grew shiny, and she sniffed.

Uh-oh. "What did I say?"

"Nothing. I'm just really hormonal and emotional. It's sweet that the dollhouse was meant for us. And I kind of hate that we're a new generation of Phillipses and Wrights, but we're evidently still fighting about the same old stuff."

And falling in love with people we can't have.

She clamped her lips shut. No way she'd share that. Besides, this wasn't love. Real love didn't include betrayal. Or sneaking around.

Her heart sank at Isabel's words. The weight of their family history, the legacy passed down through the generations, felt heavier than ever. To be honest, she longed for a different kind of love and connection. Something that seemed just out of reach.

"I know what you mean," Jovi finally admitted, her voice barely above a whisper. "Sometimes it feels like we're all just trapped in this endless loop, destined to repeat the same mistakes over and over again."

Isabel reached for her water. "I've been thinking about this a lot lately. What's the point of these family secrets and rivalries? It's like we're all clinging to this legacy that's slowly suffocating us."

Jovi stared into the crackling fire. The hands on the vintage clock Isabel and Mason had inherited from Mason's grandparents inched toward seven o'clock. She had to get going soon. Sabrina had invited her over to eat takeout and watch a movie. But she sensed there was something Isabel still wanted to say.

"I don't want to keep perpetuating this cycle." Determination laced Isabel's words. "We have to find a way to move forward and create our own legacy—one that isn't defined by secrets and bitterness."

"But how?" Jovi shifted in her chair and faced her sister.

"Well, Grammie's the only one still around, and she's not in her right mind. So as much as I hate to say this, Burke could be right. It's hard to untangle who owned what."

Jovi's stomach twisted. "No, see, that cannot be true. You honestly believe Grammie stole Lois's recipes and then opened a candy company?"

Isabel shrugged. "I don't know what happened, but in this case, Burke has a point. We don't know what happened or who the recipes belong to. What I do know is we only have a few more weeks to turn things around financially. Mom and Dad are not going to wait past the first of June. I'm sure they're about to receive an offer from the company in Germany. There's someone else in Switzerland who emails me once a week."

Groaning, Jovi squeezed her eyes shut.

"If there are two competing offers, there's no way we're going to be able to get Mom and Dad to decline them just because we think we might be able to find a missing recipe."

Jovi opened her eyes and pushed to her feet. "Isabel, why do I feel like you're slowly resigning yourself to the idea of selling?"

"I just…" Isabel sighed and drew a cozy blanket over her legs. "I don't want to sell the candy company, Jovi. I know how much it means to you, to our family. But this is exhausting. What if Burke is serious about his aunt's role in creating the original recipes? We can't afford a long, protracted legal battle with Burke and his relatives."

Jovi winced, then walked to the window and stared out. Isabel had valid points. Night had fallen, and the tree branches in the yard danced in the wind. The forecast called for another sixteen inches of snow overnight.

"I know. I just thought…" She hadn't told her sister about the kiss. "I thought things were changing between Burke and me."

"Changing in what way?"

"So we had this intense, spontaneous moment." Her cheeks grew warm just thinking about it. She turned and faced Isabel. "On Valentine's Day."

Isabel's brows sailed up. "You never mentioned that."

"I didn't know what to make of it. I instantly felt like it shouldn't have happened. And since then, we've just tried to be more like friends and neighbors. Darby Jane's a hoot, and if she needs help, I try to help, and I invite her to do things, but—"

"Oh my, this is all getting very cozy." Isabel's smile looked genuine for the first time in weeks.

"Yeah, well, nothing else will ever happen between us. Especially if he's going to be concealing crucial information. And did I mention he's included our family saga in his new book he's writing?"

Isabel's eyes widened. "I know it feels like he's being deceptive, but maybe he's just looking out for his family's best interest. Maybe he's figured out that those recipes, whoever created them, have value. Burke strikes me as a very intelligent man who respects his family's history here and appreciates Mac and Lois's legacy."

"But I'm still hurt and disappointed. I thought… I thought things would be different between us."

A car door slammed, and boots thumped on the porch, and a few minutes later, Mason stepped in. "Oh, hey, Jovi."

"Hi, Mason."

The energy in the room shifted. Mason and Isabel exchanged the kind of glances that made her feel like she needed to leave. "I'm going to head out. Thanks for listening."

"You don't have to go," Isabel said.

Mason pinned her with a long look that clearly hinted at the opposite.

She chuckled and squeezed his arm. "Don't worry. I'm leaving, buddy. Sabrina and I have plans." She put her boots back on, as well as her coat, then layered on her scarf and gloves and stepped outside. The cold air nipped at her. She tucked her chin inside her scarf and strode toward her car.

After she'd climbed behind the wheel and turned the engine on, her phone hummed. She hesitated, then pulled it from her pocket.

A long text from Michael filled the screen.

Basically, he had to choose between South Korea, Alaska, and a military base in California. And he wanted to know her preference.

Her heart squeezed. She had four weeks left on her traveler's contract. If only she'd come up with a delicious salted caramel chew by now. Then she could renew her contract to work for another thirteen weeks here. But that didn't seem realistic anymore, so maybe she'd head to Southern California next. Since Isabel was about to give up on their quest to keep the company in the family, and Burke had turned out to be a loser, why did she have to stay here? Grammie didn't know her anymore.

Before she could overthink it, her fingers flew over the screen and she responded to Michael's text.

I know that you have a child, Michael. That's not a secret you should've ever kept from me. I can't overlook that kind of deception. Please don't make any decisions about your future that include me.

In case he denied the truth, she attached screenshots of the woman's DMs claiming Michael was her baby's father. Jovi's heart hammered as she tapped the icon to send the message. Then she opened her app and looked at available positions. She could take a thirteen- or twenty-six-week assignment in Southern California starting right after Memorial Day. Rent was probably ridiculous, but she had money saved—certainly enough for her first and last month's rent and a deposit if she could find an available apartment.

Sighing, she rested her forehead on the steering wheel. She didn't want to see Michael. Or live anywhere close to him. But she couldn't stay in Evergreen either. And Burke's deception about the recipes had really taken the wind out of her sails.

Would she ever meet a man that she could trust?

"Do you want to wait for your husband?" Daisy, the ultrasound technician, wheeled her cart closer. "Or I can check the waiting room one more time to see if he's here."

Isabel lay on the table, the paper underneath crinkling as she shifted her weight. "No, that's okay. I know you have other people to see besides me. Go ahead. I'm sure he'll be here soon."

She'd left her phone in her purse hanging on the hook on the exam room wall. The lights were dim, and she stared at the ceiling, then wiped her slick palms on her leggings. Being here in this room brought back unfortunate memories of when she had had an ultrasound after her miscarriage.

Her mouth got dry, and her throat tightened. She felt tears pressing against the back of her eyelids. Oh, if only Mason were here, holding her hand, reassuring her. Just his presence would ease so much of her anxiety. What if something had happened to him? What if something was wrong with her baby? What if they couldn't hear the heartbeat? Her pulse raced and she blinked rapidly.

"Mrs. Truitt, are you all right?" Daisy's dark brows slanted. "Can I get you a sip of water?"

"No, my bladder's already super full." She forced a wobbly smile. "I'll be okay."

Daisy smiled, her eyes filling with compassion. "I have to be very thorough, but I'll also go quickly."

Isabel nodded, then drew a ragged breath and resisted the bizarre urge to grab Daisy's arm and beg her to wait.

"Do you have any fun summer plans yet?"

"Nothing planned. Lately I've been so exhausted that I can barely go to the grocery store without needing a nap," Isabel said. "Montana and Glacier National Park are on my bucket list."

"Oh, that sounds amazing." Daisy smiled. "My family has a cabin in Kalispell, and we spent a lot of time camping in that area when I was younger. It's gorgeous."

"I'd love to go," Isabel murmured.

"This gel's been in the warmer, so hopefully it won't be too much of a shock." She gently lifted Isabel's shirt out of the way, then draped her with a towel.

The aroma of the hand sanitizer Daisy had just applied filled Isabel's nostrils. Her stomach heaved. Oh, please, this was not the time to throw up.

Daisy paused and surveyed Isabel's face. "Are you sure you're all right?"

Isabel swallowed hard. "I'm fine. Just the nausea comes and goes."

"Oh, I remember. Morning sickness was all-day sickness for two of my three pregnancies." Daisy gave Isabel's shoulder a gentle pat. "As soon as this ultrasound is finished, Dr. Williams will speak with you, and then you'll be on your way, okay?"

Isabel managed a nod as Daisy squirted the gel for conducting the ultrasound onto her skin. Then she put the bottle back, jiggled her mouse on her computer and made what seemed like a dozen clicks. Isabel gritted her teeth, willed her galloping heart to take a breather, and focused on the transducer as it made contact with her rounded abdomen.

Please, please let everything be okay.

A knock at the door interrupted her silent prayer. Daisy stopped moving the transducer. "Come in."

The door swung open. Mason stepped inside. "Hey, sorry I'm late."

Tension between Isabel's shoulders loosened at the sight of her handsome husband. She offered a smile. "You made it."

"Come on in. You must be Mason. I'm Daisy. We're just getting started. You could stand by your wife if you'd like. Or grab a seat."

Mason came around to the opposite side of the table. Isabel held out her hand.

He clasped it between both of his, then leaned over and pressed a kiss to her forehead.

"Babe, this is going to be amazing." His breath smelled like spearmint gum. Stubble on his cheek grazed her temple.

"I'm glad you're here," she whispered, holding his gaze.

"Wouldn't miss it." His eyes flitted toward Daisy and the transducer. "How are you doing?"

"I'm a nervous wreck," she blurted.

"Oh, dear." Daisy gave her another empathetic glance. "This won't take long, I promise."

She guided the hand-held probe over Isabel's stomach. A rapid shooshing filled the room. "Hear that? It's your baby's heartbeat."

A sob broke loose. Tears trickled from the corners of Isabel's eyes. Mason thumbed them away. "You hear that, babe? A heartbeat."

Daisy sucked in a breath and removed the transducer. "Give me a minute, please. I'll be right back." She set the probe down on her cart and bolted from the room.

Isabel's chest squeezed. "What happened? Where's she going?"

"It's going to be all right. Just hang on, okay? You can do this," Mason said. "She'll be back as soon as she can."

Daisy returned with Dr. Williams. He stepped inside and closed the door. "Well, hi there, Mr. and Mrs. Truitt. What an exciting day."

He was all smiles, but Isabel could barely move. Terror turned her blood to ice.

"Let's see what we have here." He adjusted his wire-framed glasses, clasped his hands behind his back, then studied the computer monitor.

Daisy put the transducer back on Isabel's stomach and maneuvered it through the gel. The pressure gave Isabel something to focus on. She tightened her death grip on Mason's hand.

Rhythmic whooshing filled the room, louder this time.

"I'm thrilled to tell you that—" Dr. Williams hesitated and angled the monitor toward Isabel and Mason, "there's baby number one," he said, as Daisy moved the device around. "And there's baby number two."

"What?!" Isabel shrieked.

Mason went completely still.

"Congratulations." Dr. Williams grinned. "You're building two babies."

"That can't be," Isabel whispered. She looked at Mason. "Twins."

His mouth drifted open. Then closed. Then open again. "I—I need to sit down."

He collapsed, and the chair pushed up against the wall.

"Looks like you're about thirteen weeks along," Dr. Williams said. "The radiologist will need to see the report, and I'll have to sign off on it, of course. But I can confirm that there are two babies. Two strong heartbeats. Congratulations again, Mom and Dad. We'll be in touch."

Then he left.

"Wow. What a day, right?" Daisy smiled then gently toweled off Isabel's abdomen. "Let me print you some pictures."

Twins. Isabel couldn't stop the floodgates. Tears flowed. Mason stood and retrieved a box of tissues from the counter and brought them over.

"Congratulations, honey." His eyes glistened with unshed tears. "You're going to be an incredible mother."

"I'm not so sure about that," Isabel sobbed. She hadn't even been confident about having one child, and now she'd have two.

"Hey, hey. Listen." Mason cradled her face in his strong hands. "These babies are so blessed to have you as their mom."

She sniffed and wiped her tears with the tissues he'd brought her. They were going to have two babies at once. Thoughts of how much diapers for two must cost, endless nights with no sleep and the sheer volume of energy she'd have to muster to parent two kids at the same time assailed her.

Daisy quietly handed them the printed ultrasound pictures. "Here you go," she said softly. "Two beautiful little gifts."

Isabel took the pictures and studied them with wonder and

awe. The smooth paper displayed silhouettes of small humans, each surrounded by a circle of light. Undeniable proof of life growing within her.

Isabel managed a weak smile through her tears. "Thank you, Daisy. I just… I didn't expect this. I'm not ready."

Daisy patted her shoulder. "No one ever is."

Mason wrapped his arms around her. "I love you, Isabel." His voice was filled with determination. "We'll figure this out."

His warmth and strength, combined with his tender words, softened the razor-sharp edges of uncertainty slicing at her. He'd offered the same patient reassurance over and over these last few months, as they'd wrestled with their future plans.

"I love you too," she whispered, leaning into his strong embrace. Desperate to silence her doubts. The shock of having twins had caught them off guard. Could her body handle the physical demands of carrying two babies? Did she need to start looking for reliable childcare now? Was she supposed to quit her jobs?

The sound of Daisy's voice interrupted her thoughts. "I know this isn't exactly the news you'd expected," she said. "But I promise you, you're stronger than you think. And you have a wonderful support system here."

Isabel nodded, feeling a glimmer of hope amid the uncertainty. Daisy was right: they were not alone. They had their families, their friends and their faith to lean on.

Mason wouldn't want to leave Evergreen now, would he?

Chapter Eighteen

Burke felt like someone had forced his heart through a paper shredder.

He stood in the middle of the shed massaging his aching wrist. Yesterday's X-rays indicated that his fracture had healed. Finally. He was able to ditch the splint. Not that it mattered. He'd already slogged his way through writing forty thousand words to finish his manuscript and meet his deadline. And he'd pushed a little too hard today as he tore through Mac and Lois's possessions.

There had to be evidence of their ties to the candy company somewhere. A detail-oriented man like Mac who turned gorgeous bowls and created elaborate dollhouses from chunks of wood must've left something more substantial than a short note and a collection of ten recipes.

But what if Jovi is right?

Since their heated discussion outside his cabin, he'd come up with more questions than answers. What if Walker's version of the story wasn't accurate, and Carol had been the original creator of the candy recipes? And if Jovi was correct, had he sabotaged their relationship before it took flight?

Wow, what a sobering thought. Sadly, the notion had passed through Burke's mind on more than one occasion. He'd done his best to give it a mental shove every single time. If Mac and Lois felt they had a legitimate claim to the original candy recipes, then why did they leave them in the dollhouse?

Burke heaved a deep sigh. What a mess. He needed to find the truth, for Jovi's sake and his own. Determination rekindled within him as he resumed his search through the shed.

The plastic crates and boxes Charlie and Denise had stowed in the shed now sat in haphazard clusters. Burke had dug through almost all of them. He hadn't found anything related to the candy company. Most had been filled with paperbacks, Mac's woodworking tools and knickknacks collected over the years. Lois liked to write the date in her journals, but never made any entries. Burke had learned the hard way not to get too excited when he spotted a spiral notebook, because it was probably blank. Not helpful.

Burke sifted through the last three boxes methodically, hoping to stumble upon something significant. But there was nothing. His frustration grew, threatening to consume his resolve. He'd been out here for hours, desperate to uncover crucial details from his aunt and uncle's past. His wrist throbbed in protest, reminding him of his limitations. He ignored the pain. Darby Jane had another hour in school, then he'd have to leave to go pick her up. So he had to press on with his quest.

He turned in a slow circle, searching for any boxes he hadn't opened yet. Then he moved toward a dusty corner where an old filing cabinet stood. With bated breath, Burke tugged open the drawer, unleashing a cloud of stale air. Coughing, he riffled through folders and documents, growing increasingly disheartened with each passing second. If Mac and Lois had been involved with the candy company, it seemed they'd left no trace.

After bypassing folders full of old utility bills, bank statements and owner's manuals, he was about to give up hope. Until his fingers brushed against a rectangular envelope buried under a stack of papers. Intrigued, he pulled it out and scanned the names and addresses scrawled on the outside. The letter had been sent from Mr. and Mrs. Dennis Wright in Evergreen and mailed to his aunt at an address in Kansas. He squinted. The postmark had faded. He could just read the year: 1983.

Burke's pulse sped.

He flipped the envelope over. Its seal had never been broken. Burke hesitated. He turned it over again. As he held the unopened letter in his hands, doubt crept in. Should he open it or reach out to Jovi first? Her harsh accusations about him being deceitful and concealing his motives still echoed in his head.

He wasn't deceitful. Nor did he have ulterior motives in moving to Alaska. And oh, how he wanted to win Jovi's heart. Conflicting emotions battled inside him as he hesitated before making a decision. He'd found the letter in his aunt and uncle's shed, with his aunt's name on the outside. So didn't he get dibs?

Burke carefully tucked his finger into one corner, worked the flap loose, then removed the letter. A bead of sweat trickled down his back as he unfolded the aged paper, its edges yellowed. He scanned the faded block-print handwriting. The letter was from Dennis Wright. He wanted to end the feud and establish an agreement that granted Carol and his family permission to use a recipe to manufacture and sell a specific kind of candy. Burke kept reading. The details omitted the name of the confection, but clearly indicated Dennis's excitement about the creation of a product.

His scalp prickled.

The more Burke read, the clearer it became that there was indeed a connection between Mac and Lois and the candy company. The product Dennis alluded to in the letter sent adrenaline pulsing through Burke's veins. As he reread Dennis Wright's words, a sliver of truth emerged. He was inviting Lois and Mac to come back to Alaska and partner with his family to create this candy from her recipe. The exact ingredients weren't mentioned, but he seemed to believe the candy was something so unique and tantalizing that it could propel their family's company into unimaginable success.

So what had happened?

Burke's mind raced with possibilities. Was this somehow connected to the salted caramel chew recipe that Jovi had been looking for? That hardly seemed likely. And what was so precious about this candy that Dennis made the effort to respectfully ask Lois and Mac to collaborate?

His curiosity collided with his conscience. Had Lois been too angry and stubborn? Was that why she'd never opened the letter? She and Mac must've returned to Evergreen shortly after she'd received it. And she'd cared enough to pack the letter and bring it along. So maybe Dennis had floated his ideas in person once Lois and Mac arrived?

Except the feud clearly hadn't been resolved because Lois and Carol's friendship was never restored. He folded the letter, tucked it back inside the envelope, then left the shed. An icy wind howled across the lake, whipping up snow in frosty gales. He gritted his teeth against the wintry blast and strode across the yard to the cabin. For now, he'd stash the letter in his bedroom for safekeeping. Maybe revisit it later tonight once he'd had time to think. He had to reach out to Jovi and share what he'd discovered.

They both needed to know what this mysterious product was, why the letter had never been opened all these years and what happened between Mac, Lois and the Wrights once they all lived in Evergreen again. The unanswered questions pestered him like an itch that couldn't be scratched.

"The hidden recipes are the plot twist I didn't see coming," Danielle said, setting her disposable coffee cup on the table, then shrugging out of her jacket.

"It's unbelievable, really." Jovi shook her head as she claimed the chair across from Danielle at Alpenglow Espresso. It was the middle of the week, and thankfully not crowded. Which gave Jovi permission to speak freely.

Danielle had made last-minute arrangements and dropped her kids off at her mom's so they could meet and catch up. Exhaustion had twisted Jovi's emotions into a convoluted mess. She desperately needed her friend's help to sort it all out.

Worry carved twin grooves between Danielle's brows. "How did Burke react to finding the recipes?"

Jovi bit her lip. She felt like she had a lead weight sitting on her lungs. "He feels his family may have some claim to the original recipes, since we can't be certain my grandmother didn't use them to start the candy company."

"Yikes. Hopefully your family has retained a savvy attorney." Danielle glanced at her phone, then tucked it out of sight in her purse. "This sounds messy."

"And to make things messier, there's more than one offer on the table at this point. Because Isabel and I aren't willing to sell, our parents haven't accepted any of them. But to be honest, things aren't looking good. They gave us until the first of June to come up with a viable reason not to sell, and that's less than two months away."

"What if these recipes are the beginning of something wonderful?" Danielle's expression brightened. "Maybe you and Burke will work together to finally solve the mystery of your families' feud."

Jovi cradled her mug between her hands. "Doubt it. I accused him of ulterior motives. He denied intentionally deceiving me."

"Maybe you both need time and space to regroup."

Her throat tightened. Oh, she did not want to shed any more tears over Burke Solomon. She'd cried enough lately. Lost hours of sleep too. Why couldn't she put him out of her head? And out of her heart?

Danielle reached across the table and placed her hand on Jovi's sleeve. "Can I ask you something?"

"Of course."

"Do you want to keep the candy company? When you think about your future, do you really see yourself settling down here in Evergreen and running a business?"

Her traitorous mind projected a highlight reel of the time she'd spent with Burke and Darby Jane.

Yes. No. "I—I don't know. It's so mixed-up. *I'm* so mixed-up," she confessed, pressing her palms to her cheeks. "Sometimes I think I want to keep the candy company just because it helps me feel close to my grandparents and they are so special to me."

Empathy filled Danielle's eyes. "That's a valid reason not to sell."

"And then when I find out that my parents are considering competing offers, I'm heartbroken. Because I can't imagine some global entity or something running Evergreen Candy Company. They might be experts in developing the products, but it won't be a small-town, family-run operation anymore." Jovi slumped back in her chair. "They'll want to be uber competitive and they'll likely cut staff positions or even move operations out of Alaska altogether to save money. So not the vision I have, and not what Isabel wants either."

Danielle nodded. "Maybe the Lord has something else in mind, my friend."

"Maybe." Jovi took a sip of her coffee. If only she knew how to figure out what that was. She desperately needed His help to soothe her angst.

"The last time we hung out, you said you only agreed to be here for thirteen weeks. Where are we in the timeline of your commitment?"

"I have three weeks left, unless I reup for another thirteen.

And funny you should mention that." Jovi frowned. "Remember I was talking to Michael?"

Danielle's expression turned serious. "Tell me that's not still going on."

"Don't worry. We're not going to be communicating any longer. A woman slid into my DMs and told me that Michael is the father of her child."

"No." Danielle's reaction was so fierce that it drew curious stares from customers sitting at the next table. "You have got to be kidding me."

"Not kidding." Jovi picked at the cardboard sleeve on her cup. "I was shocked."

"Did you say anything to him?"

"At first I didn't know what to do. I thought maybe—"

"Jovi." Danielle shot her a warning look. "Tell me you didn't just let this go."

Jovi held up her palm. "Hear me out. I took screenshots of the woman's messages, but I wasn't sure how to respond. Our relationship is over. But then he kept texting me and asking my opinion on his next post, and I...got caught up in this fantasy that we'd get back together."

Danielle grimaced. "That's why I'm worried. Please, just block the man."

"I'm getting to that part. So I texted him, attached the screenshots and told him I couldn't move past that kind of deception."

"Yes." Danielle pumped the air with her fist. "That's better. Did he respond?"

"He admitted that he did have a child, and when I asked him why he hadn't bothered to tell me, he said he didn't feel like I needed to know."

"Oh, brother." Danielle rolled her eyes. "That's disappointing on many levels. I mean, why would you not tell your fiancée that you had a child? Do you think that's the real reason he called off the wedding?"

Jovi shrugged. "Possibly. I think the woman found him, and when she let him know that he was a dad, he panicked. So, needless to say, we will no longer be talking about his next post or reconnecting or any of it."

"Now you need to block him."

"Done."

"Good." Danielle's smile faded. "I'm so sorry you had to endure all that."

"Me too. I think it's time for me to put relationships on the back burner."

"Aww, not forever, I hope. I know you want to have a husband and maybe kids someday. Don't let Michael ruin this for you."

"Sadly, this isn't the first time a man has betrayed me. Before I met Michael, I dated a doctor who failed to mention that he had a wife. I'm just terrible at choosing men, Danielle, and I'm tired of getting hurt. It's so, so painful. And Burke's betrayal about the recipes is just salt in the wound."

"There are still good men out there."

"Eh." Jovi shook her head. "I'm starting to wonder if you and Isabel married the last two."

Danielle smiled over the lid on her cup. "That's sweet of you to say. Mason's a good guy, and I'm really thankful for my husband. You'll find someone if it's meant to be. God knows the desires of your heart."

"At this point, He's the only one who can make it happen," Jovi said.

The coffee shop's door opened, bringing a blast of cold air in, along with Walker. He worked his way toward her table. "Good morning, ladies."

"Hi, Walker." Jovi smiled at the older gentleman. "It's nice to see you."

He pulled off his green knitted beanie and squished it between his beefy hands. "Sorry to interrupt, but I was wondering how your grandmother's doing."

"She's all right. Thanks for asking. They had a nasty stomach flu run through her facility after the holidays, so I haven't seen her as much as I'd like. But I'm hoping to get to see her soon."

Walker nodded, then fumbled in his pocket until he retrieved a tissue. "Well, I know she has trouble with memories, but we've known each other a long time, so please tell her that Walker said hello."

"I'll do that," she said. "Thanks again for thinking of her."

He turned to go, then clutched the edge of a table nearby, and slowly turned back. "Say, Jovi, have you found anything yet?"

Jovi hesitated. She didn't want to tell him about Burke's discovery in his aunt and uncle's shed. "Nope. Not yet."

"Well, don't give up hope, sugar. Your grandmother kept track of everything. Photographs, postcards, newspaper clippings, things you and your sister accomplished at school." He chuckled, then patted her shoulder. "She had it all stashed away."

Yes, but where?

"You ladies have a nice day." Walker moved slowly toward the coffee shop's counter.

"Take care, Walker," Danielle said. When he'd moved out of earshot, Danielle leaned closer. "That was odd. What's he talking about?"

Jovi sighed. "Burke and I met with Walker, and he told us that my grandmother took Lois's recipes and started the candy company. He says she was upset because Mac and Lois fell in love and she wanted Mac for herself. I didn't believe him. Besides, I don't want to confront my grandmother. Mainly because I don't want to believe it's true, and it seems cruel to dredge up her past now."

"I wish I could help you," Danielle said. "Are you looking for a specific candy recipe?"

"The salted caramel chew was something she made when I was a kid. She said it was special, a treat she made just for friends and family. I thought it was amazing, and I'm still hoping to recreate it so we can sell it. So far my one and only attempt was lousy. Recipe development is not for the faint of heart."

"I know what you mean," Danielle said. "I have to read a recipe line by line, and even then, sometimes what I'm making doesn't turn out all that well."

Jovi wrinkled her nose. "Same."

"Sometimes I'm convinced that recipe developers leave stuff out on purpose just to make us mad."

Jovi drummed her fingertips on the table. "I really want to find that recipe. But I'm running out of time and places to look."

Danielle offered a gentle smile. "This might not be what you want to hear, but might I suggest that God is never out of time. He isn't late, and we can count on Him to provide what we need exactly when we need it."

Tears pricked Jovi's eyes. She blinked them back. "Thank you for the sweet reminder. I so need Him to show up. And soon."

Danielle's sound wisdom offered comfort and encouragement, yet doubt still threatened Jovi's peace. Her plan to find the recipe and stop the sale of the company with the iconic salted caramel chew seemed so hopelessly out of reach. Had all of her hard work been for nothing?

"Here. It's my latest attempt, and in my opinion, far better than the first batch." Jovi slid the platter of salted caramel chews across Mason and Isabel's table. They sat side by side in their cozy kitchen. Mason had one arm slung around the back of Isabel's chair. Her cheeks were flushed, her eyes weary. Growing two babies at once must be exhausting.

Jovi peeled back the plastic wrap, then stood behind her chair on the opposite side of the table. "Please, Mason, be brave."

"I'm sure they're great." He smiled and plucked one from the platter, then took a generous bite, chewing slowly. Jovi dug her fingernails into her palms, anticipation humming through her veins. She knew Mason would be kind but honest with his feedback. He chewed slowly, nodding.

Oh, nodding was good. Okay. He swallowed.

"Well? What do you think?"

He set the remainder down on a napkin then he took a sip of his water.

Jovi and Isabel exchanged worried looks.

"Please don't keep me waiting."

Mason held up one finger, then took another long sip of his water.

Oh, no. "What's wrong?" She gripped the back of the kitchen chair. Had she accidentally added too much salt? In the middle of making this batch, she'd spotted Burke and Darby Jane walking by her cabin, towing their sleds. Kids had gathered at a hill nearby, so they must've been on their way to join the fun. Regret had pierced her as she watched until they had walked out of sight. Then she'd been so distracted by what might have been between her and Burke that she'd second-guessed how much salt she'd already added.

"It's all right." He eyed the half-finished candy. "I wouldn't order a dozen or anything. But they are certainly unique."

"Definitely not five-star worthy, right? Or, like you said, something you'd want to order a batch of." Jovi picked up a chew and analyzed it like a chemist in a lab pored over results from an experiment. "There's still something missing."

"I like the caramel flavor," Mason said, infusing his voice with optimism. "It's not too overpowering. The salt on top has a nice texture."

"It should. It costs a fortune per ounce," Isabel chimed in.

She wasn't wrong. Jovi sighed and sat down. Defeated. "Who knew little flakes of salt could be so expensive?"

"Have you tried one?" Isabel asked.

"Oh, yes. Plenty. But I'm not an objective judge. If it doesn't taste the way I remember Grammie's tasting, then I'm disappointed."

Would she ever get over feeling that way? Had Grammie's chews been that tasty, or was she clinging to nostalgic memories?

"Here, I'll try one." Isabel took a bite, chewed thoughtfully, then set the rest back on her napkin. "It's all right. As Mason said, there's nothing wrong with it, but I'm not craving another one."

"Yeah, I was afraid of that. Okay, well, it's time for me to wave the white flag, I think, because I don't know what else to try. Unless I find Grammie's original recipe, I'm not sure what else I can do."

Isabel glanced at Mason. He gently squeezed her shoulder.

"What?" Jovi's gaze bounced between them. "What's going on?"

Isabel hesitated. "We received another offer. A highly competitive one. It's tough to turn this kind of money down, Jovi."

Jovi blew out a long breath. "I know. Mom sent me a text when I was on my way over here. It's heartbreaking to think about somebody else taking over our company."

"We get it," Mason said, his eyes filled with empathy. "You have all worked so hard to build on your grandparents' impressive foundation."

"But we have to think about these precious babies," Isabel said quietly, resting her palms over her rounded abdomen. "As much as I've daydreamed about handing over the reins to one of our sons or daughters someday, we have to make hard choices. What matters to us now is how we're going to provide for these kids."

Jovi fidgeted with the tassels and strings on her hooded

sweater. "But what are we going to do about Burke's theory that his aunt may have developed some of the original recipes?"

"There are no purchase orders, receipts, minutes from meetings, or contracts stating Lois and Mac held even partial ownership in the company."

"Recipes in his aunt's handwriting don't count?"

Isabel hesitated. "Mac and Lois lived here for years and never contested ownership. So unless he's legitimately claiming partial ownership in the company now, I think he's going to have to let this go."

Let this go. Had Isabel spent more than five minutes with Burke? Because that wasn't exactly how he approached life.

Jovi stood, forced a smile and reached for her jacket. "We tried, right? Sometimes that's all we can do."

Isabel watched as she struggled to put the used plastic wrap over the plate of salted caramel chews. "Are you upset?"

"Yeah, a little. I wish this had gone differently, but I realize we can't just keep rolling out batches of mediocre treats hoping to change the world. We all need to get on with our lives."

"Here, let me get you a container with a lid." Mason gently took the ball of plastic wrap from her. "What are you going to do next?"

Jovi shrugged. "I—I don't know."

"You're going to leave again, aren't you?" Isabel asked quietly.

The disappointment in her sister's voice made her wince. "If we're selling, then you really don't need me here."

"Of course we do," Mason said, bringing a plastic container and a bright blue lid to the table. "Somebody's gotta help us change these diapers and hold these babies."

"I'm going to take an assignment in California. Living close to the beach sounds like a dream."

"No," Isabel groaned. "Promise me you won't live anywhere close to Michael."

"Michael." Mason frowned. "I thought he was old news?"

"According to a social media post from a friend of a friend, Michael is transferring to South Korea, so no worries there." Jovi carefully packed the salted caramel chews into the container. "And he is most definitely old news."

Isabel folded a napkin into tiny squares and pinned her with a long look. "Are you sure?"

Jovi hesitated. "About Michael? Or California?"

"California," Isabel said. "I know you're done with Michael."

"It's just for thirteen weeks. Then I can come back. You're due in October, right?"

"The seventeenth," Mason said.

"I'll be back in plenty of time to hold those babies and change a gazillion diapers," Jovi said.

Mason turned pale. "That's a huge number."

Jovi grinned. "A slight exaggeration. It will only feel like a gazillion at first."

Mason feigned a glare. "Stop. It."

Jovi's laughter faded. "Wait. If you're worried about me leaving, does that mean you're staying?"

Mason glanced down at Isabel. "We are. Once I found out about the twins, I declined the job offer."

Isabel tipped her chin up, and he gave her a lingering kiss.

Okay, then. Jovi turned away. "I need a change of scenery, new clinical experiences, a different patient population…" She glanced at the time on her phone. If she hurried, she could make a quick trip to Anchorage to see Grammie. "Because obviously candy-making isn't my gift."

"Aww, don't sell yourself short," Isabel said. "You've done an excellent job with everything since you've been here. Thank you for coming home on short notice."

"Yes, thank you." Mason walked her toward the door. "We haven't done a great job of expressing our gratitude, but you have been a lifesaver."

"Anytime." She gave his shoulder a quick pat. "Thanks for the honest feedback. Talk to you soon."

She left their house and walked to her car. Disappointment clung to her like a weighted blanket. This wasn't how she expected her quest to end, but maybe it was for the best. Maybe somebody else could take candy-making to the next level. Because it certainly wasn't going to be her.

Chapter Nineteen

The sun had finally broken through the thick clouds, casting its pale light over the cabin and his yard. Burke had made short work of clearing the snow from last night's storm out of the driveway. Now he had to shovel out the steps in front of the cabin. He was tired of snow, and he could almost taste the savory crunch of a bacon cheeseburger and salty fries from Trailside. But as he worked, his mind was occupied with thoughts of Jovi. He had to talk to her about the letter. Avoiding her wasn't helping. They had to speak face-to-face.

He had been praying about timing and the best way to reach out. But since he'd spoken with his mother and Shane last week and they'd expressed zero interest in the whole situation, his confidence about tackling hard conversations had waned. Looking at pictures from his mother's current tropical vacation only added to his frustration and jealousy. The locals at the coffee shop and diner chattered about spring being just around the corner—they were six days into April already—but all he could see were piles of heavy white snow obscuring any signs of warmer weather. Lately he'd dreamed of escaping to a tropical paradise, away from all these problems and responsibilities. But with Darby Jane in school and doing so well with her play rehearsals and new friends, it didn't seem fair to disrupt her life with an unplanned trip. So for now, he would have to settle for imaginary beach vacations while shoveling snow in reality.

With a grunt, Burke hoisted his last shovelful of fresh snow and dumped it beside his cabin's steps. Cold air nipped at his cheeks and nose, but he barely noticed as he turned at the sound of a vehicle approaching. Jovi drove toward his driveway, her car sending exhaust puffing into the air. He leaned the shovel against the porch railing, mustered all his courage and then jogged down to the road to intercept her.

Jovi slowed to a stop and rolled down her window.

She glanced up, her mouth set in a firm line, both hands gripping the steering wheel. The late-morning sunlight filtering through the trees nearby cast dappled patterns on the ground, making it hard for him to see.

"Hey," he said, squinting as he stopped a few feet away from her. "I need to speak with you."

She pulled her phone from the console and glanced at the screen. "I'm headed to Anchorage to visit my grandmother, so I only have a few minutes. What's up?"

"I'll make this quick, then." He offered a tentative smile. At least she hadn't said no. "Have you ever considered that your grandfather may have tried to end the feud between his wife and Lois?"

A skeptical look twisted her features into a frown. "What?"

"Let me ask you this. Do you think that your grandfather knew that Lois and your grandmother had both been interested romantically in Mac?"

Jovi shrugged. "I—I don't know. Probably? Why?"

"Well, I have reason to believe that your grandfather may have reached out to Lois and asked her for help."

She didn't even try to conceal her eye roll. "And how did you come to this conclusion?"

He held up a gloved hand in defense. "Please. Hear me out. It's not a conclusion. More of a theory, really. I'm wondering if it's possible that he sought her assistance in making candy. The reason I'm asking is that I found a letter he wrote to her years ago. One that she evidently never opened."

Her eyebrows rose in disbelief. "Seriously?"

"I'd be glad to show it to you. It's inside. He sounded like he wanted to end the long-standing feud between our families. Or maybe he recognized Lois's talent for creating delectable recipes. Or both."

Jovi looked down, then heaved a sigh. "I don't know, Burke. I suppose anything's possible." She dragged her gaze to meet his. "I'm just so tired. Tired of trying to uphold my grandmother's traditions and recipes. Tired of wondering who really deserves credit for the company's success." She paused. "Honestly, I don't know if I even care anymore."

Burke stared at her, unable to speak. The pinched expression, dark circles under her eyes and the slope of her shoulders underscored her frank confession. That was not the answer he'd anticipated. "So what are you saying?"

"Like I told Isabel and Mason earlier today, I'm waving the white flag." She pulled her hand from her pocket and gave a half-hearted flourish. "I don't want to keep fighting with you. I don't want to think about why your aunt and my grandmother stopped being friends. We've come to the end of the road."

That last part landed like a punch in his gut.

She was talking like somebody who was about to leave. He swallowed hard. "What does this mean for the company?"

"Who knows?" Jovi held both palms up. "But I'm done fighting, and I'm done making mediocre candy. Isabel and my parents get to decide what to do next. If you want to make some kind of legal claim on the candy company's ownership, you might want to have your attorneys reach out to my parents. I can text you their contact information if you don't already have it."

His heart thundered in his chest. He clenched his fists inside his pockets to keep from reaching for her. "Jovi, are you all right?"

"Never better." Her forced smile didn't come close to lighting up her eyes. "I've done everything I can, and I don't know how to resolve this."

She checked the time. "I've got to go. Take care. Tell Darby Jane I said hello."

Before he could press for more information, she rolled up the window. He stepped out of the way. She waved, then drove off.

No, he wanted to call after her. *You can't give up. Not on this, not on us.*

He'd been so hopeful, so optimistic that she'd be thrilled that he might have found a different angle. Something they hadn't already considered.

He'd become the optimistic, never-give-up person, and she'd become, well, like him. Cynical, irritated, unwilling to keep trying. He walked slowly back to his cabin.

They'd come so close to untangling the mess that had their families twisted in a complicated relational knot. How could she quit? Their conversation weeks ago about what it meant to be a traveling health care worker resurfaced. His breath caught. His steps faltered. She wouldn't leave town without saying goodbye. Would she?

Her unexpected conversation with Burke had made Jovi's limited time even more precious. But when he'd run down his driveway toward her, waving, she'd been unable to ignore him. He'd looked so handsome in his gray knit hat. Those glorious prominent cheekbones flushed from exertion. Even now, her stomach tightened at the visual image.

Then he'd floated his mostly ridiculous theory.

His words had hung in the air. Waiting for her to grab on and run with the idea. As if she could just ignore everything that had happened. But now that she'd put a hundred miles between them and spent nearly two hours replaying their conversation and picking apart every word, she had to admit that his notion held potential. Part of her wanted to dismiss it as nonsense, but there was also a nagging feeling that Burke might be onto something. Grandpa hadn't grown up in Evergreen, but surely he eventually figured out that Mac had been the catalyst that severed his wife's friendship with Lois.

Jovi drummed her thumb on the steering wheel. Oh, she wasn't ready to confront these conflicting thoughts, especially when she'd already set plans in motion to leave town. Yet, despite her reservations, something about the way Burke framed the idea of her grandfather reaching out to Lois for help snagged her interest.

Grandpa was a good man. The kind of man who would've helped anyone. Was it possible he had been trying to mend Grammie and Lois's fractured relationship? Or did he truly believe Lois had a special talent for creating delicious candy and wanted to partner with her to further his company's success?

The questions swirled in her mind, leaving her torn between wanting to know the truth and fearing what it might reveal about her family's past. She shook her head, desperate to push away these conflicting thoughts. She wasn't ready to face the truth, whatever it may be.

And she really wasn't ready to say goodbye to Grammie.

Jovi sat in the car in the parking lot outside Oasis Care, staring at the doors. She hadn't enjoyed a single meaningful conversation with Grammie. The one thing she'd hoped for during her time here in Alaska. To chat like they always had.

Blinking back tears, she squeezed her eyes shut.

"Lord, please, if it's possible, help me to know if I should say goodbye or just welcome the conversation with Grammie in whatever state I find her," she quietly prayed.

Then she opened her eyes, turned off the ignition and stepped out of the car. She squinted in the sunshine and stopped to admire the bright blue sky and the gorgeous snowcapped mountains that ringed Anchorage. Moisture dripped from the roof of the building, and birds chirped from a tree nearby. The storm that had blanketed Evergreen in another three feet of powder must not have had the same impact here. Piles of dirt-tinged snow in the parking lot had been shoved off to the side, but she crossed bare pavement, and there were now puddles where she had once walked on ice.

Maybe, just maybe, they were headed for brighter, sunnier days. Not that it mattered to her. If she officially accepted her new start date for her assignment in California as a traveler, she'd have her toes in the sand in less than ten days. She hadn't planned to go just yet, but someone from HR at the hospital in La Jolla had asked if she could start sooner. They were really struggling to care for patients without enough nurses. Another traveler who'd been scheduled to start soon had had a family emergency. She'd asked for a couple of days to think about it. Even though she'd already planned on going to California, leaving in a few days was much different than leaving in June.

Her heart pinched. Could she really go? Frankly, she couldn't think of any reason to stay. Because she'd meant what she'd said to Burke. If his family claimed that they were entitled to half the proceeds of the sale, then all their attorneys would have to negotiate the outcome. She refused to believe that her grandmother would have done anything so twisted as to steal recipes. Then again, Jovi could relate to the pain of rejection. Heartache made people do strange things sometimes. Except Grammie had always been so kind and generous. And so talented. Why would she have doubted her own creativity?

She hesitated at the entrance, drew a deep breath, then

stepped through as the automatic doors parted. After signing in at the desk, she walked down the long corridor to Grammie's room. She knocked softly, then opened the door. Grammie sat in her recliner. A home-decorating show played on the television. The pleasing fragrance of peppermint wafted toward Jovi as she glanced at the diffuser, puffing a little cloud into the air. An orchid sat on the windowsill, blooming brilliant, rich pink blossoms.

"Hi there," Jovi said, shrugging out of her coat and hanging it on the hook behind the door. "How are you?"

Grammie's eyes, clear and blue and bright like Jovi remembered, locked on hers. "Oh, good, you're here. I need your help." She pointed one gnarled finger toward the two shelves under the windows. "I need you to find my scrapbook."

Jovi stopped halfway across the room. "Your scrapbook? I didn't know you had one."

"Jovi, don't be silly." Grammie chuckled. "You know I was an avid scrapbooker back in the day."

Tears pricked Jovi's eyes. Grammie knew her.

"I used to host parties, remember? Everybody would bring all their supplies to our house, and we worked on our pages together. Sometimes you'd help me. Putting the stickers in was your favorite part. I tried to always have plenty on hand, because you and Isabel would fight over them."

Jovi sniffed, then cleared her throat. "I remember. Isabel wanted an even number of stickers on every page, and I couldn't get enough of the sparkly heart stickers."

Grammie clasped her hands and tipped her head back, her sweet laugh filling the room. The best sound Jovi had heard in days.

She sank to her knees on the floor beside the shelves. "Can you describe the color or what the cover looks like?"

"Can't remember, but I'll know it when I see it."

Of course you will. Jovi suppressed a laugh and leaned closer.

"All right, then, let's see. We've got some photo albums, a couple of coffee table books featuring flowers, but I don't see any scrapbooks."

"That's odd."

Jovi straightened slowly and faced her grandmother. "What years do you think you covered in your scrapbook?"

"Oh, honey, I had so many. But the one I'm thinking of was all about the candy company. You know, Lois and I started that business together."

Jovi's stomach plummeted. Her body ran hot and then cold. "What?"

"Oh, sure, me and Lois started making candy together back when we were still in high school. Then we won a couple of competitions, prizes at the state fair, that sort of thing. So we decided to start selling candy and cookies out of her parents' place. People loved our stuff!" Her smile faded. She plucked a tissue from the box on the table beside her chair. "Of course, everything changed when she married Mac."

Jovi's heart thundered in her chest. She swiped her clammy palms on her jeans, then knelt at Grammie's side. "Can you tell me more about your early days at the candy company?"

Grammie looked away.

Jovi held her breath. *Stay with me, Grammie.*

"I suppose the most important thing you need to know is that Lois and I had the best time together. Our friendship was born from our mutual interest in baking. We both enjoyed making people happy. Even though my heart broke when Mac fell in love with Lois, and I regret that we didn't stay friends, I'll always be grateful for her creativity." Grammie's gaze met Jovi's again. She patted Jovi's hand. "Lois really had a gift. You've got to find that scrapbook, honey. Oh, the whole story is in there."

"Do you think it's someplace where you used to live?"

"Hmm." Grammie rocked slowly in her chair. "You know, I kept a lot of my treasures in an old footlocker. Like the kind servicemen brought back from the war. It's just as ugly as the day is long. You'll know when you find it. It's green, and my father's last name is printed on the outside in big stenciled letters."

"Got it." Jovi stood and retrieved her phone from her coat pocket. "Let me take some notes real quick so I don't forget what you've said."

"I can't believe I didn't bring them here. Do you know why I didn't?"

Jovi glanced up from her phone. "I don't. But I wasn't here when you moved in."

"Oh, that's right." Grammie held up one finger. "Mason did most of the heavy lifting. Isabel and your parents helped too. Well, you've got to find that scrapbook and bring it to me."

She tugged a small quilt from a footrest nearby, then smoothed it over her lap. "I hate to be rude, but I'm getting sleepy. I'm usually asleep before this show is even over. Which is a real shame, because the fella with the hammer is cute."

Jovi laughed, then she leaned over and kissed her grandmother's forehead. "I'll find your scrapbook, Grammie."

"I know you will." She patted Jovi's hand. "Thanks for coming over."

Then her eyes drifted shut.

Jovi squeezed the thin papery skin on Grammie's gnarled hand, then slipped away. She pulled on her coat and hurried out to the front desk. After signing out, she strode to her car and typed out a text to Isabel. They had to find that scrapbook.

She had looked everywhere.

Turned her parents' attic upside down, searched through all the boxes in their closets and garage and pulled everything out of the cabin's meager storage spaces.

No scrapbook about the candy company.

Now two days after her visit with Grammie, exhausted and beyond frustrated, Jovi had her suitcases packed. She towed them both down the hall into the kitchen and left them by the counter as she unplugged her phone and stowed the charging cable in her carry-on. This was it. Time to say goodbye to Evergreen and, in several hours, hello to California. She opened the airline's app on her phone and double-checked that her departure out of Evergreen was on time.

Sabrina had offered to give her a ride to the airport since she was leaving on vacation that evening as well. She'd agreed to come by in about thirty minutes. Fatigue and caffeine-fueled adrenaline hummed through Jovi's veins. The excitement for what lay ahead kept her mind buzzing with possibilities.

Maybe this move was exactly what she needed right now: a fresh start away from all things associated with Evergreen. She couldn't wait to explore California. Closing her eyes, she could almost feel the sun-kissed sand beneath her feet and imagine the warmth of the sunshine on her skin. Still, a bittersweet wave of sorrow threatened to take her under. Especially as she lingered in Grammie's kitchen one last time.

Sighing, she opened her eyes and looked around. She'd found a home again in this lovely place, spending so many wonderful weeks here. Everywhere she looked were reminders of happy memories spent with Darby Jane—from the sweet treats they'd baked together to the silly last-minute costume Jovi had fashioned for the little girl's hundredth day of school. Her heart ached. Life was going to feel so empty without Darby Jane in it.

And without Burke.

Jovi clenched her jaw, determined to sidestep those painful thoughts. Darby Jane's father had made his choice. No matter how much she longed for things to be different, a relationship between them wasn't meant to be.

Time to move on.

What a shame that an innocent young child had to get caught in the shrapnel of grown-ups' falling-out.

In an attempt to distract herself from the sadness, Jovi clicked over to her favorite social media app. Scrolling through her friend Amy's account, she admired the gorgeous photos the young woman had recently posted from a hike. They'd worked together in Chattanooga before she'd taken the assignment in Kansas City. Now Amy worked in San Diego, and she'd kindly offered Jovi a temporary place to stay until Jovi's new apartment was ready on the first of May.

A soft knock sounded at her door, interrupting her scroll. Too early for Sabrina. Surely it wasn't Burke. Or Darby Jane. Jovi's chest squeezed. She wasn't proud of her decision to leave town without saying goodbye, but honestly, her heart couldn't take the pain.

After setting her phone on the counter, Jovi crossed to the door and peeked through the window. Isabel stood on the porch.

Jovi opened the door. "What are you doing here?"

They'd already exchanged tearful goodbyes the night before.

"I know you're getting ready to leave, but please, Jovi, let's look for the scrapbook again. What if the recipe you need is in there?"

Tears pricked Jovi's eyes. "Izzy, no. We said we weren't going to do this, remember?"

"I know, but…" Isabel sniffed, then blinked quickly. Unshed tears clung to her eyelashes. "I changed my mind. I—I can't stop thinking about what Grammie said to you. How the scrapbook tells the whole story. What if you find the recipe, make the candy, and it's a game changer? Mom and Dad are ready to accept the most competitive offer and sign the papers. We have to stop the sale, Jovi. Please, help me. One last time."

Jovi sighed and stepped aside so Isabel could come in. "We've looked everywhere. There's nothing here that looks like what Grammie's describing. Besides, Sabrina will be here in twenty minutes to pick me up, and my flight leaves in two hours."

"I'll pay for you to change your ticket." Isabel turned to face her, the tears gone and a resolute look in her eyes. "And don't hate me, but I've invited Burke to join us on our final search."

"Oh, no." Jovi groaned, squeezing her eyes shut. "You didn't."

"Yes, I did." Isabel jammed her hands on her hips. "He has a right to know what's going on, and he might be able to help."

Jovi shook her head, but she knew better than to argue. Bringing Burke into this would only complicate things even more. She spotted him walking up the driveway, carrying a small paper shopping bag.

Too late now. "Let me tell Sabrina to head to the airport without me."

"Yes!" Isabel thrust her arms in the air, then raced over and swept Jovi into a hug. "I knew I could convince you."

Jovi swallowed hard against the lump lodged in her throat. She hugged her sister, then pulled away and sent her friend a quick text. A few moments later, Burke arrived at the door. Isabel let him in. His dark eyes were fixed on Jovi as he crossed the threshold.

Her heart turned cartwheels. His tousled wavy hair and the wool sweater he'd paired with dark-washed denim reminded her so much of the night they'd met in the airport.

"Isabel said you two need help looking for something?"

His gaze pinged toward her luggage stacked in the kitchen, then back to her. His guarded expression and clipped words twisted her stomach. She instantly regretted not going over to say goodbye.

She managed a brief nod.

Isabel took charge of the situation and explained their mission: find the missing scrapbook before a sale could be finalized that would potentially impact both their families. Tears welled in Isabel's eyes again as she spoke. A wave of empathy washed over Jovi. Her sister had made it her mission to save their grandparents' business and legacy for future generations. She couldn't possibly leave now.

"So you think this scrapbook might actually be here?" Burke asked as he looked around the kitchen. He scanned the old cabinets and the vintage refrigerator humming in the corner.

His wounded heart stumbled when he eyed the suitcases and carry-on beside the counter. Had Jovi been about to leave? Without telling him?

He couldn't worry about that. Not now. She was still here—looking so beautiful it physically hurt him to let his gaze linger. And the faint scent of her shampoo made his arms ache to hold her close.

Gritting his teeth, he forced himself to listen to Isabel's suggestions about where to begin.

"We can skip the kitchen," Jovi said. "I've already scoured every square inch."

Burke nodded, then turned in a slow circle, trying not to think about what had happened the last time he'd been in this kitchen. Or the discovery he'd made at Mac and Lois's place. The recipes hidden inside the dollhouse were what had gotten him into this mess.

"I've picked the shed apart twice," Burke said. "There doesn't seem to be any additional recipes or letters in Mac and Lois's stuff. I brought what I've found so far."

Jovi gave him the side-eye, obviously not convinced that he had done his due diligence. He couldn't really blame her for being suspicious. Besides, it was far too late to convince her to change her mind about him.

"Thank you." Isabel glanced at the bag as she rubbed her forehead with her fingertips. "I'd like to see what you've found after we're finished searching here. We've sorted through every photo album we own. No hints."

"Grammie insisted what we're looking for is tucked away in a serviceman's footlocker," Jovi said. "Seems like that would be hard to miss."

Burke wasn't so sure. He had searched Mac and Lois's cabin from top to bottom and hadn't been able to find any more evidence of their involvement in the candy company. Other than the letter from Dennis Wright to Lois.

"Let's have a look around," Burke said as he started toward the hallway. "Are all the cabins on this side of the lake built by the same person?"

"That's a good question," Isabel said, following him. "I always assumed each one was custom-built. Do you see remarkable differences?"

He stopped outside the hall bathroom, his mind churning. "Not really. I stopped by the library last week and did some research on the early days of Evergreen. When the homesteaders first settled here, stuff like that. There wasn't much information available about the properties around the lake. I was just thinking that if all the cabins were built by the same person, maybe there'd be some similarities between them."

He paused, considering the possibilities. "Maybe something like attic access or hidden crawl spaces that we could check?"

Isabel and Jovi exchanged glances. Isabel nodded slowly. "We're not aware of any crawl space here, but obviously there's a lot we don't know about our grandparents, so feel free to look around."

After searching for what felt like hours, they were no closer to discovering an entrance to the cabin's attic. He sensed Jovi and Isabel were getting antsy. And not a little frustrated. Did Jovi need to leave soon? The tension in the air was almost palpable. Just as he was about to give up hope, Burke noticed a tiny crack in the floorboard near one side of the door frame leading into the main bedroom. He stooped down to inspect it further. Carefully, he tugged up one corner of the shag carpet.

The subfloor looked normal, except for a strange seam bisecting the old plywood. He pressed on the wood. When he felt something give way beneath his fingers, he pulled the carpet back more and found a latch.

"Check this out." Burke glanced up at Isabel and Jovi hovering in the hallway. "Mind if I see where this takes us?"

"Please." Isabel gestured for him to continue.

He tugged on the metal ring. A rectangular panel in the floorboards lifted, revealing a staircase leading down into darkness below. "Bingo."

"Oh, my," Jovi said.

"This is bonkers," Isabel whispered.

Burke gingerly descended the stairs, one hand trailing along the wall for balance.

"Hang on," Jovi called after him. "Let me get you a light."

"Perfect. Thanks." He hesitated, the stairs creaking under his sneakers. Cold air enveloped him. The aroma of damp earth and mothballs filled his nostrils.

The bright beam from her phone's flashlight illuminated his path down into the crawl space. As his eyes adjusted to the light, he made out a compact room brimming with bookshelves, furniture and boxes of all shapes and sizes. He peered around cautiously, looking for a light bulb. A string dangling overhead with a small ring attached caught his attention. He tugged gently. The bulb lit up, casting an orange glow over the crowded space.

Jovi and Isabel followed him cautiously down into the hidden room. "This is incredible," Jovi breathed, her voice filled with awe. "How did we not know this was here?"

That scrapbook had to be here someplace.

Jovi used a flashlight she'd found in a kitchen drawer to add more light to their quest. She turned in a slow circle, eyeing the stacks of hastily labeled cardboard boxes jammed in between pieces of old furniture and a few vintage lamps.

"Oh, look." Isabel pointed. "Remember when Grammie had those chairs recovered and Grandpa hated the upholstery?"

"Yeah," Jovi said, trying to keep from crying. Why was their search making her so emotional? Somewhere in this disordered chaos of furniture and objects, they'd hopefully find the scrapbook that Grammie insisted told the story of her relationship with Lois. But could she trust that Grammie had been lucid when she'd shared the crucial details? And how would this change her relationship with Burke—or lack of it—if they found it?

Burke cleared his throat. "Where would you like to start?"

She shot him a quick glance. The hopeful expression on his face reminded her of the intimate moments they'd shared and the potential romance she'd hastily punctured with accusations of betrayal.

"Jovi?" His voice prodded her back to reality. "What exactly are we looking for?"

Jovi sighed deeply and turned to face him. "Grammie said the scrapbook is in her father's military footlocker," she said slowly. "She said that's where she kept some things with sentimental value."

"What does it look like?" Burke asked.

"It's supposedly green and ugly, and his last name is stenciled on the outside—Montgomery. It should stand out here somewhere."

Burke stilled. "Say that name again?"

"Montgomery. M-o-n-t—"

"I heard you." Burke shoved his fingers into his hair. "Any connection to the historic feud between the Harrisons and the Montgomerys?"

Jovi and Isabel exchanged looks. "Oh, yeah. The thing about the silver," Jovi said.

Isabel quirked her lips to one side. "Or was it gold?"

Then they shrugged, and Jovi swung her flashlight toward an opposite wall.

"Wait," Burke said. "Are you saying that your grandmother's family was involved in another feud that went back at least two additional generations?"

"Possibly," Jovi said. "But people either refused to talk about it or pretended that it never happened."

Burke's jaw drifted open. A few moments passed as they both stood there staring at each other. Her pulse sped. His broad frame and searching gaze distracted her. Made her wonder if things might've been different if they'd never started down this rabbit hole of missing recipes and family drama.

Before saying something she'd regret later, Jovi took a deep breath and stepped forward. "Who knows, maybe we'll find more information about both. I, for one, am determined to search every nook and cranny until we find what we're looking for."

This scrapbook could change everything—confirm who truly owned the candy company, end the feud between their families, and let her leave town with a clear conscience. They had to find it.

"I'll start moving these," she said, pointing to a pile of cardboard cartons stacked in the middle of the room. "Burke, why don't you pick a stack to move out of the way? I don't want Izzy moving anything."

Isabel reached for Jovi's flashlight. "Hand over the light. I'll be in charge of that."

"That makes sense." Burke gave Jovi a small smile before turning away to begin his search.

Jovi returned her attention to the boxes in front of her and began carefully lifting them one by one from the pile, clearing a path so she could move deeper into the space and find the footlocker. These boxes likely contained treasures to be sorted later. For now, they couldn't get distracted.

She and Isabel and Burke worked in silence, carefully squeezing between rows of boxes and stepping around other long-neglected possessions. After nearly twenty minutes, Jovi stretched and massaged her aching back muscles. "Maybe we aren't looking in the right place."

"Where else would a footlocker be?" Isabel asked, then reached for her water bottle and took a long sip.

"Did your family have any other places they stored belongings?" Burke asked, stepping away from his stack of boxes as he surveyed the room.

"Most of Grammie's valuables are at our parents' house," Isabel said.

"We've already looked there," Jovi added, then carefully blew the dust off a hardcover edition of *Little Women*. Grammie loved that book. She must've read it half a dozen times.

"What if the footlocker is hidden?" Burke asked. "It's not unheard of for people to use furniture to conceal things."

"But where?" Jovi blew out an exasperated breath.

Isabel shot her a warning glance. "We're trying to solve the problem, right? That means no suggestion is a bad one."

"It's worth considering," she admitted, avoiding making eye contact with Burke.

After rearranging everything she and Burke had the strength to move, Jovi spotted something nestled between two larger boxes along the back wall. An olive metal footlocker stenciled with a single name—*Montgomery*—Grammie's father's last name.

"Found it!"

Her heart pounding, she squeezed between the tower of boxes, then sank to her knees. She pried open the cold metal levers, flipped up the buckles, then opened the lid. The hinges squeaked. She delicately sorted through memorabilia from her great-grandfather's military service, stacks of old newspapers, and a few copies of *Life* magazine until she saw a scrapbook nestled on the bottom. "I think this is it."

"Really?" Isabel squealed and quickly worked her way over to Jovi. Burke joined them.

Jovi pulled out the scrapbook and stared at it for a moment. Its black padded leather cover had cracked near the corners.

"You open it." Jovi stood and handed the heavy book to her sister.

Isabel's eyes grew wide. She cradled it like a rare treasure in her arms, then gingerly flipped open the cover. Jovi leaned in close. A lovely sepia-toned photo of Lois and Grammie tucked behind a piece of plastic filled the top half of the first page.

Jovi's eyes blurred with tears. Page after page documented Lois and Grammie's friendship, from elementary school until early adulthood. Newspaper clippings, grainy photos and postcards from trips they'd taken together filled the heavy book.

"This is incredible," Isabel whispered.

Jovi swiped the back of her hand across her damp cheeks. "I feel like we just dug up a time capsule."

"Are these where recipes might have been removed?" Isabel pointed to the empty rectangular spaces where the background of the page was slightly discolored, indicating something had been taken out.

Goose bumps shot down Jovi's arms. Did the scrapbook hold the proof they needed to put this whole mess behind them?

Isabel set the book carefully on a stack of boxes, and Burke shone his flashlight down like a spotlight so they could all see better.

Burke carefully inspected the contents, his gaze moving from page to page. He gestured to a few more blank spots where something had been removed. "These could be where recipes were taken out as well."

Jovi leaned in and examined the odd shape of one of the blank spots.

Isabel frowned. "It would be nice if we found more tangible information other than just speculating about what's not here."

The trio flipped through the rest of the scrapbook, eventually unearthing several handwritten recipes on loose sheets of paper tucked between pages. They also found a few old recipe cards and even some product labels.

"This may be helpful," Burke said, pointing to a vintage black-and-white newspaper advertisement for a candy store in Evergreen. Underneath the logo was typed Proprietors: Lois Stevens and Carol Montgomery. The date written on the back in Grammie's handwriting was May 7, 1961.

"They would've been about twenty or twenty-one years old," Jovi said, quickly doing the math. "I'm glad we finally found proof that Grammie did, at one time, own a candy shop with her best friend. But this still doesn't lead us to a salted caramel chew recipe."

"Or keep our parents from selling the company," Isabel said quietly.

And what did this mean for her and Burke? Because finding the scrapbook didn't resolve the feud. Or excuse the fact that he'd put personal details about her in his novel. She still wasn't over that, either.

Burke sat across from Isabel and Jovi at the kitchen table. They'd moved upstairs from the chilly crawl space for more light and warmth and so Isabel could sit down.

"Here, do you want to look through more pages?" Isabel slid the scrapbook across the table. "We've sort of been hogging it."

"I'll make some coffee," Jovi said, pushing back her chair and scooting past Burke.

"Thanks." He turned the overstuffed book slowly and stared at the pages in disbelief. After months of searching for the missing clues, they'd finally discovered the link between present and past.

The rift had been well-documented. Every page served as a testament to the long history of animosity and pain between the two families. There were newspaper clippings, poems, letters and photos—all carefully arranged and labeled chronologically. Carol Wright had tracked the story for decades and presented evidence of all the devastating details. A handful of photos of Carol and Lois at community events showcased their reputation in Evergreen as the go-to source for delicious confections. Carol had included photos, letters and even a pressed flower that illustrated her teenage affection for Mac. But when he and Lois fell in love and he chose her instead of Carol, the women's friendship had obviously imploded. Mac and Lois's marriage must've destroyed any hope of reconciliation.

Burke shook his head. The shock of their discovery still hadn't worn off.

"I need a minute." Isabel blew her nose with a tissue. "Some of that is hard to read."

Walker had been right after all.

Poor Carol. He swallowed hard. She must've been so hurt and angry. A full page in the scrapbook cataloged her heartbreak. She claimed she gave Lois all her original recipes back as a wedding gift, which didn't go over well. Evidently, Lois interpreted the so-called gift as a spiteful gesture. Carol wrote that Lois kept the recipes, but only after confronting Carol the night before Lois married Mac and telling her to "grow up and move on."

Ouch. Burke grimaced. Not the kindest advice to offer someone after you'd swiped their man. After all, the recipes represented so much more than ingredients in sweet confections. They'd been the foundation of a cherished friendship. A friendship that was ruined when his uncle somehow fell in love with his aunt instead.

Burke glanced up and found Jovi staring at him from the

other side of the kitchen, where she stood adding coffee grounds and water to the coffee maker.

He stood and retrieved the bag he'd brought in with him. "So this is wild speculation, but I'm guessing the recipes I found in the dollhouse are the ones referenced here in the prewedding spat?"

Jovi's expression tightened. Then she shrugged. "Maybe."

Isabel sat across from him, her feet propped up on a kitchen chair. She looked from Burke to Jovi and back to Burke. Something undecipherable flashed in her eyes. "I think you're right. And my theory is that Grammie took Lois's hot tip to heart and rebuilt her business without her ex–best friend. Remember the photo of her and Grandpa at the ribbon cutting on opening day? No Lois. Our grandfather became her partner in life and in the candy company."

"Oh." Jovi released a soft sigh. "It sounds so romantic when you put it like that."

Warmth flushed Burke's neck. Just hearing her say the word *romantic* brought back memories of their Valentine's Day kiss. He looked away.

"At first, each page is like a tribute to their beautiful friendship, but tinged with sadness," Isabel said, reaching for her water. "So it's sort of romantic. But I also feel like Grammie got her own version of revenge because I'm willing to bet she worked from memory to recreate some of Lois's concoctions and then sold them. Since Mac and Lois didn't live here anymore, no one challenged her."

Burke shifted in his chair. He'd formulated a similar theory. Thankfully, Isabel verbalized it so he didn't have to and risk more dark looks from Jovi.

Burke cleared his throat. "I found Mac and Lois's wedding photo and an announcement stored in the shed. They married in 1963. I don't know when they left Evergreen, but Mac served in Vietnam, because I found pictures about that too."

"May I see one of the recipes, please? Let's check if it lines up with those blank spaces we saw earlier."

"Good idea." He carefully removed the stack of recipes from the plastic bag and handed them over. Jovi's gaze warmed his skin, but he didn't allow himself to make eye contact. Although part of him wanted to gauge her reaction.

Isabel flipped through a few more pages. "It doesn't look like there are too many more pictures of Grammie and Lois together after 1962, so that lines up with what you've shared, Burke. Maybe they did part ways when Mac and Lois fell in love."

She turned back to the front of the book, found the page she'd mentioned, then aligned a recipe card over an empty space. She glanced at her sister then at Burke. "It fits."

Burke nodded. "Sure does."

"Grammie must've been crushed when Lois and Mac fell for each other. I don't like the idea of anyone swiping recipes that aren't theirs, but I can empathize with her situation." Jovi poured coffee into two mugs then brought them to the table. "It's hard to imagine Grammie loving anyone other than Grandpa, yet it's obvious by the pictures and captions she wrote that she cared deeply for Mac."

"That's what I don't fully understand." A pained expression crossed Isabel's face. "If Lois got what she wanted and married Mac, why didn't she let Grammie have the recipes? Surely, she knew that her best friend had once loved her soon-to-be husband. It's too bad they couldn't work something out."

Burke sat quietly, listening to their conversation as Isabel slid the scrapbook back to him. He flipped through the last pages. Except for the final two that were stubbornly adhered together.

"I'll have to ask one of my craftier friends if there's a way to separate those without causing damage," Isabel said.

Burke nodded. "Good plan."

The scrapbook might've confirmed what Walker had told

them, but he still had to cope with the harsh reality that it had done nothing to heal the heartache between him and Jovi. He gently closed the scrapbook. Regret washed over him.

"I'd like for you both to read this letter." He fished it from the bag. "It adds another piece to the proverbial puzzle."

"You go first, Isabel," Jovi said. "I need cream and sugar."

Isabel carefully opened the letter. Blake moved the scrapbook safely out of the way and pulled his steaming mug of coffee closer. Isabel's eyes scanned the page.

Jovi brought spoons, creamer and a sugar bowl to the table.

"This is wild," Isabel whispered. "Where did you find it?"

Jovi's spoon clinked against her mug as she stirred in the cream and sugar, craning her neck to read Dennis's letter to Lois.

"It was in Lois and Mac's filing cabinet. The one in their shed." Burke lifted his mug to take a cautious sip. "No one's ever read it until this week."

Jovi and Isabel exchanged glances.

Then Isabel's gaze drifted to Burke. "Do you think this could've all been resolved if she'd just read this letter?"

He hesitated. "It's hard to say. I wondered the same thing. But maybe they talked about it in person after Mac and Lois moved here?"

"Evidently, that changed exactly nothing," Jovi quipped. "Because time marched on and here we are. Lois and Mac must've refused Grandpa's offer to work together."

So what next? Burke frowned. A scrapbook hidden in the bottom of a footlocker held all the proof they needed to confirm that Carol's heartache had instigated a feud. Even though she'd offered an olive branch of sorts, Lois's cold-hearted response must've cemented their falling out.

But what about his broken relationship with Jovi? Did he have any hope of repairing that?

Regret cratered his stomach. Their families had caused each

other so much pain because of their stubbornness and pride. Was there still hope for reconciliation among this generation? He sighed deeply. This had all been so exhausting. He had no idea how to move forward.

Chapter Twenty

"Girls, we're so impressed. You've pulled together and worked hard to keep the company afloat." Mom's voice wavered, and she blinked back tears as she reached for Dad's hand across the table.

Uh-oh. Jovi pushed her unfinished broccoli around on her plate. She exchanged nervous glances with Isabel. "I feel like I'm not going to be thrilled with what you're about to say."

Isabel carefully laid her fork across the edge of her plate.

Dad cleared his throat, his Adam's apple bobbing up and down as he fought for control of his emotions. He twined his fingers through Mom's. "It's been wonderful having our family together again."

Mason scooted his chair closer to Isabel's and draped his arm around her shoulders.

Jovi squirmed in her seat. Part of her wished Burke was beside her. How weird that she still craved the strength and stability his presence offered. Even when they didn't have a future together.

"The discovery of the scrapbook has added some interesting backstory to our family history, hasn't it? I'm thrilled that we can move forward, secure in the knowledge that our family built an incredible company from the ground up," Dad said.

Jovi frowned. "You almost sound...proud. Aren't you at all embarrassed by your mother's behavior? Seems to me Lois had a hand in creating those recipes. Shouldn't Burke's family get some credit as well?"

Dad paused. "My mother's ability to preserve photos and letters is quite impressive, but recipes aren't copyrighted. So the Phillips relatives and Burke Solomon have no legal stake in the company, if that's what you're implying. Your mom and I still want to sell."

No. Jovi's fork clattered to her plate.

Isabel leaned her head on Mason's shoulder. A tear slid down her cheek.

"Unbelievable." Jovi shoved back her chair and stood. "After everything we've uncovered—not just the recipes but also the letter from Grandpa to Lois, hinting that there's some kind of candy with a unique ingredient and incredible potential—you still want to give up?"

Mom's brow furrowed. "Jovi, honey, no one's giving up. We truly appreciate your efforts. But that letter was written years ago. How could we possibly figure out what he's referring to? Besides, you didn't hold up your end of our agreement and you're all set to leave town. So why wait until June first if you're not going to be here?"

Fury roared through her like an avalanche descending on an unsuspecting skier. "Isabel asked me to stay and help find the scrapbook. Now that Burke shared the recipes and the letter, I just need a little more time. Please. I can—"

Dad's expression softened. "I'm afraid there's no reason to wait any longer. We've attracted the attention of multiple buyers, due in part to your diligent efforts lately to boost sales. And for that, we will always be grateful. But the truth is your mom and I have been presented with an offer that we can't refuse."

"What kind of offer?" Mason asked, his tone laced with suspicion.

Dad hesitated for a moment before he answered. "A Scandinavian chocolatier with an established, reputable global supply chain. They're offering us a ridiculous amount of money that we could never hope to make if we continued running the business ourselves."

"That's still not a good enough reason to sell," Isabel said through her tears. "This is our family legacy, something that's been passed down through generations. We can't just give it away for a quick buck."

"I understand how you feel, sweetheart," Mom said. "Except our personal circumstances haven't changed. Your grandmother's care at Oasis is incredibly expensive. We're getting older, and we want to enjoy our retirement years. Selling the company will give us financial freedom to do that."

"But what about what we want? What about the fact that we're a family-owned business? That's what sets us apart from the rest," Jovi insisted, her voice thick with emotion.

"We're selling to a reputable company that shares our values and will continue to uphold the legacy that we've built." Mom's voice was gentle, but it only added to Jovi's frustration.

Jovi took a deep breath, trying to calm down. It was hard to argue with her parents' hopes and expectations for retirement, especially when she'd only been home for a few months and they'd devoted their adult lives to Evergreen Candy Company. She certainly couldn't afford to finance Grammie's care. But selling, even to a reputable company, still felt like a betrayal. She couldn't fathom putting their family's business in someone else's hands.

"I just don't know if I can give up," Jovi said, her voice breaking. "I know it's the right decision financially, but it feels like you're discrediting Grammie's heartache. Worse, you're giving up on everything we've worked for."

Mom stood, circled the end of the table and looped her arm around Jovi's shoulders and pulled her closer. "I know this is difficult to accept, sweetheart, but sometimes we have to make tough decisions for the greater good. And who knows? Maybe this is just the beginning of something even better for our family."

Shaking her head, Jovi swiped at her tears. Mom's efforts to tie this all up in a neat little bow fell woefully short. After poring over every page at least twice, there was something about the scrapbook that made her feel like they had overlooked a key detail.

She had spent countless hours searching for any clues that might point them toward an iconic recipe. Read and re-read all the recipes that Burke had brought over. Flipped through the scrapbook at least a dozen times. Analyzed every single line of Grandpa's letter to Lois. Nothing led her to the salted caramel chew.

But what if she'd missed something?

After they cleaned up the kitchen, Isabel and Mason went home. Mom and Dad went for a walk, and Jovi retreated to her old bedroom. A cleaning service had already gone to Grammie's place to prepare it for a new renter.

As she lay in bed that night, Jovi couldn't shake the feeling that they were making a mistake. She tossed and turned, trying to come up with something to convince her parents to change their minds. They'd said they were meeting with the attorneys early the next afternoon to review the terms of the offer.

Finally, in the early hours of the morning, she sat up with a start. The last two pages of the scrapbook had been stuck together. In their excitement of the discovery, she and Burke and Isabel had agreed to let it be. But she couldn't wait.

She had to know what was on those two pages.

★ ★ ★

Isabel wiped the crustiness from her sleep-deprived eyes, squinting against the sun sneaking past the drawn curtains. Their bedroom was warm and inviting in the morning light, and she reached a hand over to Mason's side of the bed. The sheets were warm. He'd returned to dayshift and started work at seven but must not have left yet.

The sound of her phone vibrating on the nightstand made her groan. She reached for it and checked the caller ID. Jovi.

"Hello?" she mumbled.

"Are you up?"

"I am now. What's going on? I thought you were leaving today?"

"I was, because I thought it would just be too hard to stay. But I couldn't sleep, so I dragged out the scrapbook. Remember those two pages stuck together in the back?" Jovi's voice hummed with enthusiasm through the phone.

"Yes. Why?" Isabel pushed herself up on one elbow, then gently eased into a sitting position and leaned against the headboard. It wasn't even six o'clock yet. How could her sister sound so excited about anything at such an unfortunate hour?

"My friend Danielle talked me through how to separate them. I figured out what the pages say, and how they're going to save the candy company. The salted caramel chew recipe was there, and a full-page story about how it came to be. Isabel, this is it."

"That's amazing." Isabel smiled, shaking her head in disbelief. "Sadly, at this point, I'm not sure there's much we can do with new information."

"But this is the recipe we need. The one that will be an instant hit."

Isabel hesitated. She really hated to pop the balloon of her sister's excitement. But Mom and Dad had a meeting to sign papers and accept the offer in less than eight hours. "Jovi, we—"

"Don't say it." Jovi cut her off. "We're not giving up. Please let me into the test kitchen. I need access to the proper equipment, and Mom and Dad can't know what I'm up to."

"Have you been up all night?"

"Um, not exactly. Why?"

"Because you're not making any sense," Isabel said, trying to sound firm but gentle.

"No, wait. Hear me out," Jovi insisted. "This is the recipe with the ingredient Grandpa alluded to in his letter. The salted caramel chew I've been looking for. It's going to put Evergreen Candy Company on everyone's radar. There's kind of a touching story about how Lois wanted a pony, but her dad brought Lois baby goats instead. Except she was so upset because she couldn't ride a goat, and she worried they'd eat everything. Which they did, but Lois didn't get mad because one day in a pinch she substituted the milk from her goat into her recipe and made the candy taste so good. Imagine the possibilities, Izzy. What if we added a petting zoo with goats to the candy company? People could take tours and see how the candy is made plus visit the animals. We'll market it as an...an experience."

Oh, brother. A petting zoo? That was a bridge too far.

Mason came into their bedroom, carrying a tray with a steaming cup of hot tea and a bowl of oatmeal. Bless him.

Isabel smiled as Mason approached. She took the cup and saucer first. "Thank you, sweetheart," she said softly. "Hold on, Jovi. Let me put you on speaker." She hit the button and carefully propped her phone against an extra pillow. "Okay, go ahead. What's this all about?"

Jovi's words tumbled out in a rush. "Okay, so I found this recipe in the back of the scrapbook, right? And it's for the salted caramel chews that Grammie used to make. Except she put goat's milk in them because that's a trick Lois taught her. Can you believe that? What a genius move."

"Interesting."

"I know, right? It's going to be the perfect blend of salty and sweet, with a smooth melt-in-your-mouth texture. People will go wild."

Isabel's stomach growled, and Mason chuckled. She eyed the tray he'd set down on the footstool beside their bed.

"Jovi, I love your enthusiasm, but we don't have any projected sales figures. This will have to be an out-of-this-world piece of candy to convince—"

"I know, I know," Jovi cut her off. "One step at a time, all right? Trust me. This is going to be amazing."

"Okay, fine. You can use the kitchen. But be careful. And you'll have to work quickly because I can't hold off the meeting with the attorneys for more than twenty minutes," Isabel said.

"I know." Jovi was nearly shouting. "Thank you, Isabel. You'll get to taste the first one off the cooling rack. Promise."

"All right, all right." Isabel laughed. "Texting you the security-system code as soon as we hang up."

"Love you. Bye!"

Isabel ended the call and took a cautious sip of her hot tea.

"Looks like we're going to be taste-testers for some goat-milk caramel chews. That girl, she's determined to save this company from being sold. I love her so much."

She set her cup on the nightstand, then texted Jovi the security code. The mattress sank as Mason lifted the covers and climbed back into bed.

"What are you doing? Don't you have to work?"

He gently took her phone from her hand. "I'm going in late."

"Why?"

His wolfish smile made her pulse race. "You'll see."

Then he gently pulled her into his arms and kissed her. Slowly. Thoroughly. Isabel soon forgot about security codes, stalling an important meeting, and their impending cost-of-living increase. Lost in Mason's embrace, all that mattered was showing him how much she loved him.

★ ★ ★

Burke stood in line outside the elementary school with Darby Jane, waiting patiently to board the buses that would take them on their field trip to a farm nearby. How was he supposed to woo Jovi before she left town if he had to chaperone a busload full of rowdy kindergartners all day?

Isabel had already told him that Jovi had changed her ticket to leave today. She'd be halfway to California before he and Darby Jane got back to Evergreen.

"Hey, Burke." Connie, the server from the diner, walked up beside him. "I didn't know you were coming along today."

"Hi, Connie." Burke shoved his hands in his jean pockets. "Thought I'd take my turn since I haven't volunteered for anything yet. Besides, Darby Jane begged me."

Connie smiled, her earrings sparkling in the sunshine. "Kids can be persuasive, can't they? That's why I'm here as well."

"Which child belongs to you?" Burke surveyed the kids goofing around on the sidewalk.

"That's my son, Tyler." Connie pointed toward a spunky little brown-haired boy demonstrating his ninjalike moves to a group of little girls. "Always a charmer, that one."

Burke chuckled.

"Say, are you and Jovi Wright still a thing?"

His smile evaporated. Heat crawled up his neck. "Sadly, no. That, uh, didn't work out. She's leaving for California shortly."

Connie's brow furrowed. "She is? Are you sure?"

"Well, not a hundred percent, but that's the latest I'd heard."

"Huh. That's odd, because she texted me early this morning and asked if I had access to any fresh goat's milk."

"Quite the request." Burke shrugged. "New dietary habit?"

"She said she couldn't give more detail, but I'm wondering why she wants the milk if she's leaving town."

"You're asking the wrong guy."

Connie hesitated, studying him. "But what if you're the right guy?"

Irritation flared. "I'm afraid I'm not following."

Connie leaned in closer, her eyes glimmering with mischief. "What if Jovi needs your help to make those candies?"

He barked out a laugh. "That's cute. Maybe you haven't heard that our families despise one another? And have for years?"

"*Despise* is a strong word, don't you think?" Connie nudged him gently with her elbow. "Maybe today's your day to put an end to all of that."

Burke's chest tightened. A ridiculous idea and the longest of all shots. But he couldn't pretend Connie hadn't piqued his interest.

"What if you showed up with goat's milk for Jovi? The one missing ingredient she needs to make those salted caramel chews she's been struggling with for weeks."

He groaned. "Someone's been reading too many romance novels."

Connie laughed. "It's a bizarre grand gesture, but you look like you need some out-of-the-box suggestions. C'mon, would I steer you wrong?"

Burke chewed on his thumbnail. The kids' excited chatter hummed around him like bees swarming their favorite flowers. Such an absurd idea. But worth a try. Because he had nothing left to lose. It was time to step forward in faith and stop using his grief as a shield. He'd been wallowing in self-pity for too long. He needed to risk his heart. He needed to win Jovi back.

Maybe Connie's plan was the push he needed.

"Okay, okay, I'll do it."

Connie clapped her hands together. "Fabulous! Now, let's get to work."

She pulled out her phone and started typing away.

"Wait." Burke held up his palm to interrupt. As if that could stop her. "What are you doing?"

She grinned. "Putting our plan in motion. C'mon, let's help these kids on the bus. I'll explain later."

Oh, brother. He did not like the sound of that. And why were so many of the other parents standing nearby staring? Or was that his imagination? He sighed and followed her toward the bus.

Once the kids were onboard and settled, he and Connie took their seats in the third row behind the kindergarten teachers and two other ladies who had also volunteered. The bus smelled faintly of socks, stale chips and whatever floral fragrances the ladies had put on. None of them smelled as appealing as Jovi.

The engine rumbled, and his stomach turned queasy as the driver drove away from the school. Thankfully, Darby Jane sat with her friends several rows back, so she couldn't see how miserable he probably looked.

Connie's phone dinged with an incoming text. Burke resisted the temptation to read the message. Her eyes roamed across the screen.

"This is working out better than I expected," she said, grinning again.

"At some point will you feel compelled to bring me up to speed?"

"Hang on." She held up one finger, but still smiled at her phone. "I need confirmation from one more person, then you'll be good to go."

Good to go regarding what, exactly? Honestly, he should have never let Connie rope him into this, whatever this was. Maybe he should have bowed out of this field trip, begged Darby Jane for forgiveness and gone and found Jovi himself. Except Darby Jane would have never forgiven him for missing the last field trip of the year.

Spending the day at a farm wasn't his idea of a good time. But he'd made so many mistakes when it came to parenting and had so many regrets about his past choices, he had known better than to back out on this. And maybe running into Connie had been the best thing that could happen to him. Still, he felt nervous sitting here next to her, riding on this stinky school bus. What could she possibly do to help him get goat's milk to Jovi? Especially when he was certain Jovi had already booked her flight to leave Alaska.

"Okay, here's the deal." She pocketed her phone. Finally. "When we get to the farm, the kids take a short tour, but after that they'll probably get antsy. So for the second half of the field trip, there's going to be some playtime. Let 'em burn off steam, run around, climb things, you get the picture. And that's when we're going to get you some fresh goat's milk and the keys to my friend Mandy's car, and you are going to head over to the candy company and show up with fresh goat's milk for Jovi."

She splayed her palm against her chest and pressed her lips together. Her eyes surveyed his face.

"You cannot be serious," he said. "That's what you've arranged?"

Her smile vanished. "Do you have a better idea, Mr. Bestselling Author? Because clearly, grand gestures are not your specialty."

"I'm not sure they're yours either."

Her mouth drifted open. Closed. Then opened again.

Regret twisted his stomach. "You're right. I'm sorry. Your plan sounds amazing. What could possibly go wrong?"

Her brow furrowed. "You are the most crotchety, uptight thing I have met in ages. Would you just work with us on this?"

"Define *us*."

"I had to call in some favors and make some deals to pull this all together last-minute. How about some gratitude? I might have just saved your love life."

A few of the teachers tittered, as they glanced over their shoulders and gave him the side-eye.

"And let me guess. All y'all are in on this?"

That provoked another wave of spontaneous laughter.

"It was the *all y'all* that did it, wasn't it?"

Connie clapped her hand over her mouth to keep from guffawing. "Burke Solomon, sometimes I think you're hopeless, but there's just enough of a little glimmer of sunshine that keeps me rooting for you."

"Wow, thanks."

Could this really work?

He wasn't in a position to be picky about his grand gesture. Because time was short. He couldn't let Jovi leave Evergreen without showing her how much she meant to him.

Why was it so hard to find fresh goat's milk? Jovi had reached out to Connie at the diner, the managers at both grocery stores, and a couple of coworkers at the hospital who had hobby farms. No goat's milk to be found in all of Evergreen.

So how was she supposed to make the salted caramel chews without it? She reread Grammie's handwritten recipe, then scrolled through her phone to the picture she'd taken of the story explaining how Lois's frustration over getting a goat had inspired the recipe's creation. Lois, and then Grammie, had most certainly used locally sourced goat's milk.

Given Jovi's lousy experience trying substitutes, she wasn't about to sub anything else. But here she stood, with only hours to spare, and every possible utensil and baking pan at her disposal in the company's test kitchen...and no goat's milk.

Jovi let out a deep sigh, then scrolled through her phone and started another internet search for alternative ingredients. Everything that popped up in the results was something she'd tried already.

The hum of the refrigerator was the only sound in the otherwise silent kitchen. Suddenly, she heard a knock on the door. Had someone complained that Isabel had given her access?

She walked over to the door and opened it.

Her breath hitched. Burke waited on the other side. Holding a glass bottle of...milk?

"What are you doing here?"

Jovi tried to ignore the way her heart raced at the sight of him. He looked as handsome as he always did. Tall and muscular, his dark hair a tousled mess, and his intense amber eyes locked on hers. He wore a snug-fitting T-shirt layered under a windbreaker and a pair of faded jeans that hugged his trim hips. Heat warmed her cheeks as she realized he'd caught her staring.

Burke offered a tentative smile and held up the bottle of milk. "I thought you might need this."

"H-how did you know?"

"Word travels fast around here. Evidently, you've made a few calls already?"

"And so you just show up with fresh goat's milk."

His shoulders lifted in a casual shrug. "I have connections."

Jovi took the bottle from Burke's hand, feeling the smooth glass against her skin. She hesitated, unsure of what to say. Did he know she'd still planned to leave for California?

His eyes drifted to her lips.

"Thank you," she murmured. "This is perfect timing."

"Good." His eyes drifted back to meet hers. "I'm happy to help."

A thrill raced through her body as she recalled the way his lips had felt on hers and the warmth of his hands when he'd framed her face and leaned in for their first kiss. Oh, how she longed to rewind time and take back those harsh accusations she'd flung at him.

She cleared her throat, determined to regain her composure. She couldn't afford to get distracted by Burke's presence or the memory of that perfect kiss. She had a batch of salted caramel chews to make, and time was ticking away.

"Thank you again." She mustered a smile then glanced at the clock. "I really need to get started on these candies."

Burke's smile faltered, but he nodded. "Of course. I'll leave you to it, then."

As he turned to leave, Jovi hesitated. She didn't want him to go. Not now. Not after everything they'd been through.

"Wait," she called out, her voice filled with uncertainty. Burke paused and turned back toward her, his eyebrows raised.

Jovi took a deep breath, gathering her courage. "I...I was wondering if we could talk. About what's happened and..."

Oh, forget it. She didn't want to talk. Not at all.

She set the milk down and raced toward him. His eyes darkened. Then he closed the gap between them and pulled her into his arms.

"I'm sorry, Burke." She swallowed hard against the emotion tightening her throat. "I'm so sorry for the terrible things I said."

"Shh, it's fine." The tenderness in his expression made her want to weep. He cupped her face gently in his hands.

"No, it isn't." She pressed both palms against his broad, firm chest. "My grandmother and your aunt were the ones who behaved badly. Not you. I'm so sorry I accused you of being a liar."

He caressed her cheek with the pad of his thumb. "Darling, I forgive you. Your devotion to your family is one of the many things I adore about you."

"But I shouldn't have—"

"Jovi?" He angled his head to one side, sending a delicious tremor dancing along her spine.

Wow, she could get lost in those golden amber pools. "Hmm?"

"May I kiss you now?"

She nodded, her eyes already drifting closed.

Burke leaned in, his lips hovering just inches away from hers. "Are you sure?" he whispered, his voice gruff.

"Uh-huh." Jovi's pulse hummed in anticipation, her senses heightened by the closeness of his body. The test kitchen, her plans to leave town, all of it faded away as they stood there, locked in a moment of raw vulnerability.

Then his mouth met hers, and it was unlike the kiss they had shared before. A soft and gentle touch that quickly deepened into a passionate embrace. It was a kiss filled with forgiveness and the promise of a fresh start. As their bodies melted into each other, Jovi felt the weight of her doubts and fears dissipate. In that moment, she knew that no matter what challenges lay ahead, she wanted Burke by her side.

Breaking the kiss, breathless and smiling, Burke grinned. "I've missed you."

"I've missed you too," she said, her fingers grazing his cheek. "I don't want to leave anymore. Evergreen is where I belong, with you."

Burke's eyes widened in surprise, a mixture of joy and relief flooding his features. "Are you serious?"

Jovi nodded, her heart swelling with newfound conviction. "Yes, I'm serious. And if it's all right with you, I'm going to use this recipe I found for salted caramel chews to stop my parents from selling the company. It was Lois's recipe originally, but Grammie put it in writing and kept it tucked away. There's no need to hide it any longer. Think of this as a combined effort, from the Phillipses, the Solomons and the Wrights."

"It's brilliant." A satisfied smile spread across Burke's face. "You have my family's permission to move forward, and I can't tell you how much it means to hear you say that you're staying," he whispered. "I've been hoping and praying for this."

"I'm truly sorry that I pushed you away." She grimaced. "I never should have doubted you or let my insecurities get the best of me. Or fussed at you because of how you chose to write your novel."

Burke's hand found its way to the small of her back, pulling her closer. His eyes searched hers, filled with a mix of tenderness and understanding. "We all make mistakes, Jovi. Including me. I should've talked to you about what I was writing, and at least let you look at the scenes before I submitted the manuscript. Please believe me when I say that you're not in the novel, but you definitely inspired the best parts. I'm so sorry I didn't think more carefully about how you might see that differently. Will you forgive me?"

"Of course I forgive you." Her chest expanded with gratitude for his humble admission and his forgiveness. "Let's not waste any more time," she added. "I want to be with you, Burke. I want to make this work."

Burke pulled her closer, wrapping his arms protectively around her. "I've wanted the same thing since the moment I met you," he whispered, resting his chin on top of her head.

Jovi nestled into his embrace, feeling a renewed sense of hope.

Together, they walked back into the kitchen hand in hand. The scent of sugar still lingered in the air, reminding Jovi of all the candy and chocolate that had been made here. Sure, there had been flops. Products that didn't satisfy some customers. But this time, with Burke by her side, she sensed they'd conquer any challenges that came their way.

As she looked around the kitchen, Jovi surveyed the array of ingredients scattered across the counter. She could almost hear her grandmother's voice whispering in her ear, guiding her with every step. It was a comforting presence that reminded her of the legacy she was trying to protect.

With renewed determination, Jovi turned to Burke and smiled. "Let's start fresh," she said. "Together."

Burke grinned and nodded, his eyes filled with unwavering support. "I believe in you, Jovi," he said. "And I'll be right here by your side every step of the way."

Epilogue

Two years later

Who knew salted caramel chews would change her life?

Jovi stood outside Evergreen Candy Company, basking in the sunshine on an unseasonably warm June day. Local residents, tourists and extended family members had gathered to celebrate the opening of the company's expanded facility, complete with a retail store, tours of the facility so customers could see their favorite products coming off the line, and a larger factory to accommodate the substantial demand for Lois and Carol's salted caramel chews.

After Jovi had discovered the recipe with goat's milk as the secret ingredient—which had produced the stellar results she'd been looking for—she'd persuaded her parents not to sell the company until they saw at least one quarter's worth of sales. Then five-star reviews and demand for small batches had been more than they could handle. Jerry and Irene had hesitated about adding a third shift to the factory's workforce. Jerry had even threatened to retire early.

But he'd settled down. Eventually. He and Irene had worked together to make adding the new shift a palatable transition for everyone. Jovi smiled as her twin niece and nephew toddled toward the inflatable bouncy house tethered to the emerald lawn nearby.

Darby Jane followed after the twins, gently offering instruction. She sounded more like she was bossing them, to be honest. Her leadership skills had developed at a fast clip ever since she'd discovered her passion for theater. She'd recently starred as Dorothy in *The Wizard of Oz* for the elementary school's spring production and had drawn a packed house.

"It's a beautiful day to celebrate people's undying devotion to sugar, isn't it?" Burke's voice made her heart beat faster, like it always did every time her new husband came close. His hands slid around her waist, and he nuzzled her neck.

"Easy there, handsome. Children are watching," she teased.

"Oh, Mrs. Solomon, you know I'll keep this family-friendly. For now."

Goose bumps danced across her skin as he held her close and gently brushed her cheek with his lips. The aroma of his aftershave sent a swirl of attraction dancing around her knees. She leaned into his embrace, unable to resist returning his kiss.

They'd married four months ago, on the beach in Mexico on Valentine's Day. The ceremony had included their families and a few close friends. Burke had wept through the whole thing. Jovi had shed a few happy tears of her own.

Their wedding also served as the first gathering of both sides of their families, and today marked the second. So far everyone was getting along well.

Burke's brother, Shane, stood with the Solomon clan not far away, holding a full plate of food from the picnic tables and chatting with Jovi's parents, who had never looked happier. Or more tan. Retirement suited them. Thanks to the incredible royalties from Burke's bestselling novel, he'd been able to buy their share of the candy company. They'd just flown in yesterday from Florida. From what her mother had shared, it seemed like all they did was play golf. But if that was what made them happy, then Jovi was glad her parents had found a lifestyle that suited them. Because she had definitely found what suited her.

"I'm so proud of you, my love," Burke said, sweeping his arm in a wide swath. "This is impressive, what you've done."

"What *we've* done." She nudged him with her hip. "We both own stake in this company, remember?"

"I know, but you mostly have been working with Isabel and the longtime employees to put this whole thing together."

"It was your decision to show up with goat's milk and sweep me off my feet," she said. "Don't be afraid to take credit for that swoonworthy grand gesture."

"If I had known goat's milk was the way to win your heart, I would've bought you your own herd the same week we met." He kissed her one more time, then pulled away, his fingers twining through hers.

She laughed. "That might've been a bit much."

Burke's second novel had been a bestseller, as well as his third, and he'd just finished writing his fourth. The two families had become equal partners, and Jovi ran the candy company alongside Isabel. Burke had sold his home in Charleston to the family that had rented it when he and Darby Jane had moved out. The funds were more than enough to pay for Grammie's care. Yet another generous gift she'd always be grateful for.

Love, courage and fierce determination had been the key ingredients that had helped them find their way forward.

She'd maintained her nursing license but didn't work in health care anymore. Between helping run the company and caring for Darby Jane, her life in Evergreen had brought more happiness than she had ever anticipated. And if her suspicions were accurate, she was fairly certain she was in the early stages of building a baby. She glanced at Burke. That was a piece of news she'd share later when they were alone, if she could manage to keep the secret for another hour or two.

Hand in hand, they strode across the lawn to fill their plates and mingle with their friends and family. Isabel and Mason walked toward them. Isabel, battling morning sickness due to her second pregnancy, had rallied to make an appearance. She had a can of ginger ale in one hand and a baggie of saltine crackers in the other. Mason pushed Grammie slowly in her wheelchair. With her white hair styled in smooth, bouncy curls, and her lavender blouse paired with bright white pants, she looked positively radiant. Dementia had taken a lot from her, and her lucid moments were few and far between, but Jovi and Isabel always made sure to bring her back to Evergreen for major family events.

"I hope Grammie knows that none of this would've been possible without her," Jovi said softly. "I'm so thankful that she's still around to see her dream live on in a new generation."

Burke smiled at her, his expression brimming with affection. "What a gift to see God make something beautiful from the bitter ashes of our heartache."

"Oh, my. That is a lovely turn of phrase, Mr. Solomon. Are you by chance a best-selling author?"

"Indeed. But I much prefer my role as your husband."

"Aww, you are the sweetest," she said. "I love you."

"I love you more."

★ ★ ★ ★ ★

Acknowledgments

Every year I map out a plan for the stories I intend to create, and every year I encounter a few real-life plot twists that alter my plans. This is not the book I thought I'd write, and yet I appreciate the opportunity because it's the one I needed to write. I've learned invaluable lessons throughout the process. Writing *A Winter of Sweet Secrets* has been a serendipitous gift. I have many generous and talented people I'd like to thank.

A huge thank-you to the whole team at Love Inspired. I'm in awe of all that you do to produce our books and launch them into the world. Thanks especially to my editor, Shana Asaro, for helping me shape and polish another story. I couldn't do this without your keen insight and attention to detail.

Steve Laube, you're a delightful human and a fantastic literary agent. I'm grateful for your integrity, kindness, and wisdom. It's an honor to be a part of your agency.

To the early readers, podcast hosts, bookstagrammers, booksellers, librarians, and publicity folks who all work so hard to help spread the word about *A Winter of Sweet Secrets*, thank you.

Your enthusiasm for romance novels makes me so happy. I'm super grateful for each of you.

Books are often written in solitude, yet there's a whole network of people behind the scenes offering their time, wisdom, and encouragement. First, I'd like to thank my sister, Heather, for giving me the secret ingredient suggestion. To my Monday and Friday morning writing pals, Lisa, Wendy, and Linda Jo, thank you for your prayers, encouraging words, and the laughs. I'm glad I get to be on this writing journey with you.

To my local church community as well as my friends and family scattered near and far, thank you for cheering me on and telling everyone you know about my books.

Finally, to my husband, Steve, and our sons, Luke, Andy, and Eli, I'm confident that it's a challenge to do life with someone who spends so much time with fictional people. Thank you for supporting my dreams with your encouraging words, graciously overlooking unfinished tasks that I've forgotten about and tackling chores you'd probably rather not do. I love you to the moon and back.

Get 3 FREE REWARDS!

We'll send you 2 FREE Books plus a FREE Mystery Gift.

Essential Inspirational novels reflect traditional Christian values. Enjoy a mix of contemporary, Amish, historical, and suspenseful romantic stories.

FREE Value Over **$40**

YES! Please send me 2 FREE Essential Inspirational novels and my FREE mystery gift (gift is worth about $10 retail). After receiving them, if I don't wish to receive any more books, I can return the shipping statement marked "cancel." If I don't cancel, I will receive 2 brand-new novels every month and be billed just $24.98 in the U.S., or $30.48 each in Canada. That's a savings of at least 26% off the cover price. It's quite a bargain! Shipping and handling is just $1.00 per book in the U.S. and $1.50 per book in Canada.* I understand that accepting the 2 free books and gift places me under no obligation to buy anything. I can always return a shipment and cancel at any time. The free books and gift are mine to keep no matter what I decide.

Essential Inspirational (157/357 BPA G2DG)

Name (please print)

Address   Apt. #

City   State/Province   Zip/Postal Code

Email: Please check this box ☐ if you would like to receive newsletters and promotional emails from Harlequin Enterprises ULC and its affiliates. You can unsubscribe anytime.

Mail to the **Harlequin Reader Service:**
IN U.S.A.: P.O. Box 1341, Buffalo, NY 14240-8531
IN CANADA: P.O. Box 603, Fort Erie, Ontario L2A 5X3

Want to try 2 free books from another series! Call 1-800-873-8635 or visit www.ReaderService.com.

*Terms and prices subject to change without notice. Prices do not include sales taxes, which will be charged (if applicable) based on your state or country of residence. Canadian residents will be charged applicable taxes. Offer not valid in Quebec. This offer is limited to one order per household. Books received may not be as shown. Not valid for current subscribers to Essential Inspirational books. All orders subject to approval. Credit or debit balances in a customer's account(s) may be offset by any other outstanding balance owed by or to the customer. Please allow 4 to 6 weeks for delivery. Offer available while quantities last.

Your Privacy—Your information is being collected by Harlequin Enterprises ULC, operating as Harlequin Reader Service. For a complete summary of the information we collect, how we use this information and to whom it is disclosed, please visit our privacy notice located at corporate.harlequin.com/privacy-notice. From time to time we may also exchange your personal information with reputable third parties. If you wish to opt out of this sharing of your personal information, please visit readerservice.com/consumerschoice or call 1-800-873-8635. **Notice to California Residents**—Under California law, you have specific rights to control and access your data. For more information on these rights and how to exercise them, visit corporate.harlequin.com/california-privacy.